High on a Hill

DOROTHY GARLOCK

High on a Hill

WARNER BOOKS

An AOL Time Warner Company

Copyright © 2002 by Dorothy Garlock
All rights reserved.

Warner Books, Inc., 1271 Avenue of the Americas, New York, NY 10020

Visit our Web site at www.twbookmark.com.

 An AOL Time Warner Company

Printed in the United States of America

First Printing: June 2002

10 9 8 7 6 5 4 3 2 1

Library of Congress Cataloging-in-Publication Data

Garlock, Dorothy.
High on a hill / Dorothy Garlock.
p. cm.
ISBN 0-446-52946-X
1. Fathers and daughters—Fiction. 2. Runaway teenagers—Fiction. 3. Prohibition—Fiction. 4. Smuggling—Fiction. 5. Missouri—Fiction. I. Title.

PS3557.A71645 H54 2002
813'.54—dc21   2001039579

This book is dedicated to
WINIFRED
(affectionately known as Winnie)

She is my constant companion, my guardian,
my faithful friend.
She also eats my leftovers.

High on a Hill

Another Annabel Lee

We came here in the dark of night,
Another step in our constant flight.
In secrecy we packed and fled.
"One last move," my father said.

I woke at dawn to sunlight streaming,
Looked down the slope to the river's gleaming.
A wooded glen, a pasture green,
The calmest place I'd ever seen.

Though my name is Annabel Lee,
I yearn for no "kingdom by the sea."
I want to stay here, quiet and still,
And make my home high on a hill.

And if "a love that is more than a love"
Should find me 'neath this sky above,
I'll rejoice in it with a heart that's free
And take from each day its own poetry.

—F.S.I.

Prologue

He knew the instant the men appeared out of the river fog and blocked his way that he was in trouble. At the time it didn't occur to him that their intentions were not to rob him but to kill him. He braced his hands on his hips and, with a sneer on his face, waited. None of the three spoke or made a move toward him.

He had been foolish to linger with his friend until after midnight. He had enjoyed the conversation and sipping a legal wine called Vine-Glo—grape juice that, when put in the cellar and nursed for sixty days, turned into wine that was fifteen percent alcohol. More time had passed than he had realized.

He peered through the fog at the men confronting him: one tall, one short and stocky, the other one a mere boy. All wore the look of experienced brawlers. Their caps were set at an angle, their feet spread wide to give an impression of immovability.

This was obviously not an accidental meeting. They had been waiting for him; waiting before confronting him until he was a good distance from the house of his friend and in an area fronting the river and boxed in by a warehouse and boat sheds.

"I'm not a bit surprised that ya come in packs of three, being the cowards ya are," the man taunted the silent, ominous ruffians.

He would not let them know that he was not at all as sure of the outcome of this set-to as he pretended. He was confident he could hold his own with one or two of them. But three was another matter. When the attack came, he would have to dispose of the third one right at the start to partially even the odds.

"Varmints." He shook his head in a gesture of disdain. "Varmints who attack in packs."

Still none of the three uttered a word. He heard nothing but the gurgling splash of a fish in the river and the faintest murmur of the wind in the pines. Then, in the far distance, the sound of a motorcar reached him and the barking of an excited dog. The night was impenetrably black. The fog that had settled down along the river shut out the sky and the earth beneath it.

He stared at the silent men, suddenly oppressed by a sense of unreality. For years he had expected this. He'd had his share of barroom brawls; this was not a brawl, but a serious life-and-death matter. These men were cold sober and intent on doing him in. It was apparent in their stance and their silence.

His eyes settled on the man in the middle, the big one with wide shoulders and long arms. He couldn't see the face clearly, but he could see that the man was in his prime and built like an oak tree. He would be the one to take down.

"Is there a one among you with the guts to take me on man to man?"

He felt a sudden, vast impatience. He knew that if they did not kill him they would cripple him so that he would be of no use to himself or to anyone else. The only chance he had, and it was a slim one, of leaving this spot alive was in his pocket. His fingers curled around the brass knuckles. They were a weak defense against three men, but they were all he had. He cursed himself for not being better prepared.

"Who is the cowardly son-of-a-bitch who sent you? At least you owe me that."

The younger man let out a giggle, which was cut short by the jab of an elbow. Without even turning his head, the middle man had moved his arm swiftly.

"Bastards! What are you waiting for? Make your move or get the hell outta my way."

Nothing. Not a sound from any of them.

They were playing with him now. Well, hell, he might as well get it over with.

He lowered his head and charged the man in the middle, boring in, driving, stomping on insteps when he got close. He swung the fist with the brass knuckles at the face of the short man standing next to him, connected with flesh and heard him yell. He took a blow to the side of his head as his other hand grabbed the sex of the man he had butted and held on, twisting, pulling, squeezing.

He felt no pain, but suddenly the strength went from his arms, his legs. He felt himself sagging to the ground and a black cloud of darkness settling over him.

"Annabel," he whispered, drifting in and out of consciousness. He was vaguely aware of hands on him, probing, searching his pockets.

Annalee. It was his last thought as he was lifted from the riverbank and tossed into the roiling waters. The strong current of the mighty Mississippi seized his body and carried it downriver with the rest of the floating debris that rode the muddy waters.

Chapter 1

Henderson, Missouri, 1925

SHE HAD NOT SEEN THE HOUSE IN THE DAYLIGHT, as they had moved in in the middle of the night. But she knew that it was high on a hill and as remote as all the other places where they had lived during the past five years.

"I know ye're disappointed to be movin' again, darlin', but this time we be stayin' for a while."

"It's all right, Papa. I'm just tired."

"Boone and Spinner will be bringin' in the furniture and helpin' ya get settled."

"Are you leaving?"

"I'll be back by noon tomorrow." He put his arm across her shoulders. The lamplight shone on his worried face as he peered into hers. "Ye're not afraid, are ye?"

"No," she said with a tired heave of her shoulders. "I'm not afraid."

"Boone and Spinner will be here and ye're not to be worryin'. Boone will be keepin' a sharp lookout."

"Why should he do that?" she asked sharply. "Are you expecting someone?"

"No. I'd not leave ya if I thought that there would be the slightest chance that ya'd be in any danger. Look over the house and see where you want things put. Boone will be settin' up yer bed."

An hour later Annabel lay in her bed with the covers pulled up to her chin and listened to the sounds of the men unloading the furniture from the two trucks. They worked without speaking, but one time she heard one of them swear.

"Dammit to hell! This cabinet's heavy!"

"Ain't as heavy as them boxes with the jars of canned stuff and that damned iron cookstove."

"Horse hockey! The dang icebox ain't no feather bed."

Annabel gazed out the window at the star-studded sky and tried to count the number of times she and her father had moved since her mother's death back in 1920. She knew the moves were necessitated by the circumstances of her father's business.

Soon we'll be havin' enough money to buy a fine house and ya can live in style. I always wanted it for yer mother but couldn't swing it while she was alive. But I'll get it for ya. I swear that I'll get it for ya.

Her father's words echoed in her head.

I don't have to live in style to be happy. I want to live in a place long enough to feel that I belong somewhere.

How could she make him understand? He was one of ten children born to a poor couple who had carried the stigma of "poor Irish trash." Hard work had sent them to an early grave. Murphy was determined that that would not happen to him or to his daughter. He knew the risks he was taking. The federal marshals would love to get their hands on him.

Annabel had told him a hundred times that she would rather be dirt poor with him than rich without him. What would she do if something happened to him? There was money put away so that she would be able to get by; her father had seen to that. But she would be without another person in the world to care if she lived or died, except maybe Boone.

Annabel drifted off to sleep worrying, as she had done almost every night since she was sixteen years old, about what tomorrow would bring.

The house looked better in the morning light, even though it was badly in need of a paint job. It was a frame building with four large rooms, a loft, a small porch stretching across the front and one in the back. From the porch Annabel could see not only the winding road going south to Henderson, but in the distance, over the treetops, a portion of the mighty Mississippi River. Behind the house, beyond the barn, a shed and another ramshackle building, was a thick forest of trees.

The two trucks that had transported their belongings from Ashton to north of Henderson were nowhere in sight, nor were Boone and Spinner. While she slept, their furniture had been put in place. Her kitchen cabinet was set up against the wall, and the boxes containing dishes, utensils and food were sitting on the big square table waiting for her to sort and put in their proper places. A bucket of fresh water sat on the wash bench beside the door. She had no doubt that her father's bed and bureau were already in the other bedroom.

As she was getting out of bed, she had heard the chimes on her clock striking the hour. It was a comforting, familiar sound. Knowing how much she treasured the clock, Boone would have put it in its regular place on the library table, leveled it, set the correct time and started the pendulum swinging.

Sighing and not relishing the job ahead, Annabel dressed and slipped her feet into her shoes. When she went to the kitchen, she carried with her the oval framed mirror from her bedroom and hung it over the wash bench.

Looking at herself critically, she saw a woman who had celebrated her twenty-first birthday last Christmas day. Her dark brown wavy hair was cut to just below her jawline, one side held back with a silver barrette. She thought that her green eyes, large and thick-lashed, were probably her most attractive feature. She was unaware that her mouth, with its short upper lip and full lower one that tilted up at the corners when she smiled, had caused many a man's eyes to follow her.

Annabel had resigned herself long ago to the fact that she was not a beauty, but she also remembered her mother saying that beauty lay mostly in expression and attitude, not God-given structure.

The cookstove had been set up in the large square kitchen and the chimney fitted into place. Boone had started a fire and the coffeepot was sending up a delicious fragrance of freshly ground coffee beans. The doors of the empty icebox stood open. Annabel washed in the warm water from the reservoir before she combed her hair and helped herself to the coffee from the granite pot.

"Mornin', girl."

Annabel glanced toward the back door. The man with the dark stubble of beard on his face was the only person in the world, other than her father, who she was sure truly cared about her. Spinner, she knew, was fond of her but, unlike Boone, kept his feelings to himself.

"Morning, Boone. Have you had breakfast?"

"Me'n Spinner had a bite or two. If ya want anythin', we'll be in the shed."

"Did I see horses behind the barn?"

"Yeah. The mare's real gentle."

"Maybe I can ride her . . . later."

"No reason why not."

"How far are we from Henderson, Boone?"

"Probably five miles as the crow flies. Ya wantin' to get somethin' from town?"

"Not just now. Later I'll need some groceries and ice."

Long before noon, the kitchen was organized and Annabel was ready to cook a meal. It would take a while for her to get used to the arrangement in the kitchen. It was much larger than the one in the house they had lived in for the past eight months.

At noon her father returned and following him was a truck loaded with hay. He stopped his car beside the house, got out and waved the driver of the truck on toward the barn.

He came into the kitchen, looked around and smiled.

"You're a wonder, darlin'. You're already settled in."

Murphy Lee Donovan was a handsome man in his late forties. He was slightly taller than average, built solidly, with a head of thick dark hair. He didn't mind hardship or discomfort. The only things in the world he loved were his daughter Annabel and, to a lesser degree, outwitting the revenue agents. It was a game to him. He sometimes wondered if he would play at it even if there weren't a great deal of money involved.

"Whose horses are those out there, Papa?"

"Ours. I've brought hay for them. I'll be in as soon as I help unload. The driver wants to get back."

The words were unspoken between Annabel and her father, but she knew that beneath the false bottom of the truck was a load of whiskey that had come down the river from

Canada. Murphy Donovan was just one of a half dozen men along the river who warehoused the illegal liquor until it was dispensed to the bars and speakeasies throughout the states of Missouri and Illinois.

Annabel knew the reason for the horses was that they would need hay, and the hay would cover a load of liquor.

Murphy was too clever to store the contraband here at the farm. A couple of cases would be left in the barn to act as a diversion should the marshals arrive. Finding it would lead them to believe Murphy was a small-time trafficker, and after disposing of it, they would be on their way. The bulk of the load would be stored in a cave or an underground storm cellar with a hidden door.

"Are the horses broken to ride?" Annabel asked as her father turned to go out the door.

"Gentle enough for you, darlin'. Just make sure Boone goes with you so you won't get lost." Murphy still, on occasion, reverted to the lilting brogue of his Irish parents.

Her father's dangerous business was never far from Annabel's mind. Murphy knew that what he was doing was illegal, but he sincerely did not believe that it was wrong.

"Darlin', the government ain't got no right to be tellin' folks what they can drink and what they can't. Prohibition is a stupid law. It can't last," he had said time and time again. "Folks is goin' to be havin' their drinks one way or the other. 'Tis best they be drinkin' fine liquor than swillin' moonshine made from rotten potatoes."

"But it's against the law and I'm afraid you'll be caught."

"Don't worry your pretty head, darlin'. I'm not hurtin' anybody or stealin' from them. How can it be wrong to help some poor workin' devil ease the ache in his back with a glass of spirits at the end of the day?"

Annabel had heard the same argument over and over,

and now it was seldom mentioned. Now and then her father drank some of the alcohol he distributed, but she had never seen him really drunk. He was generous to the men who worked for him and protective of her. She could have anything she asked for that he was able to give to her. She was careful, however, not to ask for anything except the necessities.

The things she longed for he could not give her at this time. She was lonely and yearned for friends. The few young people she knew back in Ashton, where they had lived before moving here, had been friendly, but she'd had to keep them at a distance for fear they would grow curious about her father's activities.

In her mind she considered this a holding period in her life. She was waiting for her father to do what he promised, give up this dangerous business when he had enough money to set them up in a house. It was hard to remember now that when she was younger and her mother was still alive, they had lived in Duluth, Minnesota, and her father had worked on the big ships that hauled freight on Lake Superior.

One morning, a week after they had moved to the house on the hill, Murphy told Annabel to be ready in half an hour if she wanted to go to town. She was ready in fifteen minutes and climbed happily into the car when Murphy brought it around to the front of the house.

"Ya know what ya want from town?"

"Of course. I've been making a list."

A light breeze was blowing from the south. Annabel held on to the brim of her small hat and enjoyed the feel of the wind in her face.

"We have neighbors," she exclaimed when they passed a crooked lane leading to a house set far back in the woods.

"There's no one there ya be wantin' to know," Murphy replied sharply. "I wasn't told they were there when I bought the place."

"Why wouldn't I want to know them? It would be nice to have neighbors."

"'Cause they're hill trash, that's why." His mouth snapped shut, and Annabel knew he didn't want any more questions about them.

Henderson was a quaint village on the banks of the Mississippi River, with white picket fences and cobblestone streets. A white church spire rose high above the town. Murphy parked the car in front of the mercantile. Annabel went into the store while he walked on down the street to the barbershop. The man behind the counter greeted her with a friendly smile.

"Mornin', ma'am."

"Morning. I have a list for you to fill." She placed a sheet of ruled paper on the counter. "Do you know where in town I can buy gramophone needles and violin strings?"

"I have the needles and maybe you can get the violin strings from Arnold Potter down the street at the drugstore. He's the conductor of our municipal band and he might keep a few on hand."

"Thank you."

"Play, do ya?"

"For my own amusement."

"Arnold will latch on to ya right quick." The storekeeper's eyes twinkled when he laughed, and his belly jiggled beneath the apron tied about his ample waist. "He's the beatin'est man for music. Lives for it."

"I enjoy it myself."

"I . . . ah, ain't heard of any new folks movin' to town."

"My father bought the Miller place five miles north of here."

"Ah . . . the Miller place. Ah . . . hummm. Not much land there if he's goin' to farm." The man stuck out his hand. "Luther Hogg."

"Annabel Donovan." She put her hand in his. "Nice to meet you, Mr. Hogg. Add a package of gramophone needles to my list. I'll be back as soon as I see Mr. Potter about the violin strings."

Arnold Potter was a man with a head of thick white hair and equally white eyebrows and mustache. He was as curious as Mr. Hogg about a stranger in town; and after Annabel told him about moving to the farm, she asked about the violin strings. Mr. Potter's blue eyes sparkled as they talked about music. He spoke at length about his band and he eyed, with pleasure, the slim girl in the blue cotton dress and the small-brimmed hat.

"I'd be most pleased to have you audition, my dear."

"Thank you, but I've never played with a band. I was taught by my mother and play only for my own amusement."

"We have a concert Sunday afternoon in the city park," he said while accepting the money for the violin strings, then added, "Need rosin for your bow?"

"No, thank you. I have some."

"I'll look for you at the concert," he said as she went out the door.

Annabel crossed back to the mercantile. Mr. Hogg had just finished setting the items on her list on the counter and was totaling the bill.

"Did Arnold have the strings?" he asked.

"He did. Thank you for sending me to him."

Mr. Hogg chuckled. "Bet he talked your arm off."

"Yes, sir." Annabel smiled. "He got pretty wound up talking about his band."

The bell on the screen door tinkled when Murphy came into the store. He spied Annabel and came to the counter.

"Find everything you need?" he asked, pronouncing the words carefully lest his Irish accent show.

Annabel nodded. "Papa, meet Mr. Hogg. Sir, this is my father, Murphy Donovan."

"Howdy." After the two men shook hands, Murphy spoke to Annabel.

"Look around, darlin', and see if there's anythin' you want on that table of dress goods over there. I'll be here gettin' acquainted with Mr. Hogg."

Annabel moved to the other side of the store and sifted through the bolts of material. She found a blue-and-white-checked gingham she could use to make a curtain for the kitchen door and the bottom half of the two kitchen windows. The ones she had brought from the other house would do for the top panes.

While she spread out the cloth to examine it she noticed that her father had moved close to Mr. Hogg and that they were deep in conversation. She lingered at the table of lace, ribbons and buttons, allowing them time to visit, then selected a spool of thread from the thread cabinet. As she approached with the bolt of material, Murphy stepped back.

"Find somethin'?"

"Curtain material. How much is it, Mr. Hogg?"

"Twelve and a half cents a yard, miss. It's top quality. There's some five-cent goods over there, but I can't guarantee the colors won't run."

"I'll need four yards. That'd be half a dollar. I'll look at the cheaper—"

Murphy lifted the bolt from her hand. "She wants this."

"But Papa—"

"No buts, darlin'."

Mr. Hogg unrolled the material from the bolt and measured it against the notches carved along the counter.

"I'll give ya good measure, Miss Donovan."

"Thank you."

"I'll load this and be back in to pay." Murphy picked up a box and carried it out to the car.

On the way out of town, Murphy told Annabel that he was leaving that afternoon and wouldn't be back for a week or ten days.

"Boone will be here," he said when she turned to look at him.

"Boone isn't you, Papa."

"I'm hopin' this'll be the last year, darlin'. Maybe then we can buy a house in St. Louis." When Annabel didn't say anything, he continued, "In the city ya can be the lady ya are; go to shows, parties, and maybe meet a nice young doctor or lawyer . . ." His voice trailed when Annabel laughed.

"You're the limit," she teased. "You know I would be perfectly content to live in a town like Henderson. I'm not the type for parties or meeting nice young doctors or lawyers."

"Ya be thinkin' ye're not good enough?" His voice rose in irritation. "Yer blood is good as any in the whole damn country. Yer mother was a fine woman—"

"Calm down. I didn't mean that. I meant that I'm not interested in that kind of social life. I saw enough of the jockeying around among the husband-hunting crowd in school to convince me that I'll never do it."

"I want ya to be havin' a home and a man to care for ya."

"I'd hitch with a doctor or lawyer about like a donkey would hitch with a Tennessee walking horse."

"Which bein' the donkey?" A scowl covered Murphy's face.

"Not me, Papa." Annabel's eyes teased him.

He drove another mile before he spoke again.

"I ain't goin' to always be here, darlin'."

"I worry about you being in this dangerous business."

"It won't be for much longer."

They passed the lane leading to their closest neighbors. Clothes were flapping on the line and a flock of white chickens searched for tidbits in the grass around the house. A woman wearing a bib apron stood at the corner of the house and watched them pass.

"I'm thinkin' I shoulda put ya in a boardinghouse somewhere."

"Papa, you forget I'm a grown woman. If you put me in a boardinghouse, I'd not stay. I want to be where you are."

Not another word was said until he stopped the car beside the back door.

"I'll have a word with Boone before I carry in what we brought from the store."

After the noon meal, Murphy took his suitcase to the car, then went to the barn, where he spoke at length with Boone before he came back to the stoop where Annabel waited.

"Boone or Spinner will be here. Ya got the pistol if ya should be needin' it."

"I'll be all right. Don't worry."

Murphy pulled out the choke, stepped on the starter and the motor started. The powerful engine rocked the car. Murphy adjusted the throttle and put his hand out the window to clasp hers.

"'Bye, Papa. Be careful."

Murphy squeezed her hand and drove away.

Annabel walked around the house and watched the car

until it was out of sight. Then loneliness settled over her like a dark cloak. She went up onto the front porch and sat down in the porch swing. The worry was always there. Whenever he left, she always feared that he would never come back.

She heard the jingle of harness before a wagon pulled by two large mules came from the back of the house with Spinner on the seat. He was a tall, thin man with a face that reminded Annabel of a hound dog, and he had the disposition of one: He was kind, gentle and was silent unless he were riled about something.

Boone came from around the house and stood with his hands on his hips, watching the wagon go down the lane the car had traveled just minutes before. He turned to put a booted foot on the edge of the porch.

"Boone, will we be here long enough for me to plant a garden?"

"Should be. Want me to dig ya a spot?"

"Whoever lived here before had a garden south of the house. I wish I had some chickens to tend."

"That's easy. I'll get ya some."

"We don't have a pen. A fox would be sure to get them."

"That's easy too. I'll throw up some wire next to the shed."

Annabel judged Boone to be only a few years younger than her father and an inch or so shorter. He had crisp black hair, a stubble of black beard and black eyes. She had seen his face cleanly shaven only one time during the years she had known him. At that time she had asked him why he let it be covered with the whiskers. His reply was that he didn't have time to shave every day.

"Papa said to tell you if I wanted anything. Well . . ." She paused and smiled at him. "I want a cow to milk and . . . some hogs." Her eyes teased him.

"Whoa, now. Ain't no smiles ever goin' to get me to get ya any hogs. A cow . . . maybe."

"I'd feel more settled here with chickens and a cow. But when we move, I'll hate to go off and leave them."

"It ain't been easy for ya, movin' ever' whip stitch. This ain't a business for a family man."

"I wish Papa would give it up."

"He's thinkin' on it."

"It's what he says every time I ask him."

"Keep askin'. Maybe he'll do it."

"Boone, do you know the people who live down the road?"

"What's to know about them?"

"Papa said they were hill trash and not anyone I'd want to know."

"He's . . . 'bout right. They got a still up in the hills."

"They? I saw a woman standing in the yard."

"Three brothers live there. I don't know if the woman is a sister or a wife to one of them."

"It would've been nice to have a neighbor."

Boone had come onto the porch and was relaxing against the side of the door, his hands tucked beneath his armpits.

"I've seen them watchin' us. If one comes 'round here at night, he'll get a load of buckshot." He shoved himself away from the wall and went to the edge of the porch. "I better shake a leg. Got thin's to do."

"I got dried peaches while we were in town. I'll make a peach cobbler for supper. We need cheering up." Annabel slid from the swing.

Boone's quick laugh broke with throaty vibrancy and his dark eyes shone with admiration.

"I can't think of a better way to do it than tyin' into a peach cobbler."

Boone was good company. He amused her during supper and while she washed the dishes with tales of his lumberjack days in Michigan. When the kitchen was tidy once again, they went to the parlor. She took her violin from its case, and Boone settled back in a big leather chair. She played for him but mostly for herself. An hour passed as she filled the room with music. Boone could have sat there all night and was sorry when she put the instrument back in the case.

He patted her on the shoulder and went to his sleeping quarters in the barn.

Annabel sighed and went to bed.

Chapter 2

"BOONE, DO I DARE LET THEM OUT?" Annabel proudly watched a dozen big white hens and the cocky rooster strut inside the tight fence.

"I think so. Spread some of that chicken feed around. They'll not wander far from the feed."

"Here, chicky, chicky—" Annabel pulled back the section of the fence used as a gate and threw out a handful of feed from the bucket she carried. She laughed with delight when the rooster, exerting his dominance over the hens, marched out of the opening first and began to cram himself with the unexpected offering scattered in the grass.

"Thank you, Boone." She smiled lovingly. "When will we get eggs?"

"It ain't ort to be long. The man said there was some good layers in the bunch."

"I'm going to name him Peter the Great."

"Who're you namin' that?"

"The rooster. Peter the Great was big, almost seven feet tall. And he was rude and arrogant like that rooster."

"Never heard of him."

"He was the czar of Russia back in the early 1700s."

Boone snorted.

"One of my history teachers in school was fascinated by Russian history. She sat on her desk and told us stories about Peter the Great. When he went to France, he jumped from his carriage and picked up King Louis the Fifteenth, who was a child, and kissed him. The French about had heart attacks. No one was ever allowed to touch the king, but Peter, in his arrogance, didn't care about that."

Annabel saw the bemused look on Boone's face and, realizing the subject was of no interest to him, changed it.

"What do you think Papa will say about the cow?"

"He'll snort. I'll get 'er in the mornin'. Spinner will be here. I'll ride in and lead her back. It'll be a slow walk."

"It'll be a long walk for the poor thing."

"I'll stop and let her rest now and then."

"It's going to be grand having fresh milk and eggs."

"And a chicken once in a while."

"Not one of my hens!" Annabel glanced at Boone and saw the teasing look in his eyes. "You'll have to teach me to milk, Boone."

"Yore pa won't be wantin' ya milkin'. He's wantin' ya to be givin' teas and such."

"I want to learn to milk my cow. What color is she?"

Boone's answering chuckle was dry. "Color? Hell . . . I reckon she's brown."

Annabel's eyes shone with enjoyment and Boone thought once again that Murphy should get out of business and give the girl the home she deserved.

"Did I say thank you, Boone?"

" 'Bout ten times, but ya can thank me again tonight by playin' some more tunes on your fiddle."

*   *   *

The boy had a terrible pain in his head when he woke up, lying on the bank of a small stream. He hurt all over: back, legs, arms, hands. When he was able to sit up and look around, he saw an old man squatting with his back to a tree. He also saw what was left of his measly possessions strewn near him. The old man got up and began stuffing them in the bag that lay nearby. He picked up a sheet of paper that had been wadded up and tossed aside.

"While ya was sleepin', some fellers went through yore stuff. This's yores. They couldn't read it." He put the paper in the bag. "I saw ya sleepin' here, boy. Soon as ya can, ya best get on down the road. This ain't a good place to be sleepin'."

Jack looked at him with a dazed expression on his face, then bent over and vomited. When he straightened up, he could scarcely focus his eyes.

"I . . . don't feel good."

"Looks like ya got the chill fever, boy. Don't stay 'round here. Go on, now. Find ya a place and hole up till yo're feelin' better. They took yore grub, but here's some bread and dried deer meat to tide ya over."

"Thanks," he muttered and rose unsteadily to his feet. He held on to a sapling and waited until the trees stopped dancing before his eyes, then staggered away.

He spent the next couple of days in a field south of Henderson, sleeping in a haystack and nursing his aching head. Hunger had forced him to forage in a garden at night to find food. He had considered asking for work in Henderson; but he was weak, and he feared bones in his left hand had been broken when a crate fell on it while he was helping unload a barge a few days ago. There wasn't much he would be able to do in the way of earning money.

After leaving the hayfield this morning, Jack had made his way to the riverbank and sat throughout the day watch-

ing the water roll by and wondering what he was going to
do. He was broke and weak and a long way from home. Tears
of despair filled his eyes. Refusing to acknowledge them, he
let them run unchecked down his cheeks.

From his bag he took out the letter the old man had res-
cued and read it again.

Dear Jack,

It has been a long time since we last heard from you
and I'm not even sure this letter will reach you. I wish
you would write more often. I've been worried and
Evan is threatening to come and fetch you home.

The crops are in. Evan bought a gasoline tractor. He
is like a kid with a new toy. When he isn't playing with
his son, he's tinkering with that machine. Jacob was a
year old last Wednesday and starting to walk. I wish
you could see him. Papa says he looks like you when
you were little, but he has his father's blond hair.

Corbin has quit his job as police chief. He's gone to
see his folk in Springfield, but says he'll be back.

Joy keeps asking when you're coming home. She
will start school next year if I can get her to go and
leave the baby. She thinks that he will be lonesome
without her.

I'm sorry you didn't make the baseball team but
there will be other chances to try out. The traveling
league will be back this summer. Come home and play
on the town team.

We are all well and happy here, but, Jack, we miss
you. Our family is not complete without you. Please
come home. It's been almost a year since we've seen
you. Papa is worried about you too.

If you're not ready to come home, write and let us know that you are all right.

Your loving sister,
Julie

When he finished reading the letter, he folded it and carefully put it in his shirt pocket.

I'm sorry for your worry, Sis. I'd write, but I don't even have the two cents to buy a stamp.

Knowing that he had to move, Jack got slowly to his feet, lifted his bag to his shoulder and left the riverbank. He hurt in a hundred different places and worried that he was in no condition to protect himself if he was set upon.

Trying to ignore the hunger pangs in his stomach, he put one foot in front of the other as he trudged down the dusty road. He was determined to get as far from Henderson as possible before he found a spot for the night. The cloth sack he carried on his shoulder held the sum total of his possessions. It was much lighter than it had been a few days ago before his blanket, his food, his baseball and his leather mitt had been stolen.

Twilight had darkened into night. The moon, made dim by a thin layer of rain clouds, rose over the treetops. The road Jack traveled was bounded by woods on one side and a field on the other. Just beyond the woods was the mighty Mississippi River. He knew that he had to eat, sleep, drink water and stay as far away from people as possible until he was sure he was strong enough to protect himself.

He was so tired he could hardly move when he left the road and slogged into a patch of wild chokecherry bushes. He eased the bag from his shoulder and sank wearily down on the ground. Seeing a faint light coming from a house set

on a hill above the road comforted him. He didn't feel quite
so alone.

Digging into his bag, he foraged for the green onions,
radishes and green beans he had gleaned from a garden last
night and washed this morning in the stream. He had picked
a few wild strawberries that grew back from that stream to
stave off his hunger. He thought longingly of the rabbit he
had seen that morning. He had been tempted to try to knock
it down with a rock until it occurred to him that he didn't
have a way to cook it.

Leaning on one elbow, Jack looked at the house across
the road and up the hill. The faint light glowed from one of
the windows. Was the woman of the house making supper?
About this time Julie would be cooking for Evan and Joy. Eudora would be preparing a meal for Pa, Jason and Jill. They
would sit at the table and talk about the happenings of the
day. He thought about his brother Joe, who found enjoyment
in almost everything, and wished he were here with him.

Jack chewed on the radishes and the green beans and
washed the raw vegetables down with water from the fruit
jar he carried in his bag. He had discovered that if he drank
a lot of water he wasn't quite so hungry.

When the sound of music drifted down to him on the
evening breeze, he was startled. It was so hauntingly beautiful and so unexpected that it frightened him. He got to his
feet. The melody must be coming from the house on the hill.
He went to the edge of the road to listen. Someone was playing a violin. The tune was an Irish song that he had heard
many times on Evan's gramophone. He couldn't remember
the name of the tune, but he knew it was being played by
someone who loved to play the instrument.

In awe, he gazed up the hill. The music seemed to surround him. He stood there, even when intermittent rain-

drops began to fall, only vaguely aware of the ache in his back and in his legs. When the music stopped after a series of fast tunes that ended with "Over There," the song made popular during the war, he waited for a long while beside the road before he went back to the nest he had made for himself amid the chokecherry bushes.

Lying down with his canvas bag over his head and shoulders to shield them from the rain, he let his misery flow through him. For the first time since he was a small child, he allowed himself to cry. He was eighteen years old and wished fervently that he were a child again back in the farmhouse on the edge of Fertile with the family who cared about him. His sister Julie would be fussing over him and urging him to drink hot tea. Joe, his older brother, would tell him to not worry about his chores, that he would take care of them. And little Joy would want to sit beside him holding his hand.

Throughout the miserable night Jack huddled beneath the bushes. When dawn lit the eastern sky, he was shivering almost uncontrollably. Hurt and sick, he realized that as much as he hated to do it, he was going to have to ask for help.

Annabel was checking on the biscuits in the oven when she heard a rap on the door. Sure that it was Boone or Spinner, she called out, "Come on in."

A minute later the rap came again and, thinking she had latched the screen, she went through the front room to the door. A man stood there, his arms outstretched to brace himself against the house.

"Ma'am . . ."

"Yes?"

"Ma'am, I . . . hate to trouble you, but . . ."

Annabel, seeing the fuzz on his cheeks, realized that he

was little more than a boy. His face was thin, his cheeks sunken, his eyes feverish. She pushed open the screen door and went out onto the porch.

"I apologize for my appearance . . ."

"What is the matter? Are you sick?" she said.

"Oh, I . . . ah . . . yes, ma'am. I got a touch of something. I'm sure it's not catching. I'd be obliged for a bite to eat. I'll work . . ." His voice trailed because his head was swimming and he was so weak he was afraid he'd cry.

"You're sick!"

"Yes, ma'am, but I'd be all right if I had—"

"Come over here and sit down in the swing."

He left his sack on the floor beside the door, went to the swing and sank down as if his legs wouldn't hold him for another minute. Annabel followed and placed the back of her hand on his forehead.

"You've got a fever and your . . . clothes are wet. Did you sleep out in the rain last night?"

"Yes, ma'am."

"Sit here. I'll be right back."

Annabel went through the house, stopped in the kitchen to take the biscuits from the oven and hurried out the back door. Boone came out of the barn as she was crossing the yard.

"Boone, there's a boy on the porch and . . . he's sick."

"Whata ya mean?" Boone quickened his steps.

"What I said. He's sick. He slept out in the rain last night. He needs help."

Annabel had to hurry to keep up with Boone's long strides as he headed for the house. They came around the corner to see that the boy was resting his head on the wooden arm of the porch swing. Jack's eyes were closed, but they opened as soon as Boone touched his shoulder. They were glassy and feverish.

"Pa? Am I home?"

"Oh, Boone! He's out of his head. We've got to get him into the house."

"Hold on, girl. I got to see if he's got any spots on him. He could have the scarlet fever or somethin' else catchin'."

Jack didn't seem to notice when Boone opened his shirt and looked at his chest and shoulders.

"I'd say some bones in that hand is broke," Boone said when he saw Jack's swollen left hand. "Don't reckon he's got anythin' catchin'. Don't see any spots. I'll take him to the barn."

"He's just a boy. Put him on Papa's bed for now."

"Papa?" Jack's whisper came through his puffed lips.

"He can't stay in here."

"Why not? There isn't a place for him in the barn and we can't turn him away."

"It ain't decent you bein' in here with him."

"Fiddle, Boone. You think I can't hold my own with a sick boy? Put him on Papa's bed." Annabel went to hold open the screen door.

"Can you stand up, boy?" Boone hooked his hand beneath Jack's arm and helped him to his feet. Jack's legs stiffened and he tried to remain upright, but he sagged against Boone.

"I'm sick, Pa. . . ."

"Yeah, ya are, boy."

Jack wasn't what you would call big. He was average height, stocky. Almost dead weight, he put a strain on Boone as Boone tried to get him into the house. Annabel pulled back the quilt she used as a spread on her father's bed and Boone eased the boy down to sit on the side.

"Shouldn't we get him to a doctor?" Annabel asked.

"We'll see about that later. First thing is to get him out of these wet clothes." Boone unlaced Jack's shoes and pulled them off.

"I'll get one of Papa's union suits."

"Then go fix up a toddy."

"Whiskey toddy?"

"Like the one you fixed when Spinner came down with influenza."

"Do you think he's got . . . that?"

"I don't be knowin' what he's got."

Annabel placed the union suit on the end of the bed, went to the kitchen and reached for the bottle of whiskey they kept for toddies. In a heavy cup she put several spoons-ful of the fiery liquid, added a dab of butter and a spoonful of sugar, then filled the cup with water from the teakettle on the stove.

She stood outside the bedroom until Boone told her to come in. He had stripped the boy and put him in the union suit. His wet clothes lay in a heap on the floor. As she came in, Boone was easing him down into the bed.

Boone pulled a cover up over Jack's shoulders. "Got to get him warm."

"Can you prop his head up? I'll spoon this into his mouth."

The breakfast biscuits were cold by the time they were finished with Jack and had left him to sleep. Annabel put the pan back in the oven and pulled the skillet of gravy over the flame.

"Who do you suppose he is? He was polite when he asked for something to eat. He said he would work, but I knew right away that he was in no shape to do that."

"He's a well-muscled kid. Ain't got a dime."

"Will he be all right?"

"I'm thinkin' he will. That slug of whiskey put him to sleep. When he wakes, ya can feed him, and in a day or two he'll be on his way."

"Are you going to get the cow today?"

"When Spinner gets here." Boone spooned gravy over the biscuits he had split and put on his plate.

"Where did he go?" Annabel asked with her back to him.

"Spinner? He went to buy some fence posts." Boone answered her with his eyes on his plate.

"Boone, you and Papa must think I'm dumb as a cob," Annabel said with spirit. "I know he went to get a load of booze and take it to wherever you keep it stashed away."

"Then why'd ya ask?"

"Because sometimes I like to see you squirm while thinking of a lie to tell me."

Boone looked up, and his black eyes met hers. "The less ya know, the better it'll be for ya."

"When you and Papa are caught?"

"A smart girl what knows 'bout czars of Russia and stuff like that ought to figure it out."

"Oh, Boone, I worry all the time that something will happen to Papa and . . . you. Why don't you do something else?"

"Money. Murphy's good at this and he's got connections. He'll quit when he's got enough money."

"No one ever has enough money. The richest men in the world are still grubbing for more." Her large green eyes met his and refused to look away. "Where did Spinner go?" she asked again.

"He met a barge and took a load up to a cave in the bluffs."

"Well, at last I'm getting a straight answer. Aren't you

afraid the Feds or someone roaming around in the hills will find it?"

"There's a charge set. If anyone gets close, we'll blow it. Now sit and eat and stop worryin' 'bout somethin' ya can't do nothin' 'bout."

Chapter 3

ANNABEL WAS HANGING JACK'S WET CLOTHES on the line when Spinner drove the wagon up the lane to the house.

"Come have breakfast, Spinner," she called.

He nodded as he passed and drove the team on around behind the barn.

An extremely shy man, Spinner stayed away from the house as much as possible. He was tall, with a hooked nose and a mouth that looked too wide for his narrow face. Annabel didn't know much about his background except that he must have been raised on a farm because he was very knowledgeable about horses and mules. She didn't know if he had a family or even where he was from.

Annabel liked him, though. From the deep lines in his face she guessed that sometime in his younger years he had suffered immense pain. He seldom smiled and she had never heard him laugh in all the years he had worked for her father.

Boone, on the other hand, was like a favorite uncle. It was while working on riverboats that he had met Murphy, and they had been fast friends for ten years or more. She remembered how Boone had grieved with her and her father when her mother died. He had never married, as far as she knew, and had spent the earlier part of his life in logging camps. He spoke with fondness of his sister and her family who lived in Minnesota.

Annabel picked up the letter she had taken from the boy's shirt pocket. The outside fold had been wet. Earlier she had carefully unfolded it and placed it in the warming oven to dry. She learned as she read it now that the boy's name was Jack. The letter was from his sister Julie, who was worried about him. Annabel felt guilty about reading the personal letter. She folded it again now that it was dry and left it on the table along with a jackknife and two shiny buckeyes she had taken from his pants pocket. If he'd had any money it was probably stolen while he was sick.

She had emptied the canvas sack he carried and found a pair of socks, a union suit and a pair of ankle-high shoes with spikes in the soles. She guessed them to be like the ones used by baseball players. In the bottom of the bag were a few onions and wrinkled radishes. It was no wonder the boy was weak if that was all he'd had to eat.

Annabel put a stick of wood in the cookstove and moved the coffeepot over the flame. Spinner liked really hot coffee.

Boone helped Spinner unharness the mules.

"How'd it go?" he asked as they carried the harnesses to the shed.

"All right."

"Was there anyone on the levee when you loaded?"

"Couple of darkies. They paid no mind."

"Was anythin' said 'bout when the next load would come down?" Boone knew that to get any information from Spinner he had to ask for it specifically.

"A week from next Thursday on the *Betty K.* She's bringin' down a cargo of sawed lumber."

Boone grunted a reply, then said, "There's a sick boy in the house."

This got Spinner's attention. "What he sick of?"

"Been sleepin' out in the rain. Don't reckon it's anythin' catchin'."

"How come he's here?"

"Come wobblin' up to the door. Ya know how Annabel is. She'd tend a sick polecat."

"Murphy won't like it."

"Tell it to Annabel. Remember when she took in that crippled old bum up at Ashton? Murphy didn't like that, but it didn't do him much good. The old bum give her a song and dance 'bout bein' in the war, and she fed him till Murphy sent him on down the road."

"He *was* in the war," Spinner said with more spirit than Boone had heard in a long time. "Got his foot blowed off in France. Showed me his papers."

"I ain't sayin' he wasn't in the war. I'm sayin' he drank enough of Murphy's whiskey to float a barge, and I'm sayin' Annabel's got a heart soft as goose down."

"There's worse thin's than that."

"Christ on a horse! I ain't sayin' it's bad."

Spinner ignored the outburst. "Where'd the chickens come from?"

"Farmer this side of town. I'm goin' to fetch a cow now that you're here."

"A cow? Lordy, what next? But I guess it'll be nice havin' a cow."

"Then you can milk her. I sure as hell ain't goin' to."

Spinner shrugged and started toward the house.

"Take a look at the boy. Ya might of seen him around."

Boone saddled a horse and grumbled to himself. He hated riding a horse. He would take the truck, but driving it slowly enough for the cow to walk behind it would overheat the motor. He comforted himself by thinking that on the horse he could cut off a mile going through the woods.

He led the horse to the house and tied the reins to the porch post. When he stepped into the kitchen, Spinner was seated at the table. Annabel was at the stove.

"I should be back by noon."

"Will you be going into town?" Annabel asked.

"Wasn't plannin' on it. Ya need somethin'?"

"Well . . . I thought if you were in town you could go by Mr. Potter's pharmacy and get some 666s or something for the boy."

"What's wrong with that toddy ya fixed?"

"I need something to bring down his fever."

"Get Spinner to dump him in the horse trough. It's what used to be done to brin' down a fever."

"Oh, go on and get the cow." She made an arrow of her arm and forefinger and softened the order with a smile. "If Jack's fever isn't down by night, you'll have to load him in the truck and take him to the doctor."

"Jack?"

"His name's Jack and he has a sister named Julie."

"Has he woke up?"

"No. I found a letter in his shirt pocket."

"Ya better hope the boy's on his feet and out by the time yore pa comes back."

"If Papa comes, Spinner will fix a place for Jack in the barn, won't you, Spinner?" She smiled sweetly at the man buttering a biscuit.

Boone snorted and grumbled as he left the kitchen. "If ya

asked that dumb stump to turn himself inside out, he'd do his damnedest to do it."

Boone gave the mare her head when they reached the wooded area, and she followed a faint path. He passed beneath a tall topless pine, the victim of a spring storm. An outburst of furious scolding came from a blue jay, followed by a concerted chorus of profanity from a dozen others. Then all was quiet again. The song of a thrush came from far away. After that there was only the swish of hooves cutting through a deep cushion of dried leaves.

The silence absorbed him completely.

Boone loved the woods more, much more, than he loved the river. He was acutely conscious of the overpowering solitude of his surroundings and was enjoying it.

The twitching of the horse's ears alerted him. He scanned the woods on each side of the path and saw a woman standing as still as a doe with her back to a large oak with wide-spreading branches. Her hair and her face were a light honey color. A faded print dress just barely covered her knees, and she held a small bucket in her arms.

Instinctively Boone pulled up on the reins and put his hand to the brim of his hat.

"Howdy, ma'am."

Startled, she lurched away from the tree and started running down the path as if the devil himself were after her.

"Ma'am . . ." Boone called. "I'm sorry I scared ya."

The woman was no more than fifty feet away from him when she tripped and went sprawling face down amid the twigs and leaves in the path. The bucket flew from her hand, spilling the wild raspberries she had been gathering. She lay in a tangled heap, exposing white legs and heavy black shoes.

Boone dismounted and hurried to her.

"Ma'am? Ma'am, are you hurt? I'm sorry I scared ya."

She turned over, hastily covered her legs with her skirt and cowered from him. Twigs were caught in her hair. Her face was scratched; her lips trembled. She looked at him with large, frightened eyes.

"Can I help you pick up the berries?" Boone took the two steps necessary to reach the bucket and began picking the berries up off the ground. He glanced at her when she got to her knees and then to her feet.

Boone was surprised to see that she was not a young girl in spite of her small stature. She had the rounded figure of a woman whom he judged to be somewhat older than Annabel. Her amber eyes blended with her face and hair. Her mouth was soft and open as she gulped in air.

"I'm afraid we won't find all the berries that spilled," he said, not looking up.

Out of the corner of his eye Boone could see the ragged hem of her dress and the heavy-soled shoes that laced up over her ankles. As he stood to hand her the bucket, it occurred to him that she hadn't uttered a sound, not even when she fell.

"I'm from over at the next place." He raised his hand to point in that direction.

She lifted her eyes. They were large, fringed by lashes golden and thick. Boone looked into their depths for what seemed to be only an instant, but it was much longer than that. She turned her head suddenly. Boone's eyes followed hers and saw a man on a mule hurrying toward them. He recognized the old black felt hat worn by the neighbor who had been spying on them.

"What're ya doin' out here with 'im?" he shouted angrily as he neared. "Get home! Now!"

Boone could almost feel her fear. She tried to dart around him and bumped into him with the bucket. She paused as if to apologize, then jumped when the man shouted at her again.

"Tessie! Get!"

Like a frightened doe, the woman scurried away and disappeared into the brush that grew along the path. Boone stepped into the saddle and looked steadily at the man, who was not much more than a boy. He was skinny, with narrow shoulders and long arms, and glared at him like a cornered wildcat. His furious eyes were set close together and his brows met across his hawklike nose.

"What ya doin' on our land?"

"Just passin' through."

"Ya got no right bein' here."

"I'm from the place north of yours."

"I know where yo're from."

"Sure you do. You've been watchin' us." Boone was losing his patience. "Why didn't ya come on in . . . like a decent neighbor would?"

"Bullshit!" the boy snorted. "Ya try and get next to Tessie an' ya'll get yore head blowed off!" He moved the mule nearer to the mare and she danced away.

"What the hell ya talkin' about? I never saw the woman until now. I scared her and—"

"She knew ya was comin' through here, didn't she?" He jutted his head toward Boone and let his hand rest on the rifle in the holster on his saddle.

"How would she know that? I've never seen her before. Now get the hell out of my way."

"Or what?"

"I'll jerk ya off that mule and mop the ground with ya!"

"Mouthy, ain't ya?"

"I can take care of myself, if that's what ya mean. We want no trouble with ya. We already know ya got a still in the hills. It's no business of ours unless you make it our business."

The boy's face froze. "How ya be knowin' that? Tessie tell ya?"

"Yo're about the dumbest shit-head I've come across in a long time. That woman didn't utter a word, but you'll believe what you want to. I'll tell you this—you tend to yore business, we'll tend to ours." Boone could see that he had taken some of the wind out of the boy's sails.

"Bud and Marvin ain't goin' to take it kindly that ya was spyin' on us and chasin' Tessie. I saw her runnin' from ya."

"She was runnin' 'cause I scared her. I don't give a horse turd what you think." Boone rode around the boy, wondering if he would put a bullet in his back. He turned in the saddle to look back at him and saw him going on down the path, then turning up toward the hills. "Stupid son-of-a-bitch," he muttered. "How did a woman like that get tangled up with a shit-for-brains ignoramus like him?"

Annabel was out of the house and into the yard the minute Boone rode in leading the cow. She was delighted with the animal and petted and cooed to her. She pulled fresh green grass and fed her.

"You are beautiful, just beautiful." Annabel patted the sides of the cow's face. "Look at her eyes, Boone. She knows she's found a good home."

"Confound it! She ort to. I paid out seven good dollars for her. She's lucky she ain't hangin' head down in the butcher shop."

Annabel wrinkled her nose at him, then spoke to the cow.

"And you're worth every penny, aren't you, Mildred?"

"Mildred? How'd you come up with that?" Boone rocked back on his heels and tried not to grin.

"She reminds me of a girl in school named Mildred. She had big brown eyes and big—" She glanced down at the cow's full udder. "Well, never mind. Are you going to milk Mildred?"

"Hell, no. Spinner will do it. Where's he at?"

"In the house with Jack."

"How is he?"

"Asleep. When he wakes up, I'll give him a dish of oatmeal with brown sugar on it and good fresh milk. Spinner doesn't think much of oatmeal. He said Jack needs meat to build his strength. It was good of you to get the cow, but I wish I'd remembered to tell you to go to the butcher shop while you were in town."

"I ain't goin' back to town no matter how much ya butter me up."

"I'm not buttering you up, for heaven's sake!"

"Yeah, ya are, and ya know it. It's my turn to go up to the . . . to go someplace. Ya can try and sweet-talk Spinner, but he can't leave here unless he takes ya with him."

"I know that. I can't go and leave Jack. So, how are we going to get fresh meat?"

"I'll kill a chicken."

"Boone! You wouldn't! You're teasing, aren't you?"

"Ya goin' to let them hens die of old age?"

"They're so sweet and trusting. I couldn't possibly cook one, much less eat it. Couldn't you take the truck and go to town before you go to spend the night guarding Papa's stash of illegal booze?"

Boone frowned. "Don't be sayin' anythin' like that in front of the kid."

"I won't. I know better than that. I've learned something during the years you and Papa have been . . . outlaws." Her grin told him that she was teasing.

"How long have you known about it?"

"Almost from the first. Mama didn't know."

"I'm glad a that."

"Well? Will you go to the butcher shop?"

"Now, lass—"

"It won't take long in the truck. Please, Boone. I could go with you. Spinner can stay with Jack."

"Oh, all right, but ya ain't goin'. I ain't waitin' around while ya go get yoreself all duded up to go to town, then waitin' while ya go lollygaggin' in and out of the stores. Whata ya want from the butcher?"

Annabel stretched up and kissed him on the cheek. "You're sweet and . . . almost as pretty as Mildred."

"Yo're a headstrong, schemin' little twit," he grumbled and, trying hard to keep the frown on his face, headed for the truck in the shed.

Boone drove slowly as he passed the neighbors to the south and scanned the area for a glimpse of the woman he'd met in the woods. He hadn't been able to get her out of his mind. He wanted to know if she had suffered because of their accidental meeting. He considered turning the truck up the rutted lane to the house but discarded the idea for fear he'd again bring down on her the wrath of the bully who had sent her home.

For the first time in many years Boone felt concern for a woman other than Annabel. He couldn't help wondering if the ill-mannered lout was her husband. If she was the wife of one of his brothers, he wouldn't have spoken to her like that—or would he? Tessie. Her name was Tessie and it fit her. The mouthy brute was just the type to knock around a little thing like her.

Boone felt anger boil up. He'd like nothing better than to whip the hillbilly's ass; and if he got half a chance, he'd do it.

Murphy had been told after he bought the place that the nearest neighbors, the Carter clan, had lived in these hills for generations. They were a close-knit group who had little to do with anyone other than family. The Carters had operated a still since the war. If the Feds knew about it, they chose to ignore it because it was so piddling an enterprise.

Boone went on down the road and into town. He stopped at the butcher shop and bought a ten-pound chunk of beef and another ten pounds of meat and bones to make soup, then went to the icehouse and got a fifty-pound block of ice. On the way back he slowed again when he passed the Carters', but not a soul was in sight.

When Jack awoke, the sun was hanging low in the western sky. It was pure luxury to lie in the warm soft bed. At first he thought that he was home. Then he opened his eyes. He was in a strange room, a strange house. Memory came rushing back, and he remembered his struggle to get up the hill to the house and how he hated having to ask for food.

He didn't recall taking off his wet clothes or putting on this union suit. Surely the woman . . . no, now he remembered that a man with a dark stubble on his face had helped him and that the woman had spooned something hot and tangy in his mouth. They had been kind and he had felt safe.

He heard his stomach rumble. Lord, he was hungry.

The woman came quietly into the room and smiled at seeing him awake. She placed her palm against his forehead.

"Your fever is down. I bet you're hungry." She had a pretty face and a soft, lilting voice. She reminded him of his sister Julie, except that she had short dark hair. Julie's was lighter and long.

"Yes, ma'am." The long sleep had cleared his head. The only thing that really ached now was his hand and his empty stomach.

"I'll bring you a bowl of oatmeal. Spinner has gone to milk our cow; and as soon as he comes in, you'll have a glass of fresh milk."

"Thank you, ma'am. I'll repay you with work as soon as I can get my legs under me."

"We won't worry about that now, Jack." She saw the puzzled look come over his face. "I took a letter addressed to Jack out of your shirt pocket and spread it out to dry. You are Jack, aren't you?"

"Yes, ma'am. Jack Jones. My family lives in Fertile, Missouri."

"Is that near here?"

"No, ma'am. It's in the northwest corner of the state over near St. Joseph."

"I'm not very good at geography. I've no idea where St. Joseph is."

"I'm sorry to be so much trouble. I thank you for taking me in."

"You're very welcome, Jack."

"Ma'am, I can't pay right now. I didn't have much money to start, but while I was sick and sleepin' someone took it."

"You shouldn't be worrying about paying. You should eat something like oatmeal if you haven't eaten a hearty meal for a while. Your stomach will be more able to handle it."

"Oatmeal sounds like a feast, ma'am."

"I'm cooking some beef. Later I'll give you broth." She smiled and Jack was sure that he'd never seen a sweeter smile.

"If I had my clothes—"

"I hung them on the line to dry. I'll get them after I bring your oatmeal."

"Ma'am, I can't let you wait on me. If I had my clothes I could come to the table or . . . eat on the porch."

"I won't hear of it. You'll stay right there until morning."

"But . . . this is somebody's bed—"

"It's my father's and he's away right now."

"The man that . . . helped me?"

"No, that was Boone. He's gone now too, but Spinner is here. Spinner and Boone work for my father." Annabel laughed teasingly. "Don't worry about it. There is always someone here in case you decide to get up and rob the place."

"I feel that I'm a . . . bother."

"Well, you're not. I'll go get your oatmeal." She turned to leave.

"Ma'am," Jack called. "Who was playing the violin last night?"

Annabel turned. "You heard that?"

"Yes, ma'am. I was down by the road. It seemed to be coming from heaven. It was the most beautiful music I ever heard."

Annabel beamed. "Thank you, Jack. I love the violin and play for a while most evenings. I'll play for you tonight if you like."

She disappeared from the doorway and Jack thanked God for bringing him to this place.

Chapter 4

CORBIN EXPECTED THE BRUTAL IMPACT of another bullet at any second now. He waited. But it did not come.

A burning rod was thrusting through his leg between his knee and his hip, and another in his shoulder. He staggered forward to find protection behind his car, slipped on some loose shale and fell. He struck the ground hard and felt his life crushed out of him. After that, he slid into kindly darkness.

When life came back, he lifted his hand to his head and tried to raise himself to his elbow. Pain knifed through him and he sank back down. He could see that he was in a room with plank walls, an iron cookstove and a square table. Seated at the table was a man whose face was covered with stubby whiskers as black as night, and the eyes staring at him were still blacker. The scene faded and he wasn't sure if it was real until the man spoke.

"Take it easy." The man unfolded himself from the chair and stretched out a hand to press him down on the deep soft bed of evergreen tips. He sank back and closed his eyes. Although a blanket covered the boughs he lay on, he could still smell the fragrance of the pines and vaguely recognized the sound of tree limbs swishing against the roof.

"Ya've come to. Guess I won't have to dig a hole and bury ya after all."

Corbin Appleby opened his eyes again and tried to sort out his vague thoughts. He waited until his eyes could focus before he spoke.

"Who are you?"

The man chuckled. "If you ain't knowin', I ain't tellin' ya."

"Was it you who shot me?"

"If it'd been me, you'd be dead."

"Name's Corbin Appleby."

"Ya know yore name, do ya? It's a good sign. Thought maybe ya whacked yore head, ya was out so long. Do ya want a drink of water?"

"I sure do." Corbin closed his eyes and didn't see the man go to the water pail beside the door. He was drifting toward the blackness when he felt a touch on his shoulder.

"Don't ya be fadin' away again. I'm a gettin' tired talkin' to myself."

A large hand beneath his head lifted it, and a cup was held to his mouth. The water was cool and good. He had to resist the urge to gulp. The liquid slid down his dry throat like fine wine.

"Not too much to start. I ain't wantin' to be cleanin' up no puke."

"Am I hurt bad?" Corbin's head sank wearily back down on the blanket.

"Bad enough to keep ya sleepin' off an' on most of the day."

"My head feels like someone is pounding on it with a sledgehammer."

"Don't doubt that a bit. Ya got a goose egg up there big as a good-sized horse turd. Yore head found a rock when ya fell."

"My legs!"

"They're still there."

"Did the bullet hit a bone?"

"Don't think so. Ya moved it when I dug the bullet out and yelled like a kid gettin' his butt whopped. Ya ain't goin' to be dancin' on it for a while."

"My shoulder?"

"Bullet went in and out. Scraped yore shoulder blade is all."

"Who shot me?"

The man shrugged. "Somebody that didn't want ya messin' around."

"Shit! I wasn't looking for a still."

The black-bearded man chuckled.

Corbin's hand moved to his belly. He was naked.

"Where's my britches?"

"Ya goin' some'ers?"

"Dammit, I'm buck-naked!"

"Ya ain't got nothin' I ain't seen a hundred times. What ya squawkin' about?"

"I've got to get up and go pee."

"Try it, and ya'll keel over. There's a peach can under the bed ya can use."

"I can't use it layin' down."

The man chuckled again. "I ain't much for touchin' another man's talley-wacker." He held out a rusty can. "You'll have to handle it yoreself."

Corbin reached for the can and groaned when he moved his left arm. He eased it down and reached for the can with his right. He screwed his face into a scowl at his helplessness and tried to figure out who had shot him and how he had come to be here.

His heart pounded with the effort it took to merely sit up and relieve himself in the can, then set it back on the floor. A bandage was wrapped around the thigh on his right leg. Fear knifed through him. One of his greatest pleasures was long-distance running. He had been running since his school days. *Would he ever run again?*

"Hungry? I got to get ya on your feet. I ain't sunk so low as to shoot a man flat on his back."

"Why do you want to shoot me?"

"Why not? I ain't shot nobody for a while."

"I wasn't snooping around. I stopped to pee."

"What was ya doin' up here anyhow?"

"Lookin' at the scenery. Where's my car?"

"It's down there in the woods. Ya couldn't get a car up here without wings on it. I toted ya up here belly down on my horse."

"My belly feels like it."

"Feel like eatin'?"

"Right now I feel like I could eat the ass out of a skunk."

The man chuckled, something he seemed to do often. "I can do a bit better'n that."

"What're you called? My name's Corbin Appleby."

"Ya already told me that. Ya can call me Boone 'less there's somethin' else comes to mind."

As Boone walked away, Corbin set his teeth and closed his heart against the appetite that had begun to rage in him. The man returned with a grilled trout on a tin plate.

"Best sit up to eat it. I ain't wantin' ya to choke on a bone."

"Yeah, I know. You want to get me on my feet so you can

shoot me." Corbin struggled to prop himself up on one elbow.

When he had picked the last of the flesh from the small fish, he drank the water Boone brought to him and surrendered to sleep.

Two days passed before Corbin could sit in a chair in the front of the cabin without his head feeling as if it would explode. It was such pleasure to feel the sun beating against him, warming his body, and to see the birds flying and the clouds billowing like huge ocean waves. He could sense his own strength welling up in him like a fountain.

The one-room cabin sat high in the hills and back from a clear stream that flowed down to the Mississippi River. Surrounding the cabin were thick woods. In a small patch at the side, a horse was staked out to eat the grass.

He still had no other name but Boone to put to the man who had saved his life. Nor did he know why Boone wanted to shoot him unless he was a whiskey runner and assumed that because Corbin carried a firearm he was a Fed.

This morning Corbin was able to move around with the help of the crutch made from the branch of a young sapling. Boone had left the cabin shortly after daybreak. He returned in the evening; and, although Corbin never heard a gunshot, Boone brought back a wild turkey that he quickly cleaned and put in the oven of the cookstove.

Another day after Boone left the cabin, Corbin got up the nerve to strip naked and ease down to slide into the stream. The water was cold, but nothing had ever felt as good as washing his entire body. He sat for a long time while the sun dried and warmed him. Later he hobbled back to the cabin, found a razor in a dresser drawer and shaved, observing that nothing restored a man's confidence like a bath and a clean-shaven face.

That same day he watched his companion coming toward the cabin in long purposeful strides. Over his shoulders was stretched the burden of a full-grown stag. Boone came to the stream's edge and cast down the two hundred pounds of fresh meat.

"Brought ya a little snack to eat before supper."

"Good of you. I suppose you expect me to clean it."

"'Less you want to eat it with the hide on. Gut it here by the stream, then I'll string it up so you can skin it."

"My days of lazing around are over."

"Ya got it. I ain't feedin' no freeloaders. Like a little fish first?"

Chuckling, Boone picked up the little spear he'd fashioned from a straight shaft of seasoned ash. On the end of it was a barbed head of steel. He went upstream and knelt on a rock. Swift death shot down to meet the movement of a fin in the furtive shadows of the pool formed in the bend of the stream.

Later Corbin watched and marveled as his companion prepared a spit on which to turn the saddle of venison. It was not the skill alone, it was the quiet, quick way he moved that amazed Corbin and made him wonder how long Boone had lived this life in the hills along the river.

"What are you going to do with all this meat?" Corbin asked.

"It ain't nothin' for ya to worry 'bout."

On the fourth day Corbin felt his sap rising, but still the soreness in his leg and the limited use of his arm held him back. And so he ate and slept while the red blood in his veins grew richer.

Corbin was alone at the cabin for long hours at a time.

When the two men were together, they did not talk a great deal. There seemed to be no need for it. Corbin had not thanked Boone for saving his life, nor had he asked for his reason for wanting to take it.

When at the cabin, Boone constantly worked at something. He caulked the cracks in the cabin walls with clay to make them tighter. He chopped several cords of wood and stacked it beside the house.

One afternoon he cleaned his two guns and the one he had taken from Corbin's car. He took them apart, cleaned and oiled them and reassembled the parts with hands that could have done it if he were sightless.

"Are you expecting Geronimo to ride out of the woods and attack?" Corbin casually asked that evening as they sat in front of the cabin.

"It'd more likely be a nosy lawman," Boone answered without looking up.

"You hiding something?"

"Ain't ever'body?"

"I'm not a lawman."

"Yeah?"

"Is that why you're going to shoot me? You think I'm a Fed?"

"Ain't decided yet."

"Have you heard of a boy named Jack Jones?"

"What's he look like?"

"Sandy hair, blue eyes, strong for a kid his age. He's got a real hankering to be a baseball player."

"Can't say that I have."

"His folks asked me to look for him. Last letter they got was from St. Louis."

"Big town."

"But I found him. Fellow told me he was there trying out

for their team. He said the kid was good, but not good enough, and told him to go home and come back again in a year or two. He thought he headed north."

"Yeah, well—"

"Jack didn't go home. That was four months ago."

"Maybe he didn't wanna go home."

"His folks want to know if he's all right."

"I didn't think it was the business of the law to look fer kids what didn't want to go home."

"I'm not a lawman now. I'm a friend of the family. I went down to Springfield to see my folks and came on over this way on my way back up north."

"Yo're not a Fed?"

"No. I'm not a marshal either. I was a police chief of a town up in the northwest part of the state for several years. You worried about the Feds?"

"Who isn't?"

"I'm not."

Boone looked him in the eye. "You about able to move on?"

"You're not going to shoot me?"

"Didn't say that."

"Who did shoot me?"

"I figure it was one of the hillbillies who has a still in the hills."

"Why didn't they take my car when they had the chance?"

"'Cause I'da shot 'em if they had."

"You wanting it?"

"Hell, if I'da wanted it, I'da took it an' left ya to bleed to death."

"Yeah. Sorry. I appreciate what you did for me."

"Why'd ya quit bein' a lawman?"

"I never planned to make a career of law enforcement. I took the job to catch the man who killed the girl I was going to marry."

"Catch him?"

"In a way. He's dead."

"I may know the kid yo're lookin' for."

"The hell you do? Why in the hell didn't you say so? Where is he?"

"Ain't sayin'. When yo're ready to leave, go into Henderson and I'll brin' him to ya."

"Is he all right?"

"Yeah. So far."

"What do you mean by that? Is he in trouble?"

"Not yet. He's in hog heaven, lappin' up the attention of a pretty woman."

"Goddammit, Boone. Give me some straight answers. Is he in a whorehouse?"

"I can think of worse places to be." Boone's dark eyes shone with amusement.

"The kid's fresh off the farm, for God's sake." Corbin wasn't amused.

"Yeah. He seems like a good enough kid. Needs to be home with his folks." Boone got up and stretched. "Ya can ride my horse down to yore car in the mornin'. I'll put a blind on ya. Don't want ya findin' yore way back up here. You got a problem with that?"

"No. It's better than being shot."

The horseback ride down the mountain was anything but enjoyable. By the time they reached the bottom of the mountain, Corbin's leg felt as if it were being probed with a hot poker. The wound in his shoulder kept him from supporting his thigh and he had to use his other hand to grasp the saddle horn in order to stay in the saddle.

They finally stopped.

Corbin blinked and squinted his eyes against the bright sunlight when Boone untied the blindfold. The man was gentle as he helped him from the house.

"Stay here while I take the horse and see if anyone's nosin' 'round the cars."

Minutes later, Boone was back on foot and led him to where his car and a flatbed truck were hidden amid thick foliage.

"Where's the horse?"

"I got a little place up there where I stake him out. He'll be all right if the damn Carters don't find him."

"Carters?"

"Hills are full of 'em."

"It's a wonder I didn't bleed to death when you took me up that mountain on that damn horse," Corbin grumbled.

"Ah, I knowed ya warn't goin' to die or I'd not busted a gut gettin' ya up on the horse."

Corbin reached his car and sank gratefully down on the passenger seat. It was hot. Insects were buzzing around his head. He reached for his hat, which was still lying on the seat, and slapped it down on his head.

"Are ya up to drivin'?"

"Fine time to ask me that."

"I'll back her outta here and get her pointed toward the road to Henderson. There's a couple roomin' houses there, a hotel and a right good whorehouse. I ain't been there, but any whorehouse is better'n none."

Corbin had become used to the big man's sense of humor. His mouth twitched in an effort to be serious, his eyes shone and the tone of his voice changed. Corbin was well aware he owed Boone plenty. The bootlegger had saved his life. He had no doubt that Boone was guarding a stash of illegal alcohol that had come downriver and that from time to time he would take a load out in his truck.

When Boone stopped the car, Corbin got out and came around to get under the wheel. He held out his hand and Boone took it.

"Thanks, Boone. If there's ever anything I can do for you, let me know. I'll find a room in Henderson, see the doc and wait for you. Tell the boy Corbin Appleby from Fertile wants to see him."

"Give me a day or two or three. Good luck, Appleby."

"Same to you, Boone. The way I see it, you're in more danger from the hillbillies with the still than you are from the revenuers."

Boone grinned. "You may be right." He touched his hand to the bill of his cap and walked quickly back to where he had left his truck.

Jack sat at the table and tried not to wolf down the eggs and biscuits. The good food he'd eaten and the sleep he'd gotten in a comfortable bed had helped put him back on his feet. Now he had to regain his strength. He still looked gaunt and had dark bruises beneath his eyes.

"Ma'am, I just got to do something to pay for this food."

"Tell me about your family, Jack."

"Nothing exciting to tell. We live on a farm on the edge of town. Never lived anyplace else until I left home. I went to Chicago first. I just had to see Wrigley Stadium. For the price of a ticket to see the game, I helped clean up afterwards. I even got to see Rogers Hornsby."

"Do you play baseball?" Annabel sat with her elbows on

the table, watching the boy eat. His face lit up while talking about the game.

"It's all I ever wanted to do, but I know now that only a few are good enough to make a living doing it."

"Chicago is a long way from here."

"You're telling me. I rode the train to Chicago when I left home, but I walked and got rides on the freights when I left there to go to St. Louis. I thought there'd be a chance for me there."

"No luck?"

"No. I worked at anything I could find to do in order to eat, and finally saved enough to go home. I wandered into the wrong place and got the money taken away from me and had to start all over again."

"What happened this time?"

"I'd been feeling poorly and decided to cut through the woods toward the river to spend the night. While I was sleeping someone went through my pack."

"And stole your money," Annabel said dryly as she brought a loaf of freshly baked bread to the table, cut and buttered a slice. She placed it on his plate.

"Yeah. They stole my shirt, coat, baseball and mitt too. If I ever see that mitt, I'll know it's mine and I'll get it back." Jack's eyes turned cold and he looked at her.

"Have you ever planted a garden, Jack?"

"I've done most everything that's to be done on a farm, ma'am. My pa saw to it that us kids did chores by the time we were table-high. Me and Joe—he's my brother who's a couple years older than me—got to where we could do most things Pa could do by the time we were twelve."

"We just moved here. Is the middle of June too late to put in a garden?"

"No, ma'am. I reckon you have as long a growing season here as we do at home."

"I'll pay you, Jack."

"No, ma'am, you won't. I owe you for what you've already done. Pa'd be shamed if he knew I'd let myself get in such a fix that I had to ask for something to eat and was unable to work for it."

"We'll talk about it later. My father will be back in a few days. At that time we'll have to make other sleeping arrangements for you. Spinner is going to build another bunk in the corner of the barn that's been fixed up as living quarters for him and Boone."

"I heard one of them talkin' that it wasn't fit for me to be in here with you. I agree, ma'am. I'm fit enough now to sleep in the barn if you'll allow me to stay."

Annabel got up from the table and looked out the back door when she heard a truck drive in.

"Boone is here." She went out onto the back porch. Jack followed.

Boone's dark eyes swept the yard as he stepped from the truck. Spinner came to the door of the barn and lifted a hand, a signal that all was right here.

"Brought ya some smoked fish and a hunk of deer meat," he called out to Annabel. Then he spoke to Jack as he came out onto the porch. "Looks like ya got yore feet back under ya."

"Yes, sir. I feel much better."

"Jack's going to help me put in a garden. I bought seed when I went to town with Papa."

"I told ya I'd spade up a spot for ya."

"Spinner plowed it. He was going to help me rake it today but said he had to work on the truck. Have you had breakfast?"

"A bite, but I could use a hot biscuit or two."

After giving the package of fish to Annabel, Boone took a bundle from the back of the truck. Jack stepped out to take it. Boone noticed that he winced when he used his left hand.

"What am I going to do with deer meat?" Annabel asked as Jack took the meat into the kitchen.

"Cook it."

"I don't know how."

"The boy does. Raised on a farm, wasn't ya, boy?" Boone's dark eyes honed in on Jack when he came back out onto the porch.

"Yes, sir. Ma'am, I can tell you how my sister Julie cooked it."

"Well, glory be. How was that?"

"Papa would cut off a big hunk for Sis to cook right away and put the rest in the smokehouse. She would soak the fresh meat overnight in salt water. In the morning, she'd put it in a pot with fresh water, add a hot pepper or two and boil it until it was tender. Then she'd take it out and put it in the oven and bake it for a long time. We looked forward each fall to Papa getting a deer."

"We don't have any hot peppers."

"Ya got some sage leaves, ain't ya?" Boone asked. "That'll work."

"I'll give it a try." Annabel smiled fondly at Boone. "Now come on in."

"First I got to put some water in my radiator. I got to head back in a couple hours."

"I can do that." Jack stepped off the porch, picked up a bucket and headed for the horse tank. Boone looked after him for a minute before following Annabel into the kitchen, where the aroma of freshly baked bread filled his nostrils.

"He's a nice boy," Annabel said as soon as Boone had

washed and was seated at the table. "I've asked him to stay on and help me put in the garden."

"Don't ya think ya should talk it over with your pa?"

"Why would he object? Jack's not a revenuer."

"Watch how ya throw them words around, missy."

"When are you coming back to stay for a while?"

"End of the week. Then Spinner will take a turn. Anyone been around?"

"Two men came in a truck for the load of liquor Spinner brought back in the wagon the other day."

Boone looked up sharply. "Ye're gettin' too smart for yore britches."

"It isn't polite to discuss a lady's britches with a young lady."

"And . . . don't get smarty. That kid isn't dumb. We don't need him hangin' 'round."

"If he does find out something, what can he do? Ring up the Federals?"

"He can spread it around, is what he can do. And, missy, that'd not be good."

"He's company, and he'll help me put in a garden and look after the chickens and cow. He said that he and his brother took turns milking at home. I want him to stay. At least for a while."

"I run into a feller that's lookin' for him."

"How did you do that? Why is he looking for him?"

"His folks are worried . . . the feller said."

"I've already told Jack to write to his folks and that I'd mail it."

"Gettin' pretty thick with him, ain't ya?"

Annabel glared over her shoulder at the man seated at the table.

"Boone, you and Papa make me so mad at times. You

stash me out here in the country and expect me to sit here and look at the wall. I have to depend on one of you to take me to get groceries, to church . . . for everything. You don't want me to have any company. I'm going to tell Papa I want a car and someone to teach me to drive it."

"Whoa, there. I offered to teach you how to ride a bicycle." The grin on his face infuriated her.

She turned back to the stove and didn't see that the grin quickly faded into a frown. Boone went out the door and across the yard to where Jack was coming from the horse tank with a bucket of water.

"We'd better get a rag or a gunnysack to take the cap off the radiator," Boone called. Then, when he got closer, "She's goin' to be hotter than a two-bit whore."

Jack grinned. "That'd be pretty hot."

"How'd you know that?" Boone took a gunnysack from the back of the truck and, using it to protect his hand, carefully unscrewed the cap, then sprang back when boiling water and steam gushed up.

"Oh, I hear . . . things," Jack explained.

"Yeah? What thin's?"

"This past year I learned not everyone is bad; most folks are real nice, like Miss Annabel."

"Don't be gettin' any notions 'bout her, lad," Boone warned.

"Whata ya mean? Like I want her for a sweetheart?"

"That's what I mean," Boone said bluntly. He lifted the bucket and poured the water into the hissing radiator.

"She's a nice lady and I like her . . . but not like that." Jack bristled with sudden temper.

"Don't get on your high horse. I was just warnin' ya."

"Consider it done." Jack picked up the bucket and walked back to the horse tank.

Chapter 5

Tess Carter was used to feeling ashamed of her family, herself and the place where she lived. She never really thought of the ramshackle house as being her home, because it wasn't. It was her brothers' home and they just allowed her to live there and wait on them. Deep down she felt a deep and constant resentment.

Now she was angry with herself for being so taken aback when she met the man on the horse that she had acted like a darn fool. At first she had been ashamed of the old ragged dress she wore and the shoes she'd laced up over her ankles because she was so afraid of snakes. She hoped that he'd ride on by and not see her. When he did see her, her only thought had been to get out of his sight as quickly as possible. The heavy shoes had made her trip and fall face down in the dirt. At that moment, she had wanted the earth to open up and swallow her.

At mealtime Leroy had returned and was adding to her humiliation. He would do or say anything to make himself look big in his brothers' eyes. He had stretched the story he told Bud and Marvin, making it appear she had been purposely waiting for the man to come by. Bud had lifted a hand to slap her and would have if not for Marvin.

"Calm yoreself. Ain't no harm been done that I can see. You still watchin' over there, Leroy?"

"Yeah. Man that left in the big car ain't come back. Feller came in with a wagon of hay for the horses. Feller in a truck comes once in a while. Got a right good-lookin' woman over there, Marvin. She's got good tits, white legs and swings her skinny ass when she walks. Keeps herself fixed up too."

"They fixin' to do any farmin' over there?"

"Feller was workin' on a plow behind the barn."

"Too late to start plowin'. You watchin' our corn crop?"

"Yeah. Too early for coons." Leroy's eyes honed in on his sister, who was older by eight years. "What we goin' to do about Tessie meetin' that feller? She ort to get a swat on her bare butt."

"Try it, Leroy," Tess said. "Lay a hand on me, and the first time I catch you asleep I'll cave your mud-ugly head in with a stove poker."

"Now, cut that out." Marvin looked from Tess to his youngest brother. "I'm head man here. If Tessie needs a swat, I'll do it."

Tess stood up from the table, remembering other vicious slaps and the beatings her pa had given her. Her frightened heart was pounding, and she prayed that none of the three knew it. She didn't know if it was courage or foolishness that caused her to look her eldest brother in the eye and defy him.

"I'm taking no more abuse from you, Marvin, and I'm not going to be slapped around by Bud or Leroy ever again."

"Well, now, what ya think ya'll do about it?" Bud sneered.

"I'll shoot you," Tess said calmly.

The brothers laughed. Leroy laughed so hard, he headed for the back door to spit.

"I knowed it was a mistake. Pa knowed it too. He was agin' lettin' ya go to Aunt Cora to be schooled. Shows what happens when ya let a woman get the bit in her teeth. He was plum cloudy-headed over Maw and let her have her way. Pity she didn't live to see what happened to ya," Marvin said spitefully.

"Yes, it is a pity," Tess agreed. "She worked herself to death taking care of five lazy boys and Pa."

"Ya ain't better let Calvin hear ya sayin' that. He was right fond of Maw." Bud continued to eat. He never let anything interfere with shoveling food into his mouth. He was already so fat he couldn't mount a mule. "Calvin said it was a blessin' Maw passed over before ya come back with yore belly swelled with a bastard." Bud spoke between mouthfuls of food.

"I was raped by Cousin Willard. All of you knew it and did nothing about it."

"It was yore word agin his'n." Marvin's face was a thundercloud, as it always was when this subject came up. "He said ya wanted it, begged him to do it. Willard said ya warn't no good at it nohow."

Anger made Tess's small body stiffen. Her head shot up, her fists clenched. They hadn't believed her, and they hadn't believed Aunt Cora. They wanted to believe that no-good, thieving, stinking, nasty-talking Willard Carter because he was a little better off than the rest of the Carters.

"If you had the brains of a crabapple," Tess said with a sneer, "you'd know that no woman would *want* anything from a fat, unwashed muddle-head like Willard!"

"He be a man with strong seed." Gravy ran from the corner of Bud's mouth when he grinned. "He planted one in ya on his first try, didn't he?"

"And the whipping Pa gave me when I came home shook the evil thing right out of me. I thank God for that!"

"Hear, now, don't ya be talkin' like that. It ain't Christian."

Tess looked at her fat brother with disgust. "You wouldn't know a Christian if one jumped up and bit you."

"She's bein' lippy, Marvin," Bud said. "She ain't had a switchin' since Pa died. Pa always said a woman needs her legs switched once a week."

Tess reached behind her for the butcher knife.

"Yeah. She's gettin' plumb feisty." Leroy tried to sidle behind her, but she backed up.

"Leave her be. Leroy, get on up to the still and siphon off some of that last batch and bring me a jug. I got thinkin' to do."

"Ya ain't goin' to do nothin' 'bout what she done?"

"Are you wantin' me to club ya upside the head? Get on and do what I told ya. Ya ain't in charge a Tessie. If'n yo're finished fillin' yore gut, Bud, go with him."

"But . . . Marvin, I ain't done yet."

"He won't be until the last crumb is gone from the table," Tess said, and Bud looked as if he'd like to hit her, but he didn't dare with Marvin there.

"Hitch up the wagon, Leroy. Take that case of bottles with you. This is a good batch. We'll bottle some of it. Send it back with Bud. You stay and let Cousin Arney go home."

Next to Calvin, who lived on a farm four miles west of them and ruled his family with even a stronger hand, Marvin was the smartest and the best-looking of the Carter boys. The other brother had disappeared when Marvin became the head of the family. The two had never gotten along.

Marvin had never married, although he'd had several dalliances with women from time to time. Tess suspected that they were the ones who did the breaking, because there was not one speck of softness in her brother. He was hard, demanding and cruel. He had taken over when their father died.

After Leroy and Bud left the house, Marvin lingered at the table. Tess knew him well enough to know that he was going to say something or do something he didn't want his brothers to know about. She kept the knife close, determined to use it if he attempted to whip her, even though she knew Marvin was capable of killing her.

Lord, if she only had someplace to go and some way of supporting herself without doing it on her back. If she left, she would have to go far enough away so that a Carter couldn't find her. Any one of them would delight in dragging her back to Marvin.

"I got a thin' to say. Turn around." Marvin's voice was stern.

"I figured you did." Tessie turned to face him.

"You earned a slap or two, but I ain't goin' to give it to ya yet."

"Not ever again, Marvin. I told you that. I'll hurt you if I can. If I can't, I'll hang myself. Then who would do your washing and cooking?"

Grinning as if he were really enjoying himself, Marvin pushed his hair from his forehead and leaned back in his chair.

"Cousin Judd would send over one of his girls. Maybe that little towhead."

"Ora Jean? She's only fourteen or fifteen. Cousin Judd knows that you'd work her by day and screw her by night. He wouldn't put up with that."

"Yo're gettin' smarty." The smile had left Marvin's face.

"Is that what you want to talk about . . . how smart I am?"

"No. I wanna know about the man ya met in the woods."

"Sheesh! I didn't know the man from a bale of hay. I told you that he was just passing through."

"What'd he say? Did he feel ya up? Leroy said he lifted ya off the ground."

"Leroy is lying . . . as usual. He didn't touch me."

"Dadburnit! Did he look like he *wanted* to feel ya up?" Marvin raised his voice to a near roar.

"How'd I know? I didn't look at him."

"She-it. Leroy said yore dress was up over yore butt. He looked."

"What if he did? I'll never see him again. He sure won't be making a shortcut through here. Leroy saw to that."

"Too bad. Leroy's a dumb-ass. Never uses his head."

Tess agreed but decided to remain silent and wait for whatever scheme Marvin had in mind. She didn't have to wait long.

"I want to know what's goin' on over there."

"Isn't your spy telling you enough?"

"I want you to hang around the edge of the woods. The man might come over to see if he can get some."

"I might be able to get him over here if I stripped naked and hung a sign around my neck saying 'Come on over.'" Tess grinned cockily.

Marvin's eyes turned cold. "Ya makin' fun a me?"

"Why would you think that?" Tess backed away when Marvin got up from the table.

"I'm gettin' tired a yore lip. I want ya to get friendly with them folks. Call on the woman . . . neighborly-like. See what they're up to. Leroy says there's a tall skinny feller over there and the black-haired one ya met in the woods. Get next to 'em. I don't care which one."

"I'll not be a whore for you or anyone else!"

"Why not? Ya was a whore for Cousin Willard," he shouted. "I want to know if they're tied in with the revenuers. Air ya so dumb ya can't see that they ain't but a mile or two from the still what puts food in yore belly?"

"You wasn't worried about the Millers when they lived there."

"That old man wasn't goin' to do nothin'. I scared the shit out of 'im. They moved, didn't they?"

"Didn't they own the land?"

"Banker in St. Louis owned the land. Feller named Donovan bought it. So reckon they'll be there awhile."

"I can't just go over there."

"Didn't that fancy schoolin' tell ya how to call on neighbors?" Marvin sneered.

"If it did, I've forgotten about it after being stuck here for six years and going to town less than once a year."

"Well, ya better do some thinkin' on it, and if ya shame us I'll tear the hide off your butt."

Those had been Marvin's last words before he had stomped out of the house.

Now, bent over the washtub in the yard, Tess thought about the man she had met in the woods. He hadn't tried to take hold of her or belittle her. He seemed to be genuinely sorry he'd scared her and wouldn't have been bad-looking without the whiskers. Because of her brothers' scraggly, unshaven faces, she had come to despise whiskers.

Digging her bare toes into the earth to brace herself as she pulled the heavy overalls from the water, she held the legs to the roller of the wringer attached to the tub and used both hands to turn the crank. After she hung the overalls on the line, she gazed north toward the only neighbors within five miles who were not Carters.

Not for anything did she want Marvin to know that she was excited about meeting and talking to a woman who wasn't a Carter. She had to think about what she would wear and make up an excuse for the visit. She remembered that Aunt Cora took an offering when she made a call. What could she take that a woman from town would appreciate?

The idea hit her. No woman in her right mind would turn down fresh raspberries, and she knew just the place to get them.

Marvin chose the day for Tess to call on the neighbors. A day earlier she had hurried to finish the noon dishes and had gone to the woods to pick the berries. Later she bathed, washed her hair and ironed her one good dress. With both fear and anticipation she had looked forward to the visit.

At midmorning Tess reached the edge of the woods. She stopped and stood for a while in the shadows, whipping up the nerve to go on to the house. She looked down at the print dress she had starched and ironed. The dress was all right, but she wished that her shoes were not so worn. She hoped the lady she was about to meet would think she wore her old shoes because she had to walk through the woods.

Taking a deep breath and reciting to herself what she was going to say, Tess started across the clearing toward the house. During the more than five years since she had come home from Aunt Cora's, she had not been this close to their neighbors' house. She could see at a glance that it was a well-kept-up place. No rubbish cluttered the yard, as it did over at her place. Cut wood was not tossed in a pile but was stacked neatly near the back door.

Tess's heart was pounding like a sledgehammer. What if

the woman was insulting when she called on her? What if she refused the raspberries? What if she slammed the door in her face?

Oh, Lord, why had she ever thought she could do this?

Knowing that Marvin would be watching from somewhere nearby, Tess forced her feet to move forward. As she approached the house, she could see a woman and a man working in freshly turned earth. The man was making furrows with a hand plow. They were planting a garden. The woman, wearing an old straw hat, straightened, holding her hand to her back, and called to the man.

"Will two rows of beans be enough, Jack?"

He nodded, then motioned toward Tess. The woman turned to see her in the yard and came toward her, taking off the straw hat. Her dark brown hair, cut in a short bob, shone in the sun.

As she approached, Tess could see that she was young and pretty and . . . smiling.

"Hello," Annabel called before she reached Tess.

Tess completely forgot what she had rehearsed to say. She could only nod and stare.

"Hello," Annabel said again. "You must be our neighbor on the south."

"Tess." Tess finally found her tongue. "Tess Carter."

"Annabel Donovan."

Tess accepted the hand that was extended without looking at it. She couldn't take her eyes from the woman's smiling face.

"I've been wanting to meet my neighbor."

"You . . . have?" Tess stammered. Relief made her weak. "I . . . ah . . . brought some raspberries." She lifted the bucket she had been carrying by the bail.

"Oh, my. I love raspberries. Do you have a patch?"

"The bushes are in the woods."

"You picked them for me? How nice. Thank you so much. Won't you come in, Tess?"

"Maybe . . . for a little while."

Annabel waved her hand to Jack in the garden and led Tess to the house. The woman was visibly trembling. Annabel suspected that she was terribly shy. Trying to put her at ease, she chatted about the raspberries.

"It must have taken you a long time to pick so many berries. Gracious! There's enough here for a pie, if they last that long."

Tess followed Annabel into the house, afraid that she would say or do something stupid that might cause this friendly girl to tell her to leave.

"Come in." Annabel held the door open for Tess. "I'm so glad to have a visitor, and a woman at that." Annabel hung her hat on the knob of a chair. "Sit down, Tess. Would you like a cool drink of water? It must be at least a mile over to your place."

"Thank you, ma'am."

"Oh, call me Annabel. Jack brought in a fresh bucket of water before we went to the garden." With the dipper, Annabel poured water into a glass and set it on the table. "Let's be selfish and treat ourselves to a bowl of berries. Dish them up, Tess, while I get the sugar and cream. I dipped the cream off the milk just this morning."

Annabel placed two bowls and two spoons on the table and turned her back to reach for the sugar but not before she noticed that Tess's work-roughened hands were trembling.

When they were seated at the table across from each other, Annabel smiled at the woman across from her as she put the first spoonful of berries in her mouth.

"Oh, they are so good. It was so thoughtful of you to bring them."

"I couldn't come empty-handed."

"Of course you could." Annabel laughed. "But I'm glad you didn't. Is the patch of berries far from here?"

"Not far. It's a little way behind our place."

"I'm so glad you came over. I hope we can be friends."

"I hope so too, ma'am."

"Annabel. Please call me Annabel. We're too near the same age for you to call me ma'am."

"Oh, no. I'm old, ma'am . . . ah . . . Annabel."

"You can't be much older than I am. I was twenty-one last Christmas day."

"I'll be twenty-eight next Christmas day." Tess smiled for the first time and Annabel realized that she was quite pretty.

"Papa used to tell me that Santa Claus brought me and I'd wonder how he got down the chimney when we only had a stovepipe." Annabel's unfettered laughter rang, and Tess could only stare at her.

"We have the same birthday, Tess. We can have a birthday party together . . . if we're still here."

"Are you moving . . . so soon?" Tess's eyes had hardly left Annabel's face. It was such a pleasure to look at her. She smiled all the time.

"I never know. My father . . . travels and sells things. He takes sudden notions to move."

"I hope you don't."

Tess's large amber eyes held a look of distress. Annabel noted the look and also the fact that she had a beautiful clear golden complexion that went perfectly with her hair and eyes. She was small and slim and sat with her shoulders back and her head erect as if she were listening for something. Her eyes left Annabel only occasionally to dart around the kitchen.

"Did you know the Millers who lived here before we came?" Annabel asked.

Tess shook her head. "I've not been here before. Marvin doesn't like for me to go . . . places."

"Your husband?"

Tess shook her head again, this time more definitely, and a look of distaste came over her face.

"My brother."

"You're not married?"

The head shake again. "No. I'll never marry!"

"I want to someday. I'd like to have children . . . a whole bunch of them. I'm the only one my parents had. It was lonely growing up."

"Are the men here your brothers?"

"Goodness, no. They work for my father, except for Jack. He's just a boy. He's helping me with the garden." Annabel cocked her head to listen. "That sounds like Boone's truck coming in. He works for my father."

"I'd better go." Tess got quickly to her feet.

"Don't go, Tess. Boone will probably go to the barn and talk to Spinner, the other man who works here."

"I'd better. Marvin—" Tess headed for the door with Annabel following.

They had just opened the door when Boone stepped up onto the porch. He stopped short when he saw Tess.

"Hello. I didn't know you were coming back today," Annabel said.

"I came through town and brought ya a chunk of ice." Boone spoke to Annabel, but his eyes were on Tess. He jerked the billed cap off his head. "Howdy, ma'am."

"This is Tess Carter, Boone. She lives on the place south

of us. Tess, this is Mr. Boone. He's really quite nice, even if he does look like a bear most of the time."

"I met Mrs. Carter in the woods the day I went to get the cow. Sorry about the misunderstanding with your husband."

When Tess didn't correct him, Annabel felt she should.

"You didn't tell me you'd met Tess, Boone. She isn't married. She lives with her brother."

"Three brothers," Tess said, so low that Boone barely heard the words.

"The man on the mule was yore brother?" Boone asked as if Annabel were not there.

"Leroy."

Boone grinned. "Tell ya right now, I wanted to bust his nose." He watched in fascination as Tess's eyes lit up and the corners of her mouth twitched, but the smile never materialized.

"Tess and I have the same birthday," Annabel announced. "We're going to have a birthday party together if we're still here."

"That'd be dandy," Boone said, still looking at Tess.

"I've got to go." Tess was so nervous that her stomach was fluttering.

"Don't let me run you off. The girl here needs a lady's company once in a while. How's the ice holding out?" Dragging his eyes from Tess, he looked at Annabel.

"Got a little left." She turned to the girl, who was poised as if to sprint away. "Will you come back to see me, Tess?"

"I don't know if I can."

"Come anytime. I've got goods to make kitchen curtains. I'm not sure how to go about it and would value your opinion."

"I don't know anything about curtains." Her eyes darted to the edge of the woods, where she suspected Marvin lurked with his spyglasses, then up at the big man with the dark stubble on his face. His black eyes were focused on her and she felt as if they were looking into her soul, her past, her future. "I've got to go. 'Bye."

Tess jumped off the porch and walked quickly across the yard toward the woods.

"'Bye," Annabel called. "Thank you for the berries."

Tess turned and waved. She wanted to run, but forced herself to walk until she reached the shadowed forest, then she ran as if a demon were behind her.

She hadn't gone fifty yards when Marvin stepped out in front of her and she skidded to a stop. He had a pair of binoculars in his hand. She had been right about his spying.

"What'd you find out?"

"Nothing much. They're nice folk."

"What'd the woman say?"

"Said her pa sold things and was gone a lot."

"Is one of them fellers her man?"

"No. She's not married. They work for her father."

"What's he sell?"

"She didn't say. I reckon it's stuff in a catalog."

"Ya reckon? Hell, I didn't send ya over there to reckon." Marvin grasped her arm. "Did she want the berries?"

"She wanted them. She was nice." Tess tugged on her arm, but he refused to release it.

"Go back over there. Tell her ya'll show her where ya got 'em. Offer to help make pie or somethin'."

"I can't do that."

"Ya can if I tell ya to." His fingers tightened on her arm. "I seen her up close." Grinning, he indicated the binoculars. "Pretty, ain't she? Leroy was right about one thing. She's got good high tits."

Tess had to admit that her brother was quite handsome

when he smiled, but not handsome enough. His crude ways would turn Annabel against him.

"Yes, and she's . . . nice. Leave her be, Marvin."

"Ya tellin' me what to do? Ya better heed what I tell ya. Get her over here in the woods so I can talk to her."

"How am I going to do that?"

"If ya'd used yore head, ya coulda said ya'd show her the berry patch."

"Why don't you just go over and talk to the menfolk? You could talk to her then."

"Yo're a stupid bitch. Her menfolk want nothin' to do with us Carters. They know we got a still in the hills."

"They might want to buy—"

"Ya didn't mention that!"

"No. I'd be ashamed to," she shouted.

"When ya goin' back?"

"Tomorrow . . . or the next day," Tess promised in order to get him to release her arm. "You got to take it easy with a woman like her. She's got manners."

"And . . . I don't?" The fingers tightened again.

"I didn't say that."

"Ya ain't never seen me using manners. I can sweet-talk a bitch right out of her drawers. She won't know what end of her is up when I get through sweet-talkin' her. Get home and get me something to eat. I got things to do."

Tess ran down the path toward the house. Annabel wouldn't want anything to do with Marvin. Compared to a man like Boone, Marvin was nothing but hill trash. Was Boone married? Was he in love with Annabel? She couldn't blame him if he was. She was the nicest, prettiest woman she'd ever met.

I won't let Marvin ruin her! I'll cut that thing off him first.

Chapter 6

JACK BROUGHT THE COW TO THE BARN, put her in a stall and started the preparations to milk her.

"Didn't Spinner show Annabel how to milk?" Boone asked.

"He showed her, but I don't think she's got the hang of it yet. I can do it as long as I'm here. I'm slow 'cause I can only use one hand."

"Other'n stiffened up on ya?"

Jack held it out. "I dropped a crate on it. I'm hoping there aren't any broken bones in there." The hand was swollen, his fingers looked like sausages, and the back was dark with bruises.

"If there is, I doubt anythin' could be done. Ya ort to try soakin' it in hot water."

"Miss Annabel had me do that."

"You know a feller named Corbin Appleby?" Boone sprang the name suddenly and watched Jack's expression. The boy looked surprised, then pleased.

"Corbin Appleby? Sure. He's from my hometown. How come you know him?"

"We bumped into each other. He's lookin' for ya. Yore folks sent him."

"How'd he know to look here?"

"Ya'll have to ask him. He asked if I'd seen a boy named Jack Jones. I had, and told him so. He's in Henderson. I said I'd brin' ya in."

"He's arresting me?"

Boone's dark eyes narrowed. "He said he wasn't a lawman no more."

"I guess he isn't. The letter from my sister said he'd quit and gone to Springfield to visit his folks."

"Whata ya know about him?"

"Not much. Everyone likes Corbin. He's straight as a string."

"Well, I'll drive ya in to Henderson in a day or two. He'll be wantin' ya to go home."

"He can want all he wants to. I'm not goin' till I pay Miss Annabel back for takin' care of me. I told her I'd put her in a garden and I will."

"That's up to you. Her pa might tie a can to yore tail when he gets back."

"When will that be?"

"Who knows? Murphy comes and goes."

After Boone left him, Jack sat down on an upturned box and began to milk the cow. He'd made up his mind days ago. He was staying here until he found the toughs who took his ball and mitt. He'd worked an entire summer to pay for them and he wasn't letting some polecat get away with taking them from him.

He'd not go home with his tail between his legs. His pa and Joe had thought him just a wet-eared kid, and damned if he'd have everyone say he couldn't take care of himself.

A few nights later, during supper, Boone told Annabel

that he was taking Jack to town to see a friend of his and she would have to go along because he wouldn't leave her here alone. A brief explanation brought on a barrage of questions.

"Well for goodness' sakes! Why didn't you tell me this before now? Who is he? How did he happen to ask you about Jack? Why didn't you bring him here? You're as bad as Papa at keeping me in the dark about things."

Boone looked at Jack with lifted brows. "Did ya ever know a woman who asked so many questions?"

"My sister Jill. She's nosy and mouthy."

Boone answered each of Annabel's questions patiently, being as vague as possible, then asked her to play him a tune on her fiddle after supper.

After lighting the pull-down lamp in the parlor, Boone sank into Murphy's leather chair. Jack sat on the floor because his britches were dirty. Annabel, vexed at Boone for calling her beloved violin a fiddle, started off by playing "Turkey in the Straw" and then "Crawdad Hole" and "Yankee Doodle."

"There," she said with a glare at Boone. "That's what's played on a fiddle. This is what's played on a violin."

The strains of "Blue Danube Waltz" filled the small room. Although neither Boone or Jack knew the name of the melody, they thought it was beautiful, and they could see her obvious enjoyment as she played it. She played a medley by Brahms including "Lullaby." Before she finished she played "Moonlight Sonata" by Beethoven.

Boone's eyes glittered with pride and pleasure as he watched and listened. Jack sat absolutely still, overcome by admiration.

"You sure play pretty, Miss Annabel," Jack said while she was wiping her violin off with a soft cloth and putting it back in the case.

"Thank you, Jack. When we go to town, I'd like to find out if there's going to be a concert Sunday afternoon. If so, I'd like to go."

"I ain't sittin' through no concert." Boone got to his feet and stretched.

"You don't have to," Annabel answered pertly. "You can go to the river and fish while I'm at the park."

Boone scowled, left the room and went to the water bucket.

Unknown to the three in the room, another pair of eyes had peered in through the window, watched and listened to the music played by the slender girl with long bare legs and soft, rounded breasts. When she finished playing, the watcher saw Boone leave the room and, thinking the man might come outside, moved silently to the edge of the woods and squatted down beside a tree where he could watch the house.

He would have this woman. He'd gotten every woman he'd wanted so far, and this one wouldn't be any different. It would just take a little more planning. He would have to ride into town early in the morning and go to the barbershop.

Corbin Appleby looked up and nodded a greeting as Marshal Sanford passed his table in the hotel dining room. He finished his breakfast and went to his room. Five minutes later he answered the expected knock on his door.

"Come in, Marshal."

"Good to see you, Appleby." The two men shook hands. "I was about to give up on you."

"Have a seat. Sorry, I missed the Friday meeting. Someone mistook me for a revenue agent and shot me. I was laid up for a while."

"Shot you? Are you all right now?"

"Yeah. I'll be limping around for a while, but the doctor says I'll be all right."

"I'm sorry you were shot, but it might give you a reason for hanging around."

"I thought of that."

"Here's what I wanted to talk to you about, Corbin. I need a man here to do a little snooping around. These people are clannish as hell. If they got wind you were connected to the law, you'd never find out anything."

"I told you when we talked before that I was coming over this way to look for Jack Jones. He was in the area and his folks were worried. I found him quite by accident. That will give me another reason for being here."

"The kid will spread it around that you were the police chief of Fertile."

"If it happens, I'll say I was fired and let them think that I'm seeking revenge. I might even blame my firing on you."

Marshal Sanford looked thoughtful for a short while, then nodded.

"That should work out just fine." Marshal Sanford took a package of papers from his inside coat pocket. "Look these over carefully and keep them with you. Hotel folks are naturally curious."

"What if I need to get in touch with you?"

"Write to Mrs. Ned Wicker, Box 6, Jefferson City. Let folks think she's your sister. If you need me in a hurry, send a wire saying that your Aunt Maude is sick. Sign it J. Jones. I'll get back to you. Do you plan to stay here at the hotel?"

"The rooms don't cost that much more than they do at a boardinghouse. And landladies, as a rule, are nosy. They like something new to gossip about. Here, I'm more private and still in the thick of what's going around town."

The marshal went to the door. Corbin followed and opened it. He looked up and down the hall, then nodded.

"Good luck, Corbin. I figured you'd be a good man for this job."

"Good-bye, Marshal. I'll do my best."

"That's all I ask." Marshal Sanford went quickly down the hall and into an adjoining room.

Corbin sat down in the chair beside the window and read the papers several times, committing some of the information to memory. When he stood, he opened his shirt and tucked the package of papers into the waist of his britches next to his skin. He left the room, went down the stairs and out onto the hotel porch to sit and ponder what he'd just learned.

Annabel rode into town in the truck, seated between Boone and Jack.

"Do you know where to find the man Jack is going to meet?" she asked as they approached town.

"No. But I'll find him. First I'll let you out to gab with the store clerks and spend Murphy's money."

"I'll go along with you and Jack," she said firmly, looking straight ahead, conscious that Boone was eyeing her with a frown. "We can stop at the grocery before we go home. I'll get a can of peaches and make you a cobbler." She turned, gave him a sweet smile and squeezed his arm.

"Now, Jack," Boone said seriously and turned the truck toward the hotel, "this is what ya got to look out for. A woman, pretty or not, will be contrary as a mule, then try and sweeten ya up by smilin' and offerin' up somethin' she knows yo're fond of."

"And Jack," Annabel said, equally as seriously, "it works most of the time."

Jack was silent. He had become used to the banter between Annabel and Boone. He was looking forward to seeing Corbin and hearing the news from home.

"There's his car." Boone stopped the truck in front of the hotel. "We're in luck. He's sittin' on the porch."

Annabel couldn't tell much about the man who lounged in the wicker rocking chair on the front porch of the hotel. He wore a white shirt and a Panama hat. The shoe of the foot perched on the porch rail was polished.

Jack was out of the truck as soon as it stopped. The man on the porch stood and limped to the steps to meet him. They shook hands.

"Good to see you, Jack."

"Good to see you too, Mr. Appleby. How are things at home?"

"Fine when I left a little over a month ago. Julie was fretting because they hadn't heard from you. I was going to swing over this way to see an old friend and offered to see if I could find you."

"Yeah, well, I was on my way home and ran into a little trouble. Come out to the truck. I want you to meet Miss Annabel. She took me in and maybe saved my life. Guess you already know Boone."

With the help of a cane, Corbin followed Jack down the steps and across the walk to the truck where Annabel stood waiting. He looked across the cab of the truck and nodded to Boone, then removed his hat. The sun shone on a head of thick dark blond hair.

"Annabel, this is Chief Appleby . . . rather, Mr. Appleby now. Mr. Appleby, meet Miss Annabel Lee Donovan. I owe her a lot."

"I'm glad to meet you, Mr. Appleby." Annabel held out her hand. Her parted lips showed small even teeth when she smiled. She peered up at him from beneath the narrow brim of a hat decorated with a wide blue ribbon bow. Her eyes were an unusual shade of green. It was hard for Corbin to look away from her. She sparkled.

"Same here, ma'am." Corbin held her hand briefly and released it. "Jack's folks will thank you for what you've done for him. For some reason I've not figured out yet, they're fond of him." Corbin's eyes shot to Jack's grinning face.

"I can understand why. I could become quite fond of him myself." Her smiling eyes moved to Jack, then back to the tall man. "Well, I expect you two have a lot to talk about."

"I'll be back this afternoon, Miss Annabel. I want to work up the ground so I can plant the squash and pumpkins tomorrow."

"Tomorrow is Sunday, Jack. You don't have to work on Sunday."

"Guess I forgot what day it is."

"They'll be serving in the dining room in about an hour," Corbin said. "I'd like for the two of you and Jack to be my guests for dinner. If you have nothing to do in the meanwhile, sit here on the porch while I fill Jack in on the news from home."

"Naw." Boone fidgeted. He took off his cap, then slapped it back on his head. "We'd better get on back."

"Come on, Boone," Corbin said. "I owe you a meal and you know it. I owe you much more than a meal." Corbin's eyes held Boone's.

Annabel's gaze traveled from one man to the other. Boone was anxious to be gone. She looked back at Corbin to see the teasing look he was giving Boone.

They knew each other better than Boone had let on.

"Some other time." Boone stepped back into the truck. "Let's get goin', Annabel."

"If you'd like to stay, ma'am," Corbin said when he saw her hesitate, "I'll drive you and Jack back out to your place after we've had dinner."

"Ain't ya hurt too bad to drive?" Boone asked with a sarcastic tinge in his voice.

"I'll manage."

"Ya ain't goin' to have to." Boone stepped back out of the truck and spoke to Annabel over the top. "Are you wantin' to stay?"

"It would be nice, Boone. I've not had dinner at a hotel since we left Ashton."

"All right, but we'll get what ya need from the store while we wait so we can get home after ya've et. We'll be back, Appleby. Get in, Annabel." He got back behind the wheel and waited for Annabel to get in the truck.

"Ma'am, Jack and I will be here on the porch when you get back. I'm glad you're going to join us." He opened the truck door and, with his hand beneath her elbow, helped her in.

"Thank you, Mr. Appleby. I'm looking forward to it."

Boone backed the truck out as soon as Corbin stepped away. "Shoulda let the bastard bleed to death," he grumbled under his breath.

"What did you say, Boone?"

"I said he's probably still a lawman and we ort to give him our backside."

"I like a man with good manners. Why does he owe you? You didn't tell me the whole story, did you?"

"You don't need to know ever' move I make, missy." Boone was plainly agitated.

"Did you know him before we came here?"

"No, I didn't know him before we came here. Why do you ask me thin's ya'd not ask yore pa?"

"I don't know. I'm with you more than I am with Papa. I think . . . lately, that I know you better than I know Papa." When she had started speaking, her voice was strong. When she finished, it was almost a whisper.

"This feller was a lawman, Annabel. Could still be, for all we know. I don't want him hangin' around."

"If he isn't a Federal he'd not be interested in what you and Papa are doing. What harm can it do to have dinner with him? I want to, Boone. Sometimes I feel like my life is standing still. All I do is cook, clean and wash and wait for something to happen to you or Papa."

Boone glanced at her but said nothing.

"I'd like to eat dinner at a hotel once in a while, Boone, and see a picture show and maybe go to a dance."

"Murphy tried to set ya up in a boardin'house where ya could meet young folks and do them thin's."

"Let's don't talk about that. I've told you and I've told Papa that I'm not going to be shut away somewhere in a boardinghouse."

Boone drove the block to the mercantile and stopped.

"Don't be blabbin' in the store that Appleby was a police chief or that we know anythin' about him."

"Boone! You can make me so mad. I've no reason to even mention him. Goodness!"

Boone got out of the truck and spoke to her when they met on the walk in front of the store.

"I'm going down to the repair shop and get the shoes I left to be soled. Take your time. We've got an hour to kill."

"You don't have to act as if I'm pulling your teeth," she said sulkily. "You could have gone back to the farm. He said he'd bring me and Jack home."

"Yeah. Bet he'd of liked that." Boone walked away before she could reply.

Annabel went into the store and was greeted by Mr. Hogg.

"Mornin', Miss Donovan."

"Good morning."

"What can I do for you?"

"I need a pound of dried apples, a can of peaches, a tin of cinnamon and one of nutmeg." Her eyes scanned the row of goods on the shelves. "And a box of Gold Dust washing powder."

While the grocer was setting the items on the counter, Annabel wandered over to the table that held the yard goods. She pulled out a bolt of soft blue-flowered voile, unrolled it and held it up. She decided the flowers were too large, so she rolled it and put it back in the stack.

"That'da been purty on ya."

Annabel jumped and turned. She had not known anyone was near. A man lounged against the table, his bright blue eyes on her. He was smiling and as her glance met his, he winked. Annabel wanted to laugh but managed to keep a straight face as she turned to go back to where Mr. Hogg was tallying up her bill. The man slid easily in front of her, blocking her way.

"Miss Annabel. I'm Marvin Carter, yore neighbor. Tessie said ya was right purty. She ain't right 'bout a lot of thin's, but she was shore right 'bout that."

The first thing Annabel noticed about him was that he had been to the barbershop and his blond wiry hair had been trimmed, slicked down and generously doused with hair tonic. He reeked of it. His blue shirt was new. It still had the fold wrinkles in it.

"Nice to meet you, Mr. Carter. Tell Tess hello."

"I'll tell her. I was in the barbershop when ya passed and

come up here to tell ya that I'll take ya out to the park at Riverside tonight. Be ready 'bout sundown."

Annabel couldn't hold back the small laugh. "I don't think so," she said, slowly shaking her head.

"Why not?" His face was suddenly harsh. "Ya got something else to do?"

"Yes, I do." She tried to step around him again. He blocked her with a quick step to the side. "Let me pass, please."

"Not till ya say ya'll go with me tonight." His expression changed suddenly. He winked again and smiled. "We'd have us a high old time."

"I don't know you, Mr. Carter." Her voice now was sharp, agitated. "I'm not going out with you tonight or any night. Let me pass."

"Ya think yo're better'n me? Is that it? Well, ya—"

"Miss Donovan"—Mr. Hogg appeared beside her—"did you say you wanted one pound of peaches or was it the dried apples you wanted?"

"Apples and a pound of raisins too, please."

Annabel felt her elbow being clasped by Mr. Hogg's meaty hand as he ushered her around the obnoxious man and down the aisle toward the main counter. Just as they reached it, she heard the screen store door bang shut.

Mr. Hogg looked through the window to see Marvin Carter going down the walk.

"Was he bothering you?"

"In a way. But no harm was done."

"He's trouble. All the Carters are trouble one way or the other."

"His sister is nice. She called on me and brought me a bucket of raspberries."

"We don't see much of her in town. The boys keep her close to home."

"I kind of got the impression that she was afraid of her brother Marvin."

"Your father will take care of Marvin Carter. Is he out of town? I've not seen him for a while."

"Papa is away now, but he'll be back in a few days. What do I owe, Mr. Hogg?"

"I can put it on a tab if you like. Mr. Donovan can pay when he comes in."

"I'd rather pay."

"Eighty-seven cents. Prices going up each time I order. Raisins are getting especially pricey."

Annabel said good-bye and headed for the door.

"Miss Donovan, I'd give the Carters a wide berth. They are a bad lot, and they've got kinfolk all over the county. Offend one Carter and you've offended all. They're thicker than fleas on a dog's back."

"Thank you for the advice, Mr. Hogg."

"Tell your papa to stop by if there's anything I can do for him."

As Annabel was leaving the store, Mr. Potter from the pharmacy was coming in. He backed out onto the sidewalk to talk to her.

"Hello, Miss Donovan. I was hoping to see you again soon." His white hair was parted in the middle and perfectly combed. His shirt was sparkling white, his bow tie straight.

"Hello." Annabel gave the small, rather plump little man one of her quick smiles.

"I wanted to ask you to be the guest soloist at our Sunday concert."

Annabel's laugh rang out. "Oh, goodness, no! I don't play that well, but I thank you for asking me."

"Henderson's concerts are not held in Carnegie Hall, my dear, but right here in the town square every Sunday afternoon during the summer months. Not all in my orchestra are accomplished musicians."

"I know that, Mr. Potter. I've never played for anyone but my family."

"We'll be playing Beethoven and Brahms. When we first talked, you said they were your favorites. You could play a medley or whatever you wanted," he coaxed with a twinkle in his eyes.

"They are my favorites. I love their music."

"I could tell. Will you come in sometime and play just for me?"

"Mr. Potter, don't ask me. I'd be embarrassed."

"All right, my dear. Just be warned. I don't give up easily."

"I do want to attend your concert Sunday afternoon."

"I hope you can make it, my dear. I'll be looking for you."

From the porch of the hotel, Corbin had watched the truck go down the street and park at the mercantile. He'd watched Miss Donovan go into the store and Boone walk down to the shoe repair shop.

Corbin and Jack sat in the wicker chairs and Corbin told him everything he could think of about his family, ending with Jill's graduation from high school.

"She was valedictorian. The whole family was proud as peacocks."

"She's always been pretty smart."

"Tell me how you came to know Miss Donovan and Boone, Jack."

Jack took his time telling Corbin about bedding down one night not far from the river and that thieves took his money and his baseball and leather mitt. He told about being sick and the long walk up the hill to the house to ask for help.

"It was the hardest thing I've ever had to do, to tell someone that I was hungry and to ask for food. Miss Donovan was awfully nice, Corbin. I guess I passed out on the porch and the next thing I knew, I'd been stripped of my wet clothes and was in a warm bed. Boone was there that morning. Neither one of them ever made me feel that I was a bother."

"What's Boone's connection to her? He acts like he's her father."

"He works for her father. Right now Mr. Donovan is away someplace, but they expect him back any day. Both Boone and Spinner look out for her. She's mighty fond of both of them and them of her. It's almost like she's got two extra fathers."

"Do you know what her father does besides farm?"

"He sells something, I think. He doesn't farm. That place hasn't been farmed for a long time. Miss Annabel would like for it to be a real farm. Boone got her some chickens and a cow. She hasn't had them long. She can't even milk."

"Have they hired you on to work there?"

"No. I'm putting in the garden. I've got to pay her back for taking care of me, and I've got to find the thieves who took my baseball and mitt. I'm not leaving here without getting them back."

"I plan on staying here for a while. The doctor told me not to try making the long drive back to Fertile until my leg and my shoulder heal."

"What happened to your leg?"

Corbin told the story once again about getting out of his car to relieve himself and being ambushed. He told about waking up in the cabin in the hills and learning that Boone had run off his attackers. Boone attended his wounds and several days later helped him get to the car to come to town.

"There's no doubt in my mind that they would have killed me and taken the car. If they'd left me, I'd have bled to death. I owe Boone a lot. He's a man of principle even if he doesn't want anyone to know it."

"He was gone for about a week. Annabel said he liked to go up into the hills and hunt. He came one day with a hunk of venison and some smoked fish. I had to show her how to cook the deer meat. Now Spinner has gone fishing. Spinner is the other man who works there. I thought it was strange that Boone hunted for that long."

"They may have something to hide, Jack. I think it best if you didn't ask them about their business or say anything about me ever being a police chief."

"Why? I'm kinda proud to know a police chief."

"Folks could get the wrong idea of why I'm here. Besides, I don't like them knowing my business."

"Not even Miss Annabel?"

"Boone knows, and I imagine he's told her. But if it isn't mentioned, there isn't any explaining to do."

Corbin watched Annabel come out of the store and stop on the walk to talk to the dapper little man who ran the drugstore. She was slender and poised and reminded him a lot of Julie Jones Johnson.

For the first time in a long while a woman interested him. He was looking forward to dinner.

Chapter 7

JACK AND CORBIN GOT TO THEIR FEET when Annabel and Boone came up the steps to the hotel porch. Annabel had removed her hat and looked even younger and prettier than before. Her green eyes were sparkling, her lips smiling. Corbin could hardly tear his eyes away. When he did, he caught a frowning Boone watching him.

Determined not to let the surly man spoil his pleasure in being with this exciting girl, Corbin maneuvered the cane to his other hand and offered his free arm to Annabel.

"Shall we go in?"

"Corbin . . ." Jack spoke hesitantly, even as Annabel took Corbin's arm. "I'm not dressed to go into a fancy place—"

"You're dressed just fine. This place isn't that fancy."

After putting his hat on the hall tree beside the door, Corbin led them to a square table covered with a white cloth. He held the chair for Annabel. Boone dropped his cap on the floor under his chair.

"According to the posted bill of fare," Corbin said, still standing, "they're serving catfish and corn bread today. Also chicken pie with biscuit crust. Which do you prefer, Miss Donovan?"

"The chicken pie." Corbin looked at Boone and Jack. They both nodded.

"Excuse me and I'll ask that they serve us the chicken pie family-style."

When Corbin left the table, Annabel watched him limp away. He was a tall man and lean yet muscular, with broad shoulders. He appeared to be confident, capable of handling himself in most situations.

"What's the matter with his leg?"

Boone shrugged. "Ask him."

"Are you going to pout because I wanted to come here and you didn't?"

"No, I'm not goin' to pout. I'm goin' to eat ever' dang bite I can hold, long's he's payin' for it."

"He's real nice, Boone," Jack said. "Folks back home thought the world of him. My brother and I thought he might be interested in Julie, our sister. When he saw that she only had eyes for Evan, he backed off."

"I'm not sayin' he ain't *nice*." He looked directly at Annabel. "I'm sayin' we know nothin' 'bout him."

Annabel narrowed her eyes when she looked at Boone. She had seen Corbin coming back to the table.

"You . . . behave," she whispered.

During the meal Jack brought up the subject of Corbin's love of running.

"It was a shock to some of our neighbors when they saw Mr. Appleby running down the road. They thought he didn't have any sense at all. Nobody in Fertile runs if they're not going to a fire. Then they just walk fast." Jack grinned at Corbin.

"He won't be doin' much runnin' for a while," Boone said dryly.

"You're right. I'm going to spend some time sitting on the porch here letting my leg and shoulder heal."

"Are you a runner like in the Boston Marathon?" Annabel asked.

"Not at all. I started running while I was in school, then continued while I was in France during the war. It's something I like to do."

"What happened to your leg and your shoulder? Were you in an accident?" Annabel asked.

"I guess you could say that. Someone took me for a deer and shot me."

Corbin smiled at her. His skin was bronze: He had obviously spent long hours in the sun. His eyes had little creases at the corners. She wondered what had caused the scar that ran down the side of his cheek.

"Is that true? Are you making it up? At times I can't believe a word Boone says. He loves to make up tall tales and get me riled up."

"It's true. Boone found me and . . . saw to it that I was taken care of." His gaze was fully directed on her. It was unnerving, penetrating. She was determined not to appear rattled.

Annabel turned to Boone, who was eating calmly. "You never said anything about that."

"I didn't think it was that all-fired important. Pass the butter."

"So much has happened already this morning. This certainly has been an exciting day, and it's only noon." She lifted her fork to her mouth and realized the three men at the table were waiting for her to explain.

"What's happened?" Boone broke the silence.

"Mr. Potter asked me to play a solo at the concert on Sunday."

"Harrumpt! Ya goin' to?"

"No! I wouldn't dream of it."

"She plays the violin," Jack said when he realized that Corbin didn't know what they were talking about.

"Yes, I play the violin, but I'm not a concert violinist." She could feel herself blushing. She wished that she hadn't brought it up. He would think her a braggart.

"I'd like to hear you play. During the war a fellow in our company played the violin and entertained us when possible. It was like a little bit of home. We all made sure that nothing happened to that violin. Do you attend the concerts they have here in the park?"

"I haven't yet, but I'd like to come . . . sometime, if I can talk Boone into bringing me."

"I could come for you. I can drive . . . short distances."

"I'll bring her if she wants to come," Boone said gruffly without looking up from his plate.

To change the subject, Annabel said, "Meeting Mr. Potter wasn't the only exciting thing that happened to me this morning. One of our neighbors asked me out on a date tonight. He didn't really ask me, he told me to be ready at sundown. Can you beat that for arrogance?"

"Who?" Boone spit out the one word.

"One of the Carters." Annabel spoke matter-of-factly as she split a biscuit and buttered it. "The oldest one, I think. He had blond hair and wasn't . . . too bad-looking. He'd been to the barbershop and reeked of hair tonic."

Boone dropped his fork beside his plate. "Ya . . . didn't . . . ?"

"Didn't what? Talk to him? How could I help it?"

"That ain't what I meant. Ya ain't goin', and that's that."

"Flitter, Boone. I never said I was going. I thought it downright funny that he told me to be ready at sundown."

"The stinkin' polecat! I'll bust his damn head!"

"Why are you getting riled up? You know that I'd not go out with him." She laughed a little. "He was mad as a drunk hoot owl when he left."

Corbin could see that she was enjoying baiting Boone and he could also see the man was as protective of her as a she-bear with one cub.

"Them Carters ain't nothin' but trash and ya know it."

"You didn't seem to think Tess was trash. You were looking her over pretty well the day she came to the house." There was a teasing light in her eyes and her mouth tilted at the corners as she tried to suppress a smile.

"She's different. Them brothers of hers is no good. Why'd ya even talk to him?"

"He came in the store while I was there."

"Follered ya in, did he?"

"How would I know? Stop this. Mr. Appleby will get the idea that you're my keeper."

"That's what I am." Boone looked directly at Corbin. "When her pa ain't here, I'm her keeper."

"Her pa must put a heap of trust in you."

"He does. I been lookin' out for her nigh on ten years."

"Eight." Annabel grinned at him.

"Ten," Boone said stubbornly.

"It's been eight years, Mr. Appleby. He's known Papa ten years, but I hardly saw him for the first two years. Boone, you are like my second papa . . . but you are prone to be overprotective and to exaggerate at times."

Corbin's eyes went from one to the other and he realized that the source of their bantering was the affection they held for each other.

"And yo're headstrong and as stubborn as yore pa."

"Thank you, Boone. I like you too," she said sweetly,

then turned to Corbin. "This has been a delicious meal. I'll have to cook dinner for you to pay you back."

Corbin saw the quick way Boone looked at the girl and how his shoulders stiffened.

"Please. There's no need. As soon as we've finished, they'll serve pie. We have a choice between raisin cream and custard."

Corbin stood on the porch of the hotel and watched the truck head out of town. One thing was certain, he thought: Boone didn't want him to get too friendly with Miss Donovan. What was he afraid of? Did he want her for himself? Corbin didn't think so. His interest didn't appear to be romantic, just protective. But from what was he protecting her?

Leaning more heavily than necessary on the cane he had borrowed from the hotel, Corbin limped down the street to the barbershop. He considered it an even better place than the newspaper to find out what was going on in town.

BOB'S BARBER SHOP—SHAVE AND HAIRCUT FOUR BITS. The sign was printed in gold script on the glass window.

Corbin opened the door and went inside. It was a two-chair shop and both were occupied. A mirror covered the wall behind the barber chairs. In front of it was a shelf of shaving mugs marked with their users' names.

"Howdy. Hang your hat and have a seat," one of the barbers invited. He was using the clippers on the sideburns of a dark-haired man. He stopped clipping to speak and give Corbin a careful scrutiny.

Corbin hung his hat on the rack on the hall tree and eased himself down in a wooden armchair. Several newspapers and a copy of the *Saturday Evening Post* lay nearby. Corbin picked up the magazine and glanced through it. His ears were attuned to the conversation between the barber and his customer.

"He acted halfway decent for a change. He wanted the works."

"A bath too?"

"Yeah. I told him it was thirty cents with soap and he didn't bat an eye. Just laid down his coin and went to the back." The barber jerked his head toward the cretonne curtains that hung on a tightly stretched string over an opening in the wall.

"Bet it was the first one he's had this year."

"When he came out, I shaved him and cut his hair." The barber was a small man wearing dark trousers and a white coat. The hair on his head was sparse but thick and bushy on his upper lip.

"Law, Bob, what do you reckon got into him?"

"Courtin'. I can tell ever' time when a man's got courtin' on his mind."

A disgusted grunt came from the man reclining with a hot towel wrapped around his face so that only his nose poked out. The barber stirred up a rich lather in a cup and, after removing the towel, painted the foam all over the man's face with a small brush. When it was thick enough to satisfy the barber, he picked up a murderous-looking razor and slapped it against a black strop until its sharpness suited him. With long strokes he cut into the lather on the man's face, leaving a clean path of pink skin.

"You talkin' 'bout Marvin Carter?" the man asked as soon as the whiskers were removed from his face and it was blotted with a warm towel.

"Yeah. Do you know him?" The barber splashed a spicy-smelling liquid on his hands, rubbed them briskly together and applied the bay rum to the man's skin, slapping it smartly. He then raised the man to a sitting position.

"I know all the blasted Carters. They are the beatin'est bunch you ever did see. Stupid and mean. Clannish as hell. They keep their womenfolk beat down and spitting out kids. Marvin's brother Calvin, who lives over west of here, already has six or eight and I hear he ain't no more'n twenty-five or -six years old."

"He musta started young."

"He did. Them Carters are a randy bunch. All that's on their minds is whiskey and fornicatin' with their woman or someone else's." The man got out of his chair and reached for his coat. He stopped and looked intently at Corbin. "Do I know you?"

"Might. I've been around."

"Was it around St. Louis?"

"Nope. Only been through there."

"Were you in the war?"

"Western Front. Second Division under General Omar Bundy."

"Well, I'll be a pissed-on polecat!" The man sprang forward with an extended hand. "I was sure I'd seen you someplace. It was in that hellhole. You fought at Belleau Wood? So did I. Name's Sergeant Craig Travis."

"Lieutenant Corbin Appleby." Corbin got slowly to his feet and the two men shook hands vigorously.

"Good to see you, Lieutenant."

"Corbin or Appleby now, Travis. That lieutenant stuff is all behind me."

"Me too. I consider myself lucky to be alive. In three weeks of fighting we cleared the woods, but eighteen hundred of our men were killed and seven thousand wounded."

"Whoever said that war was hell knew what he was talking about."

"I came out with just a scratch or two. I see that you wasn't so lucky." Travis gestured to the cane Corbin had hung on the chair.

"I got this in the war." Corbin drew a line down the scar that sliced his cheek. "This"—he patted his leg—"is something different. Fellow took me for a deer when I stopped along the road a few days back."

"Hellfire! He shoot you? You sure he thought you were a deer?"

"No, I'm not sure." Corbin saw that the two barbers and the man in the chair were hanging on every word that passed between him and Travis. "Maybe they wanted my automobile. Another fellow came along and scared them off. Now I've got to wait around here until the doc says I'm fit to drive several hundred miles."

"The doc here is as good as there is."

"I've found that out."

"It was good meetin' up with you, Appleby. Where you staying?"

"The Riverfront Hotel."

"I run the butcher shop. Drop in anytime. I want you to come over to the house before you leave and meet my wife. She'll cook up a big slab of beef with potatoes and carrots. She's the best cook in town, even if I do say so."

"Thank you, I will."

Corbin remained standing as Craig Travis left the shop. He glanced at the barber behind the empty chair, went to it and eased himself down onto the comfortable padded seat.

The barber whirled a white cloth around him as the door opened again. A man with a brown hat smashed down over a head of thick gray hair came into the shop. Wide red suspenders held up trousers that were several inches too big around his ample middle. A gray mustache curled down on each side of a mouth that had a toothpick protruding from the corner. A big tin star was attached to his shirt.

"'Lo, Stoney." The barber spoke to the man's reflection in the mirror behind the chairs. "Got a *Post-Dispatch* this morning."

"Figured ya did." Stoney sat down, laid his hat on the seat beside him and picked up the St. Louis newspaper. He scanned the headlines. "Nothin's been done in Washington since Harding died."

"Things seem to be goin' pretty good."

"That fool Coolidge is sleepin' at the switch. They say he takes a four-hour nap ever' day. Sleepin'," Stoney snorted with disgust, "while racketeers take over the country."

"This is Henderson, Stoney. Not Chicago or St. Louis. I ain't seen a racketeer this mornin'." The barber winked at Corbin.

"That ain't sayin' they ain't here. Think they go 'round with a sign on their backs sayin' they're racketeers? They could be preachers, doctors, anybody. The college boys who killed that Frank kid in Chicago wore nice suits and ties. Their daddies was rich. They got them that rich lawyer feller to get 'em off. Didn't do no good, though."

"I've not heard that Clarence Darrow was so rich." The barber winked at Corbin again.

"Ridin' around in fancy cars? He's rich. You can't tell 'bout folks these days. Coolidge better be doin' somethin' 'bout crime in this country instead of sleepin' and lettin' the country run itself."

"What do you want him to do, Stoney?"

"I want him to keep his fingers on things. Not pilin' up in the bed sleepin'."

"He's had a bad time since he's been in office. It's not easy losin' a boy to blood poison."

"Didn't say it was. I just don't see why we have to pay a man for sleepin' on the job four hours a day. It ought to be taken out of his pay. Our government is a joke."

"Will Rogers says that he don't make jokes, he watches the government and reports the facts." Bob stuck his tongue in his cheek and waited for Stoney's response. He was disappointed to get only a snort of disgust from him.

Corbin listened to the conversation and wondered if Stoney was the only lawman in Henderson. If so, he understood why Marshal Sanford wanted him to hang around and see what he could find out.

Corbin's mind drifted to Annabel Lee Donovan and he wondered if she was named after the girl in Poe's poem. He remembered having to memorize it in school.

She was a child and *I* was a child,
In this kingdom by the sea,
But we loved with a love that was more than love—
I and my Annabel Lee—

"Where you from, mister?" The barber broke into Corbin's thoughts.

"Over near Springfield."

"Never been that far west. I've always lived along the river."

Corbin let the conversation lag. He watched as the man in the other chair got up, put on his hat and left.

"He's been comin' to the shop regular as clockwork lately," Stoney remarked as soon as the door closed.

"His business, Stoney," the barber replied. He shook the

cloth, then got out the broom and swept hair into a pile in the corner.

"Monkey business. He was gettin' hisself all smelly up nice for that woman he's seein' down on Cedar Street."

"What woman?" The ears of the barber working on Corbin perked up. "There aren't any single women on Cedar Street that I know of."

"Is Alex Lemon sleepin' with another married woman, Stoney?" Bob asked and stood the broom in the corner. "The damn fool has broke up one family already."

"How about his own?" the other barber asked. "He's got a nice little wife and two kids. His woman can't be so dumb she don't know what's going on."

Stoney ignored the conversation, opened the paper and continued to read.

Chapter 8

I SHOULDN'TA TOOK YA. I shoulda let the boy take the truck and go in by hisself." They were seated at the supper table.

"Why shouldn't you have taken me? Did I do something to embarrass you?"

"No." He glared at her. "Murphy won't like it a bit when he finds out you were seen in town in that rat trap of a truck."

Boone had stayed away from the house after they returned from town and had only come in to supper after Annabel went to the barn and urged him to come in and eat.

"What in the world are you talking about?"

"Has he ever took you to town in the truck?"

"You know he hasn't. He takes me in the car."

"See there? See there? That's what I'm talkin' about. He's got his sights set high for ya bein' kind of highfalutin and havin' folks seein' ya in that rat-trap truck ain't how he wants 'em to think of ya."

"That's the silliest thing I ever heard. Boone, are you sure you feel all right?"

"Just wait till he hears. He'll rake both of us over the coals."

Jack wasn't sure what to make of the conversation. He was suddenly dreading the return of Mr. Donovan. Was he so high-toned that he would be angry that Annabel went to town in the truck?

"I've decided to go to the concert Sunday afternoon. If you don't take me in the truck, I'll have to walk or ride one of the horses." Annabel dished up the peach cobbler and brought a pitcher of cream to the table before she sat down. Over Boone's head she winked at Jack. "Jack, tell me about Mr. Appleby. Was he a longtime friend of your family?"

"You might say that."

Annabel glanced sideways at Jack and then at Boone. The boy kept his head down.

"How long?"

"Ya might as well tell her, boy." Boone reached for the sugar bowl. "She's goin' to pick at ya till ya tell her what she wants to know."

"What's that?" Annabel asked. "What are you two trying to keep from me?"

"Appleby was a lawman back in Fertile. Could still be a lawman, far as I know," Boone said grumpily. "He's got a easygoin' mouth and eyes like a hawk."

"He was the police chief in our town," Jack said. "But he quit after he got the man who killed the girl he'd been going to marry. It was a shock to folks in town when they found out there was a murderer among us. The man had fooled everyone, even me. He could be nice as pie but really was a terrible man and had done a lot of bad things."

"Thank you, Jack. That's more information than I'd've gotten out of Boone in a month." Annabel sent Boone a cynical smile, then tilted her head to listen. "Do I hear a car?"

Boone got quickly to his feet and went to the door. Annabel crowded in close behind him. Boone blocked the door until a big black car rounded the house and stopped beside the back porch.

"It's Murphy," Boone said, stepping out of the way.

"Papa!" Annabel dashed out onto the porch and waited for the big, dark-haired man to get out of the car.

"Hello, darlin'. You got some supper for your papa?" He came up the porch steps and hugged his daughter. He had a stubble of beard on his face and his clothes were rumpled.

"I'm glad you're home, Papa."

"I'm glad to be here."

"You were gone a long time."

"I know, darlin'." His eyes looked past her and found Jack. Annabel felt the arm around her tense.

"Papa, this is Jack Jones. He's helping me put in a garden."

"You don't say? A garden, huh?"

"Glad to make your acquaintance." Jack wasn't sure what to do. He seemed to be pinned to the floor by a pair of piercing dark eyes that finally swung back to Boone.

"Things all right around here?" The question clearly referred to Jack's presence.

"Yeah."

"I'll pen up the chickens." Jack began to edge around the two big men.

"Chickens?" Murphy looked to Boone again.

"And a cow," Annabel added happily.

"A cow?" Murphy echoed, then began to laugh. "She talked you into getting a cow?" He spoke to Boone with his arm across his daughter's shoulders.

Boone moved out of the way so that Jack could go down the porch steps and didn't answer until the boy had disappeared into the barn.

"Yeah, a cow. I'd like to see ya stand against yore girl

when she's got her neck bowed and her head set on havin' her way."

"I think it's a good idea. Chickens, a cow and horses. Looks like we're real farm folk." His big hand squeezed Annabel's shoulder. "I'm hungry as a bear, darlin'. I've not eaten since morning. I was in a hurry to get here."

"I'll have you something in three shakes of a dog's tail." Annabel hurried to the kitchen, leaving her father with Boone.

Murphy's eyes held Boone's. "The boy?"

"He's all right. Been good for Annabel to have him here. I'll fill ya in after ya've et. Go give some time to Annabel. She's been frettin' 'bout ya."

"Is he wantin' me to leave?"

Jack spoke worriedly to Boone when he came to sit beside him on a box near the barn door. Boone had had a long talk with Murphy. He told him about finding Appleby shot beside his car and about his being a former lawman looking for the boy. He told about Jack's being sick and coming to the house. After listening to Boone's report that two loads of whiskey had gone out and that Spinner was expecting the barge bringing more down from Canada tonight, Murphy had gone back to the house.

"He didn't say so," Boone said in answer to Jack's question. "I reckon ya can stay awhile and help Annabel with the garden. The girl means the world to him; and if she wants a garden, he'll get her one come hell or high water."

"After we get the garden in there won't be much for me to do for a while. I'll go to town and get a job of some sort. I'm not going back to Fertile until I get my baseball and my glove back."

"How ya goin' to do that?"

"There's not a glove like it anywhere. I'll know it when I see it. Corbin said that Henderson has a ball team. Someone may be using it. It'd be a glove to brag on."

"Coulda been someone from upriver that stole it."

"Or downriver."

"Not much downriver but hill folks, and they ain't much for playin' ball."

"They might have sold it to someone. Makes no difference, I'll get it back."

"Stubborn little cuss, ain't ya?" Boone's eyes had been focused on a light spot at the edge of the trees for the past few minutes. Someone was there watching the house. "Stay here, boy. I'm goin' through the barn and out the back. Someone's spyin' on the house. I'm hopin' it's that clabberhead I met in the woods the day I went for the cow. I been wantin' the chance to bust his head."

"Is there anythin' I can do?"

"Naw. Just sit here like you're waitin' for me to come back out."

Boone walked slowly to the barn door and disappeared inside. Once inside, he hurried to the back entrance and peered out to see if he was visible to the one standing at the edge of the woods. When he was reasonably sure he couldn't be seen, he hunkered down and went quickly to the brush that grew along the fence line that enclosed the cow pasture. He followed it until he could turn into the woods and come up behind the person watching.

Sounds amplified by the stillness of the forest drifted to Boone's ears as he moved as quietly as possible. He heard the rustling of brush as some unknown creature sought to hide itself from him. He heard the sound of birds nesting in the trees and the far-off hoot of a train whistle. He moved swiftly and cautiously toward the unknown watcher.

He neared the tree line and saw the blur of white ahead. On closer inspection he became aware that it was the skirt of a woman's dress held against the trunk of a large cottonwood by the slight breeze. He had expected it to be a Carter but not Tess Carter. Anger flowed out of him, and in its place a kind of excitement made his pulses race. He had thought about her. Now he pondered how to approach her without scaring the daylights out of her.

Watching her, he softly whistled a tune and saw her slip around to the other side of the tree. Fearing that she would bolt and run, he called out.

"Miss Tess, it's me . . . Boone. Can I talk to you for a minute or two?" There was no answer. He waited for a moment, then he said, "I won't come any closer than you want me to."

When she didn't speak, he made a wide circle around the tree and approached it from the front so that she could see him. He stopped a dozen feet from her.

"Hello, ma'am. I'm sorry I scared you. I saw someone over here and didn't know who it was."

"I was . . . just looking."

"I know that." Boone laughed a little. "Ye're welcome to come over anytime ya want." *Good Lord, he was as nervous as a kid meeting a girl for the first time.*

"I couldn't."

"Annabel would like it if you did."

"I couldn't," she said again.

"Will your brothers be out lookin' for ya?"

"They've gone off somewhere."

"Aren't ya afraid out here in the woods by yourself?"

"What's there to be afraid of?"

"Some no-good son-of-a—some man might catch ya out here by yoreself."

"No one ever came through here but Carters until you."

"Ya've nothin' to fear from us. Annabel liked you. She's hopin' ya'll come callin' again. She gets lonesome."

"She's pretty and . . . nice."

"Yeah, she is."

"Are you going to marry her?"

"Marry Annabel?" He laughed again. "I'm almost old enough to be her pa."

"That don't make no never mind to some folks."

"She'd think it funny you'd think that."

There was a long silence, then Tess said, "I didn't mean to make a . . . funny."

"I meant strange. Annabel'd think it strange anyone would think that. I've known her since she was 'bout this high." He held his hand out even with his waist.

"You're fond of her."

"Yeah. She's like my own kid . . . if I had one. I hope she'll find a good man someday, get married and have kids of her own."

"If he's not a good man what'll you do?"

Boone came closer to where she was standing with her back to the tree.

"I'll beat hell outta him . . . if there was anythin' left after her pa got through with him."

"She's lucky." Tess's voice was a mere whisper.

"Do you have a beau?"

"No." She shook her head.

"Why not? You're a pretty girl."

"No, I'm not!" She frowned. "I'm old."

"Old? Are you fifty?"

She almost smiled. "I'm twenty-seven."

"I've lived exactly ten years longer than you have. Do you think that's old?"

"Not for a man."

"I like talking to you." Boone was near enough now that he could see her face clearly. He looked at her, letting his eyes wander over her face. Her breathing was jerky, but she didn't move or say anything for a long moment. When she did, it was a low, breathless whisper.

"I don't have much to talk about."

"Tell me about you. How long have you lived here with your brothers?"

She shook her head, then said, "Long time."

"Have ya always lived here?"

She shook her head again.

"I lived up north in Minnesota for a while," Boone said, wanting to keep her talking.

"I know where it is."

"It gets pretty cold up there."

"It's by Canada."

"My sister lives in Minnesota."

"I don't have a sister. Just brothers."

"Tess, do you ever go to town?"

She shook her head. "Marvin won't let me."

"Why not?"

"Ah . . . he—" Embarrassed, she looked away from Boone.

"Will you meet me here again so we can talk?"

"Just talk?" She tilted her head and looked into his face.

"Just talk. Don't be afraid that I'll force myself on you, Tess. I won't. I swear it."

"Marvin swears to things. It don't mean anything."

"I'm not Marvin," Boone said firmly. "My word is my bond."

"What does that mean?"

"It means that when I give my word, I keep it."

"All right."

"You'll meet me?"

"I don't know when they'll be gone."

"What would happen if I came to the house to call on ya?"

"Oh, don't!" Her voice was panicky. "They'd know and be awful mad."

"Would they hurt ya?"

"They'd be awful mad," she repeated and edged around the tree.

"Tess, don't run off. I won't do anythin' to cause ya trouble." Boone didn't understand the unfamiliar feelings that were spiraling through him. He desperately wanted to be with her again, talk to her. His mind worked frantically to find a way. "You can signal when you're here. I'll be here five more days, then I'll be gone for a while. Wear something white and stand there by the tree."

"Marvin comes here sometimes."

"To spy on the house?"

"He likes her. He likes to look at her and listen to the music."

Boone snorted. "He met Annabel in the store."

"He likes her," Tess said again. "He was fit to be tied when he came back from town. He swears he'll have her. He usually gets the women he wants. Tell her that . . . he ruins girls."

"He'll not ruin Annabel. I'll kill him first. Ya can tell him that."

"No! I can't tell him I talked to you. He'd be sure to . . . to . . . do something."

"What would he do?"

"I've got to go. Bud will be back from the . . . from the—"

"I know they've got a still, Tess. I don't care if they have a dozen stills."

" 'Bye."

"Tess?" Boone placed his hand on her arm and she didn't flinch away. "If things get too rough for ya, come over. If I'm not here, Annabel will be and a fellow named Spinner. He'd do his best to help ya, and he'd get in touch with me. I'd come, Tess. You can count on it."

"Who was the man who came in the big car?"

"Annabel's pa. He's a straight shooter. If ya get in trouble, ya could count on him to help ya."

She searched his face with large amber eyes, then said, " 'Bye."

Boone watched her run lightly down the path until she was out of sight. Something about her had gotten to him. Whether it was her softness, her sincerity or an odd kind of sadness, he didn't know. He had felt an instant attraction to her that day in the woods, then when he saw her in the kitchen with Annabel, his heart had thumped. Tonight, it had thumped with gladness when he realized that it was Tess standing beside the tree.

Good Lord! What was he thinking? What was she thinking? He rubbed his hand over his whiskered cheek. He didn't look any better than any hillbilly who roamed these hills. Somehow he had known that she was a few years older than Annabel . . . but not that old. She didn't look it. One thing was sure: She was too old to have brothers dictate her every move.

She was afraid of them! Did they knock her around? By God, he'd better not find out that they did. He'd pick the bastards off one at a time and beat the holy hell out of them.

Boone turned and walked slowly back to the barn, where Jack was waiting. He'd have to warn Jack and Spinner to be on the lookout for Marvin Carter and not leave Annabel alone here at the house. The son-of-a-bitch had been here at night to listen to the music. One night he'd catch him and he'd not be pleasuring himself for a month of Sundays.

Boone debated telling Murphy about Marvin's liking for Annabel and decided against it. The Irishman had the temper of a treed wildcat when Annabel was threatened in any way. He might march over to the Carters, drag Marvin out and beat the daylights out of him. Stubborn and short-tempered, Murphy could stir up a mess of trouble.

Deep in thought, Boone shook his head. If they had an open clash with the Carters, it would make life miserable for Tess, and he suspected that that little woman had all the trouble she could handle.

Chapter 9

CORBIN ATE HIS DINNER IN THE HOTEL DINING ROOM and visited with a drummer who sold ladies' underwear and swimsuits and liked to talk about it.

"I'm making a swing up through St. Louis and on to Chicago. I doubt I'll get many orders in this hick town for the kind of lingerie I sell." He lifted his brows several times in a lecherous gesture. "What I'm showing is more for the modern girls, if you know what I mean. Lace and see-through stuff is what sells in the city.

"The crotch on the panties is about this wide," he said in a low confidential tone, holding his thumb and forefinger an inch apart. "With the short skirts the girls are wearing these days, it makes for a high old time for some lucky fellow whose girl is wearing R. L. Daniels underwear. If you know what I mean." The man lifted his brows up and down again in the gesture that was beginning to irritate Corbin.

I know what you mean. You crude son-of-a-bitch. Corbin continued to eat his dinner and tried unsuccessfully to block out the salesman's voice.

"Last year our swimsuits were worn by the girls in the Miss America Pageant in Atlantic City. The girl that won, a

Miss Malcolmson, was a looker. Her waist was no bigger than this." His curved fingers formed a small round hole. "Some thought she'd cinched her waist in to make it so small. But I don't think so. Her titties weren't pushed up. They hung there just right."

"Did you see her?" Corbin was bored with the conversation and, knowing that he was under no obligation to listen to the blowhard, placed his napkin beside his plate.

"Well, no. But a friend of mine did. He was within a few feet of her and—"

"Excuse me." Corbin picked up his cane and went to the counter to sign the bill for his meal, then made his way out onto the hotel porch.

Later in the month it would be hot and sultry, but today was a beautiful warm summer day. Corbin went down the walk to the riverfront. The river fascinated him. He stood for a long while watching the water out in the channel moving on its way to the sea. As a lover of history, he knew the part this mighty river had played in the development of the country.

From its banks Lewis and Clark had launched their expedition to the Pacific Ocean and Zebulon Pike had been dispatched to the Southwest to explore the Arkansas and Red rivers and obtain information about the Spanish territory. LaSalle, the French explorer, had claimed all the region watered by the great river and its tributaries for France, naming the region "Louisiana." Later it was purchased by the United States for less than three cents an acre. A bargain, if there ever was one.

Corbin shook himself out of his reverie and took one last look at the water rolling on past him out of that far land, then turned back toward town. He happened upon a small barefoot boy who had come to the bank with a long cane pole. Corbin stopped and watched him attach a wiggling worm to the hook on the end of a string and waited until the line was thrown out and the cork was bobbing on the water.

"What are you fishing for?"

"Anythin' I can get."

"Is this a good place?"

"Yes, sir. Caught me six bullheads here yesterday." The boy lifted a heavily freckled face to look at him, and his grin revealed widely spaced teeth.

"Well, good luck." Corbin patted him on the head and walked on.

His life had suddenly become very empty. He felt hollow inside. For some time now he had longed for a wife and children: a freckle-faced boy to go fishing with, a pretty little girl to run to meet him when he came home, a soft, sweet-smelling woman to hold in his arms at night.

There wasn't anyone who depended upon him and he had no one to depend upon. He loved his sisters who lived in Springfield and he knew that they loved him. But they had their own families and he was only on the fringe of them. He thought of the Jones family back in Fertile and the loving care Julie Jones had given her brothers and sisters. He longed to be part of such a family.

"Howdy, sir." He was greeted cheerfully by the pharmacist who, Corbin had been told, was the conductor of the Henderson municipal band. He was carrying a large instrument case. "Glad to see you giving that leg some exercise."

"I don't dare let it stiffen up on me."

"Come to the concert this afternoon. We'll play you a tune to jig to."

Corbin laughed. "I'm not ready to jig, but I plan to be there."

He walked on down the street and looked into the windows of the five-and-dime store. He lingered at the picture show next door to read the poster attached to the wall. GLORIA SWANSON IN "HER GILDED CAGE," PLAYING ON TUESDAY, WEDNESDAY AND SATURDAY. Corbin had seen the show when it came to Fertile last year.

The tall shoeshine chair was empty and the window blinds down when he passed the barbershop. He crossed the side street to the limestone bank building. A black marker two feet high on the corner was a reminder that the river had overflowed ten years back and that muddy river water had flooded the town.

Corbin's mind wandered to the assignment given to him by Marshal Sanford. Who in this town was connected to a murder-for-hire scheme? Who in this small, peaceful town was connected to brothels and opium dens? Even the jolly bandmaster could be one of the criminals. Murderers came in all ages, shapes and sizes and from all walks of life. It was a depressing thought.

The day stretched ahead.

Not wishing to go back to the hotel, where he would risk running into the underwear drummer, Corbin walked to the tree-lined city park. The square, fronting Main Street, had been set aside by the founders back in 1850. A Civil War cannon occupied a place of honor on the corner. A pyramid of cannonballs was stacked neatly beside it. Branching out from the bandstand in the center of the park were rows of green-painted benches and a scattering of sturdy picnic tables.

A few cars were angled facing the park. A half dozen families were finishing picnic dinners. Some of the womenfolk were busy packing baskets and taking them back to the cars. Children chased each other in a game of tag; boys rolled hoops and girls played jacks on the sidewalk surrounding the park.

The scene was peaceful, families enjoying the day in the park. Children's laughter and the voices of the women calling to them were cheerful sounds, but they made Corbin feel lonely. He stood watching until a young boy ran into him. He reached to steady the lad.

"What do you say, Jimmy?" the mother called.

"Sorry," the towheaded boy shouted as he ran to catch up with his friend.

His mother threw up her hands. "All he's got on his mind today is play."

"I envy him," Corbin replied and tipped his hat.

Corbin found a bench set well back beneath a large oak tree, eased himself down on it and took a deep breath. He missed his two- or three-a-week runs. He'd give anything to be able to take off down the road and run and run and run.

Running had been his way of relieving stress since his school days, during the war and while he was police chief of Fertile. Waiting for his leg to heal was frustrating. Even if he were able to run, he shouldn't and wouldn't. If folks thought that he was well enough to run, he would lose his excuse for staying here.

Corbin felt the thin leather envelope tucked inside his shirt. Inside the envelope were the notes he'd been making about each of the people he'd met here so far. He had jotted down his impressions of the two barbers and the lawman. He had ruled out the hotel employees. Their jobs were too menial for the man he was seeking. He wanted to find out more about Craig Travis, the sergeant who was in his division in France. He planned to call upon him this next week and to accept the invitation to dinner if it was extended again. He also wanted to know about the man they called Alex Lemon who was sleeping with another man's wife.

Corbin was almost certain that Boone wasn't his man. Nor were the Carters, the clan who lived in the hills surrounding the town. From what he'd heard about them, they were not smart enough to play with the big boys in Chicago.

Time passed while Corbin's thoughts tumbled over each other. The park benches were beginning to fill up with people. He wondered if Annabel would come to the concert. He was unaware of a smile that hovered about his lips when he thought of her, or that he had stored her image in the dark regions of his mind to bring out and enjoy

But we loved with a love that was more than love—
I and my Annabel Lee—

Why couldn't he get those lines of poetry out of his mind? He had no business thinking about that woman. He had no business thinking about anything but doing the job assigned to him, then getting the hell out of here.

Even as he was thinking about her, he saw her coming down the sidewalk clinging to the arm of a man wearing a black suit and a brown felt hat that tilted jauntily forward. Corbin was surprised to feel a sharp pang of utter dejection on seeing her with the well-dressed man.

She was wearing a blue dress of soft material that swirled around her calves as she walked. A narrow matching blue ribbon had been slipped beneath her hair in back and brought around behind her ears and tied on top of her head. Her feet were light, her head high and she was taking two steps to her companion's one.

As they neared, Corbin could see that she was smiling and talking excitedly. She appeared to be as happy as a kid on Christmas morning. The man held her close to his side in a proprietary manner. His head was canted toward hers, and he was paying close attention to what she was saying.

Watching her, Corbin saw the instant she spotted him. She lifted her hand and waved. He tipped his hat in greeting. Annabel tugged on the man's arm and pulled him toward where Corbin sat on the bench. He got to his feet and took off his hat as they approached.

"Hello, Mr. Appleby."

"It's nice to see you again, Miss Donovan."

"I've been telling my father about the lovely meal you treated us to at the hotel."

Her father. Corbin straightened his shoulders to keep them from slumping in relief.

"It was nothing compared to what you did for Jack."

"This is my father, Murphy Donovan. Papa, Mr. Appleby, Jack's friend."

"Glad to meet you," the men said in unison as they shook hands.

On closer inspection of Murphy, Corbin saw a man of considerable strength, rough-hewn and obviously proud of his daughter. Who could blame him? Annabel, with the friendly demeanor, sweet body and beautiful face, was a girl any man would cherish. He turned to see that she was smiling at him as if she were genuinely glad to see him.

"Did you come in for the concert?" he asked, thinking that he had to say something when all he wanted to do was look at her.

Annabel laughed. "We did. Poor Papa. He humored me. He'd rather be anywhere but at a concert."

"Now, darlin', that's not true."

"Are you staying for the concert?" Annabel asked Corbin.

"I thought I would."

"I doubt that there's much else going on in Henderson on Sunday afternoon," Murphy said.

"Do they have a ball team here?" Corbin asked.

"I don't know. Most towns this size have a team. I hear that your young friend fancies himself quite a ball player."

"I wouldn't put it like that," Corbin said bluntly. "He likes the game and is a pretty good player. If he wears out his welcome, let me know and I'll come get him."

Murphy rocked back on his heels and studied the tall man leaning on the cane. This was a man somewhere near thirty years of age who had been down the river and around the bend. He knew how to take care of himself.

According to Boone, Appleby had been a lawman in a small town in the northwest corner of the state. Was he a federal marshal now? Had he planted the kid out at the farm to get information before he called in the marshals? If he was a Fed, he would have to work fast, Murphy thought now. If things went the way he planned, this time next week he would be out of the bootlegging business with enough money to buy Annabel a nice modern house in town and open up a legitimate business.

"Boone told me about someone taking a couple of shots at you. Do you have any idea who it was?" Murphy asked after a short pause.

"Never saw a thing."

"Boone thought maybe someone wanted your car."

"They could have asked me for it. They didn't have to shoot me. I'd have died right there if Boone hadn't been around. I owe him." Corbin looked directly into Murphy Donovan's probing dark eyes.

"How long do you plan to stay around?"

"Until my leg and shoulder heal."

"What kind of work are you in?"

"None at the present. I studied to be a journalist, but the war got in the way of that."

Corbin leaned on his cane. His eyes were drawn to Annabel. He couldn't stop looking at her and he didn't give a damn if Donovan liked it or not.

"What division were you in?"

"Military Police attached to General Bundy's division." Corbin's eyes switched to Donovan and stayed there. The man's expression never changed.

Good Lord, I hope Annabel's father isn't the man I'm looking for. But hell, he fills the bill more than anyone I've met so far.

"I understand you've just moved to the farm. Do you plan a cattle or a grain operation?"

"There isn't enough acreage for grain. I'm looking into buying some adjoining land."

Corbin could tell by the way Annabel looked at her father that this was news to her. She opened her mouth to say something, then closed it and looked toward Mr. Potter, who was coming down the walk carrying a slide trombone.

"Hello, Mr. Potter."

"Miss Donovan," he called. "Dare I hope you changed your mind about playing with us?"

"No, sir. I've not changed my mind, but thanks for asking me."

"Don't run off after the concert. I'd like you to meet some of my musicians."

Annabel waved to him and watched him waddle down the walk toward the bandstand.

"Papa, let's go sit down."

"You go ahead, darlin'. Save me a seat and I'll be along after I see to a few things."

"It was nice seeing you again, Mr. Appleby."

"It was a pleasure seeing you, ma'am." Corbin tipped his hat and watched her walk away. Murphy lingered.

"You married, Appleby?"

"No. Why do you ask?"

"I saw how you looked at my daughter. I've looked at a few women like that myself." Murphy took a cigar from his pocket, bit off the end and struck a match on the sole of his shoe.

"No law against looking," Corbin said tightly. "I'm sure a lot of men look at her. She's a pretty girl."

"She is that. Pretty, smart and . . . wholesome. Any man I'd approve of courting her would have to have the means to support her in style."

"In other words, she's out of my class. Is that what you're getting at?"

"Something like that."

"Don't worry. I have no plans to come courting. I'll not be here long enough."

"I'm glad to hear it."

"I'll tell you this, Donovan, your approval or disapproval wouldn't mean spit to me if I decided she was the woman I wanted."

Murphy nodded. "Now that that's cleared up, I'll bid you good day." With his cigar clenched between his teeth, he strolled up the street toward the business section of town.

Murphy was troubled by thoughts of Corbin Appleby. The man had made no bones about serving with the Military Police. Many of the men who had served in that capacity during the war had been recruited by the Federal Bureau. Was he one of them?

What bothered Murphy the most was Appleby's obvious interest in Annabel. Would he be devious enough to use her as a pawn to get to him? She was as innocent as a babe where men were concerned. His Annabel might be attracted to a worldly man like Appleby. If he broke her heart, Murphy would kill him. It was as simple as that.

In the world in which Murphy traveled, it was believed that the Feds worked both ends against the middle and would stop at nothing to get what they were after. The same ruthlessness was true of the racketeers who provided the bootleg whiskey to the saloons, bawdy houses and gambling joints. Prohibition had scarcely been born before the gangsters began to capitalize on it. Murphy never considered himself like those men. He had merely seen an opportunity and taken it.

Tipping his hat to the few people he met on their way to the concert in the park, Murphy walked leisurely on as if he had all the time in the world. He went into the post office, lingered in the small room as if looking for his box, then slipped through the rear door. He walked quickly through the building and out the back door. After a hurried scan of the alley, he knocked on a wooden door, which was immediately opened.

Murphy stood inside the room to allow his eyes to adjust to the dim light. The man who had opened the door now closed and locked it with a steel bolt.

"I wasn't sure you'd come." He sat down on a sagging old cot.

"I said I'd be here."

"Well, sit down. I don't like having to look up at you. And for God's sake, put out that cigar. It's smelling up the place."

"It smells better than dirty feet," Murphy grumbled, but he dropped it on the floor, ground the toe of his shoe in the end of it, then put it back in his pocket. "I don't have much time. What have you heard from the top man?"

"We've been going over your list of contacts. So far, so good. If we take over your operation here, we want you out of the area . . . pronto."

"I plan on it. How about the money?"

"Fifty thousand and that's it."

"I know. I agreed on the amount. When and where will I get it? You've already inventoried what I've got stored in the hills."

"How do we know you've not been shipping it out since then?"

"You don't. How do I know you'll come through with the money?"

"Memorize and burn this." The man dug a paper from his shirt pocket and passed it and a key to Murphy, who gave him a disgusted look.

"I've been in this business for seven years. I know the ropes." He read the paper carefully: *June 1st. United States Bank of Tennessee, Memphis. Use the name TC Brown and ask for Thurmon Rice. Money will be transferred at that time.*

Murphy struck a match and held it to the paper and set it aflame. When he could no longer hold it, he dropped it to the floor, watched it burn, then rubbed the sole of his shoe in the ashes.

"I'll send a couple of men up to the cave to take over."

"No. Not until the money is in my hand."

"That'll be a week. We have orders to fill."

"Too bad. Not until the money is in my . . . hand," Murphy said with emphasis.

The man's eyes narrowed angrily. "Don't get too smart, Donovan. You're just a drip in the puddle to the organization."

"So are you. Stay away from my supply until I come back

with the money." Murphy pinned the man with his dark eyes before turning to the door.

"Don't cross us," the man warned.

"My reputation for square dealing is far better than yours." It was Murphy's parting shot.

He looked up and down the alley. Finding it clear, he went out and heard the door close softly behind him.

Chapter 10

ANNABEL HAD BEEN EXCITED at seeing Corbin Appleby again. She had felt his eyes following her when she went down the walk toward the row of benches that faced the bandstand. Her father had been on his guard when meeting him, and she had hesitated about leaving them alone together. No doubt Boone had told him about Corbin's being a former police chief, which would automatically make her father suspicious of him.

Annabel found an empty bench near the sidewalk and sat down. The musicians were warming up and she watched with interest. So far she hadn't seen a violin player and suspected Mr. Potter's band was a marching and not a concert band. She was greatly relieved that she wasn't playing a solo. She could just sit back and enjoy the music.

The band had just begun playing a rousing march when Annabel's attention was pulled from the music to movement beside her on the bench. She glanced at the man, frowned, then moved to make more space between them.

Marvin Carter, his hair slicked down and wearing a freshly ironed shirt, folded his arms over his chest, stuck his booted feet out in front of him and crossed his ankles.

"The skinny one on the big horn is puffin' so hard he's 'bout to blow his brains out," he said, as if they had been carrying on a conversation. Marvin puffed out his cheeks and said in a loud voice, "Boom, boom, boom."

Mortified, Annabel reined in her anger and refused to acknowledge him.

"Ya sure do look purty today, sugartit." He leaned so close, his breath brushed her cheek. "You smell good too."

Annabel moved until she was at the end of the bench and glanced around to see if the people sitting nearby were noticing the loathsome lout who was bothering her.

"Settle down, honey. Yo're as flighty as a whore in church. I ain't goin' to hurt ya. I just want to be with ya. Ya been givin' me a *hard* time—if ya know what I mean."

Her head swiveled around. "You're disgusting," she snapped. "Get away from me."

"Ya ain't wantin' me to do that. I'm gonna be yore new beau."

"That's a laugh. You don't stand a chance."

His grin was wide and confident. "Who says?"

"I say. Now leave me alone."

"All yo're doin' is playin' hard to get. I ain't blamin' ya for it. When I get ya off by yoreself and give ya my special lovin', ya'll be pantin' after me like a mare in heat."

"I don't like you, Mr. Carter. Please leave me alone."

"That ain't what Tessie said. She said ya liked me fine."

"I don't believe that. You were not even discussed."

He chuckled. "I'm takin' ya to the picture show Saturday night. Ya'll like me after that. I know how to pleasure a woman."

When he moved an inch closer and lifted his arm to the back of the bench behind her, Annabel jumped to her feet. By the time she had reached the sidewalk he was beside her,

her elbow clasped in a tight grip. She walked as fast as she could. He kept pace with her, holding her close to him.

"Slow down, honey. Ya don't want folks to think we're havin' a lover's spat, do you?"

"Get away from me, you . . . you . . . stupid lout." She tried to jerk her arm from his grasp.

"Just walk along nice-like. Folks are lookin'."

"Let them look. Turn loose my arm or I'll scream loud enough to wake the dead."

"I like a woman with spunk. We'll hitch good together."

"I'd rather be hitched to a rattlesnake," Annabel countered.

Suddenly Corbin Appleby appeared on the walk in front of them. His cane was in his hand.

"I'm sorry I was late, sweetheart," he said casually and held his hand out to Annabel, who took it. He tugged gently in an attempt to pull her to his side.

Marvin refused to release her arm. Instead he tried to steer Annabel around him. Corbin stayed in front of them.

"Butt off, she's with me," Marvin snarled.

"I'm not!"

"The lady says she's not with you. Get your hands off her."

"Get the hell outta the way. She's my girl!"

"I'm not," Annabel cried again.

"Let her go or you'll get this cane upside your head."

"Yo're a cripple! Ya fixin' to take me on?" Marvin sneered.

"If I have to."

Corbin's eyes flicked to Annabel. He saw her wince. *The bastard was hurting her.* An almost unreasonable rage came over him. In a lightning-fast move, he reversed the cane and struck Marvin on the kneecap. The blow was so sharp, so hard and so unexpected that Marvin's leg went out from under him. He fell to the ground. Only Corbin's hand prevented Annabel from going down with him.

"Ohhh . . ." Marvin howled. "Ya son-of-a-bitch!" He rolled on the ground holding his knee, then struggled to his feet. He was so angry that his eyes were unfocused. His lips lifted from his teeth in a snarl and he drew back a clenched fist.

"I don't advise you to fight me." Corbin released Annabel's hand, extended an arm and pushed her behind him. "I was with the Military Police during the war, and I know ways of taking you down before you have time to spit. And I can hurt you real bad in a place you . . . treasure."

"Ya shit-eatin' bastard! I'll kill ya for this."

"Watch your mouth or you'll lose some teeth . . . now!" Corbin said quickly. Then, "Get away from here or I *will* break your leg."

Marvin glanced around to see that several people had stopped to gawk at them.

"What're ya lookin' at?" he snarled. He took a few limping steps toward the street and turned with a look of pure hatred on his face. "I ain't forgettin' this," he said to Corbin. "I got first claim on her and I'll have her."

"Not unless she wants you."

Corbin and Annabel watched him limp across the street and disappear behind the blacksmith shop.

"He's mean!" Annabel gasped.

"Is he the one who bothered you in the store?"

"Yes. He, his brothers and a sister live on the place next to us. I don't see how Tess, the sister, could be related to such an obnoxious man."

"Don't let him catch you alone."

"Boone or Spinner are usually at the house. And now I have Jack. I've never been afraid before."

"Does your father travel a lot?"

"He's usually gone part of each week. This time he was gone longer." She laughed nervously. "My knees are shaking."

"Come sit down. I'll stay with you until your father comes back."

"Thank you for what you did. I wasn't sure how I was going to shake him," Annabel said after they were seated on the bench Corbin had hurriedly left when he saw her with Marvin.

"You would have been safer to stay with the crowd."

"I was embarrassed and thought I'd meet Papa coming back. It's probably best that I didn't meet him. I don't know what he would have done. He's got a hot temper."

"Maybe Carter was lucky this time. He only had to put up with me."

Annabel turned to him. At first she smiled, then she burst out laughing. Corbin couldn't take his eyes off her. She was as pretty and as sparkling as a spring morning. A smile lit his eyes and tugged at the corners of his lips. In that instant Corbin fell completely, eternally in love with her . . . and he didn't even know it.

"Only you! You handled yourself pretty well for a . . . cripple!" She began to laugh. "You sure took him by surprise."

"Yeah. Surprise was on my side. The cane came in handy too."

"Watch out for him. He might try to do something really . . . mean. I'll worry now that you'll get hurt on my account."

Corbin sat on the bench for a long time after she left him.

Murphy Donovan had stopped on the walk and waited for his daughter to join him. They talked for a few minutes. She turned and waved to Corbin, and her father nodded his head before they got into the car.

Corbin's eyes followed the car until it was out of sight, and he tried not to resent what Murphy had said before he went uptown. The man loved his daughter and wanted to make sure that whomever she married would be able to take care of her. He had been straightforward. He had to give him that. *Maybe,* Corbin thought, *if I had a daughter as pretty and sweet as Annabel Lee, I would feel the same way.*

He felt a stirring in the region of his heart and cursed softly.

"Why didn't you tell me about Carter insulting you?"

"I suppose Boone told you he met me in the store."

"It's Boone's job."

"Mr. Carter didn't actually insult me. He was obnoxious in a flirty sort of way. But today he held on to my arm and wouldn't let go until Mr. Appleby hit him with his cane." Annabel laughed. "You should have seen him, Papa. He was madder than a flitter."

Murphy swore.

"It's over and done with. He'll not bother me again."

"I'll see to it," Murphy said in an angry tone.

"I really like Tess Carter. I think her brothers might be mean to her. When she brought me the berries, she was shy and scared and acted as if she expected the door to be slammed in her face."

"The Carters have been in these hills for generations. Everyone I've talked to says they are clannish, inbred and ig-norant. I was told that when I bought the place and thought they would stay on their side of the fence."

"Tess isn't trash. I like her."

"Believe me, darlin', an apple don't fall far from the tree. She's like her kin. I was told that she was away for a while and when she came back she was in the family way. No one seems to know what happened to the babe. She got rid of it somehow. She's trash, and I don't want you to have anything to do with her."

Annabel remained silent. Seldom did her opinion go against that of her father. However, she believed him to be wrong this time.

They were driving out of town when she asked, "How did you find out about Tess?"

Murphy shrugged. "A fellow here in Henderson told me."

"Who?"

Her persistence surprised him. He glanced at her. She was looking straight ahead.

"Why are you bein' stubborn about this? You were raised with quality folk, went to school with quality folk. You be knowin' the difference." Off his guard, Murphy lapsed into his Irish brogue.

"I feel that it's unfair to Tess to call her trash. She can't help it if her brothers . . . have an unsavory reputation."

Murphy slowed the car because the one ahead was in the middle of the road and moving at a snail's pace. He pressed on the horn. The driver of the car, an old stripped-down Model T Ford, didn't move over, deliberately refusing to allow Murphy to pass.

"It's him," Annabel blurted, leaning toward the windshield to get a better look.

"Is he the son-of-a-bitch that's been botherin' you?" Without waiting for an answer from his daughter, Murphy swore, loud and long.

"Let him go, Papa! Don't do anything!"

"Hold tight, darlin'." Murphy's temper was up. He was not in a reasonable mood.

He increased the speed of the powerful car and rammed the back of the lighter Model T. Annabel saw Marvin Carter's head snap back, as she was propelled forward. Murphy, his hands gripping the wheel and a string of curses coming from his mouth, continued to push the car.

"Papa! Stop!"

"I'll teach that son-of-a-bitch to put his hands on my girl."

Murphy put his foot on the brake and let Marvin's car go ahead a short distance, then speeded up and connected with it again with a jarring impact.

"Don't . . . Papa!" Annabel cried in a shrill voice. She was holding on to the door with one hand and bracing herself against the dashboard with the other.

"Bastard! Goddamn hill trash!" Murphy shouted.

The Model T was shoved off the road with the second impact. The car careened through the brush until it collided with the trunk of a thick ash tree. Marvin jumped out just as the radiator burst and boiling water spewed out. Murphy pulled the car to a stop and stepped out.

"Papa, don't! Please don't!"

Murphy paused beside the sedan and looked at his daughter's anguished face. Tears were running down her cheeks. He looked back to see Marvin Carter lifting a heavy tire iron from the wrecked car.

"I'll kill you!" Maddened almost to the point of insanity, Marvin ran toward them, swinging the weapon.

Realizing not only the danger to himself but to Annabel, Murphy jumped into the car, slammed the door shut and stepped on the gas. They shot around the crazed man, who threw the tire iron at them as they passed. It bounced off the hood of the car with a loud thump.

Annabel cried out in alarm.

"It's all right, darlin'. He won't hurt you."

"I'm not worried about myself, blast it all! I'm worried about you."

"Don't worry. We'll be leaving here in a couple of weeks. I'm goin' to be buyin' you a house in St. Louis. What do you think of that?"

"Are you going to be there?"

"Yes." He turned up the lane toward the house. "I'm thinking about buying a hotel."

"You're giving up the . . . business?"

"I'm selling it." A broad smile softened his features.

"Papa! I've prayed that you'd do that. You don't have to buy a house. If you're going to run a hotel, we can fix up a suite of rooms there."

"No. You're going to be havin' a proper home where folks will be lookin' up to you. You can entertain with musicales and afternoon teas just like the hoity-toity folk. I'll be able to afford havin' household help, darlin' girl. What do ya be thinkin' of that?"

Annabel gazed at his beaming face and into eyes that looked back at her with all the love his heart could give. He had been risking his freedom, his life, all these years in order to give her this. She didn't have the heart to tell him that living in a big house in St. Louis and entertaining with musicales was her idea of a perfectly awful existence. So she said, "That will be nice, Papa."

"I promise you, darlin', that you'll never again be livin' in a house without electric lights, indoor toilets and such." He stopped beside the back porch. "In a few days I'll be leaving to finish up the deal."

"How long will you be gone?"

"Only a few days. A week at the most. Then we'll go to St. Louis and look for a house. While I'm gone, Boone will be stayin' with you every minute. I'm goin' to tell him to shoot that mangy polecat if he gets within a stone's throw of you."

"If you're afraid for me to be here, why can't I come with you?" Annabel asked before she went up the steps to the porch.

"No, no, darlin'. I'll be busy and be feelin' better knowin' you'll be here with Boone. Go on in and fix your papa a glass of tea while I be havin' a word with him."

Boone was sitting on a box beside the barn door.

"What happened to the hood of your car?"

"Long story. Where's the boy?"

"Out on the horse. I told him to stay off Carter land."

Murphy snorted. "If that son-of-a-bitch steps foot on this land, I want you to shoot him."

"Jack? What's he done?"

"Carter! The big one with blond hair. He pestered Annabel, put his hands on her!" Murphy was still so angry, his jaws quivered. While pacing back and forth in front of Boone, he related all that had happened. "She says we owe thanks to Appleby, the lawman you found shot. He forced Carter to turn loose of her and sent him on his way."

"Then she's right. We owe him our thanks."

"I ain't trustin' him."

"You don't have to. He won't be around for long."

"I'm not sure. He was eyein' Annabel."

"Eyein' Annabel? Ya can't blame him for that."

"She's not for the likes of him. I told him so."

"Hell, Murphy, why'd ya go and do that for? It'll just get

his back up. It might make him want to come here and court her just to spite ya."

"If he shows up out here, send him on his way. Keep her away from him while I'm gone."

"I'd bet my life he's a decent man. He'll not go where he ain't wanted."

"He's a man, isn't he? If she be on his mind and he gets his sap up, he'll be after her. Hell, you be knowin' how it goes when a man needs a woman," Murphy said heatedly.

"There be places a man can go when his sap is up without botherin' a decent girl." Boone looked off toward the woods that separated them from the Carters. He didn't believe for a minute that Appleby would try to court Annabel if she didn't want him.

"I'm not likin' that he's interested in her."

"Ain't nothin' ya can do about that. Probably nothin' he can do about it either. When you leavin'?"

"Soon. The sooner I go, the sooner I get back."

"When'll that be?"

"Five or six days. Annabel can start packin' up. We can stay at the hotel while we look for a house."

"She ain't goin' to like that. She thought we'd be here awhile." Boone stood and fumbled in his pocket for his pipe. "She's got right fond of that cow. Even give her a name. Mildred."

"Mildred? Where the hell did she get that? She'll forget about a stupid cow when she sees the house I'm going to buy in St. Louis."

"What're ya goin' to do with this place?"

"Sell it, if I can."

"I ain't a hotel man, Murphy. I'll buy the place for what ya paid."

Murphy's head turned slowly toward his friend, and his mouth dropped open in surprise.

"Buy this dirt-poor farm? What kinda livin' can ya hack out here? Ya know why I bought it."

"I know. Ya bought it 'cause Spinner knew 'bout the cave in the hills."

"And I'd be havin' a better chance sellin' out here. Spinner knew that."

"That's between you and Spinner. Like Annabel, I'm tired of movin'. I've been savin' up to buy a place. I like it here. I like Henderson. With a few cows and a little luck, I can make a livin'."

"I thought ya hated cows."

"I do. I don't have to love the stupid things to feed 'em and milk 'em."

"You never said ya wouldn't be goin' with me when I told you about the hotel."

"Never said I was either. I been thinkin'."

"Well, be thinkin' some more. We've been together for a long time."

"Yeah, we have. But yo're movin' on to the upper way of livin'. It's time I found a spot of my own. I ain't gettin' no younger."

"You're not as old as me."

"Hell, ain't nobody old as you are," Boone said with an easy smile and clapped Murphy on the shoulder.

Murphy whistled through his teeth and the familiar gleam of humor lit his eyes.

"I only got about five years on ya, but I be a hell of a lot smarter than ya be!"

"Well, now, I be doubtin' that," Boone replied, mimicking Murphy's Irish brogue.

"When is Spinner comin' in?"

"He's due in Saturday. I ain't seen hide nor hair of him for a week."

"He'd rather stay up there than here."

"Why wouldn't he? He built it. 'Tis his home."

Chapter 11

'Bye, papa. i'll be ready."

"That's my girl. This is the last move. I promise."

"Don't make promises you may not be able to keep," Annabel chided gently.

"The last couple of years have been hard on you, honey, but the end is in sight. I'll be back in less than a week and we'll go over to St. Louis. I've not completed the deal on the hotel. I want you to see it first. Meanwhile we can take rooms there."

"Are you sure that this is what you want to do, Papa?"

"Absolutely sure, darlin'." Murphy put his suitcase in the car. "Boone will be with you. Don't stray from the house. If you go to the barn, be sure that he or the boy is in there."

"Oh, Papa—"

"Mind me, darlin'. I wouldn't put it past that Carter trash to sneak over here, wait in the barn and waylay you. Boone will be on the lookout. I trust him to take care of you or I'd not leave."

"Don't worry. I'll be all right. Hurry back, Papa."

Murphy kissed his daughter on the forehead, got into the car and started the engine. With a cheery wave, he turned around in the yard behind the house and headed down the lane toward the road.

Annabel walked to the front porch and watched the car until it was out of sight. The heavy hand of loneliness gripped her, wrapping its icy fingers around her heart. She loved her father with all her heart, but at times she didn't understand him.

She felt at home here and didn't want to move to another strange place. The house could be modernized and made comfortable for a lot less money than it would cost to buy a house in St. Louis. She wished that she had suggested to her father that he try to buy the hotel in Henderson or possibly buy out another business.

She heaved a sigh. It was too late now to do anything but pack and be ready to move again when he returned.

Twilight was fading when Jack came around the corner of the house and found Annabel sitting on the porch, pushing the porch swing back and forth with one foot, the other curled beneath her.

"Miss Annabel, I'm sorry that you and Mr. Donovan are moving. I know you like it here."

"We won't be needing a garden now, and I'll have to say good-bye to Mildred. I've even become fond of that strutting rooster." She sounded so dejected that Jack squinted through the near darkness to get a better look at her face to see if she was crying.

"Boone said he hoped to stay on here and that I could go ahead and plant the potato eyes tomorrow. It's the dark of the moon and the best time to plant root crops."

"What's the moon got to do with it?" Annabel dried her eyes on the end of her apron.

"Eyes make more potatoes and less vine if planted during the dark of the moon. It's what we did at home. Above-ground crops are planted during the light of the moon."

"I've never heard that. When did Boone say he was staying here?" Annabel stopped the swing. "He always goes with us when we move."

"Just now when I said it was a shame that you'd go off and leave the garden we just put in."

"I thought we'd be here awhile. Where's Boone?"

"He walked out back. He told me to stay here and not let you out of my sight and, if we needed him, to shoot off the gun you keep in the kitchen. So I guess you've got to put up with me for a while."

"That won't be hard to do. He and Papa are afraid one of the Carters will come over."

"Mr. Donovan was awful mad when he told Boone about Carter pestering you in town. He said that he'd fixed him by pushing his car off the road."

"Marvin Carter was angry when Mr. Appleby hit him with his cane. But after Papa pushed his car into a tree he was crazy mad and threw a tire iron at us. I'm afraid Tess Carter will never come back over now."

"Boone asked me to stay until Mr. Donovan gets back. I think he expects trouble from the Carters."

"Do you mind?"

"Heavens, no. I'm staying anyway until I get my glove back."

"Is Mr. Appleby staying until then?"

"He said he was in no hurry and that we could go to as many ball games as we know about in hopes we might sight it. It's a special glove. I'd know it in a million."

Annabel got up out of the swing and stood looking off toward the woods that separated them from the Carters.

"I wonder why Boone didn't come in for supper."

*   *   *

Boone wasn't sure why he had told Murphy that he
wasn't moving with him and Annabel to St. Louis. He had
been thinking about breaking with him for some time. He
would have done it a while back if not for Annabel. The little bootlegging business Murphy had run had gradually
turned into something bigger than Boone wanted to be involved with.

He was too old to play games with himself. Tess Carter
had a lot to do with his decision to hang around here. He
liked her. He had felt something he hadn't felt for a long time
when he was with her. She stirred up his protective instincts.
She was a woman, yet she was a girl too. He didn't know a
hell of a lot about women; but he knew men, and the Carter
men were at the bottom of the barrel in his estimation.

It was dark when Boone stepped over the line onto
Carter property. Knowing the volatile nature of the clan, he
moved cautiously and silently through the woods toward the
house. What was driving him to take this chance was that he
wanted to make sure Tess was all right. The thought that she
might have been the one to suffer Marvin's wrath after his
encounter with Murphy worried him.

Boone found a spot where he could see the back of the
house and hunkered down. He didn't dare go closer until he
found out if they had dogs. He wished now that he had asked
Tess about that. A light shone from a window and he could
see someone moving around inside.

He scanned the slovenly homestead. The woodpile was
scattered, fences sagged, and discarded rusty machinery sat
amid the weeds that grew south of the barn. The place was
as he had expected it to be after he'd met the one Carter
brother in the woods. Looking around, he located the out-

house leaning precariously beside the chicken house. There was a chance Tess would go there before she went to bed.

One of the brothers came out onto the back porch. He stood on the end of the porch and Boone heard the unmistakable sound of his relieving himself. *Crude bastard was too lazy to move away from the house.*

"Goddammit! No wonder it smells like piss around here!" The shout came from the doorway. A man came out onto the porch and shoved the man fumbling with his overalls, causing him to step down off the porch.

"Now look what ya done. Ya made me step in it."

"If I catch ya pissin' off the porch again, I'll rub your nose in it. Now get the hell out and bridle those horses. We're goin' over to Calvin's."

"Ah, Marvin. Can't we take the car?"

"No, ya dumb clabberhead! We can't take the car. The radiator is busted all to hell. Why do ya think I dragged it to the house?"

"Make Bud go. I wanna stay here."

"Do as yo're told. We're goin' by the still to get some lightnin' for Calvin. He'll call in the Carters. By God, that Donovan will soon know what he's up against."

"Ain't ya sweet on the woman? Ya kill her old man—"

"Shit! Ya got 'bout as much brains as a suck-egg mule. Get out there and get the horses." Marvin stuck his head in the door. "Bud, keep yore eye on Tessie. If she gets sassy, ya can slap her around some. Don't hurt her bad. Hear? Tomorrow's wash day. She's taken to runnin' off at the mouth more'n she ort to. I might not be back tonight, but Leroy will." He let the door slam shut, then opened it again. "Ya behave, Tessie. Mind Bud, or next time ya'll get the strop on yore skinny bare butt."

An almost unreasonable fury flared up in Boone. *The no-*

good piece of horse dung had taken his rage out on that little woman. With an effort he remained perfectly still, his thoughts busy with what he planned to do to Marvin Carter when he caught him alone.

It seemed forever before Marvin and his brother mounted the horses and rode west into the hills. Boone waited awhile longer before he stood and moved closer to the house. He had not gone ten feet before he stopped abruptly. Tess had come out, hesitated, looked back into the kitchen, then jumped off the porch. She ran from the house as if the devil himself were after her. Boone ran to catch her. He didn't dare call out until they were a good distance from the house.

"Tess," he called softly. He saw her hesitate, then run on. "Tess, stop. It's me, Boone."

She slowed, then stopped and stood as if poised to run again. Boone was winded when he caught up with her.

"Lordy, girl. Ya can run like a deer."

"Mr. Boone! What're you doing here?"

"I've been waitin' down by the house hopin' to see ya. Hopin' you'd come out. Were you comin' to the edge of the woods?"

"You shouldn't be here. Marvin—"

"I saw him leave. How about the brother inside the house? Will he come looking for you?"

"I gave him a loaf of fresh bread and a jar of berry jam. It'll take him a while to eat it. You shouldn't come here," she repeated fearfully. "Marvin is madder and meaner than I've ever seen him. He won't rest till he gets even with Mr. Donovan for pushing his car into the tree and the man in town who hit him on the knee."

"If I'da been there I'd of done more than hit him on the kneecap. I'd of rearranged his face!"

"He'll try to get Annabel alone and . . . ruin her. It's what he's planning. Watch her every minute," Tess pleaded.

"If he does, Tess, I'll kill him. I want you to know that right now."

"It's what he'd deserve, even if he is my brother. He's going to kill someone, Mr. Boone, and I don't want it to be you."

"Did he hurt you, Tess?"

"Ah . . . no. I'm all right."

"I heard him tell someone he could slap ya around," he ground out angrily.

"Bud's so heavy and slow on his feet, he couldn't catch me."

"Holy hell! If he'd followed you out, I'd have laid him out with a club."

"You'da done that?"

"Damn right. Tess, Tess . . ." He said her name just because he liked saying it.

Boone put his hands on her shoulders so he could turn her to him. She tried to keep her head averted so that he'd not see her injured face and the tears that filled her eyes. She had never hoped to hear such a tender, caring tone in a man's voice when speaking to her, and she wanted it to go on for as long as possible.

"Look at me, Tess."

"Don't make me. I don't want you to see me," she whispered brokenly.

"Let me see what he did to ya." With a gentle hand beneath her chin, Boone held her face so that he could peer into it. Her lip was split and swollen. Big, quiet tears were creeping down her cheeks.

A crude oath slipped from his lips. Anger at what had been done to her caused his heart to hammer in his chest.

Unable to stop himself, he slipped his arms around her. She leaned against him, her face against his shoulder, her arms at her sides.

"Tess, Tess, sweet girl," he crooned.

His strong warm body was like a safe haven in a storm. He didn't grab at her breasts; he didn't pinch her bottom; he didn't try to kiss her. He held her so gently and so protectively that she couldn't stop the tears that continued to fall. It didn't even occur to her to pull away.

"Tess, girl. What can I do?" His voice was a whisper in her ear.

She rolled her forehead against his shoulder. "You can't do anything."

"I'll pound his face to mush for doin' this to ya." Boone pulled a handkerchief from his pocket and, holding her away from him, dried her eyes.

"Please don't fight with him. I'm used to it . . . in a way."

"Don't ya ever want somethin' better, girl?"

"For a while I did. Now I don't dare dream of something better." For the life of her, Tess didn't know why she was talking to him like this, why she wasn't afraid of being with him in the dark woods. Her eyes traveled over his face. "Mr. Boone! You shaved off your whiskers."

He grinned and rubbed his fingers over his face. "Yeah, I feel kinda naked. I'd got used to 'em coverin' my ugly face."

"You're not ugly," she said quickly, and, unbidden, her fingertips stroked his cheek.

He caught her hand and held it there. "I wish ya didn't have to go back. I'll be worryin' 'bout ya."

"I'll be all right. As long as I feed Bud, he won't hurt me. He lives to eat." She would remember as long as she lived the feel of Boone's face against her hand. "But I thank you for worryin' about me. Nobody's ever worried 'bout me but my mother and my aunt."

"Will you meet me again?"

"Yes. But I don't know when."

"The Donovans are movin'."

"Oh—"

"But I'm stayin' here."

"Why're you doing that?" she asked after she had caught a sharp breath. He had released her fingers, and without realizing it, she was stroking his upper arms.

"I've been wantin' to settle someplace and . . . this seems to be a good place."

"I'm . . . glad you're staying. Don't get the Carters mad at you. There's a lot of them and they stick together."

"I'm not afraid of them."

"They don't do anything out in the open. They'll sneak and do it. You don't know how mean they can be." Her voice rose and her hands gripped his arms.

"Don't worry about it. It could be that Donovan won't sell me the place."

"Then . . . what will you do?"

"Find another place."

"Be careful. I'd rather you go than be hurt."

"Tess, I can't remember when anyone but Annabel worried about me."

"I liked her. She was nice."

"She's a fine lass. I think the world of her."

"Will she . . . stay here with you?"

"No. She'll go with her papa."

"I guess I won't see her again." Tess tilted her face up to his and he felt the warmth of her breath on his chin. "I'd better go," she whispered.

"Tess . . . can I kiss ya? If ya don't want me to, say so. I'll not force ya—"

"I know that. I've not done much kissin'."

"I've not done much kissin' either, so we're even. I've thought about kissin' ya since the other night." His voice was a hoarse whisper. Boone instantly read her fear in the large amber eyes he found so transparent. "I won't do it if you don't want me to," he said again.

"I . . . I want ya to."

The arm around her waist drew her close; his hand tilted her face up to his. He lowered his own, slowly, inevitably. His lips brushed hers in feather-soft exploration, his breath mingling intimately with hers. He repeated the caress again and again, being careful not to press hard on her swollen lip.

Boone discovered that he had been trembling and that now his heart had settled down into slow, heavy thuds. In all his life he had never been so moved. He was acutely aware of the slim, vulnerable figure pressed close against him—of the warm sweetness of her mouth. A few days ago he hadn't known that this sweet woman existed. Now her soft breasts were pressed to his agitated heart.

After placing several gentle kisses on her lips, he finally felt hers move beneath his. He lifted his head to look down into her serious face. He didn't have a name for the feelings that swamped him. All he was sure of was that she had become tremendously important to him.

"Tess, you don't have to take being cuffed around in order to have a roof over your head. If things get rough, come to me." His hands gripped her upper arms and held her away from him so he could look into her face. "Promise?"

"I promise."

"I'll be out here tomorrow night."

"I'll try to come out." She tugged on her hand. "But . . . I don't know. Marvin—"

"We'll help ya. Me and Annabel. We'll hide ya from him."

"I don't know . . ." she said again and tugged her hand free of his.

Boone watched her run back toward the house. When she stepped onto the porch, she turned and waved, then slipped into the house.

On Monday morning, leaning heavily on his cane, Corbin walked to the post office. He really didn't need the cane because his leg was much better, but he wanted to continue to use his injured leg as an excuse to stay in town. The post office was a small white-painted building with a United States flag fluttering from a steel post in front.

"Morning, Mr. Appleby."

"Morning, Mr. Brighton."

The postmaster, in a white shirt and black bow tie, worked behind the bars that separated the office from the lobby. He was a thin man with rounded shoulders and long arms. He smiled so constantly that Corbin surmised he wasn't a man to be trusted.

"Nice bright morning. How's the leg?"

"Coming along . . . but slow. I need a stamp." Corbin pulled a letter addressed to Mrs. Ned Wicker, Jefferson City, Missouri, from his shirt pocket. "I thought I'd better let my sister know I'm doing all right." Corbin placed two pennies on the counter. The postmaster took the letter, looked at the address and, with the smile still on his face, looked up at Corbin.

"Jefferson City, huh? Do you know the Greenfields who live there?"

"No. I've never lived there. My sister moved there when she married."

"Hummm. Greenfields are my wife's second cousins. I wonder if they know the Wickers."

"It's possible. Jefferson City isn't Chicago."

"Plan to be around for a while?"

"Awhile. I'm not sure how long."

"Must be nice to hang 'round not havin' to do anything."

"Yeah, it is. Well, good day." Corbin put his fingers to the brim of his hat and left the post office, remembering to lean heavily on his cane.

He stood on the walk in front of the post office for a minute. The postmaster's too-friendly smile and probing questions bothered him. He wouldn't put it past the man to steam open his letter to Marshal Sanford. Thank goodness he'd said only that his leg was healing and that he would be getting in touch again soon. Let Brighton make something of that.

Chapter 12

CORBIN WALKED ON DOWN THE STREET toward the butcher shop. It was time he called on an army buddy, although he wasn't even sure Craig Travis *was* an army buddy. He didn't remember ever seeing him. In that hellhole of Belleau Wood, all soldiers, alive or dead, looked alike.

The butcher shop was empty when Corbin entered. A half of pork and a quarter of beef rested on the long butcher's block alongside a large slab of smoked side meat and a small tub filled with joined wieners. An assortment of meat saws hung from hooks over the block and a thin layer of sawdust covered the floor. Signs were posted with various cuts of meat suspended on hooks attached to the back wall.

CHICKENS DRESSED 5 CENTS EXTRA.
SOUP BONES WITH ORDER OF TWENTY CENTS.
RIVER BASS ON SATURDAY.
DOG BONES ON SATURDAY.

Corbin heard male and female voices just outside the back door, where, in a crate, live chickens of all colors—red, white, black and speckled—were cackling excitedly.

"That one," a female voice said.

"Yes, ma'am. That one's a dandy."

After a series of squawks, Travis came in the back door holding a live chicken by the feet. Following him was a woman with a large bosom and a small head topped by a black straw hat. Travis smiled broadly on seeing Corbin.

"Lieutenant Appleby. Good to see you. Be with you in a shake." The butcher weighed the chicken on his scales. "Four and a half pounds, Mrs. Schuler." Without waiting for the woman to reply, he disappeared into another room. The sound of the chop came a minute later and the chicken ceased squawking. Travis reappeared with the headless chicken wrapped in newspaper.

"Did you put the head in?"

"Sure did, Mrs. Schuler."

"Filmore would be disappointed if he didn't get the head. He likes to gnaw on it. Course, I have to take the feathers off. Put it on our tab, Mr. Travis. Mr. Schuler will be in at the end of the month to settle up."

"Yes, ma'am."

The woman eyed Corbin with suspicion as she approached the door. Corbin raised his brows in question after the door slammed behind her.

"Filmore?"

"Her dog."

"I thought maybe Filmore was her husband."

Travis's laughter rang out. "I'd almost swear that Filmore's got more sense than Schuler. At least he ain't henpecked. That man's so henpecked he don't know if he's swimmin' or ridin' a bicycle half the time. How's the leg doin'?"

"Coming along . . . slow."

"You itchin' to get somewhere?"

"Not really. I stopped by Henderson to pick up the son of a friend. He's helping out on a farm north of town and isn't ready to leave just yet."

"What farm? I know most everyone around."

"Donovan. I hear he just moved here a short time ago. The place is next to a family named Carter."

"Know the place. I couldn't figure out why a city fellow would buy the place. No accountin' for what folks do with their money."

"Jack's helping out with chores for a while. We'll be moving on soon."

Travis hoisted the quarter of beef to a broad, muscled shoulder and hung it on an overhead hook, a feat that took considerable strength. Corbin realized that it took a lot of muscle to cut up so much meat every day.

"How long you been here, Travis?"

"Three years now. My wife's uncle had the shop and taught me the ropes."

"You found your niche. A lot of veterans were not so lucky."

"I thank God every day that I came home to my girl. My cousin was gassed in the Argonne; my uncle is buried in Flanders Field. I'm thankful for every day I have with my wife and my boy. Say . . . we want you to come to dinner. Tomorrow noon be all right? I close the shop from twelve to one."

"Fine. How well do you know Brighton at the post office? He looks familiar, but I can't place him."

"He came here a couple of years ago after our postmaster slipped on a muddy bank, fell in the river and drowned. He was a nice old man. 'Twas a shame. He loved fishin' more than anything."

"How come a new postmaster wasn't picked from here?"

"Hell, I don't know. You know how the government works. Brighton was assistant postmaster up at Hannibal before coming here."

"I've been through Hannibal a few times. Might have seen him there."

"He'd kind of like to run things here. He ran for mayor and lost out to Ed Lewis, who owns the ice house. His main cause was getting a real lawman in town. He's at odds with Stoney Baker, our sheriff. Doesn't think he does his job."

"Baker was elected, wasn't he?"

"Yeah. No one run against him."

"Where does the mayor stand with this?"

"Stands with Stoney."

"I've heard the name Alex Lemon a time or two. Is he a councilman?" Corbin asked, knowing full well that he wasn't.

"He was in the barbershop gettin' all smelly up to call on Mrs. Zeadow. Her husband's a railroad man and is gone a couple nights a week."

"Lordy! Does everyone know everyone's business in this town?"

Travis laughed. "Sure. We're all waiting for Eldon Zeadow to come home some night, catch him and either shoot him or beat the stuffings out of him."

"The barber said Lemon had a wife and child to support."

"Doesn't seem to worry him. I was told that he's broken up two other homes. Mrs. Lemon is as nice a lady as you would meet anywhere. Why she puts up with him is a mystery to me." Travis stopped to hone the knife he was using to cut thin strips from the smoked side meat on the block and greeted the woman who opened the screen door and came into the shop.

"Hello, Mrs. Zeadow."

"Hello. I'd like three pork chops, please."

When the woman bent to look at the slab of smoked meat, Travis winked at Corbin.

Corbin took special notice of the woman having the affair with Alex Lemon. She was a small, shy woman, well-rounded and with rich brown hair and rosy cheeks. Modestly dressed, she didn't fit his idea of an adulteress; but, as he had learned from previous experiences, you couldn't tell from the outside of a person what lurked on the inside.

"Anything else? How about a slab of smoked bacon to season up a pot of beans?"

"Well . . ." She hesitated. "A piece about this thick." She held her thumb and forefinger a half inch apart.

Travis cut the meat with one slash of his knife. "Could I interest you in a nice fresh chicken?"

"Not today."

"That'll be fifteen cents for the chops and a nickel for the side meat, Mrs. Zeadow." Travis took the chops from his hanging scale and wrapped them with the bacon in white paper. He tied the bundle with a string he pulled from the cone of twine suspended over the butcher block. "There you are, ma'am. They'll cook up real nice for you."

"Thank you," she murmured, then placed the coins on the counter and hurried out.

"Don't it beat all," Travis said, shaking his head. "Lemon's wife is almost a copy of that one. Same size, age, hair, kind of shy. I don't understand the man . . . or the woman, for that matter."

"Yeah, well, that's how some people are. They want what they don't have. What does Lemon do?"

"He has the photography shop over next to Mrs. Freeman's Hats and Gowns. Does good work. We had him take our family picture."

"Has he been around here long?"

"Don't know. He was here when I came."

"Every town has its Lothario."

"Lothario? What's that?"

"Lover boy, seducer of women."

Travis laughed. "He's that, all right."

"I'd better get along. I'll see you at noon tomorrow, and thanks again for the invitation."

Corbin hung the cane over his arm and walked out. Watching him, Craig Travis drew in a deep breath and grinned.

Why, that sly dog. He doesn't need that cane any more than I do. I wonder what he's up to.

The dinner with Craig Travis and his family was enjoyable. Mrs. Travis, pleasant-looking though not beautiful, wearing an embroidered apron over a freshly ironed dress and her dark hair pulled back with a ribbon, welcomed her husband with a kiss. She greeted their guest warmly while Travis stood proudly by.

"Welcome to our home, Mr. Appleby." She reached for his hat to hang it on a hall tree beside the door.

"Thank you for inviting me, ma'am."

Travis had a cozy, neat home, a loving wife and a son he was proud of. The dinner of ham, cabbage and freshly baked bread was a welcome change from the hotel food. The table conversation centered on the coming events in Henderson: ball games, concerts, and later the county fair.

After the meal, Corbin walked back to the butcher shop with Travis.

"You've made a nice place for yourself here, Travis. I envy you."

"I know how lucky I am. I'm grateful for coming through the war and for having the good sense to leave my wild ways behind me. Maxine and little Kevin are my life."

"We've all sowed a few wild oats in our time. It's only a fool who won't admit it."

"Mine were more than a *few*. When I got out of the army, I was more or less at loose ends and got hooked up with some pretty powerful fellows who were on the wrong side of the law. I hope to God I've shook them off."

They stopped in front of the butcher shop. Travis unlocked the door and looked at Corbin with twinkling eyes and a wide grin.

"By the way, Appleby, if you want folks to think you need that cane, you'd better not forget to use it."

Corbin stared at him for a minute, then laughed. "Guess you're right. I'm not much of an actor."

"Thought you needed reminding, in case it was important."

"Thanks. How far is it out to the Donovan place? I may drive out and see my young friend."

"'Bout five miles. The first place on the left set back in the woods is the Carters'. The second place on the left is the old Miller place that Donovan bought. A long lane leads to the house."

"Thanks again. Be seeing you, Craig."

"You betcha." The butcher then greeted a potential customer approaching his shop. "Good afternoon, Mrs. Fallon. Come right in."

Corbin drove slowly, mulling over in his mind the bit of information about Craig Travis at one time being hooked up with powerful men on the wrong side of the law. Corbin was reasonably sure that if he still had contact with them, he would have been more careful about dropping the information. Yet it was something to think about.

If Travis could tell that he was faking the limp, Corbin reasoned, others might as well, especially the doctor. The cane had served its purpose and had been left at the hotel. He chuckled while thinking about the look on Marvin Carter's face when he whacked him with it. During the war he'd used a billy club. That had been six years ago. He took pride in the fact that he hadn't lost his touch.

Corbin drove through the streets of Henderson. He wanted to get a feel for the town. He passed blocks of neat houses behind white picket fences. Flower beds were blooming, apple trees blossoming and clothes fluttering on lines. He drove through the colored community of small unpainted houses and waved back at the children playing in the street who stopped to watch him pass.

On the western edge of town beyond the redbrick schoolhouse was a ball diamond. He would bring Jack here Saturday night and watch the game between teams sponsored by the Henderson Ice Company and Brower Dairy. He knew how proud the boy had been of his baseball glove and hoped they would be able to spot it.

After circling the town, he drove along the river road. It was good to be away from the hotel. Out in the open Corbin longed to run. It was one of his greatest pleasures. He remembered the people of Fertile shaking their heads to see their police chief running down the road as if he were going to a fire.

He was tempted to stop the car and give running a try but thought better of it. No point in being foolish because his body, with the exception of his leg, craved activity.

His mind the last several days had been plenty active. It had gone over again and again the events of Sunday afternoon. Murphy Donovan had eyed him with suspicion. No doubt the reason was that Boone had told him that he had been in law enforcement. To Corbin that meant the man had something to hide. It was strange that Donovan had not even thanked him for preventing Carter from walking off with his daughter.

For the last couple of nights, Corbin had lain in his bed and stared up at the ceiling of his room, faintly lit by a street-light in front of the hotel, and envisioned the face of a slim, brown-haired girl with an endearing smile.

He didn't understand himself. Here he was—a man of twenty-seven years interested in a sheltered young girl not much more than twenty. As yet, he wasn't ready to admit that he was enamored of her. If not, he asked himself, why in hell had the lines of Edgar Allan Poe's poem lingered in the back of his mind? *But we loved with a love that was more than love— I and my Annabel Lee.*

The only way to find out whether this was love was to see Annabel again. He hoped that when he did, he wouldn't make a fool of himself. Surely Murphy Donovan wouldn't object to his coming out to see Jack, and while there he just might come to a better understanding of the man who was Annabel's father.

Corbin passed the Carter place. A woman who was hanging clothes on the line stopped to watch him pass. Down the road a quarter of a mile was the lane leading to a square white house with a porch stretching across its front. Going slowly to keep from stirring up dust, Corbin drove the car up the lane toward the house, wondering what kind of welcome he'd get from Murphy Donovan.

Boone came out onto the porch and waited for him to

stop the car, then came down the steps to lean in the window on the passenger side before Corbin could get out.

"What can we do for you?" Boone asked in a voice that was anything but friendly.

"Good afternoon to you too." Corbin noticed that the man looked much younger without the whiskers.

"Guess if ya can drive, ya'll be leavin' soon."

"Are you wanting to be rid of me, Boone, after all we've been through together?"

"Biggest mistake I ever made. Ort to a let ya lay there and bleed to death," he growled.

"You don't mean that. You're just being your usual ornery self. I owe you, Boone," Corbin said pleasantly. "I've been thinking of ways to pay you back. What say I move out here and give you a hand . . . farming this big place?"

"Whata ya mean by that?"

"As I said, I owe you. I always pay my bills."

"Horsecock! Ya wantin' to see Jack or what?"

"I want to get out and stretch my leg."

"Ya don't see me stoppin' ya, do ya?"

"I'm thinking you might try. You're like a mule with a burr under its tail every time I see you. Are you ever civil?" Corbin got out of the car as Annabel came out onto the porch.

"Hello, Mr. Appleby."

"Howdy, ma'am."

"When you finish your business with Boone, come in for a glass of tea."

"I'd like that—that is, if Boone doesn't shoot me with that gun he's got under his shirt."

"Boone! Why are you carrying a gun?" Annabel exclaimed, eyeing him warily.

"'Cause I might find a snake that needs shootin'," he answered belligerently.

"Well for goodness' sake. Come in, Mr. Appleby. You too, Boone. I'll put extra sugar in your tea in hopes of sweetening you up. You've been like a cat on a hot griddle since Papa left."

So Donovan wasn't here. He was in luck.

Behind Annabel's back, Corbin grinned at a scowling Boone, then followed her through the neat but sparsely furnished house.

"Sit down at the table, Mr. Appleby," Annabel said when they reached the kitchen. "I'll call Jack in. He'll want to visit with you."

"Fix the tea," Boone said from behind him. "I'll get the boy."

The table where Corbin sat was covered with a white linen cloth edged with crocheted lace. It looked out of place in the primitive kitchen with the wood-burning stove and kerosene lamps, as did the dainty bowl of lilies of the valley that sat in the middle of it.

A shrill whistle issued from the porch, Boone's signal to Jack. Boone came immediately back into the kitchen.

"Want me to chip ice?"

"No, sit down. I've got a chunk for the pitcher."

Corbin watched Annabel. Boone watched Corbin. Then Jack bounded up on the porch and burst into the kitchen and both pairs of eyes turned to him. He skidded to a stop.

"Oh. I thought something . . . was . . . well— Hello, Corbin."

"Howdy, Jack."

Jack looked down at his bare chest. "Oh, gosh! Sorry, Miss Annabel. I forgot to grab up my shirt. I'll run back—"

"No need. Here's one of Spinner's." Annabel handed the

boy a shirt from a pile of folded clothes on the ironing board at the end of the kitchen. She was aware that Corbin Appleby was watching her closely, and it made her nervous.

Mercy me! I hope that he doesn't notice how nervous I am. My hands are shaking and my tongue feels like it's thick as a bed slat.

Corbin was unaware of either of those things. It was difficult for him to take his eyes from her. He found her looks fascinating—far more fragile than he remembered. He had been puzzled by her, puzzled by his own reaction to her. And the fact that he had not been able to shake her image puzzled him all the more.

Chapter 13

Do you take sugar in your tea, Mr. Appleby?"

"No, ma'am."

"Neither do I. Boone, however, takes a little tea with his sugar." She glanced at the scowling man, then uttered a soft, teasing laugh.

"How long do you plan to stick around?" Boone asked bluntly.

"I've not decided. I like it here. It would be a good place to plant roots." Corbin's eyes flicked to Annabel and saw that she was watching him intently and was well aware that he was goading Boone. He wondered how her eyes could look so green.

"Harrumpt!" Boone snorted. "Tell that to the man behind the barn."

"Miss Annabel and her father are moving to St. Louis," Jack said in the silence that followed.

"Leaving soon?" With a feeling of acute disappointment, Corbin's eyes went to Annabel.

"Papa's gone to make arrangements." She looked down at the table as she spoke.

Corbin felt the full force of her eyes when she looked up

again and encountered his gaze. He knew immediately, sensing the hint of sadness in her eyes, that the move was not to her liking.

"Have you been to St. Louis, Mr. Appleby?"

"Passed through there, is all. I'm not much for the big city. This tea hits the spot." Corbin drank from the tall glass, then turned to Jack. "Are you staying on until they move?"

"I'll stay as long as Miss Annabel wants me to. Boone isn't moving. I might even stay longer if I can give him a hand. I'm going to stick around here until I find my glove."

Corbin's eyes swung to the man sitting at the end of the table. "Going to take up farming, Boone?"

"Maybe. Ya got any objections?"

"No. You'll get along well with a team of mules. You're about as stubborn as they are."

"Bullfoot!"

Annabel let out a sigh of exasperation, annoyed by Boone's rudeness.

Corbin spoke to Jack. "They have ball games in Henderson on Saturday evenings and again on Sunday after the concerts in the park. We could be lucky enough to spot your glove."

"I'm going to beat the daylights out of whoever took it." Jack's voice rose in anger.

"Whoever took it will probably not be the one using it." Corbin's voice was calm and reasonable.

"He's just as guilty if he bought stolen property."

"Maybe not. He might not know that it was stolen."

"How'll ya know if it's your glove?" Boone asked.

"I'll know if I see it, and besides, I burned my initials on the inside of the strap."

"That should be identification enough."

At the sound of a car, Boone pushed back his chair and went quickly to the window.

"It's Spinner."

"Tell him to come in," Annabel called as Boone went out the door. "Spinner works here . . . for my father," she explained to Corbin.

As soon as Boone left them, Corbin invited Annabel to go with him and Jack to the ball game Saturday evening. He didn't know if he'd get another chance to ask without Boone hovering over her.

Color rose in Annabel's cheeks. Corbin wondered if he had spoken too bluntly, then was relieved by her answer.

"I'd like to go." The words came from not-quite-steady lips. Her fingers plucked at the lace on the pocket of her dress.

"Good." Corbin smiled with his mouth closed, creases appearing on each side of it. "Maybe between the two of us we can hold this wild man in check if he spots his glove."

Annabel liked Corbin's face, his steady eyes and the way he had of smiling at times as if remembering something pleasant. A tightness crept into her throat, and she thought how foolish she was to believe that he might be interested in her. He had asked her to go to the ball game because he would be driving out to get Jack, and it was the polite thing to do.

He was silent for so long that a queer little shock of something almost like panic went through her. *Had he asked her on impulse and was sorry that she'd agreed to go?* To cover her confusion, she got up to peer out the window to see that Spinner and Boone were standing beside the truck.

"You should hear Miss Annabel play the violin," Jack said.

"Jack, I swear!" Annabel returned to the table. "You're a

regular . . . blabbermouth." She smiled to take the sting out of her words. On seeing the affection she had for the boy, Corbin felt something warm and exciting deep in his belly.

He had not been mistaken about her.

"It's not a secret," Jack protested. "Corbin heard you tell about the conductor wanting you to play with his orchestra." He grinned at Corbin. "Sometimes after supper she plays just for me and Boone. Maybe she'll play while you're here."

"And maybe not," she said flippantly with a toss of her head to hide her confusion.

The truck started up. Annabel went to the door to see Spinner moving it up to the barn and knew that they were going to load something they didn't want Corbin Appleby to see. What were they up to now? Although nervous chills ran up her back, she had a smile on her face when she turned her back to speak to the two men at the table.

"Jack, do we have enough ice to make a freezer of ice cream?"

"I don't know." Jack got up and lifted the lid on the icebox. "I got this chunk yesterday. We would need most of it."

"That's all right. We can get another chunk tomorrow. We've got eggs and milk. I'll stir up the custard if you'll fire up the stove so I can cook it."

"What's up?" Boone had asked as soon as he reached Spinner's truck.

"Some city boys are nosin' 'round up in the hills."

"Lookin' for the stash?"

"They ain't there lookin' for goobers."

"Murphy's gone to get the money."

"He come by and told me. I need a few sticks of that dynamite from the barn. The charge is set at the cave. They get close to it, I'll blow it to hell and back. I need the sticks in case they get to nosin' 'round my place."

"How many?"

"Men? Four, so far."

"Godamighty! Don't kill any of 'em 'less it's you or them. Did they find the mules?"

"Naw. They're up at my place. If they mess with 'em, they'll get a blastin' stick up their ass. The wagon's in the cave."

"I'd come give ya a hand, but Murphy had a run-in with one of the Carters, and I don't dare leave Annabel."

"He told me. Who's here?"

"Appleby, the man who was shot up near your place."

"Ain't he a lawman?"

"Used to be. I think he's sweet on Annabel. Hell of a lot of good it'll do him. Murphy's movin' her to St. Louis."

"Poor little gal. Murphy's been a-draggin' her from pillar to post."

"He says it's the last time." Boone's eyes strayed to the woods that separated them from the Carters'. Tess hadn't come out the previous night, and he was worried about her.

"Hell, I don't believe it. Murphy likes the excitement of outwittin' the Feds."

"I'm goin' to try and buy this place from him."

"Ya are?"

"He says he's sellin'. I can rake up what he paid for it."

Spinner took off his battered old felt hat, slapped it against his thigh to rid it of dust, then put it back on.

"I done told him I'm through after this. It's got too hot for me. Never thought ya'd quit on him."

"Hell. I ain't quittin' on him. I don't want no truck with them big torpedoes in Chicago. I want to settle down and not have to worry 'bout someone bustin' in and bustin' my head."

"Why here?"

"Why not here? I ain't a city man."

"I ain't either. Get them sticks so I can get back."

"Why didn't Spinner come in?" Annabel asked as soon as Boone came back to the house.

"He had to get back."

"Isn't it your turn to—"

"No. I'm staying here." Boone's dark eyes flicked to Corbin and saw that he was listening to something Jack was saying. "Come out on the porch," he said in a low tone to Annabel and picked up the water bucket.

Annabel followed him to the porch. "I swear to goodness, Boone. It's rude to leave a guest."

"He ain't no guest. He's a lawman," Boone growled. "Be careful what ya say and stop bein' so damn friendly to him or he'll stay all night."

"What do you think he can do, for heaven's sake?"

"He can notify the Feds, is what he can do."

"About what, Boone? Even I don't know what I could tell the Feds. I've asked him to stay for supper. Jack and I are making ice cream," she said defiantly. "And you . . . behave."

"Holy hell! Why'd you do that for? Murphy won't like it."

"Papa isn't here, and I asked him because I wanted to."

"If yore pa comes home while he's here, look out. He told me to keep him away from you."

"Why, Boone? Why?" Her large green eyes filled with tears. "The two of you treat me like I didn't have any brains at all. I'm tired of it! I'm tired of staying put where you tell me. I'm tired of not having any friends."

"It's been hard on ya, youngun. I'm just doin' what yore pa told me to do. It'll be all over soon."

"Will it?"

"Lord, I hope so. Truth is, I'm tired of it too," he said to her back as she flounced into the house again.

While Annabel cooked the custard to make the ice cream, Boone penned up the chickens. Jack and Corbin carried the big block of ice to the back porch and chipped it to go around the drum once it was set in the freezer.

"Boone doesn't like me much," Corbin said as soon as he and Jack were alone.

"He's not said anythin'." Jack looked at him with a puzzled look on his young face.

"Is he . . . interested in Miss Donovan?"

"Like, ah . . . being sweet on her?"

"Something like that."

"He watches over her like a mother hen, but I don't think it's . . . 'cause he's sweet on her. It's more like he was her uncle or something. He and Spinner look after her when her pa isn't here."

"Is her father gone a lot?"

"He's only been here once since I've been here. Boone is worried about the Carters. He's afraid one of them will slip over here and . . . hurt Annabel."

"Hurt her?"

Jack told Corbin about Murphy Donovan pushing Marvin Carter's car off the road into a tree and busting up the front end.

"Ruined his radiator, did he?"

"Last couple of evenings Boone has disappeared. I think he's watching the Carters to see what they're up to. He told me to stick close to Annabel. We sit in here in the house without a light on."

"What does she think of that?"

Annabel came out onto the porch before Jack could answer. "Is the freezer ready? The custard will be cool soon, and you can start cranking."

Later she poured the custard into the drum and added the milk to fill it to within a couple inches from the top. Then, while Jack milked the cow, Corbin turned the crank on the freezer. Annabel added salt to the ice and covered the top of the freezer with a folded quilt.

"I wish we weren't moving to St. Louis," she said as she sat down on the edge of the porch.

"Why St. Louis?"

"Papa is buying a hotel there."

"I hear the hotel business is good right now. A lot of people are on the move."

"Have you moved around a lot?"

"I lived in Springfield all my life until I went up to Jefferson to school, then into the army. When I came back from France, I went home to Springfield for a year, then took the job of police chief in Fertile. I was there until a few months ago."

"Jack said you are well thought of in Fertile."

"I don't think some of the drunks at the river dives would agree with him." He tipped the freezer and let the water from the melting ice run out onto the ground.

"Are you going back into police work?"

"I've not decided. Keeping the peace in a small town is satisfying work. It's also confining unless the town is big enough for you to have an assistant. You're always on call."

"You didn't have an assistant in Fertile?"

"No, and after the town was cleaned up, the challenge was gone."

"Ah . . . so you liked the excitement of putting the crooks in jail."

"It was really more satisfaction than excitement." It was comfortable talking to her like this. "Are you leaving as soon as your father comes back? Jack said you had started packing up."

"Probably." She swallowed hard and concentrated on not letting him see the deep ache within her.

"You'll still be here Saturday night to go to the ball game?" A sharp feeling of apprehension suddenly struck him.

"Unless . . . unless Papa comes home and wants to leave right away."

"I hope that doesn't happen. I'm . . . looking forward to us going to the game."

A stillness followed. Only the green, thick-lashed eyes and the faint color that spread across her cheeks betrayed the fact that her heart was soaring like a bird. She hoped that he was unaware of the turbulent feeling his presence inspired. She looked into his piercing, sunlight-squinted eyes. They seemed endowed with the ability to look a hole right through a person. She had to get her mind off the man and put a lid on her thoughts that perhaps, just perhaps, he might be attracted to her, or after she left here she'd be in for more heartache than she could handle.

"Tessie!"

The kitchen door slammed and Tess heard her brother's heavy boots coming toward the pantry-sized room where she slept.

"Where the hell are you?"

The door was jerked open. Tess got up off the bed, where she had been sitting looking out the window remembering the kiss she had shared with Boone and knowing that another night would go by and she would be unable to meet him at the edge of the woods.

"What do you want? I left your supper on the table."

"I want you to get over there and find out what's goin' on. That bastard that hit me is there honeyin' up to my girl." A stubble of whiskers covered Marvin's cheeks and his hair looked as if he had come in out of a windstorm.

"Over to the . . . Donovans'?"

"'Over to the Donovans'?'" he mimicked. "Ya dumb-ass! Where else?"

"I can't go over there if they've got . . . company."

"You'll do as I tell ya, gawddammit!"

"It . . . wouldn't be polite, Marvin, to barge in on folks who have company."

"Who the hell cares 'bout polite? Get your skinny ass over there and see what's goin' on." His hand lashed out and fastened on her arm.

"Why don't you send Leroy?"

"Leroy ain't got no reason to go over there. You're goin'. Put on a clean dress. Fix your hair. I ain't wantin' her to see my kin lookin' like they've been sleepin' with the hogs."

"Please, Marvin. What if they know you took their horses?"

"What do you know about that?"

"Only what I heard Leroy and Bud talking about. Calvin came and got them, didn't he?"

"What if he did? Donovan's goin' to pay for what he did to my car. Before the week's out he'll know not to go pissin' on Carters." Marvin's face turned uglier than usual; his nostrils flared and he ground his teeth in frustration. "Cousin Willard'll take care of him. I ain't tellin' ya again to get yoreself fixed up."

"Then get out so I can change." Tess tried to pull away from him, but he pulled her up close and stuck his face in hers. The sour mash on his breath sickened her.

"Don't be shamin' me. Hear? And watch what ya say to 'em. If ya let out a peep 'bout what goes on here, I'll hear about it, and then . . . and then I'll beat yore ass to a bloody pulp!"

"Why are you stealin' from her? It wasn't her fault—"

"Not from *her*, ya stupid bitch. They was her old man's. I'm gonna have her and when I get 'er I'll screw her brains out. She'll be hangin' on me like a leech before I'm done."

"She's not like the other women you've had, Marvin. Can't you find someone else?"

"Ya think I'm not good enough? Huh? Huh?" He twisted her arm until she cried out, then shoved her from him. "Get movin'. Find out who that son-of-a-bitch is and what he's doin' there."

It was dark in the woods.

Tess was more afraid of the brother who walked beside her than she was of the dark. Something sinister had happened to Marvin since he had been rejected by Annabel Donovan, bested by her crippled friend and pushed off the road by her father's car. To the delight of Leroy and Bud, he told and retold, in detail, what he was going to do to Miss Donovan. For two days he had been drinking whiskey as if it were water, and tonight he was carrying a bottle with him.

Calvin had insisted that the Carters could create such havoc that the Donovans would pack up and leave, and it wouldn't be necessary for them to kill anyone. If the Donovans didn't go, the Carters would make other plans. The scheme had worked with the previous owner of the property. This afternoon Carter cousins had stolen the horses while they were at the far end of the pasture. It was the beginning of the harassment.

Leroy had reported what Calvin had said. "Fair is fair. An eye for an eye. We'll sell the horses to pay for fixing the car, and Marvin can have the pleasure of gettin' his own revenge from the man who hit him."

Calvin had no words of wisdom to offer about Marvin's courtship of Annabel or Tess would have heard about it from Leroy, who relished the telling. Women in the Carter clan were not held in high respect. They were to be used and enjoyed as the males saw fit. Calvin was fond of saying that with a sack over her head, one woman was the same as another.

Tess wondered what Marvin would do if he knew the Donovans had already decided to move. *Hurry! Hurry and get away from here, Annabel! If my brother gets to you . . . you'll never be the same again.*

At the edge of the wood, Marvin grasped Tess's arm. "Stay till ya find out how the wind blows. Act friendly like ya was just out walkin' and saw the lights. Don't be doin' nothin' dumb. I'll be waitin' here." He leaned back against the tree and took a deep swallow from the bottle he was carrying.

A knot of apprehension twisted Tess's stomach as she walked out of the shelter of the woods. Light from the kitchen shone on several figures sitting on the edge of the porch. She could hear the murmur of male voices and Annabel's girlish laughter. Tess walked slowly, dreading to approach and wondering what in the world she would say.

Tess's uneasiness grew into full-fledged fear when she realized that Mr. Boone was standing and looking directly at her. She didn't know why she knew it was him. The distance between them was too great for her to see anything but the shape of him. Then he was coming to meet her and she prayed that he wouldn't call out to her.

With her finger against her lips, Tess hurried to meet him.

"Sshhh, sshhh—" she hissed. "He's watchin'." Tess's heart was beating like that of a trapped rabbit.

Boone nodded that he understood. "Ma'am, is somethin' wrong?" he asked in a tone slightly louder than normal.

"Oh, no," Tess said with a forced laugh. "I . . . wanted to ask Miss Donovan . . . something."

"Come on over. She's here on the porch." Boone turned and walked beside her, keeping a distance between them. He waited until they were almost to the house before he spoke. "Is something wrong?" he asked in an anxious whisper. "Did he hurt you?"

"No. He made me come to see what's going on." There was an embarrassed hesitancy in her voice. "Don't stop! He can see us," she said when Boone paused.

"How long can ya stay?"

"Until I find out what that man is doing here."

Annabel stepped off the porch as they approached.

"Hello, Tess. You're just in time for ice cream. We've all had one helping and are getting ready for another."

"Oh, no. I didn't come to—"

"Come up onto the porch. Jack, will you get a chair for Tess?" Annabel reached for Tess's hand. "You know Jack and Boone. This is Mr. Appleby. Corbin, Tess Carter is our neighbor."

"I'm pleased to meet you, ma'am." Corbin looked down at the small woman with the delicate features and could hardly believe that she was the sister of the lout who had bothered Annabel in the park.

"Likewise," Tess said when she finally got her tongue unstuck from the roof of her mouth.

Annabel led her up on the porch to the chair Jack had placed next to hers.

"I brought out another bowl, Miss Annabel."

"Then dish up the ice cream before it melts. We're running out of ice," she explained to Tess.

Tess was glad that it was dark. She couldn't stop trembling. Her teeth chattered against the spoon when she put the first bite in her mouth. Only Boone knew why she was here. Marvin would go right out of his head if he knew that she had talked to Boone, that he had kissed her. Her eyes clung to him as she listened to the voices that floated around her.

"We always took out the dasher at home," Jack was saying. "The kids would fight over who got to lick off the ice cream."

"Yo're the only kid here. We'll let you lick it." Boone tried to hand the dripping dasher to Jack, who refused to take it. There was a lot of laughter and horseplay that was foreign to Tess. This sort of thing at the Carters' would result in a fistfight.

"I'm glad you came over. I've been wanting to see you again."

Tess tore her eyes from Boone when she realized Annabel was speaking to her.

"I . . . didn't know you had company."

"Mr. Appleby isn't exactly company. He stopped by to see Jack and we decided to make ice cream."

"It's good."

"I used cream. Our cow gives good rich milk."

"You ought to keep her close by . . . because of . . . because of coyotes or . . . wild dogs."

"Wild dogs? Oh, my. I'd be sick if anything happened to Mildred. I'll ask Boone if he's seen any wild dogs or coyotes around."

Tess's eyes flashed quickly to Annabel's. They looked as if they were seeking something. Sadness sagged the corners of her mouth as she turned away to fasten her remarkable amber eyes on Boone. His face was a blur in the dark, but she knew he was looking at her . . . wanting to help her, protect her. She wished she could go to him, ask him what to do.

"If everyone has finished, I'll take in the bowls. Corbin can wash out the freezer at the pump."

Jack stepped up onto the porch as Annabel got to her feet. "I'll take in the bowls. You wash the freezer."

Jack held the bowls out of her reach. "Not until you promise to play for us."

"Jack Jones! You're getting to be more like Boone every day."

Chapter 14

ANNABEL DIDN'T WANT THE EVENING TO END and if prolonging it meant she had to furnish the entertainment, then that's what she would do.

Corbin didn't want the evening to end either. He was determined to have a short time alone with her, but he wasn't sure how he was going to manage it. Boone had watched him like a hawk until Tess Carter arrived. Now he watched her and wasn't hanging on to every word that passed between Corbin and Annabel. Almost every time he looked over at the man, Boone's eyes were on the small woman. And when Tess wasn't speaking to Annabel, she was looking around for Boone.

Something interesting was going on here. It didn't take much figuring to come to the conclusion that the two of them knew each other better than they were letting on.

"I'd better go," Tess said and pulled back when Jack held the door for the ladies to go into the house.

"Oh, no," Annabel exclaimed. "Stay a little longer. Boone will walk you back home. Won't you, Boone?"

"Sure. As long as yo're here, ya might as well stay awhile." His hand on her back urged her into the house.

Carrying the lamp, Annabel led the way to the front

room. Tess held back to allow Jack and Corbin to pass with
the kitchen chairs.

"I can't let you walk me back," she whispered. "Marvin's . . . waiting at the edge of the wood."

"What's he wantin' to know?"

"If Mr. Appleby's courting Annabel. Marvin calls her *his*
girl."

"Bullfoot! He sent ya over here to find out that?"

"I ought to go."

"Ya've been here this long, it'll not hurt if ya stay a little
longer."

"He's drunk and . . . kind of crazy."

"Don't worry. I'll think of somethin'."

Boone was aware that Corbin, looking over his shoulder,
saw that he and Tess were exchanging whispered words and
kept himself between them and Annabel. Boone guided Tess
ahead of him into the living room and toward a chair. His
black eyes darted a glance at Corbin, and he was relieved to
see that he had eyes only for the girl getting her beloved violin out of the case.

Marvin Carter was right. Corbin Appleby had come
courting Annabel. Well, hell. He wasn't a bad sort. He just
got under Boone's skin at times.

"She really plays pretty. She can play most anything on
that fiddle: waltzes and funeral songs—"

"Funeral songs! Jack Jones, I've never played funeral
music, and this *violin* is not a *fiddle*." Annabel playfully
tapped him on the head with her bow, then put it to the
strings and played "Little Brown Jug."

At the proper time, Jack began to clap and sing.

"Ha, ha, ha, you and me. Little brown jug
don't I love thee—"

Soon Corbin was clapping with him and Annabel's foot was keeping time to the music as she played. When the song ended, she removed the violin from beneath her chin.

"That was fun!" Her green eyes were sparkling. Corbin was fascinated. "I'll play something more soothing. Later I'll play Jack's favorite."

"What's that?" Corbin asked.

"You'll see."

She swayed as she played two Irish melodies: "I'll Take You Home Again, Kathleen" and "Danny Boy." The music was hauntingly beautiful. The four people listening sat breathlessly still.

"Those two songs are my father's favorites . . . naturally, as he's Irish." She laughed a little. "Boone likes western ballads. These are his favorites." She played the medley: "Red River Valley," "Strawberry Roan" and "The Wide Missouri."

The entrancing music filled the room and spilled out into the night, where Marvin Carter sat hunched down beside the window. He burned with resentment that he had to squat outside the window to listen, while the bastard that had hit him was in there sitting on one of the fancy chairs. He slunk away, his head filled with plans to get even.

Annabel closed her eyes and played as if she were off in another world. Corbin was amazed; not so much that she played beautifully, but because there was not a sheet of music in sight. She played from memory and because she loved it. *She is an extraordinary woman*, he thought. *A jewel, a treasure.*

When she finished the medley and opened her eyes, they dwelled on Corbin. She took a few deep breaths and let the arm holding the bow fall to her side.

"What type of music do you like?"

"All types."

"How about this?"

He smiled and she put the bow to the strings and began to play "Sweet Georgia Brown." When she finished, they laughed. Eyes still holding, she began to play "I'll See You in My Dreams." Sure that none here knew the words, she poured her heart into the music; and when she finished, her cheeks were flushed.

"Do you have a favorite, Tess?"

Tess came out of her trance-like state and shook her head. She had been to musicales while she was in school and thought that she never again would be privileged to hear such music. She wanted to cry. She wanted to crawl under the bed and stay here forever.

"I'll play "Indian Love Call" for you, and then Jack's favorite."

Corbin was enchanted. She had been playing for almost an hour. He glanced at Boone from time to time when he could take his eyes off Annabel. The man had something on his mind besides music. He hadn't uttered one gruff remark since Tess Carter had arrived.

When she finished, Annabel let her tired arm swing at her side and spoke to Jack. "I'll play the lead-in, and then sing out." She played a few bars of a recognized tune, then lifted her chin. "Now, Jack."

To Corbin's amazement, Jack stood beside Annabel and sang in a surprisingly good voice.

"Listen to the jingle, the rumble and the roar,
Riding through the woodlands,
to the hill, and by the shore.
Hear the mighty rush of engines,
Hear the lone-some ho-bo squall.
Riding through the jungles on the Wabash Cannonball."

Jack sang several verses and seemed to be totally at ease and enjoying himself. Annabel's fingers worked the strings on the violin while the bow caressed them. She tapped her foot on the floor in time with the music. Corbin realized the two of them had done this before and thought what a great thing it was for the boy to have found this place when he was sick and needed help.

When the song ended, Corbin clapped his hands. "The two of you should get a job on the stage."

Jack, with a wide grin on his face, took a bow. "Didn't I tell you she could play? The night I was sick and lyin' down by the road, I heard the music and at first I thought I had died." Jack's voice quavered a little, remembering.

Annabel laughed. "We could perform on the street corner, Jack, and you could pass the hat." She carefully wiped the violin with a soft cloth and put it in the case.

"I've got to go. Thank . . . you . . ." Tess headed for the back door. Annabel hurried after her.

"I'm glad you came over. I'll be moving away soon."

Tess's amber eyes flew to Boone. "I . . . guess I'll not see you again," she said to Annabel.

"You can come over again . . . or I could come see you before I go."

"Oh, no! Ah . . . sometimes I'm not there. I had a good time. 'Bye." She darted out the back door.

Boone grabbed Tess's arm. "Annabel," he said over his shoulder, "stay close to Jack and Appleby till I get back."

"Mr. Boone!" Tess whispered urgently after they stepped off the porch. "Let me go. Marvin could be right around the corner . . . listening."

"Be back in a little while," Boone called, should Marvin be nearby. "I'll walk Miss Carter part of the way home."

"What'll I tell him?" Tess whispered.

"Tell him Appleby came to see me and Jack."

"When is she going away? I wish it was tomorrow."

"Why is that?"

"'Cause . . . Marvin won't give up till he's . . . ruined her."

"Bastard," Boone gritted between clenched teeth.

They fell silent as they neared the woods. Tess's eyes searched for her brother but saw no sign of him.

"He was going to wait."

"Where?"

"Over there."

Boone's eyes followed her pointed finger. His night vision was exceptionally good. "He isn't there, Tess." He reached for Tess's hand and pulled her to him.

She twisted away. "He's around here somewhere," she whispered.

"I'll walk you home," he said in a conversational tone. "Annabel is by herself. I shouldn't be gone too long."

"Ah . . ."

He squeezed Tess's hand and steered her off the path into the bushes, where he would have a clear view of the area between the woods and the house. He drew her close to him and whispered in her ear.

"If he's here, he may hotfoot it over to the house. We'll wait and see."

"If he heard you, he'll go and fight Mr. Appleby."

"Appleby can take care of himself. And I'd be right behind him." Boone settled her back against his chest and wrapped his arms around her. "Now tell me, are they treatin' ya all right?"

"I've been all right."

"I came lookin' for ya the last two nights."

"I couldn't come out. Marvin is on a tear. He talks about

getting even with the man who pushed him off the road and the one who hit him. He tells Leroy and Bud what he's going to do to . . . Annabel. Nasty things. Take her away from here," Tess pleaded.

"Don't worry. Annabel and her pa will be leaving soon. Meanwhile, I'll watch her every minute."

"Marvin will find a way. He's got the rest of the Carters helping him."

"They stole the horses, didn't they?"

"How'd you know that?"

"The fence was cut. Horses don't cut fences and walk away."

"He told me not to tell you."

"Ya didn't tell me. Tomorrow I'll discover they're gone and in a day or two go in and report it to the sheriff."

"Watch the cow. She'll be next."

"Tess . . ." He turned her around in his arms. She went to him willingly and placed her head on his shoulder. "I'll not be able to stay here now, even if Donovan would sell the place to me. There would always be trouble between me and the Carters."

"They don't trust anyone that isn't kin."

"Could *you* trust me? We haven't met but a few times and never out in the open. When I leave here, will you go away with me?" He spoke with his lips close to her ear.

Rigid with surprise, Tess pulled away from his warm strength. *Go away with me.* A man like Boone wouldn't ever consider marrying a woman like her. He just wanted her to go away with him. He'd not use her rough like Cousin Willard had done, but he'd use her.

"You don't know anything about me. You'd be ashamed . . . after a while." She choked back the sobs that rose in her throat. "And . . . they'd come get me. I've got to stay and . . . pay—"

"Pay for what?" Boone peered down into her face.

Realizing she'd said more than she should, Tess hid her face against his chest, her mind searching for a plausible answer.

"Pay for what, Tess?" Boone insisted.

"For . . . my keep." She whispered the lie, praying that he would believe it.

"Ah . . . sweet girl." Emotion flooded Boone's heart like none he had felt before. He hugged her tightly to him and kissed the top of her head. He silently vowed that if this golden girl who had seeped into his heart would come with him, he would love and protect her for as long as he lived.

Love. The word had just popped into his mind. He'd not even thought the word before. Love was a new word for him. But, by God, he loved her!

"I want to take care of you. We can go where they can't find you. Tess, look at me." He put his fingers beneath her chin and lifted her face. "You don't have to care for me, but trust me to take care of you." He put his mouth gently on hers and kissed her. "I want to keep you with me. I've been alone for a long time."

"You've had Annabel."

"Annabel isn't mine. She'll marry someday and have a family. I'll be like an . . . uncle. Appleby is smitten. He couldn't keep his eyes off her. He'd not be a bad choice for her, but her pa would never allow it."

"So he *is* courting her."

"I think he wants to. Will you tell your brother?"

"No. I'm afraid he'd waylay him and hurt him."

"He might just meet his match. Appleby bested him once."

"Yes, he's the one who hit Marvin on the knee."

"He knocked his feet right out from under him." Boone nuzzled his face in her hair. "Marvin hasn't showed himself. Can ya stay awhile longer?"

"For a while. But Annabel . . ."

"It'll give Appleby an excuse to stay. He won't go until I get back. I want to hold you and kiss you, sweet woman. I was worried sick when you didn't come out last night."

Jack had brought the lamp to the kitchen table and now sat straddling a chair.

"It's strange that she'd walk over here in the dark." Annabel turned back from the door with a puzzled look on her face. Her eyes went to Corbin, who stood in the doorway.

"Her brothers may have sent her over thinking Boone would walk her back through the woods and give them a chance to jump him."

"I thought of that."

"Would you feel better if I went out and looked around?"

"I can do it. I know the lay of the land," Jack said, getting to his feet. "I'll take the gun and go out the back door of the barn and snoop around over by the woods. If there's any trouble, I'll fire off a couple of quick shots."

Annabel went to the kitchen cabinet and took a small pistol off the top shelf. She checked to be sure it was loaded, then handed it to Jack.

"Be careful, Jack."

Jack tucked the pistol in his belt. "Stay close to her, Corbin," the boy said seriously. "Boone always told me not to let her go into another room by herself. He doesn't trust the Carters at all."

Corbin's eyes left Jack, caught and held Annabel's.

"Trust me, Jack. It'll be the most pleasurable chore I've had in a long time."

"For goodness' sake!" Annabel sputtered, color coming up her neck to spread across her face. "Be careful and don't shoot yourself," she cautioned as the boy went out the door. She stared out into the darkness for a moment, wondering what she was going to say when she turned around.

Corbin filled in the void. "Shall we blow out the lamp?" he asked with a chuckle.

"I don't think we have to go that far. You probably never intended to stay this long when you came out to see Jack. I'm sorry you got . . . stuck . . . here with me," she finished in a rush.

"I'm thinking I'm damn lucky. I've been trying to figure out a way to get you out from under Boone's watchful eyes so we could get to know each other. The chance fell right into my lap."

"Well, for goodness' sake." She didn't know what else to say.

"Let's sit in the swing on the porch. If someone is coming at me, I want to see him coming."

Annabel turned out the lamp and led the way through the house to the porch.

"Will you be warm enough? It's cool at night this close to the river."

"I think so."

She sat down in the far corner of the swing. When he sat down, she felt strange being this close to him in the darkness, even though they were not touching. A curiously warm, exciting feeling fluttered in her stomach.

Corbin was determined to make the most of this time alone with her. She had crept into his heart and his mind and lodged there. He tried to think of something to say that would put her at ease.

"How long have you been playing the violin?"

"Since I was about ten years old. My mother played and taught me to read music."

"Tonight you played for almost an hour from memory. It was amazing."

She laughed a little. "It isn't amazing at all if you have an ear for music."

"The only ear I have for music is for the enjoyment of it."

"That's the most important part." Her voice came softly out of the darkness.

Corbin decided that he'd better act soon before Jack or Boone came back. She either liked him or she didn't. It was time to find out.

Annabel's heart almost stopped when he moved over closer to her and reached into her lap for her hand. He held it tightly in both of his.

"One of the first rules I learned when I was a lad and started noticing girls was always to hold the girl's hand if we were sitting in a porch swing."

"Whose rule was that? I never heard of it."

"*Appleby Family Rule Book on Courting,* written by my grandfather back in 1870."

"Corbin Appleby! You're making that up!" Her soft girlish laughter delighted him. "What was the second rule you learned?"

"Number two, if she jerks her hand away and slaps you, cry loud and long. She'll feel sorry for you and might even let you put your arm around her."

Annabel released another breath of soft laughter. "Did you ever give that second rule a try?"

"Not yet, but the night's not over."

"I'm thinking that you're full of blarney, Mr Appleby."

"You called me Corbin a couple times tonight."

"I did? How rude of me."

"You don't think you know me well enough? I think about you as Annabel Lee."

"How did you know Lee was my middle name?"

"My friend Edgar Allan Poe told me."

"The . . . poet?"

"I know him well." He quoted: "*'She was a child, and I was a child—'*"

"*'In this kingdom by the sea.'*" Her voice was a mere whisper.

"*'But we loved with a love that was more than love—'*" Corbin paused.

"*'I and my Annabel Lee—'*"

"*'With a love that the wingèd seraphs of Heaven/ Coveted her and me.'*" He finished the verse in a soft, intimate whisper.

The silence that followed was broken only by the squeaking of the chains holding the porch swing. The hand holding hers was never still. His thumb stroked her knuckles, her palm and her fingertips.

"Is Lee really your middle name?" he asked.

"Yes, it is. My mother loved the poem. Her name was Annalee."

"Annabel Lee and Annalee are both beautiful names."

"I used to wonder what the word *seraphs* meant when my mother read the poem." Her voice was strong, but she was quivering inside. "I looked it up when I went to school."

"Let me guess. It means a whole herd of angels."

Her laugh was low and musical. "Not a whole herd, but a few. I'm not sure, but it may mean the angel's wings. I'll have to look it up again."

He gazed at her profile and wanted to tell her that sometimes thinking about her made him feel all mixed up and shaky inside, and at other times he was surprised by the flood of happiness that washed over him. He was afraid that if he attempted to say any of those things, he would make a mess of it and scare her away.

"I think it's time to test the third rule," he said lightly. "You're cold. I felt you shivering." His arm arched over her head and pulled her close. "If I hold your hands tight enough, it says in the rule book, you can't slap me."

"I've never slapped anyone in my life."

"That's good to know. I thought I'd better do this before Boone comes back and punches me in the nose."

The sound of his voice in the warm, dark night was so reassuring she lost her self-consciousness and relaxed against him.

"This is nice," he said in a low whisper. "I've wanted to do this since that first day when we met in front of the hotel. After that day, I couldn't get you out of my mind."

"More blarney, Mr. Appleby?"

His fingers came up to silence her lips. "I shouldn't have said that so soon. Have I ruined my chances with you?" His voice was husky and had the sound of a plea in it.

"Nooo . . ." She drew the word out because she was breathless.

The word gave him the encouragement to continue. "Want the truth? I've been mooning over a girl with sea-green eyes, a sweet smile, and beautiful dark brown hair, a girl whose father would like to flatten me out like a pancake."

"I'm sorry—"

"You've nothing to be sorry for. If I had a sweet and pretty daughter like you, I'd guard her like Fort Knox. He doesn't know me. I could be a flimflammer, for all he knows."

"Are you a flimflammer?" Annabel's heart was beating so hard and so fast that she was sure he could feel it.

"When he gets back, I'll tell him my life's story, show him my army records and get a horde of preachers to vouch for me, tell him about all the old ladies I've helped cross the street, and maybe he'll let me come courting when you get moved down to St. Louis."

"You'd come all the way to St. Louis?"

"Didn't Napoleon come home from the wars to be with his Josephine? Didn't George Washington cross the icy Potomac to be with his Martha? Didn't the gallant Sir Walter Raleigh throw his coat over a mud puddle to protect the feet of Queen Elizabeth?"

He felt her body tremble with laughter. It was in her voice when she spoke. Corbin was enthralled with her.

"It's pure fiction that Sir Walter Raleigh threw down his coat for the queen to walk on. I'm glad he didn't, because a few years later she had his head cut off."

"The ungrateful wench." The arm around her tightened a bit. "The lesson here is never throw down your coat for a lady to walk on."

"Especially if she's a queen."

Corbin was happier than he could remember being in a long time, and his foot moved the swing gently. He held her firmly to his side, loving the feel of her soft body against his. This was more, much more than he had hoped for when he left town to come here. He was sure now that she didn't object to his attention. Her father was the obstacle he would have to overcome.

Sitting close to Corbin, her shoulder behind his, her hip and thigh snugly against him, Annabel had no thoughts except of him. She was gloriously, foolishly happy. He had not said that he would come to St. Louis to see her, but he had indicated that he would. By then her father would be out of the bootlegging business and would have nothing to fear from a former police officer. After he got to know Corbin, he would like him. *Oh, she hoped so.*

She turned her head to look at him and found him looking down at her. There was a mingling of their breaths and she was sure that he wanted to kiss her.

Then Boone's voice came rumbling out of the darkness.

Chapter 15

H ELLFIRE! I figured I'd better get back here."

Corbin swore under his breath and refused to remove his arm from around Annabel.

"Boone, one of these days I'm going to bust you in the mouth. You can count on it."

"Yeah?" Boone came up onto the porch. "Who're ya goin' to get to help ya? Where's Jack?"

"He's around here somewhere."

"Got rid of him, did ya?"

Annabel got suddenly to her feet. "Good night, Corbin," she said briskly. "Thank you for watching over me while my *guardian* was away."

"You're very welcome, Annabel. And thank you for supper and the concert and the ice cream. I'll be out Saturday to take you and Jack to the ball game."

"What's this about?" Boone demanded.

Ignoring him, Corbin said, "Good night, Annabel." And he walked off the porch.

Boone followed him to the car. "Yo're askin' for trouble, Appleby. Annabel's pa told me to keep her away from you."

"Yeah? Why didn't he tell me himself?"

"He will. Don't doubt it."

Corbin leaned back against his car and lit a cigarette. He waited until he saw a light in the house before he spoke.

"Boone, to my way of thinking prohibition is a stupid law, but it's law. I don't know how deep you and Donovan are into the bootlegging business, but I'll tell you this. Be careful how you play with the boys in Chicago. They're tough. They squash little operators like bugs if they get in the way."

"Yo're a Fed."

"I'm not a Fed. I've told you that. I've no interest in Donovan other than he's Annabel's father. If he thinks he can compete with the big operators out of Chicago and St. Louis, he'd better be careful. He could get you all killed."

"He's gettin' out."

"I'm glad to hear it."

"What are you doin' here?"

"Courting Annabel, or trying to."

"Hell, I know that. I'm not blind. I mean what're ya hangin' 'round Henderson for?"

"Waitin' for Jack to be ready to go home."

"Horse hockey! Ya might fool them rubes in Henderson, but ya ain't foolin' me."

"I'm not trying to. What's going on between you and the Carter girl? She's a fine-looking woman even if she does act like a cowed pup. Been meeting her on the sly? Can't say that I blame you."

"It's none of yore damn business." Boone's voice rose angrily.

"Then stop sticking your nose in mine." Corbin dropped his cigarette on the ground and stepped on it. "Better get back to town."

"Good idea. Watch out for Carter. He sent Tess over to

see what ya was doin' here. He's layin' claim to Annabel and don't want ya chiselin' in on him."

Corbin's head jerked up. "He'll pay hell claiming her! If her pa can't put a stop to it, I can."

"Tess says he's crazy about her and he's layin' for ya for what ya did last Sunday."

"She told you that? You two must be cozier than I thought."

"If ya let it be known she warned ya, it'll go hard with her. Might get her killed. Then I'd come for ya—"

"Tell Miss Carter I thank her for the warning." Corbin got into the car, reached under the seat and placed a revolver on the seat beside him. "Use your head, man. Bring Annabel to town. She can wait for her pa there."

"Ya'd like that, wouldn't ya?"

"Don't be more of an ass than you are, Boone. If things get rough out here and you need me, send Jack."

He started the car and drove down the lane toward the road. At the end of the path he stopped for a moment and wondered if there was a way to get to town other than going by the Carter place. He had not heard of a road that went around the town and didn't relish the thought of wandering around at night looking for one. He turned south toward town.

The headlights on his car picked out the rough spots in the road to avoid but didn't reach into the brush that grew along the roadside. He traveled down a small incline and rounded a slight bend in the road that brought him even with the Carter place. He increased the speed of the car, then on down the road he slowed down again, his eyes peering into the dark ahead of the headlights.

His keen night vision allowed him to see the obstruction in the road ahead just as the headlights reached the large pile of brush and tree limbs. He stomped on the brake, put the car in reverse, backed up and stopped. Then out to the side he caught a glimpse of someone on a balking mule.

They were trying to box him in with another tree limb.

He tromped down on the gas pedal and the car sprang forward, the headlights bouncing on the deadfalls that had been dragged across the road.

Without hesitation, Corbin gunned the motor and jerked the wheel. The car bounced as it hit the ditch and the brush that grew alongside the road. At the last second he saw another mule, but it was too late to keep from hitting it. The fender of the car hit the hind legs of the mule trying to get out of the way. The man riding it was thrown off and hit the side of the car with a loud thump.

Corbin thanked God for the powerful motor that kept the car plowing through the brush until he could steer it back up onto the road.

The bastards had been waiting for him!

He slowed the car and reached down for the gun that had bounced off the seat when he hit the ditch. He regretted hitting the mule, but he hoped that whoever was on it got his head busted when he hit his car. The bastard deserved to have his neck broken.

There wasn't a car in sight when Corbin drove down the main street of Henderson on his way to the hotel. The light was on in the telephone office, the billiard parlor and Alex Lemon's photography shop.

Corbin parked in front of the hotel, sat for a minute or two, then tucked the gun inside his shirt and got out. The front fender of his car had a good-sized dent, as did the door on the passenger side. He wasn't sure without touching it, but there could be a couple spots of blood on the door.

On the way to town he had decided to report the incident

to the sheriff in the morning. Corbin was almost sure that the Carters wouldn't report that he'd hit the mule unless the man on it had been badly hurt.

Tess knew that something had happened when she heard the cursing on the porch. She jumped out of bed the instant her name was bellowed by one of her brothers and pulled her dress on over the petticoat she slept in.

"Tess, get yore skinny ass out here, light a lamp and hold open the door."

"I'm comin'." She parted the curtains and hurried to the table where the lamp sat beside a box of matches.

As soon as she replaced the chimney on the lamp and the room was flooded with light, she went to the door. Bud and Marvin, carrying Leroy on a flat board, stood on the porch. She held back the screen door and stepped out of the way.

"What happened?" Leroy's face and head were covered with blood. Ignoring her question, they carried him to the bunk at the end of the kitchen where he had slept since he was a child and eased him down.

"Is he dead?" Tess peered over Marvin's shoulder at the bloody figure of her younger brother.

"No, he ain't dead," Marvin yelled as if she were out in the yard instead of standing beside him. "Get some water and wash him off."

"We should take him to the doctor."

"We ain't got no car to take him to a doctor. Wash him off. I told the shit-head to stay back outta the way. He got what he deserved for not takin' orders." Marvin went to the water bucket and filled a dipper with water, drank some of it and poured the rest on his brother's bloody face. Leroy didn't move. "He's still out. Wash him off before he comes to. He'll be yelling like a sick whore."

"Marvin, I don't know if I can. I've not got much stomach for—"

"Do it and shut up bitchin'. Yo're a woman, ain't ya? Women are supposed to do such things."

"Is he hurt anywhere else?"

"No broken bones . . . at least I don't think there is. That son-of-a-bitch drove right into the mule he was on. Broke both the mule's legs. I had to shoot it."

"What're we goin' to do with it, Marvin?" Bud seemed to be thoroughly subdued.

"Drag it down to the river." Marvin paced back and forth. "I got to go talk to Calvin. Somethin' ain't right. Somethin' sure ain't right."

"Whata ya mean?" Tess was glad Bud had asked the question. Marvin turned his anger on him.

"Ya slack-jawed, pig-fat dumb-ass! That feller that run Leroy down ain't no ordinary city feller, is what I mean. That car he's drivin' cost a pretty penny too, and he learnt how to drive it."

"I ain't never said he was, Marvin."

"Lud and Arney said he was. They'da got his car if that black-bearded feller hadn't started shootin' at 'em."

"Was they gonna kill him and take his car?" Bud asked.

"What the hell ya think, fat boy? He'd stopped up in the hills to pee and Arney got him in his sights. They'd only got off a couple shots when that other feller stuck his nose in. Ya can break a car like that down and sell the pieces for a right good sum of money."

"I'm not for killin' a man to get his car." Bud spoke to Marvin with more conviction than Tess had ever heard.

"Nobody's askin' ya to. Ya ain't got the guts of a sick cat nohow."

Tess placed a pan of warm water on the floor beside the

bunk where Leroy lay. She wet a cloth and laid it over his bloody face. The top of his ear was torn off. She had to swallow repeatedly to keep from throwing up.

"I wonder why he doesn't wake up. He may be hurt worse than we think." Tess voiced her fears aloud.

"He ain't hurt bad. His head is hard as a rock." Then, as if suddenly remembering, he took Tess's shoulder and spun her around. "Ya stayed long enough over there. What'd ya find out 'bout that feller?"

"He was visitin' with Mr. Boone."

"I watched through the window. Looked to me like he come a-courtin'."

"I honestly don't know if he did nor not. He talked to the others as much as he talked to her. I think he was there to see Mr. Boone and Jack, the boy who works there, and they invited him to stay for ice cream."

"Ya think! Ya don't know shit from corn bread. Was anything said about the horses?"

"No." Tess dipped the cloth in the water and kept her head down.

"They ain't discovered them gone yet. Dumb shits." Marvin went to the room he had taken over after their father died. Tess heard the squeak of the springs as he threw himself down on the bed.

"Ya think he's hurt bad?" Bud came to look down at Leroy. The worried note in his voice caused Tess to look up.

"I don't know. He should be waking up." She lifted the cloth from his torn face. "We should get him to a doctor so he can sew his ear."

"Ya want me to get ya some fresh water?"

"Throw this out and get some out of the reservoir." Tess was surprised by Bud's offer to help.

He returned with a pan of warm water, set it on the floor and pulled up a chair.

"How did Leroy happen to be down on the road this time of night?" Tess spoke in a low murmur.

"Marvin made us go with him to block the road so he could get at that feller that was over at the Donovans'," Bud whispered, looking toward the room where his brother slept. "We was goin' to block him in, but he gunned the car and went for the ditch to go around. He hit the mule Leroy was on."

"Did he stop?"

"Hell, no. He beat it on down the road. Marvin was crazy mad."

"Look at Leroy's face. He's never going to be the same again." Tess clicked her tongue sadly. "He wasn't good to look at anyhow. Bud, do you think you could take hold of his nose and straighten it?"

Tess turned her head while Bud's pudgy fingers worked at straightening Leroy's nose.

"It looks straight. Leroy ain't a bad kid. He just tries to be like Marvin."

Bud wiped his hands on the wet cloth. His fat face was lined with concern. Leroy's arm was hanging off the bunk. Bud lifted it and placed it beside him on the bed.

"Why do you and Leroy want to be like Marvin?"

"I dunno. Folks look up to him."

"Not decent folks. They think he's hill trash." Bitterness crept into Tess's voice.

"How do you know that? The Carters, all of them, look up to him."

"Don't you ever want to know anyone other than Carters?"

"There ain't nothin' wrong with the Carters. Ya better not

let Marvin hear ya say that. Carters is kin, and kin stick together."

Tess realized that she may have said too much. Bud and
Leroy had lived under the rule of the Carters all their lives.
It was too much to ask of them to see things differently.

Leroy stirred and cried out. He opened his eyes and
looked at Tess bending over him.

"Sis . . . Sis . . . I . . . hurt."

In her heart Tess damned Marvin. Leroy was a stupid,
foolish kid trying to live up to what was expected of him,
and Marvin had almost gotten him killed.

Annabel stayed in bed when she heard Boone and Jack in
the kitchen cooking breakfast. She wasn't sure if she would
ever speak to Boone again. He had done his best to ruin the
most perfect day of her life, and she didn't think she'd ever
forgive him.

Like most girls, she had longed to meet someone with
whom to share her joys and her sorrows; someone who
would love her and whom she would love with all her heart.
She had been attracted to Corbin when first they met. He
had said that it was the same with him. She believed him.
Admittedly, she didn't know much about men, but Corbin
didn't seem the type to say things he didn't mean.

She only had to close her eyes to see his features: high
cheekbones, squared jaw, blue eyes and thick dark lashes
and sandy hair. His eyes were like deep pools, clear and fath-
omless, as though they reached to the center of him. The
thin scar that ran from his hairline down through his eyebrow gave him a sinister look until he smiled. She wished
she had asked him about it. Maybe someday she would get
the chance again.

Annabel relived the time they spent in the swing on the

porch, recalling every word and every touch. She had been happy, feeling safe and warm sitting close to him with his arm around her. She could have stayed there forever.

Last night she had been riding on a cloud. Corbin was not only good-looking, he was fun. He had been about to kiss her when Boone returned and spoiled it. If only he hadn't come back when he did, she would have the kiss to remember when she was in St. Louis.

Annabel left her room when she heard the back door slam. Thinking Boone had left the house, she was surprised to find him sitting at the kitchen table.

"Thought maybe ya'd sleep all day." His tone was light, teasing.

"You hoped," she muttered. "You could guard the bedroom door and Jack the window. It would save you some trouble." She poured a cup of coffee and turned to go out onto the porch.

Boone was in front of the door when she reached it. "Sit down, youngun. We got a problem with the Carters."

"Isn't this something new?" She backed away from him, her tone heavy with bitterness. "You shouldn't be admitting family problems to the *youngun*. Remember? She doesn't have sense enough to do anything but sit on a shelf and . . . be dusted off once in a while."

"Don't be funny. This problem concerns ya, and don't be gettin' yore back up. I only do what your pa tells me."

"Horse hockey! That's going to change as soon as he comes back. I'm twenty-one years old, for God's sake! And I'm going out and get a life of my own and if . . . you and Papa don't like it you can . . . you can kiss my foot!"

"Ya'd better not let him hear ya swearin' like a drunk sailor." Boone took the cup from her hand and set it on the table. "Ya ain't too old to get a heavy hand on your butt."

"That's what I mean. You and Papa think I'm nothing more than a child who can't think for herself. I guess it's partly my fault for letting you get away with it."

"I know for a fact that he wants ya to be more and have more than he had. That's one of the reasons he takes the risks he does."

"What do you want to talk about?" she asked bluntly. "I've things to do."

"Like what?"

"Like packing to move away from here, that's what! We finally get to a place that I like and we have to move again. It's the story of my life."

"You've wanted Murphy to get out of the business."

"Yes, I've wanted him to stop bootlegging for a long time and I'm glad he's doing it. But why can't we stay here?"

"Ya wanna stay because of Appleby? Don't take him too seriously. He'll be movin' on. He's a man who's put some miles on his feet."

"What do you mean?"

"Well . . . he's been a lot of places and . . . done things."

"I've been a lot of places, but I've not done much." She picked up her coffee cup again and raised it to her lips.

"Marvin sent Tess over here last night to find out what Appleby was doin' here. She said Marvin's crazy and determined to have ya. Guess he overplayed his hand in town and got set down by Appleby. It didn't set well with him."

"He's a . . . puffed-up jackass. I'd not have him if he was gold-plated!"

"He's crazy mean . . . at times. Tess is scared to death of him."

"Why doesn't she leave?"

"It's easier said than done. They slap her around whenever they take the notion." Boone's black eyes came alive with anger. His tone was more bellicose than usual.

It suddenly dawned on Annabel that Tess could be the reason that Boone had started shaving every few days and why he had been so amiable last night after she arrived. *He had fallen for Tess Carter.* That was why he wanted to buy this place. He wanted to settle down and have a home, a family. While she was trying to adjust to the idea of Boone being romantic with someone, his voice interrupted her thoughts.

"They stole our horses."

"They what?" Annabel jumped to her feet. "The Carters stole our horses?"

"It'll be the cow next."

"They'll not get Mildred! I'll shoot them if they try!"

"Sit down. I want ya to go into town with Jack this morning and report to the sheriff that our horses have been stolen. I'd send the boy by himself, but I don't know how much weight he'd carry. Besides, it'll give ya somethin' to do to get yore mind off Appleby."

"Why don't you go?"

"Because I'm afraid those sneakin' Carters will come over here and burn the place down, that's why."

"You think they would?"

"Damn right they would. They're a mean bunch."

"All but Tess." Annabel watched her friend closely and saw his eyes narrow and his lips press tightly together.

"Jack can take you in the truck. When you get to town, go right to the sheriff. Tell him that someone cut the back fence and took the horses through the woods. I followed until the tracks met up with another bunch of tracks and headed west."

"Shall I tell him it was the Carters?"

"Tell him I trailed them across Carter land. If ya see a

Carter in town, stay with the sheriff and send Jack to get Appleby."

"I thought you didn't like him."

"I didn't say that. I said your pa told me—"

"—to keep him away from me. I've heard that a couple of times now. But you trust him to protect me from Marvin. Is that it?"

"That's it." Boone got to his feet.

Chapter 16

In the light of day, Corbin surveyed the damage to his car and walked down the street to the courthouse square. He turned the corner and followed the walk to the small, squat building that served as the police station and county jail.

Stoney Baker, the sheriff, leaning back in a chair with his booted feet on the top of a scarred desk, looked over the top of his newspaper when Corbin entered.

"Morning, Sheriff."

"Mornin'." Sheriff Baker scanned a few lines in his newspaper before he spoke again. "What's on your mind?"

"I want to report an accident. I ran into a mule last night out on the river road."

"Yeah? Too bad for the mule. Whata ya think about that Scopes fellow over in Tennessee teaching the kids that humans come from monkeys?" Baker snorted and turned the page of his paper. "A kid's got enough foolishness stuffed in his head without thinkin' about his grandpa swingin' from a tree by his tail. I hope they nail that know-it-all's hide to the barn door. It he gets away with this, the next you know they'll be teachin' that God was colored and pigs can fly."

"The court will settle it. Sheriff, there was a man on the mule I hit. He may be injured."

"If he is, he'll come in." The sheriff shook his paper, then spoke from behind it. "I'll swear I thought Clarence Darrow had more sense than to defend that brainless schoolteacher. What's the world comin' to? Him and that other lawyer, William Jennings Bryan, are nothin' but old farts, is what they are. They ort to be sitting in a rockin' chair or out fishin'. It's what I'd do if I had their money."

When Stoney said nothing more, Corbin sat down in a chair and lit a cigarette. He looked around for a place to put the ashes, then flicked them on a floor littered with ashes, cigarette butts and balls of wadded-up paper.

Twenty minutes or more went by. Corbin sat patiently, waiting to be acknowledged again. Stoney Baker turned the pages on his paper and continued to read. From time to time a grunt of approval or disapproval, Corbin couldn't tell which, came from him.

Finally the scuffed boots were removed from the desk and Stoney carefully folded his paper.

"You still here?"

"I was the last time I noticed."

"Pee-waddle! Whatta ya want?"

"I want to report that last night on a road north of town, I came upon a pile of tree limbs blocking the road." Corbin spoke slowly. "Trying to get around them, I went down in a ditch and hit a mule. The rider was knocked off and hit the side of my car. I don't know if the man was badly hurt. The mule certainly was."

"Whatta ya want me to do about it?"

"Investigate it. Isn't that what you normally do when an accident is reported?"

"No. I ain't runnin' around all over the country because some fool let his mule out on the road."

"The *fool* was *on* the mule. The *fool* had set up a road-block thinking I would stop. I didn't."

"Why not?"

"For one reason, the main one, I didn't want my head bashed in."

"Good reason." Stoney got to his feet and stretched his arms up over his head. "I got to get on down to the barbershop. It's about time for the *Post-Dispatch* to come in."

Corbin stood. "Sheriff, don't you think you should go out and have a talk with Marvin Carter?"

"You tellin' me how to do my job?"

"No. I'm suggesting that you talk to the Carters and tell them if they try to waylay me again, I'm coming out of the car shooting."

"Hummm . . . How do you know it was the Carters? Did you see them?"

"No, I didn't see them, but I had a set-to with Marvin Carter in the park last Sunday, and I'm reasonably sure he and his brothers were responsible for the roadblock."

"I heard about that. Fightin' over a woman, was ya?"

"He was forcing the lady to go with him. I intervened." Corbin snarled the words.

"What are you doing here in Henderson?"

"Waiting around for a friend."

"We don't tolerate bums here. You got a job?"

"Not at the present."

"Lookin' for handouts in Henderson is against the law. You could find yourself in my jail."

"I'm not looking for handouts!"

Corbin was having difficulty holding on to his temper and was about to tell the sheriff what he thought of him when, through the dirty windowpane, he saw a truck pull up and Annabel get out. She came toward the sheriff's office with Jack close behind her. He lingered outside while she pushed open the door and came in. Her eyes met Corbin's.

"Ah . . . morning, Mr. Appleby."

"Ma'am." Corbin quickly removed his hat.

Annabel turned to the other man. "Are you the sheriff?"

"Sheriff Stoney Baker."

"How do you do? I'm Annabel Donovan." She extended her hand. "My father and I live north of town on the old Miller place. Sometime yesterday or last night two of our horses were stolen."

Stoney folded his arms across his chest. "They probably wandered off. We ain't had no horse thieves around here since before the war."

"They didn't wander off. The fence was cut, and Mr. Boone, who works for my father, followed the tracks over onto the Carter land next door. The tracks then mixed with those of several horsemen headed west."

"They're long gone by now. My advice is to take the loss and forget it." He went to the door and turned. "Next time, young lady, keep an eye on your livestock if ya want to hold on to 'em." He waited with the door open for them to pass through, then locked it, put the key in his pocket and walked away.

"He isn't going to do anything about our horses. Can you beat that?" Annabel stood with her hands on her hips, looking after the sheriff as he leisurely walked down the street.

"I think I can. Beat that," Corbin added, when she looked at him. "Hello, Jack. Can you stay in town for a while?" he asked both of them.

"Boone didn't say anything about hurryin' back." Jack looked at Annabel for confirmation and she nodded.

"Was there anything else you wanted to do while you're here?" Corbin asked.

"Get ice before we go back. We used it all last night."

"Then what would you like to do for an hour or so? Go for a ride? Sit in the park? Walk along the street and see the sights?" He smiled into Annabel's eyes and she almost forgot they were standing on the sidewalk in front of the sheriff's office.

"Any of those is all right with me."

"You're going to let me decide?"

"Why not? You've only three choices."

"Jack, why don't you park the truck up by the hotel. Annabel and I will walk, and on the way we'll decide what we want to do until dinnertime."

"I'll amble on over to the billiard parlor and watch the fellows play a game of pool. Boone said if I saw a Carter in town, I was to get you, so I think he'd trust you to take care of her for a while. I'll meet you at the hotel about noon."

"We'll have dinner there. All right with you, Annabel?" When she nodded, Corbin reached for her hand and tucked it into the crook of his arm. "I'm beginning to like you more and more, Jack."

"Thanks." Jack grinned and shrugged. "When Evan was courting my sister Julie, Joe and I learned that at times we needed to make ourselves scarce."

"Smart boys. We'll see you at noon."

Walking beside Corbin, her hand held firmly in the crook of his arm, Annabel was unable to keep her foolish heart from fluttering like a caged wild bird. Nothing seemed real. She felt as light as a cloud.

"I've decided to be selfish and keep you all to myself for a while."

"How will you do that?"

"We'll take the car and go south along the river road away from town, find a shady spot to park and smooch."

"Smooch?" She looked up into laughing, teasing eyes. "I haven't heard that word for a long time."

"Then you know what it means?"

"Of course I know what it means, but that doesn't mean that I'll do it."

"I'm bigger than you are."

"I'll tell Boone."

"Don't do that! I promise to behave. That wild man would be after me with a buggy whip."

Corbin pressed her hand tightly to his side, inhaled deeply and let the air escape slowly from his lips. She was every sweet dream he had ever dreamed. Engrossed in each other, they passed the drugstore, the photography shop and the meat market without even knowing it and continued on toward the hotel.

From different directions, two pairs of interested eyes followed Annabel and Corbin down the street and noted that the pair were totally absorbed in each other. The watchers didn't take their eyes off the couple until they were out of sight.

When they reached the car, Corbin opened the door and helped Annabel inside, then hurried around to the other side. Before starting the motor, he turned his head to look at her. Their eyes held. Time seemed to stop. Without the slightest embarrassment, Annabel looked at him until she was sure that his features would be imprinted in her memory forever. A sudden smile formed on his lips and spread to his eyes.

"Last night, I forgot to tell you rules three and four in the *Appleby Rule Book on Courting.*"

"Are they important?"

"Absolutely essential, according to the author. When your sweetheart rides with you in a car, she is to sit close to you as soon as you leave town," he quoted. "That's rule three. Rule four is: Get out of town as quickly as possible." He started the car.

Annabel's delighted laughter filled the car and flowed over him like a warm blanket.

Corbin drove to the edge of town; and as soon as they passed the last house, he reached for her and pulled her over close to him. She came willingly and tucked her shoulder behind his.

"Isn't that better?" he asked with mock seriousness.

They rode in silence, content to be together. When they came to a little-used road, Corbin stopped the car in a spot overlooking the river and turned off the motor.

"We have so much to talk about. I want to know all about you and I want you to know all about me." He turned and placed his arm along the seat behind her.

"There's not much to tell about me." She spoke as if talking around a large lump in her throat.

"I already know you like music. I want to know what you like to eat, to wear, to read, to talk about."

"I'll write it all down . . . someday."

Corbin felt a surge of pleasure. She overwhelmed him, driving all logical thought from his mind.

"What would you do if I tried to kiss you?" he asked suddenly.

"What does the rule book say?" Annabel's heart jumped out of rhythm.

"Rule five says, in so many words, if you like him . . . let him." His voice came on the breath of a whisper.

She turned her face and silently offered her lips. His arm

slipped off the seat and around her shoulders. He kissed her, gently, reverently.

"I don't know if I can stop with one."

"What does the rule book say?" she asked again.

"It says kiss your sweetheart as many times as she'll let you."

"Two or three . . . is all right." She lifted her lips, sweet and softly parted, to his.

The tenderness of his lips on hers bespoke his determination to express gentleness ahead of the desire to crush her to him and drink thirstily from her sweet mouth. When he finished, he cradled her face with his hand.

"I'm crazy about you." His voice was quiet. "I hadn't meant to say it like that, but I mean it with all my heart."

"We don't know each other—"

"I know all I need to know about you. You're sweet and caring and loyal and about the prettiest thing I've ever seen."

"You're pretty too."

"Beauty is in the eye of the beholder, sweetheart." He hugged her to him, his cheek pressed tightly to hers. "'But we loved with a love that was more than love—I and my Annabel Lee—'" he murmured in her ear.

Gradually a strange quiet enveloped both of them. Corbin lifted his head and looked into her eyes, green and shimmering and beautiful. She lifted trembling fingers and traced the scar on his face.

"Where did you get this?"

"During the war. A soldier went out of his mind and cut me while I was trying to subdue him."

"Will you tell me about it sometime?"

"Sometime. I want to share everything with you."

He kissed her lips again, gently. Then he sat back, holding her close to his side.

"I'm rushing you. This feeling I have for you came on awfully fast. I'm going to hate it when your father comes back and takes you away."

"I'll hate it too."

"It will be good for you to get away from here. I'm worried about Marvin Carter. He's prone to do crazy, unpredictable things, and we can expect no help from the sheriff."

"I can see that."

"I went in to report that I'd hit a mule last night. The rider was thrown off and flung against the side of my car. The sheriff wouldn't even talk about it. I can't help but think that he's in somebody's pocket."

"You think it was one of the Carters on the mule?"

"I'm sure of it. Boone told me before I left last night that Marvin had sent his sister over to find out what I was doing there. The roadblock was set up a little past their place. I drove down into the ditch to avoid it and hit someone on a mule."

"Jack and I saw a dead mule beside the road this morning and a bunch of tree limbs pulled to the side."

"I figured someone would have to destroy the mule. I hope the man wasn't badly hurt. That wasn't my intention. I just wanted to get away before I had to shoot someone."

"Do you think it could come to that?"

"I hope not. Miss Carter told Boone that her brother was claiming you as his girl."

"Boone told me that this morning. It's scary. I don't want you to get hurt on my account."

"I suggested to him that you should stay in town until your father gets back. He didn't seem to think much of the idea. He thought I wanted you in town to be near me. Which, by the way, was partly true." He picked up her hand and laced her fingers with his.

"Papa will be back soon. If he got to know you, he would like you."

"He doesn't like me much now, but I'm going to do my best to change his mind." He bent his head and looked into her face. "I'm not going to let you get away from me until we decide if we're right for each other."

"I want that too," she whispered, her eyes on his mouth. She lifted them to his and saw aching tenderness there.

"We must wait, sweetheart, and see if what we feel is just mutual attraction or something more."

"I know. It's happened awfully fast."

He kissed her then, a gentle sweet kiss that would allow her to turn away if she wanted. Her lips moved beneath his. He ended the kiss and lifted his head to look into her glazed eyes. She was so open, so loving and as innocent as a babe.

"We'd better get back to town," he said softly. "Jack is probably at the hotel waiting for us."

To all appearances, the two men who stood on the street corner had met there by chance and were passing the time of day. They were both well-known in town and it was a perfectly normal thing for them to do.

"Looks like that fellow staying at the hotel is hot for Donovan's girl."

"I saw them head out of town. Didn't stay long. They're at the hotel now."

"Reckon she's givin' him pussy?"

"She don't hardly look the type, but you can't tell about women these days."

"What'd ya find out about him?"

"Was Military Police during the war, then a policeman in a small town. Quit a few months ago. Went to Springfield to

visit family. Came here to get the kid that's working at Donovan's."

"It could be that he didn't know the Donovans when he
came here."

"I'm not a believer in chance. I say he knew him or about
him and set it up with the kid."

"I just got word a barge is coming down in a few days
with a hundred barrels."

"And I got word that we'll have help in a day or two."

"I wish he'd let us handle it. Some of his goons get out of
hand. They like bashing heads too much for my liking."

"We should decide what to do about Appleby."

"You want to get rid of him?"

"Humm . . . not yet. Marvin Carter's blowing about what
he's goin' to do to him. He might do it for us. If not, we'll
take care of him when the time comes."

Annabel was so happy she was almost giddy. During the
meal at the hotel she laughed often, teased Jack, and her
eyes, shining green between a hedge of thick lashes, danced
over Corbin's face. Corbin wondered how it was possible
that this slip of a woman, with her sweet smile and soft, musical laughter, could make him feel so damn good.

Nothing was said about the Carters until the three of
them left the hotel dining room and were standing on the
sidewalk in front of the truck.

"Jack, I've been thinking that I should follow you back to
the house. Marvin Carter may know that you and Annabel
came to town and plans to stop you on the way back."

"I hadn't thought of that. You may be right."

"Annabel can ride with me. We'll follow you."

"I figured that's what you had in mind." Jack's freckled
face lit with a grin. "I'm going by the ice dock on the way out

of town to get a chunk of ice. Maybe Annabel will make us some more ice cream."

"Go ahead. We'll be right behind you." Corbin waited until Jack was driving away before he opened the door of his car for Annabel. "What do you think of my fancy maneuvering to get you alone?"

She waited until he came around and got in the car before she answered.

"Is that what you were doing?"

"I was going to follow you home; this way I can have you to myself a little longer. Boone will probably come barreling out and want to send me crackin'. I don't chase easily, and he's going to have to get used to it."

"He's been with my father for a long time and feels responsible for me when Papa's gone."

"As much as his attitude irritates me, I'm glad you've got him to look after you . . . when I'm not around." He reached for her hand and held it tightly.

They followed the truck along the river road, staying well back to avoid the dust it stirred up. When they came to the place where the Carters had set up the roadblock, Corbin slowed the car, and they could see that the dead mule had been dragged away.

Corbin drove slowly up the lane to the house on the hill, his eyes searching for anything out of the ordinary. Jack drove the truck to the back and Corbin followed. Boone came out of the house and walked up to the car before Corbin could get out.

"What're ya doin' here?"

Corbin's eyebrow lifted in an arch. "I'm running for governor. I came to ask for your vote."

"Bullsh—"

"Watch your language," Corbin said quickly and pushed

open the door. Boone backed out of the way and Corbin stepped out. Annabel scooted under the steering wheel and stood beside him.

"Did you know the Carters tried to waylay Corbin last night?" she said.

Boone shrugged. "Must not have worked. He's here."

His low, emotionless voice irritated Corbin, but he tamped down his annoyance for Annabel's sake.

"I hit someone on a mule. It could have been Tess."

Boone's head jerked around. When he saw the smug look on Corbin's face, he snarled. "Gawdamn ya."

"I got your attention, didn't I? The sheriff isn't going to do anything about your horses or about me hitting someone on a mule. You're on your own out here. From what I hear, the Carters are clannish as hell and may pull in their kin. Annabel could be in more danger than you realize. I think you should consider letting her stay in town."

"Her pa will be here tomorrow or the next day. He'll handle the Carters. Seems like yo're the one they want. If I was ya, I'd pull foot and hightail it out of here."

"You're not me." Corbin swallowed his anger. "I'm staying as long as Annabel and Jack are here. You can like it or lump it."

"Thanks for bringing me home, Corbin, and for the meal at the hotel." Annabel's throat was so clogged she could hardly speak. She loved Boone—he had been a second father to her—but she couldn't understand his attitude toward Corbin.

Corbin saw the shimmer of tears in her eyes and reached for her hand. He pulled her to him and put his arm around her, looking over her head to Boone and silently daring him to make an objection.

"I don't know what's put a burr under your tail, but this

girl has come to mean the world to me. I've got to leave her in your care until her father comes back. Then I'll talk to him. Meanwhile, if your stubbornness causes any harm to come to her, I'll come after you and not stop until you're a bloody pulp."

Corbin bent his head and peered into Annabel's face.

"'Bye, honey. I'll be here tomorrow. Meanwhile, stick close to this big bobcat with bristles on his belly. Don't give Carter a chance to get to you. Before I go, I want to speak to Jack." He glared at Boone. "Any objections?"

Annabel stood in the yard beside Boone and watched Corbin walk to the shed where Jack was getting the chunk of ice out of the truck. She dug into her pocket for her handkerchief.

"Why don't you like him and accept his help? Why are you so mean about . . . things?"

"Ah . . . law! I do like him. I just can't let things get out of hand while Murphy's gone. But it looks like I done failed in that."

"I like him. Hear? I may even *love* him. What do you think of that?"

"I'm thinkin' it's between ya and Murphy."

"You're wrong, Boone. It's between me and Corbin."

"Yore pa'll be home—"

"What in the world—"

Boone followed Annabel's gaze to see Tess running out of the woods toward them. She was calling to him. A feeling of dread washed over him.

Chapter 17

Tess SAT IN THE CHAIR AND DOZED. She had been up all night with Leroy. Bud had sat with her part of the time. At midmorning, he and Marvin had left the house and hadn't returned for the noon meal. The whimpers and groans that came from Leroy were like the sounds made by a small wounded animal. Tess went to the cot and bent over him. He looked up at her with one eye. She feared he might not ever see out of the other again.

"Do you want something, Leroy?" She leaned closer when she saw that he wanted to say something.

"I . . . hurt . . . so bad." He could barely move his lips.

"I know you do and I wish I could help you. I really do." She stroked the hand lying at his side.

His face was so raw and swollen he hardly looked human. It was a wonder to Tess that he could speak at all. She had thought his jaw was broken. During the night and this morning, she had squeezed water into his mouth from a cloth.

"Doc-tor."

"I begged Marvin to let me go ask Mr. Boone to come

take you in his car, but he won't let me. I'm sorry, Leroy. I did the best I could."

Tess saw a tear slide from the corner of his eye, and her soft heart filled with pity for the little boy she remembered. He had been cuffed and scorned by Marvin and Calvin because he was small for his age. He had tried to copy Marvin, thinking to win the respect of the family, and he had turned into a resentful, defiant, smartmouthed kid who gave the elder Carters even more of an excuse to browbeat and belittle him at every opportunity.

"I . . . hurt all over."

"I'll ask Marvin again when he comes in. I'm sure Mr. Boone would take you to the doctor in his car."

Leroy closed his eye. "Marvin . . . don't care 'bout . . . me. Nobody . . . does."

"I care about you, Leroy."

"Am . . . I goin' to die?" His eye opened. It was blurred with tears.

"I don't think so. But I'm not a doctor."

"I'm sorry . . . for bein' mean to ya."

"It's all right. You were doin' what Marvin expected you to do."

"I . . . don't want to die—"

"Oh, Leroy . . ." Tears filled Tess's eyes and ran down her cheeks.

"I wish . . . I wish . . . I'd not gone—"

"You didn't have a choice."

Marvin had been in a frenzied state last night, drunk and fiercely jealous of Corbin Appleby. He had forced Bud and Leroy to go with him to set up a roadblock. He had bragged that he would beat Corbin senseless, then drag him back to the Donovans' behind his car. It hadn't worked out as he'd planned, and he blamed Leroy and Bud.

"Marvin is mean to all of us," Tess whispered angrily. "We shouldn't have to be afraid all the time. Maybe when you're better we can go off someplace—"

"No. I'll . . . die here."

"You won't, if I can help it!" From somewhere came a surge of courage Tess didn't know she had. "I'm going to get Mr. Boone. He'll take you to the doctor. You'll be by yourself for a little bit. I hate leaving you . . . but I'll have to."

She leaned down and kissed the top of his head, something she had not dared to do since he was a little boy.

"Sis . . . hurry—"

Tess ran out the door, fear giving wings to her feet. She didn't care if Marvin beat her, and she was sure he would. She had to get to Boone and get Leroy out of the house before Marvin returned. She couldn't let Leroy lie there and suffer, maybe die, without trying to help him. She ran through the woods as if the devil were after her. When she came out into the clearing, she saw Boone and Annabel standing beside Corbin Appleby's car.

"Boone, Boone," she called.

Boone ran to her. "What's wrong?"

She was panting and could hardly get her breath to speak. "Leroy is hurt . . . bad. Please take him to the doctor. Please. Marvin wouldn't take him and wouldn't let me ask you to. I had to . . . had to—"

"Does Marvin know yo're here?"

"No. He wouldn't let me come this morning. He and Bud have gone off somewhere. Marvin doesn't care about Leroy. I'm afraid he'll die."

Corbin's long strides took him to where Tess stood in the shelter of Boone's arms.

"Was Leroy on the mule I hit last night?"

"Yes. His face is all busted up and his ear . . . is almost off."

"I'll take him to the doctor. I'm the one who hit him."

"Ya'd better let me do it. Marvin would go crazy if he came home and found ya there. It'll be bad enough if he sees me, but I think I can convince him to be reasonable."

"Please hurry." Tess was crying.

"Take my car. It'll ride easier than the truck. Do you need me to help get him in the car?"

"No. Tess and I can handle him. Come on, Tess."

"Is there anything I can do?" Annabel asked.

"Watch out for Marvin," Tess muttered and got into the car.

"Stay close to Annabel," Boone said as he passed Corbin. Then, "Sheesh! It's like askin' the fox to guard the hen-house."

"Damn you, Boone—"

"I don't know when I'll be back."

"Next month would be fine with me. There's a gun under the seat, if you should need it."

"Thanks. There's a rifle and a shotgun in the barn and a pistol in the house."

Corbin, Jack and Annabel watched the car, a dust cloud trailing, go down the lane and wondered what kind of reception Boone would get at the Carters'.

"Which one is Leroy?" Corbin asked.

Jack answered, "He's the young one. Boone said he was younger than me. Small, mouthy, mean as a cornered pole-cat."

"God, I hate it that I hit the kid. I wouldn't have cared a bit if it had been Marvin."

*   *   *

Boone drove as fast as possible down the rutted road and turned up the path to the Carter homestead when they reached it. Tess sat on the edge of the seat, her hands on the dashboard in front of her. Her eyes scanned the yard for signs that Marvin and Bud had returned. She saw none, and when Boone stopped the car beside the back door, she ran into the house ahead of him.

"I'm back, Leroy. Mr. Boone is going to take you to the doctor."

"I . . . thought ya wasn't comin' back—"

"I hurried. He brought me back in the car."

He saw Boone and said, "I can't . . . get up."

Boone had seen a lot of things, but never had he seen such a pitiful sight. Leroy wore only a pair of drawers. Bruises covered his body, his skinny legs and his feet.

"Ya don't have to, boy. I'll carry you. Tess, get a sheet or something to cover him."

Boone waited until Tess was holding open the door before he scooped Leroy up in his arms. The boy's scream of pain shook him. He gritted his teeth, cradled Leroy against him as gently as he could and hurried through the door to the car. Tess ran to open the door and crawled inside. Boone laid Leroy on the backseat, his head in his sister's lap. He covered him with the sheet.

As soon as they were settled, Boone started the car. He was anxious to be away. At that moment he believed he would take the gun from beneath the seat and shoot Marvin Carter if he came and attempted to stop him from taking the boy to the doctor.

On the way to town, Boone concentrated on avoiding the rough spots in the road and tried to close his ears to the pitiful whimpers at what must be excruciating pain coming from the backseat. After what seemed forever to Boone, they reached Henderson. He drove down Main Street, turned after he passed the mercantile and stopped at a big white house on the corner. He had seen the sign—JOHN H. PERKINS, M.D.—on a previous trip to town.

"Sit tight, Tess. I'll see if the doctor's in."

Boone hurried up the walk and around to the office door. As he entered the small reception area, a man who looked more like a lumberjack than a doctor came through another door, wiping his hands on a towel. He was as tall as Boone and looked to be strong as an ox.

"You the doc?" Boone asked.

"Yes. What can I do for you?"

"I've got a boy in the car. His face is smashed up and he's hurtin' a-plenty."

The doctor threw down the towel. "Bring him in."

"He's in bad shape, Doc. I'll have to carry him."

"I'll be ready for him. Marlys," he called. "Get ready for a patient."

A slim blond woman was waiting at the door for Boone when he carried Leroy up the walk from the car.

"Go on through to the other room," she said.

The doctor was waiting and helped Boone ease the boy down onto an examination table. Boone stepped back and removed his cap. The doctor looked closely at Leroy's face, lifted his eyelid and gently turned his head first one way and then the other. Leroy made small grunting sounds. His one eye followed the doctor's movements. If the doctor was shocked by the extent of the injuries, he didn't show it.

"When did this happen?"

"Last night. A car hit the mule he was on."

"Last night? Thunderation!" The doctor swore under his breath, then turned to the woman getting supplies out of a cabinet. "Get anesthesia ready, Marlys."

Boone motioned for the doctor to step away from the table and follow him to the door.

"Doc, my name's Boone. The boy is Leroy Carter. I live on the place north of the Carters'. The boy's brother is Marvin Carter. You've probably heard of him. He's a mean, unreasonable son-of-a-bitch. That's his sister out there. Marvin wouldn't let her get help for the boy last night or this morning. She came for me as soon as Marvin left the house. You might have trouble with him when he finds out I brought the boy here."

"Let him come," the doctor said confidently.

"Marvin had the kid out helpin' set up a roadblock so they could waylay a feller. Man refused to stop and hit the mule the kid was on."

"A man who'd not get help for a kid hurt that bad isn't worth a bucket of spit. The boy's ear has got to be sewed on. I doubt he'll hear out of it again. I'm not sure about the eye. I'll do what I can for him, then worry about the Carters."

"He might call in his kinfolk. I hear the Carters are a clannish bunch."

"Let him. I've got a few friends myself, and some of them are tough as shoe leather."

"Ya'll not be alone, Doc. I've been in a few brawls and got pretty good at bustin' heads."

"Stay with the sister. My wife is a nurse. She'll help me." Dr. Perkins went back in the room and closed the door.

Tess, looking like a small frightened child, sat with her hands tightly clasped together. Her hair, in a thick blond braid, lay over her shoulder. When she saw Boone, she smoothed the sides of her hair back from her face with her hands. She had removed her bloody apron and wadded it in a ball. Boone sat down beside her.

"What did he say about Leroy?"

"He said that he was going to sew his ear on. The doctor's wife is a nurse and will help him. The anesthetic will put him to sleep so that he'll not feel anything."

"I'm glad of that. Did you tell him that . . . Marvin might come and make a fuss?"

"I told him. Don't worry. I'm thinkin' the doc can handle himself. His only concern now is for Leroy. He'll fix him up the best he can and give him somethin' to ease the pain."

"I couldn't stand it, Boone. Leroy has swaggered after Marvin since he was little-bitty, trying so hard to be like him. And Marvin didn't care that he'd got hurt. He ranted about him and Bud not stopping Mr. Appleby's car."

"It's a good thing for Marvin they didn't stop the car. Appleby would have come out shooting, and one or all of them could be dead." Boone took her hand. "Marvin will take out his anger on you. I don't want you to go back there."

"I've got to go back and take care of Leroy. Bud would do it, but he won't stand up to Marvin."

Boone put his fingers under her chin and turned her face toward him.

"He hit you, didn't he?"

"He slapped me this morning because I wanted to come get you. He said that if Leroy died, it was Mr. Donovan's fault because he wrecked his car."

"That makes a hell of a lot of sense." Boone held her hand in both of his. "Tess, honey, I don't want you to go back there," he repeated. "If Marvin lifts a hand to you again, I might . . . kill him."

"The Carters will find me wherever I go. They're scattered all over the Missouri hills."

"I've got to stay here until Murphy gets back. When he does, we'll leave here and go far away."

"I can't leave Leroy while he's helpless." The emptiness in

her voice brought an unexpected ache to Boone's heart. "He said that he's sorry for the way he treated me."

"It may not be too late to change him."

"What do you mean?"

"Folks change, but they have to want to."

"I think he and Bud finally saw Marvin for what he really is. But that doesn't mean they'll do anything about it. They know nothing but to live the way they've always lived, and they're scared of Marvin; they'll do what he tells them to do."

"But you know there are better ways?"

"Yes. I lived with my mother's sister, my aunt Cora, for a while and went to school. Then—"

"Then . . . what—"

He heard Tess gasp.

"What is it? Honey—" He pulled down the hand she had clapped on her mouth.

"I just thought about something. I don't have money to pay the doctor, and Marvin . . . won't pay him."

"Lord, ya scared me. If Marvin won't pay him, I will. Don't worry about it."

"I can't let you do that. It was good of you to bring us here and good of Mr. Appleby to lend his car after what Marvin tried to do. He'll be madder than ever at Mr. Appleby and now you."

"Marvin is a bully, honey. How many men my size has he come up against?"

"You don't understand him. He wouldn't go up against you man to man. He says that's stupid. He'd sneak and do something."

"Yo're not to worry about it, hear?"

Too tense to talk, they sat quietly, waiting for the door to the surgery to open. When it did, the nurse came out. They both stood.

"The doctor will be out soon." She smiled reassuringly. "Meanwhile, I need to know a few things, like name and age and so on."

"Ma'am, this is Tess Carter, the boy's sister."

"How do you do? Please take a chair." The nurse sat down behind a desk and pulled out a blank chart. "What is the patient's full name?"

"Leroy Carter."

"Age?"

"Eighteen."

"Do you know if he's had the smallpox vaccination? His arms are so bruised the doctor couldn't find a scar."

"I'm sure he hasn't. Our folks didn't believe much in doctoring."

"They were not alone." The nurse smiled. "Since we came here, we've discovered many families from the surrounding hills who have never been to a doctor." She continued to write, then looked up again. "Are you the next of kin?"

"One of them. Our parents are dead."

The doctor came into the room, closing the door behind him. He stood behind his wife and read what she had written. His glance shifted to the delicate features of the small woman standing beside Boone. She didn't fit at all with what he had heard about the Carters. The man with her had alert black eyes that missed nothing. His hand was on her back in a proprietary kind of way that suggested the two were more than just friends.

"Ma'am, your brother had injuries other than those to his face and ear. His nose was broken, and a cheekbone. I don't know yet if he has lost the vision in one eye. His ribs are cracked. Thank God they were not broken or one of them would have punctured his lungs when Boone carried him in here. He has a broken collarbone and several broken bones in his left hand."

"Is he . . . going to die?"

"He has lost a lot of blood, and there is the danger of infection," the doctor said, avoiding answering her question. "We have two rooms here we use for patients. One of them is empty. We'll keep him here for a while. He's resting now. When he wakes up, we'll give him some nourishment through a straw."

He wasn't aware that the woman was crying until he saw the tears sliding down her cheeks. She was holding her head erect and had not made a sound. Proud as a game rooster, he thought.

"I can't pay cash money," she said, refusing to allow the tears to thicken her voice. "But I will find a way to pay you."

"Get us a bill, Doc. We'll pay." Boone's hand moved up to Tess's shoulder.

"We can talk about that at a later time. Do you want to see him before you go? He's sleeping."

Without waiting for an answer, Dr. Perkins opened the door and stood back. Boone followed Tess into the room. Leroy had a bandage wrapped around his head covering his ear and his damaged eye. His rib cage was bound from beneath his armpits to his navel. More wrap encased his broken hand.

Tess stood beside her brother for a moment, touched his hand, then turned to the doctor.

"Thank you."

"Doc . . ." Boone waited until she left the room before he spoke. "Are you sure ya can handle what might come from Marvin Carter? I could stay—"

"It isn't necessary. I've got a shotgun and two stout men

who would like nothing more than to tie into that man after they see the boy."

"Will the sheriff help out?"

Dr. Perkins laughed. "As an officer of the law, Stoney Baker is as useless as teats on a boar."

"Why in hell did folks elect him?"

"Politics. Kaiser Bill could be elected if no one ran against him."

"It's a sorry state of affairs, if ya ask me." Boone went to the door. "Thank ya, Doc."

"Come back tomorrow. We'll know by then if we got to him before an infection set in."

Chapter 18

As soon as his car disappeared down the road trailing a cloud of dust, Corbin began to plan on what to do if Marvin Carter mustered some of his relatives and came looking for Tess and his brother after discovering them missing.

"Jack, get the shotgun and the rifle out of the barn. Annabel, do you know how to handle the pistol?"

"Boone taught me."

"Good. Get it and check to be sure it's loaded."

"Do you think we'll need guns?"

"I don't know. But I want to be prepared. When Marvin finds Tess and his brother gone, he's going to guess that she had help from here. If he comes looking for them, it'll not be a friendly visit."

Corbin sat on the edge of the porch, checked both barrels of the shotgun and put several extra shells in his pocket. He looked over the rifle. The firearms were in good condition; he expected them to be, considering how well Boone cared for his weapons while they were in the cabin in the hills.

"Do you know how to handle this?" he asked Jack.

"I've been hunting since I was knee-high to a short frog."

"Got extra shells?"

"In my pocket."

"Is there a place in the barn where you'll be out of sight and still have a good view of the yard?"

"The hayloft."

"You'll be my backup. It may be necessary for you to show yourself so they'll know I'm not here alone. If he comes, he'll have some of his kinfolk with him."

"If I see anything, I'll signal." Jack put two fingers in his mouth and whistled. "One if he's alone. Two or three depending on how many he has with him." He flung the sling of the rifle over his shoulder and went to the pump for a drink of water before disappearing into the barn.

Corbin walked around the house several times during the afternoon. Seeing the front door standing open, he told Annabel to shut and lock it. He checked to make sure that there were no spots in the approach to the house that Jack couldn't see from the hayloft. Satisfied he had covered most, if not all, possibilities of surprise, he went back and sat down on the back porch.

Days were long this time of year. Several hours had passed when he looked toward the west and saw the sun disappearing beyond the horizon. A raucous mass of gulls flew over on their way to the river to spend the night. Then a formation of ducks, high in the sky, passed overhead. Corbin watched a hawk soaring on the prowl, and the thought struck him that this house on the hill was a very pleasant location for a home. The only drawback was that it was surrounded by Carters.

The events of the entire day seemed unreal to Annabel. She couldn't imagine that they were preparing to defend themselves with *guns*. Corbin knew what he was doing. He must believe they were in a dangerous situation to make such deadly preparations.

The last rays of sunlight came through the kitchen door and bounced off the wall. She sat on a chair at the table, folded her hands, put her chin on them and stared at the light playing on the wall and kitchen floor.

Papa, come home. Corbin shouldn't have to fight our battles with only a boy to help him. None of this would be happening if you hadn't lost your temper and pushed Marvin Carter's car off the road.

Corbin came to the door and saw her sitting at the table, her shoulders slumped dejectedly. He called to her.

"Annabel? Are you worried?"

"A little . . . about Boone." She arranged a smile on her face so he wouldn't know how really worried she was about Boone, Tess, all of them. "Did you notice how concerned he was for Tess? I think he's in love with her. In all the years I've known Boone I've never heard him mention a woman or seen him give one a second look."

"It happens that way sometimes. A man sees a woman and knows right away that she's the one for him."

"I hope his . . . wanting to be with her doesn't cause him to get crippled up or . . . killed." *And you, my love. Being here with me could get you killed. I couldn't live with that.*

"Your father must think he's a pretty tough nut to crack or he'd not left you here with him."

"Boone and Spinner may be the only two people in the world besides me that Papa trusts. I'm very fond of Boone. He was with us when Mama died. I've spent more time with him and Spinner these past few years than I have with my father."

"From what I've seen of Boone, he's a levelheaded, capable man who has been in tight spots before and knows how to take care of himself."

"Why do you and Boone snap at each other?" she asked suddenly.

He answered her frankly. "It irritates me the way he tries to keep me away from you. I like the big galoot, but I don't want him to know it."

"He said he liked you, but Papa told him . . . to look out for me."

"Your papa told him to keep *me* away from *you*. I won't stay away until *you* tell me to." His face slowly broke into a grin like that of a young boy, and it was endearing.

"I don't want you to stay away," she replied softly.

"It's what I hoped you'd say." He opened the screen door and reached for her hand. "Why don't you come out and sit on the porch with me?"

"I need to feed my chickens."

She went out onto the porch with a small bucket and dipped it into a feed sack. She really needed to go to the privy. She hadn't gone since she left the house this morning to go to town with Jack. As soon as she scattered the grain, she would slip into the outhouse.

Before she could step down off the porch, Corbin said, "I think we should get a few things out of the way before it gets too late." Looking off toward the woods, he continued, "Why don't you feed your chickens and go to the outhouse? I'll go when you come back." He spoke as matter-of-factly as if he were talking about the weather.

Unable to utter a word, Annabel left the porch. She scattered the feed inside the fenced area for the chickens, then hurried to the small building next to the chicken house. *Oh, Lord! Had he read her mind or was it written on her face how badly she needed to go to the privy?*

Corbin watched her go, the skirt of her dress dancing around her bare legs. The truth was he was anxious for relief himself and hadn't wanted to leave his lookout position to make the trip to the outhouse. He was sure that she was embarrassed by his suggestion, but in a situation like this there was no help for it.

The more time he spent with Annabel Lee Donovan, the more certain he was that she was the woman with whom he wanted to spend his life. Her ready smile and quick wit were a constant source of pleasure for him. *But we loved with a love that was more than love—* The phrase played over and over in his mind.

His fascination with Annabel, however, had not made him forget his responsibility to find out as much as he could about the criminal element in Henderson for Marshal Sanford. The marshal had information that a wing of the operation set up by George Remus, titan of the bootleggers in Chicago, was in the area.

Remus, having been trained as a pharmacist before getting his law degree, had cashed in on his early learning by buying up dozens of distilleries in Missouri, as well as in Ohio and Kentucky, that the law had allowed to remain in business for the purpose of making medicinal alcohol. If his *stolen* pure booze later ended up in speakeasies, it was not the fault of George Remus.

He had taken control of the flow of alcohol along the Mississippi River and would tolerate no competition. The federal marshals feared his criminal dynasty was spreading to Kansas City and points west.

Corbin felt the flat leather envelope that lay next to his skin. In it were his observations of Murphy Donovan and four other men in town. His hope was that Annabel's father had been involved in selling only cases or kegs of illegal booze to saloons and speakeasies and not in the wholesale business where the big money was to be found and murder was almost commonplace.

If Murphy was selling out to Remus, he was getting out at a good time and Corbin was glad for Annabel. It was a relief to him to know that after he gave the information to Sanford he would be through with it.

Annabel stopped by the pump on her way back from the outhouse and drank a dipperful of water, delaying the time she had to face Corbin with him knowing where she had just come from. *Heavens!* she scolded herself. *Even people in love have to do that sometimes.*

As soon as she returned to the porch and sat down, Corbin went to the small building. Annabel was careful to keep her eyes away as he entered the privy. She scanned the edge of the woods, her face devoid of expression. Inside she trembled.

Corbin returned. He was either gone a mere few minutes or her mind was so busy she had lost track of time. He took her hand and pulled her to her feet.

"Are you afraid I can't take care of you, honey?"

"It isn't that."

"If they come over, I want you to go inside the house and not show yourself. Will you do that?"

"I'll do whatever you say," she answered in a shaky voice. "But Papa should be here, or Boone and Spinner. It's not your—"

His hands gripped her shoulders and he looked down into her upturned face. "Don't say it isn't my place to be here with you. Haven't I made my feelings clear enough?" he asked quietly.

"Yes," she whispered, and her forehead dropped to rest against his shoulder. "I just don't want you to get hurt."

"Sweetheart, I—"

Three short whistles came from the hayloft. Corbin's head jerked up. Three riders had come out of the woods and were riding toward the house.

"Inside, honey. Stay there."

Annabel ducked into the house. Corbin picked up the shotgun, walked out into the yard and stopped in front of the barn. Two of the riders were on horses, the third on a big gray mule. All three rode bareback and stopped a few dozen feet from Corbin.

Marvin Carter's eyes were hate-filled, his nostrils tight with anger. Corbin's eyes flicked to the other two men. One was a kid, sixteen or less; the other was a man Marvin's age who looked a lot like him.

"You movin' in here?" Marvin's face was red and bloated. A stubble of beard covered his cheeks.

"What's it to you if I do?"

"Ya'll see what's it to me. Ya run Leroy down last night. Killed the mule he was on. Ya hurt him bad. We Carters ain't lettin' that stand."

"How bad is he?"

"That ain't none of yore business."

"You set up the roadblock to stop me. I'd a been a fool to stop and let you jump me. Too bad it wasn't you on that mule."

"We was pullin' the limbs off the road."

"Liar!" Corbin met the man's angry gaze without a flicker of the emotion that tensed every nerve inside him.

"We come for Tess and Leroy."

"They're not here."

"I'll see for myself." Agile as a cat, Marvin slipped from the horse and started for the house.

"Stay where you are!" Corbin's voice was as sharp as the

crack of a rifle. He jacked a shell into the chamber of the shotgun.

Marvin turned and laughed nastily. "Ya takin' on all of us?"

"Take a look in the hayloft. The fellow up there with the rifle can shoot the pimple off a jaybird's ass. With both barrels of this shotgun I can cut the legs out from under two horses and a mule."

"He ain't goin' to shoot, Calvin. I'm gettin' Leroy and Tessie." Marvin swaggered toward the house.

"Stop right there." Annabel appeared on the porch, walked out into the yard, aimed the pistol at Marvin and pulled the trigger. The bullet nicked the toe of his boot.

He jumped back and yelled. "Ya . . . gawddamn . . . bitch!" The curse burst from his lips. "I'll beat hell outta ya!" He took a step toward her, his face red, his jaws shaking, his fists knotted.

"The next one will shatter your kneecap. Get off this place and stay off." Holding the gun on Marvin, she came to stand beside Corbin.

"Good shooting, honey. Hold the shotgun." Corbin shoved it in her hand, took two steps, grabbed Marvin and spun him around.

With a whining cry of fury, Marvin went for Corbin with both arms flailing, but he never laid a hand on him. Corbin's left fist chipped him on the chin with a crack like that of a blacksnake whip. Marvin fell to the ground, and he lay there shaking his head.

"That was for what you called the lady. Now get up and get the hell out of here." Corbin's cold eyes met those of the man on the horse. "You dealing in?"

"Not . . . with a rifle on me. A man's got a right to look for his kin."

"They're not here."

"But ya know where they are."

"If I did, I'd not tell a piece of manure like that." Corbin jerked his head to where Marvin was trying to get off the ground.

"I ain't a forgettin' this," Marvin snarled his favorite threat, got to his feet and reached for his horse's reins.

"That's up to you. Anytime you've got the guts to meet me man to man, I'll be glad to accommodate you." He took the shotgun from Annabel's hand.

"You stole our horses and we want them back." Annabel's usually smiling face was set in lines of resentment. Anger burned in her eyes. Although her hand was steady on the gun she held pointed at Marvin's chest, her heart was racing like a runaway train.

"I don't have 'em."

"Some of your kin do." Her eyes shifted to the other man on the horse. He was grinning at her.

"I'm Calvin, ma'am. Brother to this un. I do admire a woman with spunk."

"I've reported you to the sheriff."

Calvin laughed. "Old Stoney ain't goin' to do nothin' 'bout nothin'. Where ya think he gets his booze?"

"I'll report you to the federal marshals. We know you've got a still and where it is."

"Things happen to folks who do that. Like grass fires that burn up barns and . . . houses, like bein' taken for a deer—"

"Get off our land." Annabel made a jabbing motion with the gun.

Marvin grabbed a handful of the horse's mane and sprang up on its back. He glared at Corbin. His fury was about to push him beyond the bounds.

"I'll be back to get my girl."

"You . . . you filthy hog!" Annabel's head was erect and she looked him in the eye. "You're rotten through and through. I wouldn't walk on you if you were dirt!"

"I'll learn ya to keep yore trap shut." He would have said more, but he glanced at the man holding the shotgun. His eyes were like two frozen ponds.

"If you even speak to her, you'll get a load of buckshot." A burst of anger exploded in Corbin and his finger tightened on the trigger.

Everything in Marvin rebelled against backing down, but self-preservation won over pride. Marvin turned his horse to leave. The others followed.

A shot came from the hayloft and plowed into the ground inches from the mule's hind legs, sending dirt clods spraying up onto its belly. The frightened animal lowered its head and kicked out, throwing the rider to the ground.

By the time he'd gotten to his feet, Calvin had grabbed the mule's reins and had him under control. Thinking that Annabel or Corbin had fired the shot, the boy shook his fists at them, then climbed back upon the mule.

Not a word was said until the trio disappeared in the woods. Then Corbin reached over and took the pistol from Annabel's hand.

"Why didn't you tell me you could shoot like that?"

She was trembling and started to laugh. She couldn't seem to stop. Holding on to Corbin's arm, she hid her face against him until the giggles subsided.

"I wasn't . . . aiming at anything. I was nervous and the gun went off. I was more surprised than Marvin."

"Good Lord! I'm glad I didn't know that. You can sure run a bluff. I was ready to put down the shotgun and let you take over. On second thought . . . why didn't you stay in the house like I told you to?"

"There were three of them. I figured there should be three of us."

Jack came out of the barn, a smoldering look of anger on his face.

"That kid had on my shirt. He's one of them who stole my glove."

"I suppose your gun just went off too."

"No, by damn. The second shot woulda took off his hat or his head if the mule hadn't bucked him off."

Corbin shook his head. "You two are about as helpless as a couple of rattlesnakes," he said, but he was smiling.

"What will they do to Boone and Tess? They should be back by now."

"It's out of our hands, honey. All we can do is wait and hope for the best."

It was the twilight time of day. Boone and Tess sat in the car in front of the doctor's house.

"The doctor didn't say that he'd be all right." Tess's large amber eyes watched Boone's face anxiously.

"He couldn't say that. He has to wait and see if infection sets in. If it does, Leroy will be right there where the doctor can treat him."

"What if Marvin and Calvin and some of the others come to get him—"

"The doctor won't let them take him."

Tess snorted with disgust. "They'd not ask."

"He said they'd not take him. Honey, the doc's no pushover. I imagine he's seen plenty of rough-and-tumble times." Boone started the car and drove slowly along the streets of Henderson. "I wish we didn't have to go back, but first we're going to have a few minutes alone together."

He drove down to the end of the park and stopped the

car. Turning to her, he opened his arms. Without hesitation, she went into them. Her arms moved up to encircle his neck. He groaned her name, then covered her lips with his and left them there while he whispered, "Sweet, sweet girl—"

"What would I have done without you?" She clutched him tightly, her hands biting into the solid flesh of his back.

The feel of his strong body, the stroking of his hands, the warm moistness of his breath and the love spilling from her heart left no room in her mind for anything but him. With her fingers tangled in his black hair, she held his head to her, never wanting to leave him.

For long moments there were no words between them, only the sounds of labored breathing and moaning kisses.

"Tess, sweetheart." Holding her tightly, he spoke in her ear when finally he could talk. "I can't take ya back there. Let me take ya to Annabel. Murphy will be back tomorrow or the next day. He'll look after his daughter and we'll go where the Carters can't find ya."

"I'll remember forever that you offered to do this, but I can't let you—"

"Yo're the most important thin' in the world to me, darlin'. I wasn't goin' to St. Louis with the Donovans. I want a home, with ya as the mother of my kids. I'll take care of ya. I swear it."

"There's so many of them—"

"Are they all like yore brothers?"

"Some of the Carters south of Henderson are different. They don't have much to do with the Carters around here."

"If I take ya back to Marvin and he hurts ya, I'll kill him and end up gettin' hung or in the pen for life."

"But they'll know I'm there and will come to get me. They set a whole woods on fire once 'cause a man stole a barrel of their whiskey. Burned him out. I don't know what happened to him or his family."

"Jack, and prob'ly Appleby, will be there, and Murphy will be back tomorrow or the next day. If he isn't back, I know a place where you and Annabel will be safe."

"What . . . will she think?"

"She'll think it was the smart thin' to do. She likes ya. I hope that ya like her. I think the world of her, not as my sweetheart, but as a kid I've watched grow up into a nice young lady."

"You're awfully smart, Boone. You could have any woman you want. Why are you bothering with me?"

Boone laughed, hugged her, then held her off so he could look into her face.

"Have ya looked at yoreself in the mirror lately? Yo're all gold from head to foot: hair, eyes, skin. Yo're pretty as a gold nugget, not that I've seen many. 'Sides that, ya've learned how to live with what ya have to put up with. Ya've got spunk too. It took spunk to come to me today. I like it that yo're concerned for your brother even though he's been mean to ya. Ya can see what made him what he is. I could tell ya more—"

"I like hearing it even if it's not all true."

"It's true, sweetheart. Every dadgum bit of it. Now can I ask why yo're botherin' with an ugly old river rat like me?"

"You're not ugly! Not old!" She caressed his cheeks with her fingertips. "I never knew that there was a man like you. I knew it that first day when I ran and fell and you didn't pounce on me like I expected. I was embarrassed for you to see me . . . and the way Leroy acted—"

"Sweet girl . . ." Boone could feel her heart pounding against his.

"If I don't go back now . . . I can never go back," she

whispered. "Before I go with you, I have to tell you about me. You may not . . . want me."

"If ya want to tell me, do it and get it off your chest. Nothin' ya say will make a difference."

Chapter 19

T ESS BEGAN TO TALK, realizing that what she had to tell him would surely mean the death of the sweetest interlude in her life. But she couldn't take the chance that he would find out later on and hate her.

"According to the Carter family I have to work and pay for being . . . a slut. That's what they call me." Her voice dwindled until Boone could hardly hear it, then it strengthened with her resolve to tell all. "My mother sent me to live with her sister, my aunt Cora, in St. Charles when I was twelve. She was afraid some of the Carters would . . . ah . . . violate me. I loved it at Aunt Cora's. They lived in a nice house and she and Uncle Don got along well together: laughing and talking and sometimes hugging each other. It was different from the way my family treated one another. I lived there until I finished high school.

"Aunt Cora wanted me to learn to be a telephone operator. Uncle Don got me a job in a little town west of St. Charles and a room in a rooming house for ladies. I'd been there a month or two when Cousin Willard came to call. He's the son of one of Papa's cousins. His wife had died and he was on the prowl looking for another one. He had a son not much younger than me. To make it short, he raped me." Tess's voice quavered. "I was afraid to tell Aunt Cora and . . . he did it again."

"Ah . . . honey, ya don't have to talk about it."

"I want to. I have to. When I learned I was in the family way, I had to tell Aunt Cora. By then Cousin Willard had found a widow lady he wanted to marry. Aunt Cora sent me home with a letter telling what Cousin Willard had done, thinkin' my pa and my brothers would punish him. Mama had died and Papa, after talking to Cousin Willard, believed that I lied when I said it was him. He was convinced that I'd become a whore and had been with many men. He beat me . . . bad. I lost the baby. Papa said I was to stay on the place and work for the rest of my life to pay for the shame I brought down on him and the boys. After Papa died, Marvin took over. I've been there six . . . almost seven years and today is only the third or fourth time I've been to town."

Boone's mind was almost blotted by a heavy cloud of rage at how she had been treated by her own kin. The muscles along his jaws rounded into hard knots. He took a long, deep breath to steady himself.

"The filthy, rotten-minded sons-a-bitches!" His big hand cupped her head and held it to him. "Ya'll not go back there. Hear me? Someday I'll meet that low-life bastard and nail his balls to a stump!"

"Can't you see why I can't go with you? They won't rest until they get me back."

"Sweet girl . . . you have to!" His voice was loud in the car. "If there was a way for me to wed ya right now, we'd do it. Then they'd answer to me."

"You still . . . want me after—"

His lips cut off her words. His kiss was hard and quick.

"I want ya more than I've ever wanted anythin'. I'm mad

as hell at what happened to you, but, good Lord, it makes no difference in how I feel about you. Someday, I promise you, I will find Willard, and when I get through with him, he'll know he's paid for what he did to ya."

"Marvin and the Carters all kowtow to him. They think he's grand . . . because he has money."

"That'll do him no good. Ya'll marry me, won't ya, sweet girl?"

"I can't believe ya want me, but if ya do, I'd be so proud to marry you."

"I'm not a ruttin' moose like Willard, sweetheart. Ya don't have to be afraid that I'll force ya to be a wife to me. Ya'll never have to be with me in any way ya don't want."

She kissed his face time and again. Having someone who cared about her was so new, so wonderful that she could scarcely catch her breath for the excitement that beat through her.

"Honey," Boone said, holding her away so he could look into her face. "If yo're goin' to be Mrs. Boone, ya better know yore husband's first name. Ya won't laugh, will ya?"

"Cross my heart," she said solemnly.

"It's . . . it's Amsterdam."

"Amsterdam? Like the city in Holland?"

"Yeah. My mother was from there and homesick to go home when I was born. When I was a kid they called me Am. Now I'm just Boone. Or when I have to be, A. Boone."

"It's a grand name! Not everyone gets named after a city. Amsterdam Boone."

"You won't tell anyone?"

"Not if you don't want me to. I'll never do anything you don't want me to do, Amsterdam." She giggled happily when he bit her gently on the neck.

"I'd like nothin' better than to sit here with ya all night, darlin', but we got to be gettin' back. The doc told me a way to go around Henderson and come out north of town so that we can get to Donovans' without passin' the Carter place. The bastard might have another roadblock set up."

As Boone was headed south out of town, Calvin Carter, in a topless, stripped-down Model T, drove into town from the north. Marvin was with him, as were Judd and Arney Carter.

"If they ain't a light in the jail, old Stoney'll be at his place yonder behind the ice house." Marvin's voice was slurred. On their return from the Donovans', he had downed a glass or two of liquor before Calvin put a stop to it.

"Don't look like no light in the jail."

"You fellers stay in the car," Calvin said when he stopped in front of a small house surrounded by a sagging picket fence. "Me'n Marvin'll talk to him."

After several loud thumps on the door, it was flung open.

"Whatta ya want?" Stoney demanded.

"Want to tell ya somebody's got my brother and sister and won't let 'em go."

"Kidnapped 'em?"

"It's what I said."

"Who's got 'em."

"The folks livin' north of us. The shit-eatin' Donovans has got 'em."

"How do you know that? Have you seen them over there?"

"No, but gawdammit! Who else'd have 'em?"

Calvin nudged Marvin aside. "Sheriff, Leroy, our young brother, met with an accident last night and was hurt bad. We want to make sure he's all right."

"Was he the Carter on the mule that was hit by a car?"

"Yeah. He was out pulling dead limbs off the road."

"Horseshit!" Stoney snorted. "Whatta ya think I am? A pickled fart? Ya was fixin' to bushwhack that feller that's been stayin' at the hotel. He was here this mornin' tellin' me about it."

"He run down the mule Leroy was on and hit him with his car," Marvin shouted.

"I ain't deaf. Whatta you want me to do about it?"

"Find 'em, gawdammit! We been good to ya, old man. Ya've had plenty of jugs from our still."

"You threatenin' to cut me off? Your'n ain't the only place around here to get booze."

"I'm tellin' ya I wanna know where my kin is at."

"A man was brought to doc this afternoon. Go over and see if it's who you're looking for."

"Get yore hat. Yo're goin' with us."

"No, I'm not. There's not been a crime that I know of. I'm stayin' and listenin' to my radio show. 'Sides, the feller they brought in may be a rowdy off the river, for all I know."

"Old man—" Marvin reached to jerk open the screen door, but Calvin caught his arm.

"Folks'll not take it kindly if you get rough with the sheriff," Stoney said and shut the door.

"Come on, Marvin. We found out what we want to know."

They drove the two city blocks to the doctor's house, and when they knocked on the door, it was opened by his wife.

"We come to see the doctor," Marvin said.

"Come in. I'll get him."

Inside the reception room, Calvin removed his cap and nudged Marvin to remove his. Arney and Judd dragged their caps from their shaggy heads.

"I'll do the talkin'," Calvin said. "Leroy's my brother too."

Marvin frowned but said nothing. He was the eldest and didn't like Calvin taking over. They had waited for what seemed a long time, and Marvin was getting more irritated by the minute, when a tall man came through the door. He wore a shirt open at the neck with the sleeves rolled up beyond his elbows. He looked more like a barroom brawler than a doctor.

"What can I do for you?"

"We come to see the doctor."

"You're looking at him."

"Ya ain't him," Marvin sputtered. "Doctors is . . . are—"

"Little old men with spectacles? Sorry to disappoint you." Dr. Perkins looked at each of the four men crowded into his reception room. *So these were the notorious Carters, the bullies who refused to get help for a boy suffering unimaginable pain.* "Which one of you is in need of my services?"

"We are lookin' for our brother. Stoney said a man was brought here."

"Men who are hurt come here all the time. What were the nature of your brother's injuries?" *I'll make you tell me, you hard-ass bully.*

"He got knocked off a mule," Marvin blurted. "A son-of-a-bitch run him down."

"You must be looking for the boy whose face was smashed in, his nose and hand broken, ribs cracked and cuts and bruises all over his body, the boy whose brother wouldn't bring him in for help. What do you want to know about him?"

"We come to take him home."

"Why do you want to do that? Are you trying to kill him?"

"Carters take care of their own, mister," Calvin said.

"Miss Tess Carter signed him in. I'll release him only to her."

"What's that whore got to do with men's business? We come to take Leroy home and we're takin' him."

Marvin took the necessary steps to reach the inner door. The doctor was there ahead of him and threw it open. Two big, brawny men stood there with stout clubs in their hands.

"Which one you want, Doc?"

"I'll take the stupid one with hair that looks like a haystack. On second thought, I'll take two of them. That'll leave one for each of you."

"Wait just a minute. We ain't wantin' to fight nobody," Calvin said. "We come to see about our brother is all."

"You said you came to take him. You'll not move him out of here. It's as simple as that," Dr. Perkins said. "The boy was badly hurt. I can't be sure he'll live."

"He'd better," Marvin yelled. "He warn't hurt so bad when I left home this mornin'."

"Jesus, my God! I've run into ignorant jackasses in my time, but these lunkheads go beyond stupid."

"Ya better be careful what ya call us, Doc," Calvin said. "There's more Carters in these hills than you could shake a stick at."

"You'd better not threaten me. I'm the only doctor within ten miles in either direction. The boys here"—he nodded toward his friends—"and a hundred others want to keep me in working order because they might need me sometime. Now I suggest you go home and cool off. If your brother lives through the night, it means he has a chance. Move him and he'd not live to get out of town."

"We ain't payin' ya nothin' for keepin' him."

"I've not asked you to pay anything. As a matter of fact, my fee has been paid."

"Who paid it? The whore that brung him ain't got no money. We ain't takin' no handouts from nobody." Marvin slapped his cap back on his head.

"Come on, Marvin." Calvin urged his brother toward the door. "We'll come back in a day or two."

The two men with clubs followed the Carters out the door.

"We didn't get to have no fun a-tall," one of them complained. "Can't we bash just one or two heads, Doc?"

"If they give you any lip, let 'em have it."

Corbin and Annabel sat in the swing on the porch of the darkened house. Jack, having returned from a tour around the house, sat down on the steps and placed the rifle beside him. The night sky was peppered with a million stars. From a distance came the faint hoot of an owl, the only sound to disturb the quiet.

"I feel like a prisoner in my own house," Annabel said from the shelter of Corbin's arm.

"You should be in town. When Boone gets back with my car, I'm taking you there."

"I have to stay here until Papa gets back. Surely he'll be here tomorrow. I'm afraid that when he finds out the Carters have stolen our horses, he'll go storming over there. I have to stop him, if I can. Papa can talk a dog off a meat wagon when he wants to; but when his temper is up, he's ready to fight."

"Car comin'," Jack said quietly.

"Maybe it's Papa."

Corbin stood and went to the edge of the porch. "It sounds like my car." He watched the car come slowly up the hill. "Stay out of the headlights, Jack, until we're sure who it is."

But that wasn't to be. The driver stopped the car a good hundred feet from the porch, backed up and turned the wheels so that the headlights shone on the front of the house. He then came on ahead and stopped at the porch, cut the motor and turned off the lights.

"No lights in the house made me leery," Boone said, as he stepped out and reached his hand in for Tess.

"We had visitors."

"Did they give you any trouble?"

"Nothing we couldn't handle."

Boone urged Tess up the steps to the porch. "I ain't lettin' her go back over there," he said to Annabel. "She'll have to stay here. We'll hide her somewhere until Murphy gets back. After yo're packed up and ready to go, me and Tess are leavin' this part of the country."

"I'll be trouble to you." Tess was clinging to Boone's hand. "Marvin and Calvin won't rest until I'm back over there doin' for them."

"They've been here, Tess. If they come back, they won't take you. Corbin and Boone will see to it. I'm glad you're here with me," Annabel assured her. "Tell me what happened, but first, have you had anything to eat?"

"I forgot all about eating."

"I didn't," Boone said. "What've ya got, youngun?"

"I'll find something."

"Are ya leavin' now, Mr. Appleby?"

"Not on your life, Mr. Boone. I'm not leaving here without Annabel, and she wants to stay until her father gets back."

"That's what I was afraid of," Boone said in a dejected tone of voice and winked at Annabel when she turned to glare at him.

*   *   *

It was midnight when Annabel and Tess went to Annabel's room and closed the door.

Jack, Boone and Appleby were each going to take a two-hour watch, with Jack taking the first one. Corbin pulled off his shoes and lay down on Murphy Donovan's bed. His training during the war to take his rest when he could get it served him now, and he fell into a light sleep, waking only when Jack came into the room to tell him it was his turn to take the watch.

The night passed uneventfully.

When morning came, Annabel, with help from Tess, cooked breakfast. Jack came in with the morning milking.

"What'll I do with it, Annabel?"

"If we won't be using it, I suppose we'll have to pour it out. I've got to think about what to do about Mildred and my chickens. I can't just go off and leave them here."

"I can crate up the chickens and take them to town," Jack said. "I could lead the cow to town if I had a horse to ride."

"We've got mules and a wagon . . . somewhere." Annabel's voice trailed. "Maybe Spinner will come today."

Boone came in with a plucked chicken.

"Weasel got one of your chickens, Annabel. Make us some dumplin's. Can't let it go to waste."

"Oh, the poor, poor thing."

On the way out the door, Boone winked at Jack.

Tess finished dressing the chicken and put it on to boil. She and Annabel spent the morning making over one of Annabel's dresses. After Annabel told Tess that the dress was several years old and much too tight for her, Tess consented to try it on. Annabel pinned it at the waist and adjusted the hemline for the much shorter woman. Then, while Annabel darned socks, Tess labored at putting in the hem with tiny neat stitches.

Boone looked in from time to time and was pleased to see the two women he cared about with their heads together, talking and occasionally laughing. Without that encounter with her in the woods, he realized that he wouldn't have met Tess, nor have discovered the wonderful feeling of loving and being loved.

He glanced up at the open doors of the hayloft at the top of the barn, where Corbin sat with the rifle. He had to admit that he was a good man to have on your side. Murphy wouldn't find a better man to take care of his daughter.

Annabel made big fluffy dumplings to go with the chicken and Tess made a peach cobbler with the last two cans of peaches in the cupboard. When Tess protested the extravagance, Annabel said, "We might as well use up as much as we can. There will be less to pack when Papa gets here."

Jack offered to be lookout while Corbin and Boone ate with the women.

"Don't let those two big clabberheads eat everything up, Annabel."

"I'll put yours away before I let the two *clabberheads* have a go at it."

"You're giving that little brat all the best pieces," Corbin complained when Annabel brought Jack's plate to the table, filled it with chicken and dumplings and set it on the back of the stove to keep warm.

"He's a growing boy," Annabel retorted in her imitation of a schoolteacher's voice. "Besides, there's plenty for you and Boone."

"I'm a growing boy and I don't get the attention he gets." Corbin managed to put a sulky expression on his face.

"Oh, poor, poor you. Keep complaining and you'll leave the table without any of Tess's cobbler."

The good-natured banter continued through the meal. Tess's eyes went from one to the other. Sweet memories of being with her aunt and uncle came rushing back. Would she ever be able to erase the last six years and be as light-hearted again as she had been when she lived with them?

Annabel's eyes passed over Tess and went to Boone. He had a light in his dark eyes she'd not noticed before. *He was happy!* She smiled at Corbin when she caught him looking at her. *She was happy!* Annabel wished that her papa were here. He would like Corbin if he ever got to know him.

Chapter 20

Jack came down from the hayloft and called to Corbin, who was throwing grain to the chickens through the fence: "Marvin is sitting over there at the edge of the woods."

"Is he alone?"

"So far."

Corbin threw the last of the feed and hung the bucket on a fence post. "How long has he been there?"

"Half hour. He's got a jug and keeps nipping at it."

"Keep an eye on him. I'll pass the word on to Boone."

A little light still lingered in the western sky, but it was fading fast. Corbin went to the water pump, worked the handle until the water came, then ducked his head under and sloshed water over his head and face. He wanted a bath and a change of clothes, but this would have to do.

Boone came out of the house and stopped a short distance from where Corbin was shaking the water out of his hair.

"Jack says Marvin's sitting over there at the edge of the woods with a jug. I doubt it's water he's drinking."

"Bastard!" Boone turned toward the woods. "I oughta go

over there and stomp the shit outta the mean, lily-livered son-of-a-bitch!"

"There's a big red anthill over there." Corbin grinned and put his hat back on his wet head. "Suppose we'd be lucky enough that he's sitting on it?"

"As soon as it's good and dark, me'n Tess are goin' to do a little lookin' around. If he's still there, I just might smash his balls."

Corbin laughed. "It's all right with me. What are you and Tess going to look for?"

"She thinks they may have taken the horses to a place up near their still. If they have, we're gonna steal 'em back."

"Jack's keeping his eye on Marvin. He won't come in here unless his kinfolk show up to back him." Corbin headed for the house, stopped and turned. "I'm going to be with my girl for a while, and you keep the hell away from us."

With her hand clasped tightly in his, Tess and Boone melted into the darkness behind the barn and slipped quickly into the shelter of the woods.

"The still is this way," she whispered and tugged on his hand.

"I want to make sure where Marvin is before we go any farther. I don't want to bump into him . . . not now any-how."

Tess walked with an easy stride and almost noiselessly, keeping close to Boone. If Calvin and Marvin got hold of her, she was sure to be beaten severely. She was anxious but strangely unafraid. If she died within the hour, she'd already had more happiness with this man than she had ever dreamed of having.

"I don't see him," she whispered.

"I do." Boone had exceptional night vision. He stopped

and put his lips next to Tess's ear. "He's sittin' over there under a tree."

They watched for several minutes. When Marvin didn't move even to take a nip from the jug, Boone crept closer. He dropped Tess's hand and with his hands on her shoulders motioned for her to stay put. He crept up behind Marvin, then shuffled his feet to create noise. When there was no movement by the man under the tree, he whistled.

Marvin was either dead or dead drunk.

Boone moved around and put his foot against Marvin's upper arm and pushed him over. The jug fell from his hand. Boone picked it up.

"He's dead drunk, Tess. The jug's empty."

"Are you sure? He doesn't usually pass out."

Boone prodded Marvin with his foot. When there was no reaction, he reached down and touched his fingers to the pulse in his neck to make sure he was alive.

"He's alive, but dead to the world. We'll not have to worry about him for a while." Boone picked up the jug and flung it against a tree. "Dirty low-life skunk! If he wasn't drunk, I'd beat hell outta him for the way he's treated ya. When I do it, I want him to know who's doin' it and why." He took Tess's hand and pulled her to him.

He lowered his head and kissed her.

BOOM! At the sound and the flash of bright light in the sky, Boone instinctively ducked his head over Tess and hugged her to him.

"Godamighty!" He raised his head and looked around.

"What was that?" Tess asked anxiously.

"Godamighty," he said again when he realized what it probably was. "It was an explosion . . . up in the hills." He held her away from him and looked at the sky as if expecting another blast. "I've got to go. Come on."

With Tess keeping pace with him, Boone loped toward the house. He feared for Spinner and hoped that he had moved far enough away from the cave to be safe before it blew up. He was panting when he reached the yard and saw someone running out from behind the barn.

"Boone! It's me, Jack. What happened?"

"Explosion . . . in the hills."

"Boone," Annabel called. Then, "Jack!" Corbin and Annabel were on the back porch.

Boone ran up to the porch. "I've got to go—"

"What happened?" Corbin asked.

"You sure you don't know?" Boone snarled, his worry for Spinner making him unreasonably suspicious.

"How would I know?"

"You tell me, Mr. Federal Man."

"You still singing that song?" Corbin responded angrily.

"We had no trouble till ya started nosin' around. Damn ya to hell! I gotta trust ya to stay with the women while I go see about Spinner. I'll take Jack. I might need help with Spinner if he's hurt. You won't have any trouble with Marvin. He's dead drunk."

"I want to go with you." Tess clung tightly to Boone's hand.

"Honey, I don't know what I'll find up there."

"I don't care."

Boone looked helplessly at Annabel, then back at Tess.

"Honey, this could be dangerous."

"I don't care," she said calmly, but the frantic look on her face tore at his insides. Then it dawned on him. *She was afraid that he'd leave her and not come back.*

Boone took Tess and headed for the shed. A minute later he drove the truck out.

"You might need this." Jack pulled the pistol from his belt and extended it to Corbin. "I've got the rifle."

"Keep it. I'll get the one I have in the car."

Boone paused by the porch. "Get in, Jack. You too, Annabel."

"Me? There's not room."

"Sit on Jack's lap."

"Annabel isn't going." Corbin held on to Annabel's arm.

"She's goin'." Boone jacked a shell into the chamber of the shotgun. "I'm not leavin' her here with a damn sneak."

"Boone, what's the matter with you?" Annabel exclaimed. "What are you talking about?"

"He thinks I'm responsible for the explosion," Corbin said. "When he thinks about it, he'll see how wrong he is."

"Why do you think that, Boone?"

"I don't have time to argue. I don't want to leave you here with *him*."

"Why? He was with me all day yesterday and last night. I'll be all right."

"If she isn't"—Boone spoke to Corbin in a voice cold as ice—"I'll hunt you till the day I die."

Annabel watched the truck leave, her thoughts tumbling. Why had Boone turned so quickly against Corbin? He called him Federal Man. And why was he so concerned about Spinner? It had to do with the *business*. Damn, damn the business. Why didn't they ever tell her anything? She felt Corbin's hand on her shoulder.

"You're shivering. Do you want to go back in and get a wrap?"

"I didn't realize that I was cold." She turned and looked up at him. His face was a blur in the darkness. "Boone thinks you had something to do with that explosion."

"Is that worrying you?" He put his hand on her shoulder. "I don't know why he suddenly got a bee in his bonnet, but he's wrong."

"I thought maybe it was going to end." She lowered her head and gazed at the top button on his shirt. "They don't tell me anything," she said, slowly speaking her thoughts. "They treat me as if I were two years old."

"They're protecting you." His hand moved down her arm and clasped her hand.

"I've been an adult for quite some time. I deserve to know what's going on."

"They don't want you involved. I understand that."

"How can you, when you don't know what's going on— or do you?"

"Let's walk around the house to the car."

"So you can get your gun?" she spat out angrily.

Instead of answering, he said, "Why don't we sit in the car for a while."

Corbin opened the door and reached in for a coat lying on the seat. After putting it around her shoulders, he helped her into the car, shut the door and hurried around to the other side.

"I think I'll move the car over behind those bushes where we can watch the house."

He started the car and backed it across the yard until it was partially concealed behind a hedge of honeysuckle bushes but still gave them a view of the front of the house and the road. After they parked, Annabel sat quietly, saying nothing for several minutes.

"I'm not a child, even if my father and Boone treat me like one." Her voice came out of the darkness.

"I know that. You're a sweet sensible woman. I wish you'd sit over here close to me." His hand reached for her arm, but she resisted.

"I know that you're a lawman. Maybe not a federal marshal, but a lawman with contacts with them. My father has been engaged in an illegal business. You probably know that. The explosion may have something to do with it, or Boone wouldn't have been in such a lather and worried about Spinner."

"I am a lawman, but my coming here had nothing to do with your father. Come sit close to me. You're shivering."

"I'm not cold."

He moved close to her and put his arm around her. She remained unyielding, with her face turned away from him.

"Have you decided you don't trust me, Annabel?"

"I want to trust you."

"I've been honest with you and Boone. I've held nothing back, even that I knew something illegal is going on here. Boone can't get it out of his mind that I was once a police officer."

"Maybe he's afraid I'll tell you something. That's a joke, because I don't know anything."

"Your father and Boone have nothing to fear from me because I was a lawman. I'm not a federal marshal. I came to Henderson looking for Jack. I stopped along the road and someone shot me. I owe my life to Boone. He ran off the bushwhackers and took care of me for a week in a cabin in the hills. Although I never saw it, I think there's a cave near the cabin that's used as a warehouse for their booze. Boone may think I slipped the location to someone, but I didn't. I'll not cause Boone or your father any trouble because they do a little bootlegging."

"So you know?"

"It wasn't hard to figure out. The booze comes downriver and is stored in the hills. Boone and Spinner take turns guarding it."

"What does Papa do?" she asked softly.

"I can't tell you for sure, but someone has to sell the booze to the saloons and the speakeasies."

"When I was younger, I didn't think about what Papa did. Later, I was afraid to ask, for fear they would tell me something I didn't want to hear." Suddenly Annabel melted against him and laid her head against his shoulder. When he pressed his cheek to hers, he felt the wetness of her tears.

Her whispered voice came against his throat. "Papa wants me to live in a big house and mix with high-toned people. What will they think when they find out that I'm the daughter of a bootlegger?"

"Former bootlegger," he corrected. "They'll think that you're sweet and pretty and that you play the violin like an angel. If your being the daughter of a bootlegger made any difference to them, they wouldn't be worth having for friends anyway."

"I don't want to mix with high-toned people, but I can't disappoint Papa. He's worked to get that kind of life for me for so long."

"Have you told him?"

"I can't. I'm all he's got. He hated that he couldn't provide more for my mother. Now he wants to do it for me."

"Don't worry about it now. Things have a way of working out. Sweetheart, it hurts like hell to think you don't trust me. I promise you that I'll never keep anything from you." He held her head against his shoulder, kissed her lips, then pressed his cheek to hers.

They sat quietly for a long moment, then Corbin said urgently, "Annabel, honey, listen closely to what I'm going to say. There's a car coming down the road. It may be coming here and it may not be, but I want you to get out of the car and run for that high grass there on the other side of that open place. Lie flat on the ground and cover yourself with my dark coat."

"Oh, but—" She lifted her head to look.

"Do as I say. I'll tell you everything I know as soon as I know it. You've got to help me. Understand?"

"It could be Boone—"

"Not truck lights. Go!"

As soon as Annabel was out of the car, Corbin reached beneath the seat for his gun. He got out and yanked up the hood covering the motor and pulled out the cushion from the front seat. He looked around and saw that Annabel had done exactly as she had been told.

Leaving the doors of the car open so that it appeared to be an old wreck, he bent over and ran toward the shelter of a pile of dead wood, where he could see both the front and back of the house as well as the tall grass where Annabel was hidden.

His hunch had been right.

The car sped up the lane toward the house. It was a sedan with powerful headlights. It stopped beside the house and three men sprang out. Two of them, one with a flashlight, went up onto the porch and, with guns drawn, entered the house. The third man ran around to the back.

"No one's here." The shout came minutes later as the men emerged out onto the back porch. "Check the barn and sheds. Morey, take a look at that car over there behind the hedge."

Corbin sidled around the woodpile and watched as the man, with gun drawn, ran toward his car. He flashed his light inside. After a quick search of the car, he backed away, then, holding the gun out in both hands, fired into the gas tank.

The fire from the explosion lit the area. Corbin was

caught in the light momentarily and moved quickly around the woodpile, keeping it between him and the fire. From where he was concealed, he was relieved to see the man moving back toward the house away from where Annabel lay in the grass.

"You damn fool! Why'd you do that for?" The angry shout came from a man coming out of the barn.

"It'll let him know we mean business."

"Horseshit!"

"Fire the house."

"Use your head for something more than to hang your hat on. We can come back and burn it if we don't find him. It might be a draw to bring him out."

"I fired his car. If he leaves, he'll be walkin'."

"Let's get out of here before that bunch of hillbillies next door comes to see about the fire. We're in a hell of a mess as it is."

As soon as Corbin saw the taillights of the car at the end of the lane, he caught up a feed sack and hurried to beat out the flames eating at the short grass before it reached the tall dried grass where Annabel lay.

"Annabel, they're gone. Get out of that grass," he shouted. A minute later she was beside him, gasping and coughing. "Use my coat and beat out the flames on this side." They worked for several minutes, then Corbin grabbed her hand and ran with her toward the barn. "That's all we can do. The fire will go toward the lane and burn itself out."

Inside the barn, out of the light of the burning car, Corbin put his arms around her and held her tightly. He could feel the pounding of her frightened heart against his. Her head lay nicely on his shoulder, and her face fit into the curve of his neck. Thankful that she was safe, Corbin closed his eyes and let his lips caress her forehead before he spoke.

"You did good, honey."

"Why did they burn your car? Who were those men? How did you know they were coming?"

"They burned the car out of pure meanness. It was logical to me that if someone knew about the stockpile, they knew where Donovan lived. That's why I moved the car. The marshals didn't blow up the cave. I'm sure of that. They don't operate that way. The men who were here were looking for someone, possibly your father or Boone. They were going to burn the house but decided not to because whoever they are looking for may come back. They may change their minds, return and leave a man to lie in wait. We should get away from here fast."

"Oh . . ." She wrapped her arms around his waist. "I was so . . . scared!"

"We're all right for now. Don't be scared. What's in the house that you treasure the most?"

"My mother's picture and my violin," she answered without hesitation.

"Get them and a blanket. Get a jacket for yourself, and do you have a heavier pair of shoes?" When she nodded, he said, "Put them on." The fire was dying down when he looked out the door. "Run to the house, get those things and hurry back. I'll watch. I'd not put it past those thugs to stop and come back through the woods."

"Boone, Tess and Jack might come back."

"We'll wait down along the road in case they do. Hurry, now."

Corbin was waiting for her at the end of the porch with a feed sack and a tarp when she came out of the house. He put the violin case and pictures in the sack and wrapped it securely in the tarp. At the deadwood pile, he pulled out several tree limbs and a large number of small branches, buried the sack in the hole and covered it with the limbs, piling more and more on until it was deep at the bottom of the pile.

"I think they'll be safe there even if they fire the barn and the house. There would be no need to fire a woodpile."

"Do you think they will?"

"I don't know, honey. I just don't want you here if they do. We're going to have to hurry. Are you up to it?"

"Yes, but how about your leg? Only a few days ago you were using a cane."

"It's sore." He grinned and pinched her chin with his thumb and forefinger. "I promised I'd not lie to you. If I think it's going to give out on me, we'll stop."

Corbin tied a cord to the blanket and adjusted it on his back so that his hands would be free.

"What if Papa comes back? I should leave a note and tell him what happened."

"You can't do that, sweetheart. If your papa is as savvy as I think he is, he'll take one look and get the heck out of here."

"He'll be worried about me."

"When he sees that the truck is gone, he'll figure you're with Boone."

"I was hoping he'd come home; now I hope he doesn't . . . for a while anyway. I hate leaving Mildred and the . . . chickens."

"I propped open the back door of the barn so that the cow can get out if something scares her, and I made an opening in the wire so your chickens can get out too. In the morning they'll be scattered all over. The rooster, Peter the

Great, will keep his women together," he added in an attempt at humor.

"Thank you." She didn't smile and looked so sad that he bent his head and kissed her, then took her hand and they walked away from the farmhouse.

Chapter 21

TWO MILES NORTH OF THE FARM, Boone turned the truck onto a little-used road leading toward a high wooded area that lay in the bend of the river. The comforting pressure of Tess's shoulder and hip against him had eased his anxiety and given reason to his thoughts.

Spinner had set off the charge that blew the cave. Knowing the man, Boone reasoned that if marshals had found the cache, Spinner would have let them take it and been glad to escape arrest. This looked like gang warfare, and Boone feared that Murphy had been double-crossed. Had the deal gone as expected, Murphy would have brought the representatives of the new owner to the cave and turned the inventory over to them himself.

He had been wrong to accuse Corbin Appleby.

"Corbin didn't have anything to do with blowing up anything. I don't like it that you accused him." Jack's curt voice broke the silence.

"Maybe. Maybe not," was Boone's answer. He wasn't ready quite yet to admit aloud he had been hasty in accusing Jack's friend.

"I've known him longer than you have. He isn't a sneak. If he was a marshal, he would have said so."

"I might've been hasty." The truck bounced over the rocky upward trail.

"I've got a right to know what I'm getting into." Jack held on to the truck door to keep from crowding Tess, who sat between him and Boone.

"Yeah, ya do." Boone didn't answer until he drove the truck into a thick stand of brush and turned off the headlights. "We've been storin' bootleg whiskey in a cave up here. Murphy went to sell it and our contracts with the speakeasies we supply to a big dealer out of Chicago. He may have been double-crossed. If anyone other than Murphy came to the cave, Spinner was to blow it. I think that's what happened. We walk from here. I dunno what we'll run into."

"Then why did you accuse Corbin?"

"Forget it, kid. Give the pistol to Tess and get the rifle. Honey, can you shoot?"

"I know about guns. I can shoot."

"Good. Stay between me and Jack. If I tell you to lay flat, do it. If I tell you to stay behind me—"

"I'll do what you say," she answered calmly.

Boone took a small lantern from the back of the truck, shook it to be sure it had fuel, then lit it. He turned the wick until there was just a faint light, then picked up the shotgun. They fought their way out of the brush that hid the truck and headed north.

The sound of a motorcar reached them, and Boone stopped to listen. When the sound faded, he moved on. The path he followed was steep and rocky. Jack was puffing when they came up and onto a grassy bench. Boone hurried across the open space and into the trees, where he stopped and blew out the lantern.

"Are ya holdin' up, Tess?"

"I'm all right."

"It's not far now. Spinner has a cabin about half a mile from here. Are you rested enough to go on?"

Tess nodded; then, realizing that he might not have seen her, she said, "Yes."

Jack wondered how Boone could tell where he was going in the almost pitch-dark of the wooded area. Jack couldn't see beyond Tess, who was directly in front of him. The pace was slow but steady. When Boone stopped and held out his arm, Tess ran into him.

"The cabin's just ahead. Between here and the cabin is a small stream. It's only about ankle-deep, or was the last time I was here. When we get there, hunker down. I'll go on and see if Spinner is there."

"I want to go—"

"No, Tess," Boone said firmly. "Yo're to stay with Jack. I'll come back if the coast is clear." He hugged her for a minute, then spoke to Jack. "If I get pinned down in there, could ya make yore way back to the truck?"

"Not in the dark, but I think I could find it in the daylight."

"I think what we're dealin' with is city boys. They'll not know how to handle themselves in the woods. If ya have to hide out, follow Tess's lead. She knows how to get through the woods as silent as a ghost."

"We'll make out," Jack said. "Be careful."

They followed Boone and when he held out his arm, Tess and Jack stopped and he went on. Tess reached for Jack's arm. She was trembling violently, her eyes on the place where Boone had disappeared and the faint outline of the cabin beyond.

Tess was almost too frightened to breathe. Her heart

thumped and goose bumps climbed her arms. The rough but gentle man with the dark whiskers on his face had taken over her heart, leaving no room for anyone or anything else. To her he was like a drink of water to a man dying of thirst. A strangled sob escaped her.

Oh, God, Boone. Come back. Please come back. I love you so damn much.

"He'll be all right," Jack whispered.

It seemed like forever before a dim light came from the cabin. Then the lantern was waving, and Boone whistled shrilly. He loped toward them.

"Spinner is hurt. Watch your step. There's a log foot-bridge." He stopped and held the lantern low so Tess and Jack could cross on the logs. "He's in bad shape. Come help me get him into the cabin. He looks like he's been through a sawmill."

For an instant Tess's sensitive nature rebelled when she first saw Spinner lying on the ground in front of the cabin. She turned her face away. His face was blue-black as if covered with coal dust. His eyes were swollen shut. His hair was matted with blood. The buttons had been ripped from his shirt. Blood oozed from a hundred cuts on his shoulders and chest.

His split lips parted and he whispered, "Tell ya nothin', ya sons-a-bitches." He continued to mutter unintelligibly.

"Spinner, it's me, Boone." Boone, kneeling beside him, put his hand beneath his head and lifted it.

Spinner tried to open his eyes "Boone? I blew . . . it."

"I know you did. Did they come here?" When Spinner didn't answer, Boone asked him again, "Did they come here?"

"Caught me . . . by the cave. Beat me . . . shot me. Lookin' for ya. I got to the plunger and . . . blew the sons-a-bitches. . . ." His voice trailed. His hand fell away from his side and blood oozed from a wound. Boone realized that he'd been shot as well as beaten.

"We've got to get him inside. Tess, go in and light a lamp. Jack, put your arms under his knees and I'll get the rest of him."

When they lifted him, he groaned. Boone cursed. Tess held the lamp as Boone and Jack gently placed Spinner on the built-in bunk.

"Strip him, Jack, while I get things ready to sew up that wound in his side."

"He's got a bullet in his thigh that should come out while he's unconscious," Jack said.

Tess built a quick fire in the stove and set a pan of water over the flame. She found vinegar, whiskey and what looked to be a torn bedsheet.

"Can you wash him off with vinegar water, Tess? There's a box around here somewhere with a needle, thread and alcohol. I've got to boil this knife before I probe for the bullet in his leg."

"Looks like they worked him over with a blackjack and brass knuckles." Jack had pulled off Spinner's britches and covered his privates with a corner of the sheet.

"Why do you reckon they didn't kill him?" Jack asked later as he and Boone bent over the man.

"Might've thought they did. When they left him, he managed to get to where he'd hid the plunger. He blew them up."

"Plunger?" Jack had washed his hands and was holding the wound closed while Boone stitched it.

"Charges of dynamite had been set in the cave and a wire run out to a plunger. Somehow he made it there, then here to the cabin. I don't know how in hell he did it, the shape he's in. He's lost a lot of blood."

"Shouldn't we try to get him to a doctor?"

"How? We can't carry him out of here tonight. It's a mile to the truck. We'll see how he is tomorrow. I may have to go fetch the doc. There's a horse and two mules a little farther up in the hills if those bastards haven't killed them."

"I hope the blast got all of the gutless devils!"

"It took more'n one or two to do this to Spinner. Even if someone was holdin' a gun on him, he'd not stand still and let them beat him. I'm done with the sewin', Tess. There ain't much we can do for the gash on the head but douse it good with alcohol and tie a pad against it to stop the bleedin'. We've got a bottle of laudanum. I'll try to get him to swallow a couple drops in a sip of water."

After they had done all they could do for Spinner and he was sleeping, Boone covered the windows with blankets and set the lamp near Spinner's bunk.

"Do you think they all died in the blast?" Tess asked after they had settled down on the step in front of the cabin.

"We can't be sure. I don't want to take the chance. I doubt they found this place, or they'd've stayed the night and waited to move out in the mornin'."

Boone put his arm around her and held her close to his side. She had strength. He was proud of her. She had followed his lead without question. He kissed her forehead and silently swore to spend his life taking care of her. This love that had come to him was so wonderful, so unexpected.

Boone hoped that Tess hadn't caught Spinner's words about the men looking for him. He reasoned that Spinner knew that he, Boone, could take care of himself, but Spinner's fear had been that if he told where to find Boone, they would have come to the house and hurt or possibly killed Annabel.

Boone hadn't really thought about it before, but it made

sense to him that the Remus organization would know that he knew as much about the operation as Murphy did. Unless they had planned a double-cross, why would they be interested in him? He didn't want to think about it, but it was becoming clear: Their intentions were to eliminate any future competition in this area.

"I don't understand any of it."

Annabel had not said much since leaving the house. Corbin slowed his pace as soon as they had crossed the field and were away from the farm. He led the way to the road because it was easier to walk along, and he would be able to see the lights of a car or hear it in time for them to hide in the bushes that grew at the side.

"I don't understand much of it myself, but I know this: It isn't federal marshals we're dealing with."

"Were the men looking for my father?"

"I couldn't tell from what I heard if it was your father, Boone or Spinner they were looking for. I heard one of them say that they were in a hell of a mess, which to me means they are accountable to whoever is calling the shots and they hadn't completed what they had been sent to do."

When they reached a small rise in the road, Corbin stopped. He looked ahead, behind and then at the house. He could see in all directions. A thick stand of cedars lined the west side of the road.

"We can wait here until morning."

He took her hand and, shining his light ahead of them, led her off the road. Corbin spread the blanket where within a few seconds they could hide behind the thick screen of cedars. They sank down wearily. He took the gun from his belt and placed it and the flashlight within easy reach, then, without conscious thought, rubbed his aching thigh.

"Does your let hurt?"

"Naw—"

"You said you'd not lie to me."

"I said that and I meant it. I'll never lie to you. I was going to say, 'Naw, not much.'"

"But it hurts. Let me rub it." She placed her hand on top of his. "Is this the place?" He moved her hand to the inside of his thigh and she gently rubbed the aching flesh. "Am I too rough?"

"Feels good."

"Corbin," she said after a long silence, "do you think my father is mixed up with . . . gangsters?"

"I don't know that, honey. He may have been trying to sell out to them so he could get out of the bootlegging business."

"Then why would they blow up the stockpile?"

"Spinner may have blown it up because they hadn't paid the money . . . or something like that. I'm just guessing."

"I'm . . . afraid Papa won't come back." There was a sob in her voice. "I'm always worried when he goes away, but this time . . ."

Corbin put his arms around her and drew her close. She snuggled her face in the curve of his neck. He could feel the wetness of her tears.

"Ah . . . honey. Don't cry. Your papa is a smart man or he'd not have been able to stay in the business as long as he has. He knows how to take care of himself."

"He used to tell me he sold things out of a catalog. He stopped telling me that when I got older, but he never came right out and said that he . . . bootlegged."

"Some folks don't think it's such a terrible crime. Prohibition is not a good law. Everyone knows that, but it's a law and should be obeyed until it's revoked. It's making the big racketeers rich and ruining the lives of people who drink their rotgut whiskey."

"My papa is a good man. He loved my mother to distraction. It almost killed him when she died."

"If your mother was anything like you, I can understand that." Corbin pulled on her arm until it circled his chest. His lips moved over her forehead.

"I remember how they were with each other. When Papa came into a room, there wasn't anyone in it but her. His eyes would find her. He'd go to her and greet her first no matter who was there. He never went by her that he didn't reach out and touch her. She was his life; then he had only me and was determined that I'd be what he called 'somebody,' not Irish trash, as he'd been called when he was young."

"I've dreamed of finding a love like that." Corbin's lips caressed her cheek. "I don't have to dream about it any longer."

She was quiet. "Papa put money away and told me where it was just in case . . . something happened to him."

"Did you hear what I said, sweetheart?"

"You said something about . . . finding a love like my Mama's and Papa's."

"I said I've found my love. It may not be like the love they shared. No two loves are the same."

He lifted her chin with his fingers and placed his lips on hers. At first his mouth brushed gently over hers in soft lingering kisses, then his fingertips stroked the tender skin at the nape of her neck.

"*You* are my love," he whispered against her mouth. His hand moved down her back and over her hips, pulling her closer. She could feel the pounding of his heart against her breast. "I thank God every day that I found you."

"We've not known each other very long."

"I feel like I've known you forever. Do I seem like a stranger to you?"

"No. You've never been a stranger to me."

"We may have met in another life. You were a princess and I was the knight who adored you."

"Or you were a king and I was your chambermaid."

"Never that! Tell me, sweetheart. Tell me what I want to hear."

"You know that already. I've said that I love you in so many different ways." Her hand moved up to cup his cheek and hold her trembling mouth to his. "I wouldn't be here with you like this if I didn't love you."

"Are you real, or am I having a wonderful dream?"

"Oh, love," she breathed against his lips. "Even dreams aren't this wonderful!"

He turned and bore her down on the blanket, leaned over her and gathered her close. His kisses came upon her mouth warm and devouring, fierce with love and passion. Annabel closed her eyes in bliss as his greedy mouth sparked her every nerve with intense excitement. She heard his hoarsely whispered words of love.

" 'But we loved with a love that was more than love—/ I and my Annabel Lee—' "

She opened her mouth and felt the first exciting touch of his tongue along her inner lips.

"My beautiful Annabel Lee," he breathed, almost in reverence. His face was inches from hers. "You love me? Say it again."

"I love you. I've never said the words before . . . not even to Papa or Mama. Now I wish I had. I'll tell you every day that I love you, Corbin Appleby."

"I'll never leave you. Never! You are my mate for as long

as I live. Here in this quiet place, I give you my love, pledge my protection, vow to be faithful and never lie to you."

"I will guard these treasures you have given me and offer myself into your keeping."

"You will be my treasure."

Annabel's eyes were soft with love as she gazed at him. Her breath was warm against his face. He felt as if she had given him the world. His lips moved slowly and lingeringly from her mouth to her earlobe to her eyes and back to bury her mouth with his.

He turned on his side, holding her breasts, belly, hips and thighs tightly against him. Her head was pillowed on his arm. He kissed her gently, lovingly. Her soft mouth parted with yearning, and the kiss deepened and went on and on. She pressed on the hand caressing her breast and shivered with an excitement that was sheer heaven.

Annabel had been sheltered, but not so much that she didn't know what throbbed against her belly. It was his sex, large and firm, straining against the buttons of his britches. His hand moved down her back to her hips and pressed her tightly against it, rocked for one delicious moment, then he released her and rolled onto his back, taking deep gulping breaths.

"I've shocked you." His voice was a groan. The arm that held her against his side loosened so that she could move away if it was what she wanted to do.

"Not as much as you think. You want to do more than kiss me. You want us to love each other like husband and wife." She placed comforting kisses along his jawline.

"Sweetheart, I'd not be human if I didn't want that. It's something a healthy male longs to do with the one he loves."

"Are you surprised that I know about such things?"

"I'm glad you know. Do you fear it?"

"My mother told me things that she was afraid no one else would tell me after she was gone. She knew that she was dying, and she wanted me to know that for a woman to mate with the man she loves was one of God's greatest gifts. She said the coming together of two people in love was a beautiful thing—each time you gave a little bit of yourself to the one you loved. Does that answer your question?" Annabel's whispered words came against his cheek. "It will be that way with us."

"When that time comes, I'll make it as beautiful for you as I can." He caught her hand and held it against his chest. Emotion weakened his voice. "We'll be married as soon as I can speak to your father."

"He will not be happy. He said it was just as easy to love a rich man as a poor one."

"I don't have much, but I don't consider myself poor. I have earning skills I've not used very much. I studied to be a journalist but got sidetracked by the war. I've been asked to come back to Fertile as their police chief. But secretly I've always wanted to start a small newspaper. I'm confident that I can take care of you. I'll have to convince your father of that." He was quiet as a sudden thought chilled him. "What will you do if he refuses to give his consent?"

"I'll marry you anyway," she said without hesitation. "I'm an adult. Later, Papa will come to accept you when he sees how happy I am."

"Ah . . . sweetheart . . ." He hugged her tightly to him and thanked God that Jack Jones had come to Henderson.

In the darkness beneath the evergreen tree, Corbin cuddled her warm body against his while she slept. He was elated by her trust in him, the maturity of her thinking, her acceptance of his sex, which had sprung up between them when he held her and kissed her. She was more, far more, than he had ever wished for. God help him never to disappoint her.

In the far distance he heard a dog barking and later the swishing of branches overhead disturbed by a winged creature. His senses were alert to sounds or lack of them. His mind reviewed the events of the day and every word that had been said by the men who came to the house and fired his car.

He and Annabel had no way to get to town unless they walked. If they did that, they might encounter the whole clan of Carters. He didn't want to shoot one of them unless it was absolutely necessary.

What a hell of a note, he thought, that Annabel was in danger both from the Carters and from the thugs who had come to the house. The thugs had been given a mission. They wanted to get it done and go back to Chicago or wherever they came from. If they didn't find Boone in the hills, they would go back to the house, he had no doubt about that.

Lord, he hoped Boone had enough savvy to keep Jack and Tess safe. If anything happened to Jack, the Jones family back in Fertile would be devastated.

His mind suddenly recalled something Boone had said about Spinner coming back to get a few sticks out of the barn. Dynamite sticks? If that were the case and he hadn't taken all of them, he and Annabel were not as helpless as he had believed.

That was a little something to hope for as the long night slowly passed and the girl he loved, and had promised to keep safe, slept in his arms.

Chapter 22

With the early morning sun warm on their faces, Annabel and Corbin approached the farm buildings from the rear. They had circled around through the woods north of the house and now paused amid a clump of tall chokecherry bushes.

From their vantage point, they could see across the barn lot to where Mildred stood patiently chewing her cud and switching her tail to brush away the pesky flies that plagued her.

"Poor Mildred should be milked."

"Stay here while I check out the barn."

"I would rather go with you." Annabel looked at him with eyes ringed with dark circles.

"Honey, I don't think there is anyone here; but in case there is, I'll need to concentrate on them. If you're with me, I'll be worried about keeping you safe."

"I understand. I'll wait here. Just be careful."

Corbin dropped the blanket and put both arms around her. He cuddled her to him and kissed her forehead.

"You're worn out. Sit down here on the blanket, and I'll

be back as soon as I can. I don't think you've anything to fear from the Carters. Marvin is probably sleeping off his drunk."

"Be careful," she cautioned as he dropped his arms and pulled the pistol from his belt.

Corbin ran across the open space, heading for the back of the barn. It felt good to run again. His leg didn't bother him except for muscles stretching the healing flesh. He reached the back door and, with the pistol at the ready, darted inside. The barn was cool and smelled of animal manure and hay. He listened and, after hearing no sound, searched the building systematically as he had done while looking for the enemy during the war.

While in the hayloft, he peered out the loft door. There was no sign of a car and no activity around the house. He climbed down and went into the tack room, where on his initial search he had seen a heavy wooden box. With a thankful sigh, he discovered four sticks of dynamite with long fuses. He wrapped two sticks in a feed sack and carried them to the loft. He placed the remaining sticks in a bucket and hung it on a nail in one of the stalls.

The rooster and his flock of fluffy hens were scratching in the yard when he crossed it to reach the back door of the house. They scattered with a flutter of wings. Still cautious, he moved silently to the door and peered into the kitchen through the screen.

A plaid, billed cap lay on the table.

Corbin eased open the door and stepped into the kitchen. He waited, listened, then on the balls of his feet moved to look into Annabel's room. It was small and neat and empty. The floor creaked as he crossed it to the parlor doorway. One glance told him that no one was there. The door to the bedroom off the parlor was open. He flattened himself against the wall, then peered into the room.

A man in black pants and a white shirt lay sprawled on the bed. He was sleeping soundly, with his mouth hanging open. A shoulder holster and gun lay on the bed beside him. His shirt was open to the waist and his tie was looped around a bedpost. He had a swarthy pockmarked complexion, thick black hair and a hairy chest and arms.

Corbin's eyes scanned the room and listed in his mind what he was going to do before he tiptoed into the room. Holding his gun at the ready, he reached for the weapon on the bed, slipped it from the holster and tucked it into his belt.

The man slept on.

Keeping his eyes on the intruder, Corbin took the tie hanging on the bedpost. In one end he tied a slip knot and looped it around the man's foot. He knotted the other end of the tie to the bedpost.

Corbin moved around to the side of the bed and shook his head in wonder that the man was still sound asleep. He slept as if he hadn't closed an eye in forty-eight hours. Figuring that he hadn't much time left before the others returned, Corbin stuck the barrel of his gun beneath the man's chin with such force the man's eyes popped open.

"Wake up, sleeping beauty. The big bad wolf is here."

"Huh! What!" The man tried to rear up, but the barrel beneath his chin held him down.

"Are you going to behave, or do I blow a hole through the roof of your head?"

"Whatta ya want me to do?" The man spoke with difficulty because of the pressure of the gun barrel.

"I want you to sit up and put your hands behind your back." Corbin moved the gun barrel to beneath his ear. He grabbed a handful of the man's hair and lifted him. "I'd like nothing better than to blow a hole through your rotten head. So watch yourself."

Using one of Murphy Donovan's ties, he tied the man's hands securely behind his back, then went to the end of the bed and pulled on the end of the tie holding his foot.

"Get up. Keep in mind that you'd be less trouble to me dead. Move." Prodding him with the gun, Corbin followed him into the kitchen, snatched the cap from the table and slammed it down on the man's head. "Out. I don't want to kill you in here. It would make too much of a mess."

"Who're you?"

"I'm the man who's going to kill you if you don't tell me what you're doing here. Meanwhile, get out the door."

In the barn, Corbin prodded him to the last stall, one that hadn't been mucked out for so long that manure was a half foot thick on the floor.

"Phew! Nasty, isn't it? You can lie down in it or you can tell me where the hell you're from and who the hell you're after."

"I'm visitin' these folks."

"Yeah? Where are you from?"

"Across the river."

"That doesn't tell me anything. Whose bully boy are you?"

"You'll find out."

"Are you the one who burned my car last night?"

"I ain't tellin' no hick nothin'."

"Suit yourself. I'll not waste any more time on you. Open your mouth or I'll bust your eardrum." Corbin emphasized his words by tapping the man behind the ear with the barrel of his gun. He took the handkerchief from the man's hip pocket and stuffed it in his mouth. When the man was securely gagged, Corbin knelt down, took the end of the tie hanging from one foot and wrapped it around the other and tied it. Then he gave him a shove. Unable to catch himself, the swarthy man fell heavily in the muck.

He struggled and managed to turn on his side and lift his head. Corbin had moved into the other stall and made a loop from a rope he took from a nail on the wall and dropped it over his prisoner's head. He pulled it through the rails that separated the stalls and tied it.

"Now listen to me, you sleazy son-of-a-bitch. If I hear one small sound out of you, I'll pin your belly to the wall with that pitchfork. If you understand that, nod your head. All right. Now, I'm afraid you might get cold lying in that shit, so I'll cover you with some nice fresh hay."

Five minutes later, his prisoner covered with a bale of mildewed hay, Corbin was back in the house removing every trace that the man had been there. When he was satisfied, he went back through the barn and out the back to wave for Annabel to come to him.

With his finger against his lips, he signaled for her to be quiet as she followed him through the barn and to the house.

"Do you have anything in here ready to eat?" He took the pillowcase from her bed. "Put it in here. I'll watch out the front. If I yell, drop everything, run for the barn and climb up into the loft."

"Oh, shoot!" Annabel exclaimed when she saw the puddle of water on the floor. "The ice pan has run over."

"We don't have time to empty it, honey. Hurry and find us something to eat."

Ten minutes later they were at the barn door. Corbin carried the pillowcase, a fruit jar filled with water he had drawn from the well as they passed, a blanket and the two guns.

"Don't say anything until we get up in the loft. I've got a

man tied up in that last stall." He grinned. "The one that's so full of manure even the chickens avoid it."

"Ah . . . phew . . ." A teasing glint came into her eyes and her lips tilted. He couldn't resist bending and placing a kiss there.

"Come on. I've a lot to tell you and we've got to make plans."

While they sat on the blanket beside the loft door and ate bread spread with butter and jam, Corbin told her about finding the man asleep in her father's bed and about tying him up and leaving him in the stall.

"He was dead to the world. Probably hadn't slept for a couple days. He's a hard case. Wouldn't tell me a thing, and I didn't have the time to try and persuade him. He should have taken his chances with me. If the gang gets to him and finds out that I took him while he was asleep on the job, his life won't be worth a plugged nickel."

"You were right about them coming back."

"If I'd known there was only one man in the house, we could have hidden out here in the barn. I thought it more likely they'd all come back, stay until morning and then fire the house. I never saw a car approach the house last night. He may have come through the woods, thinking to surprise us."

"You don't think they are local, do you?"

"No, honey. They are not local, but they have a contact here. I'm sure of that."

"The others will come back for the man they left here," she said with a worried glance out the loft door.

"Yeah, but we're ahead of the game now. We know that they're coming, and we've got the means to protect ourselves."

"I'm still afraid that Papa will come or Boone with Tess and Jack."

"I was hoping Boone would be back by now or that he would have sent Jack. We'd head for town in the truck."

"We could walk through the woods."

"Honey, the woods are alive with Carters. Marvin hates my guts. He or one of his kin might shoot me on sight. I can't take the chance of leaving you to them. Besides, my life is suddenly more precious to me now that I have you. I want to live and be with you until we're old and gray."

Annabel hugged his arm. "I can't bear the thought of you being hurt again. So much has happened to you because of me."

"But look what I've gained, sweetheart. I've found the woman I want to spend the rest of my life with." He put his arms around her, held her close and kissed her, trying not to scratch her face with his whiskers. "We'll get out of this and someday we'll tell our grandchildren about it."

"Oh, I hope so. I'm worried about Papa. He's got such a temper and . . . bulldozes his way through things."

"Maybe the thugs will give up and leave before he gets back," he said, but he didn't really believe it.

Corbin checked the pistols for the third time that morning and placed them on the blanket near at hand. He considered his options before he mentioned them to Annabel.

"Promise me"—he took her hand and laced her fingers with his—"if there's any shooting, I want you to get over behind that pile of junk; and if I tell you to get down that ladder and out the back door and run for the woods, promise that you'll do it without argument."

"Why . . . in the world would you want me to do . . . that?"

"Because the walls of this barn will not stop the kind of

bullets they'll be using. Now promise that if I get shot or pinned down, you'll go. Marvin Carter is in love with you. If he finds you, he wouldn't kill you, but the men who were here last night would."

"I'd not leave you. Don't ask me to." She slid her arms around his chest and clung to him.

"I hope it doesn't come to that, but I wanted to prepare you just in case." Corbin's ears picked up a sound. He moved quickly to peer out the hayloft door. "A car is coming."

"Is it . . . them?"

"I can see only one man in it."

"Who is it?"

"I don't know yet."

The man went up the steps to the front porch and was out of Corbin's sight. A few minutes later he came out the back door and stood looking around.

"Dammit to hell," Corbin muttered as a thought penetrated his mind. *A friendly visitor who had not been to the house before would not have gone inside if there was no one at home.* "Annabel, ease over here and take a look, but don't make a sound."

Annabel peeked out through the crack, then drew back with a big smile.

"It's Mr. Potter from the drugstore," she whispered.

"I thought that was who it was."

"He'll take us to town."

"I . . . don't think so. . . ." Corbin was frowning.

"Why not? He's come to ask me to play in his band . . . but it's a marching band and I don't—"

"Shhh—"

"Call to him before he leaves."

"He isn't leaving. There's another car coming up the lane. He's waving for it to come on, as if he were expecting it."

"Oh . . . if it's them . . . they might hurt him. You've got to warn him."

"Shhh," he murmured in her ear.

Corbin's arm snaked around her waist and drew her back against him. Standing back in the shadows beside the loft window, they had a good view of the area between the barn and the house. While the small, plump bandleader waited for the car to stop, he removed his Panama hat and dabbed at his forehead with his handkerchief. His thick white hair was parted in the middle; his white shirt, tucked smoothly into the waist of his dark trousers, sparkled. He wore a jaunty black bow tie.

"No one is here," Potter said as soon as the two men got out of the car. "Not even that brainless idiot you left here."

"Goddamn that son-of-a-bitch!" The driver of the car cursed loud and long, then went into the house. "It doesn't look like he's ever been here. If that bastard took off after we let him out . . . I'll strip off every inch of his mangy hide," he said when he came out.

"Morey wouldn'ta run out, Benny."

"Did you look in the barn?" Benny, the driver, barked at Potter.

Without waiting for Potter to answer, the other man strode toward the barn door, scattering the group of cluck-ing hens searching for tidbits in the house yard.

"Morey," he shouted after he threw open the door. "Morey, you whopper-jawed piece of shit, are you in there?"

He stood for a minute in the doorway, then walked be-tween the stalls to the back and looked out. When he came out, he slammed the door shut.

"Ain't nothing there but a pile of shit and a cow out back." He lifted his pant legs and looked at his shoes. "I can hardly wait to get out of this hick country and back to the city. How do you stand it?" he asked Potter.

"I'm paid to stand it and so are you," Potter answered frostily.

"Yeah, but—"

"Shut up, Lester." Benny wasn't as tall or as heavy as Lester, but it was evident from his tone that he was in charge. "Your carping is getting on my nerves. What could have happened to Morey?" He turned and spoke to Potter. "What the hell is going on?"

"What's going on," Mr. Potter said coolly, "is that a bunch of soft city boys were sent out here to deal with men who know what they're doing. You lost forty thousand dollars' worth of valuable inventory when that cave blew up. I wouldn't like to be in your shoes when you get back to Chicago."

"We lost three men and a damn good car too."

"What the hell did the men amount to?" Potter sputtered. "I doubt any one of them knew their ass from a hole in the ground, or they'd not have gone up there and got themselves and the warehouse blown up."

"They were sent out there to guard that hooch. You didn't tell them that it was wired."

"Don't be throwing that botched-up job back at me. How in hell would I know it was wired?" Potter's voice was raised in anger. "There was one man out there. Couldn't your *boys* take care of one man?"

"They were not my boys, although I knew them."

"Who burned out that car? It looks like the one that belongs to a fellow staying at the hotel."

"Morey shot into the gas tank last night."

"Christ Almighty! That took brains." Potter shook his head in disgust.

"He did it on his own. I never told him to."

"Can't you control the men you brought with you, for God's sake? Things were going smooth as silk around here until you smart city fellows showed up."

"If things were going so smooth, how come you didn't keep a closer tab on Boone?"

"If you fool around and bring the federal marshals in here, there'll be hell to pay. Donovan's isn't the only operation going on around here."

"We're doing the job we were sent to do."

"Then why aren't you up in the hills looking for Boone and that other fellow who works for Donovan?"

"Because you told me they'd be here."

"You'd better find them—and the girl, and the boy that's been staying here."

"It's why we're here, goddammit!"

"When they blew up that cave, I heard the blast all the way to town. It isn't hard to figure out that they heard it here and went up to see about it."

"Are you giving orders now?"

"Damn right I am. If you don't want to follow them, get your ass back to Chicago and I'll find someone here to do the job."

"I wasn't told to get rid of the girl, just the men."

"Are you too chickenshit for the job? She's got chummy with the owner of the car you burned and probably spilled her guts to him."

"Who is he? Nothing was said to me about a third man, just the boy."

"He came into town a few weeks ago. I'd not be surprised to find out that he's a revenue agent and playing up to the girl to see what he can find out about Donovan. The man's a cold-eyed bastard. He's not going to stand still and let you shoot him."

"*Me* shoot him? What's the matter with you? Don't you have the guts for it?"

"Don't be talking down to me, you half-cracked dude." Potter's voice rose again in agitation. The dapper little white-haired man with the rosy cheeks looked like a gentle Santa Claus, but he was tough, mean and very much in charge.

"No one told me that you were the boss here."

"Well, I am. And if you get any ideas about taking over, I'll remind you that there are two of us running things in this county."

"How come your buddy ain't out here stickin' his nose in?"

"He will be if you can't handle things. He's handled small-caliber thugs before. I don't doubt he can handle you."

"You listen to me, old man—"

"Looky here what's comin'," Lester broke in, glad to have a reason to defuse the tension between the two men. Both men turned toward the woods.

"Now, there's a hayseed if I ever saw one," Benny muttered.

Chapter 23

ANNABEL WAS TREMBLING FROM THE SHOCK of hearing the harsh words from the band director she had admired. Silent little gasps came from her lips; her hands seemed frozen to Corbin's shirt. Corbin held her tightly to him and whispered in her ear.

"Quiet, honey. We can't let him know we're here."

"He wanted me to play in his band—and now he wants to kill us!"

"I'm shocked too, but we can't let it throw us. Sometimes people are not what they seem to be."

"There's another man working with him."

"Contact men usually come in pairs in case something happens to one of them. What he said about me isn't true. You know that. You're my love, my life. I don't care if your papa is Al Capone."

"I know, but I'm . . . scared."

"So am I. We'd be fools not to be. We have to sit tight until they leave. But if they don't, remember that you promised to go out the back and run if I tell you to."

"They want to kill Boone and Spinner and even Jack. I

don't understand. . . ." She rolled her face back and forth on his shoulder.

Corbin peered out the side of the loft door. "Marvin Carter is coming," he whispered, his lips close to her ear. "He's on horseback."

"Is he alone?"

"Yes. I hope he doesn't shoot off his mouth and get himself killed."

"Hey," Marvin shouted as he neared the house. "What ya doin' here?" He gaze swept over the two strangers and the druggist.

"Who wants to know?" Lester answered belligerently.

"He's one of the Carters," Potter explained. "The hills around here are loaded with them."

"Ain't you the man from the drugstore?" Marvin pulled up on the reins and stopped the horse a few yards from where the men stood.

"You know that I am. I'm the band director as well."

"What're ya doin' out here?"

"I don't think that's any of your business. What are you doing here?"

"I'm callin' on Annabel, and it ain't none of yore's."

"She isn't here."

"Where is she?"

"I only know that she isn't here."

"I ain't believin' ya."

"You calling him a liar?" Lester's voice was curt.

"I ain't talkin' to ya, shit-head. So shut up. I'm looking for my sister. She was here with Annabel."

"See for yourself. She isn't here."

Marvin slid off the horse and headed for the house. He stepped up onto the porch and went inside. A few minutes later he came out and stood in the yard, looking toward the barn.

"Believe me now?" Mr. Potter said with an excessive amount of patience.

"Hey, hayseed, did you look under the bed?" Lester asked with a sneer.

"Haw'd ya like me to smear yore mouth all over yore ugly face?" Marvin snarled.

"Think you can?"

"Want to find out?" Marvin snarled, before turning back to Mr. Potter. "Some city slickers was here last night. They burned the jaybird's car. If they took Annabel and Tess, they'll be shittin' bullets when I get through with them."

"It's a tough man we got here, Benny," said Lester.

"What jaybird?" Potter asked.

"The feller who was callin' on my girl," Marvin shouted angrily.

"Who's Tess?" Lester asked. Then, "There was two women here? Hot diddle-dee-damn, Benny. We'll have us one apiece."

"Annabel is my girl. Tess is my sister, ya dumb-ass. Ya keep yore hands off 'em."

"Or . . . what?" Lester goaded.

"Or ya'll be gettin' yore asshole stretched over that washtub." Marvin stepped off the porch and crossed the yard to look into the shed. After a glance inside, he went to the barn, flung open the door and disappeared inside. He walked the length of the aisle separating the stalls and looked out the back door.

On the way back he heard a rustling in a pile of hay in the back stall and paused. Then, thinking it was only a rat, he passed the stall and went to the ladder leading to the hayloft. Remembering that the loft door was open, he climbed quickly.

The instant his head cleared the loft floor, Corbin pressed a gun to Marvin's temple.

"Let out a sound and I'll blow your head off."

"What . . . the hell?"

"Be quiet!" Corbin snarled.

"What're ya doin' up here?" Marvin's eyes found Annabel.

"Trying to stay alive and keep her alive."

"Who're them men?"

"Killers out of Chicago. Potter is one of them." Corbin spoke quickly and in a whisper. "There were three besides Potter. I've got one of them tied up in that back stall."

"Why—" Marvin's eyes found Annabel again. She was hunkered down next to the wall.

"Donovan's a big-time bootlegger, and they want his business. They want to hold Annabel and force him to come to them. You know what they'd do to her in the meanwhile. Then they'd kill her. I'm here to see they don't get their hands on her."

"Horse cock! I ain't believin' ya."

"You stupid bastard! There was two carloads of them. One carload got themselves blown up. This bunch would just as soon kill a man as look at him. Get on your horse, get out of here and bring us some help."

"Ya been tryin' to court her—"

"Shit a brick!" Corbin said in exasperation. "Listen, I can hold them off long enough for Annabel to get out the back way. Meet her in the woods and take her to town," he whispered, not wanting Annabel to hear.

"Marvin, please, help us," Annabel murmured.

"Give me your word, or I'll blow your head off now."

Marvin looked at Annabel again. "Ya got it."

He backed down the ladder, went to the back stall and looked at the pile of hay, kicked at the man beneath it through the stall slats and, satisfied Corbin had told the truth, left the barn. He blinked when he came out into the bright sunlight.

"What took you so long, Carter?" Potter asked.

"Lookin' to find me a bottle of whiskey," Marvin replied and headed for his horse.

"Don't you drink the stuff you make? Stoney Baker seems to like it."

"Stoney'd drink piss if it was in a liquor bottle."

"Where you goin'?" Lester asked when Marvin took the reins of his horse.

"What's it to ya, shit-head?"

"I'm gettin' tired you callin' me that."

"What're ya goin' to do about it, shit-head?"

"Kill him," Potter said.

"Huh?" Lester looked at Potter.

"You heard me. Kill him."

Before Marvin had time to open his mouth, the bullet to his heart slammed him back against his frightened horse, who shied, whinnied and took off running toward the woods.

"Good shooting." Potter gazed down at the man on the ground.

"Damn right."

"Don't get a big head. Anyone can hit the side of a barn."

"Now, look here, old man. I'm getting tired of your mouth."

"And I'm getting tired of yours." Potter headed for his car.

In the loft Annabel let out a gasp that was cut off by Corbin's hand over her mouth.

"Hold on, honey," he whispered against her ear. "Don't give way." He turned her face into his shoulder.

"Did they . . . did they kill him?"

"Yes, they did."

"Is he . . . dead?"

"I believe so."

"He was going to help us, and they just . . . shot him."

"Try not to think about it." Corbin grasped her shoulders, held her away from him and shook her gently. "Listen to me. I've got a couple sticks of dynamite, but I don't want to use them if I don't have to. If I do, I want you to get behind that pile of junk and stay there. If I tell you to run, get down that ladder and run. Understand?"

Annabel looked at him with dull, unfocused eyes. Corbin feared that she was going into shock. He'd seen it happen during the war.

"Annabel," he hissed. "Listen to me. Dammit, I need you to help me."

She blinked her eyes. "What do you want me to do?"

"I know this is hard for you, sweetheart. But we've got to work together if we're going to get out of this."

"I'll do what you say. I'm . . . sorry—"

"You've been great. Sit down, honey, I've got to see what's going on," he said when he heard a car door slam.

Corbin peered out to see that Potter was now in his car. The man called Benny stood at the car window. After a moment he moved away. Potter started the car, drove it into the space in front of the barn, backed up and headed down the lane. Benny then moved the big black car behind the house so it wouldn't be seen from the road.

"What're we going to do with the hayseed?" Lester asked.

"Why did you shoot him?"

"Potter told me to."

"I know that. Why are you suddenly taking orders from that little dandy?"

"I wanted to shoot the mouthy bastard. Besides that, I've not shot anyone lately." Lester's lips curled into a grin, but his eyes were hard.

"I thought that you'd rather bury a man in a barrel of cement," Benny said dryly.

"That's fun too. What'er we going to do with him?" Lester jerked his head toward the body lying on the ground.

"Nothing. We'll leave him right there. The Carters will come looking for him. Potter said they're a mean bunch and stick together like glue. They'll blame it on Boone and tear up jack around here. They know these hills. If Boone and Donovan's girl are hiding out anywhere near, the Carters will find them. All we got to do is sit back and wait."

As Corbin watched from the loft, Benny took a bag from the car and went to sit on the end of the porch. Lester was pumping water at the well. It didn't seem to bother either of them that Marvin Carter's body lay in the yard not a dozen feet away.

Benny opened the bag and took out a Thompson submachine gun. It had a handgrip under the barrel and, in front of the grip, a round drum. Corbin was familiar with the weapon known as the tommy gun. It was deadly and the favorite weapon of the modern-day gangster.

Realizing that the barn walls would be no protection against the powerful weapon, Corbin was tempted to toss down a stick of dynamite and end it. But he was not sure of the effect the blast would have on the barn if it went off close enough to get the men. The walls of the barn might come down and bury them.

Leaving the window, Corbin quickly moved the blanket and food sack over behind the pile of junk. Annabel was sitting on the floor with her back to the wall. She looked up at him with lifeless eyes. Her face was dirty, her hair tangled. Corbin knelt down beside her.

"Sweetheart, are you all right?"

"Poor Marvin. He didn't deserve to be shot down like a dog."

"No, he didn't, but you can see now the type of men we're dealing with."

"Do you think they found Boone and Jack and Tess?"

"No, honey, I don't. It was a mistake for us to come back here, but at the time I thought it was the thing to do. Now we're between the men out there and the Carters, who will blame us for killing Marvin."

Annabel made a move to get to her feet, but Corbin put his hand on her shoulder to hold her down.

"Rest. If they go into the house, we'll make a run for it out the back of the barn and take our chances of running into the Carters."

"I'm worried that Boone or Papa will come. I expected Papa the day before yesterday; surely he'll come today."

"We'll leave here as soon as we can and get down to the road to warn him."

"Can't we go now?"

"Honey, the barn door is open and they can see through to the back. We'll have to wait until they go in the house." He put his fingers beneath her chin and lifted her face. He kissed her lips, held her cheek against his and whispered, "I love you."

"I keep thinking that God wouldn't be so cruel that he'd

take you from me now that I've found you," she murmured. "I couldn't bear it if something happened to you."

"Nothing is going to happen to either of us. Soon we'll go somewhere and have a good bath, a warm dinner and find a soft bed. When we get to town, I'm going to find a preacher to marry us so that you'll truly be mine to take care of."

"I want that too."

"Your papa will just have to like it or lump it."

"He'll lump it for a while, but he'll get used to it." A half smile tilted her lips. "I'll tell him how much I love you and how happy I am."

"I love you too." He placed another gentle kiss on her lips and went to look out the door again.

An hour passed. Lester and Benny were sprawled on the back porch. Corbin decided that they were waiting for the Carters to come looking for Marvin. He was worried about Annabel. She had been strangely quiet since Marvin was killed. He turned from the window to look at her and was startled to see a man's head coming up out of the hole in the floor.

Corbin jerked the gun from his belt and held it on the man coming up the ladder. "Hold it right there," he ordered.

"Shit, man. Don't shoot me." He continued on up until his knees were against the floor of the loft.

"You're a Carter."

"Calvin Carter. I was here the other day. I'm lookin' for Tess." His eyes searched the corners of the loft.

"She isn't here. Only me and Miss Donovan. Did you see what they did to your brother down there? He was going to help us get out of here."

"Bud saw it. He was watching with his spyglass." Calvin came on up out of the ladder well and squatted on the floor. He had a long-barreled pistol tucked in his belt.

"Thank God for that. We were sure you'd blame it on us."

"Bud said another man was here, but the tall one in the striped shirt did it."

"Did he recognize the other man that was here and left in the one-seated car?"

"He said the gray-haired man from the drugstore was here, and a woman and a man was up here in the hayloft. He could see ya with the spyglass. He thought it was Tess. I come to get her outta here before the shootin' starts."

"Tess is up in the hills with Boone and Jack."

"Why'd them fellers shoot Marvin?"

"Potter told the other fellow to kill him and he did. Maybe it was because he saw Potter and could connect him to the killings when they killed us. They're out of Chicago looking for Donovan. Marvin was going to help me get Annabel out of here."

"They'll get what's comin' to 'em. The little cocksucker from the drugstore will get his too." Calvin's face was hard as stone.

"He's their connection here."

"Did they blow the cave where Donovan kept his hooch?"

"I think Donovan's man blew it up to keep them from getting it. They want to get their hands on Donovan's girl and hold her so they can get to him and Boone."

"Why're ya stickin' yore neck out?"

"Because I'm going to marry Miss Donovan." Corbin spoke firmly while looking Calvin straight in the eyes.

"Ya're the one who run down Leroy, ain't ya?"

"Yes, I hit the mule Leroy was on, but it wasn't intentional. I was trying to avoid the roadblock." Corbin thought it best to tell the truth.

"I ain't sayin' ya done right, but I ain't holdin' it agin ya . . . now. Who's tied up in that last stall down there?"

"Is he still tied up? It's one of them. I found him in the house before the others got here. How did you get in here without them seeing you?"

"Come across the cow lot behind a pulled-up bush. My papa taught me that. I climbed over the stall boards next to the wall instead of comin' down the middle. When I stepped on a pile a hay, it moved. Found a man under it, tied and gagged and wallerin' in cow shit. He was a dressed-up dude. I figured he was one of 'em and kicked a bit more shit in his face."

"I've got to get Miss Donovan out of here." Corbin went to the loft door and looked out. "They're still on the porch and can look straight through the barn."

"I'll signal Bud. When the ball starts rollin', get'er out the back."

"What ball?"

"Ya'll see. Carters take care of Carters. Ain't nobody guns down a Carter and lives to tell it."

"Are you comin' out with us?"

"Naw, we got a little surprise for 'em. We didn't have time to gather up many of our kinfolk, but we got enough to do the job."

"They've got a tommy gun."

"Them fellers ain't leavin' here alive if'n they got a dozen tommy guns." Calvin was at the side of the loft door waving his cap. "Bud will be comin' with a hay wagon and they'll be watchin' it. When I tell ya, take the woman and get out the back."

"Thank you, Calvin. I'm sorry about Marvin." Annabel had come to stand beside Corbin.

"Ya suckered him in, girl. He was 'bout as foolish over ya as Pa was over Ma."

"I'm sorry that I couldn't . . . like him."

"Ya woulda in time. My woman didn't like me much at first. Now she's wild for me." There was no brag in Calvin's voice. He sincerely believed what he was saying was true. "Marvin was a wild one. It's said Pa was wild too when he was young, but Ma settled him down. Tell that Boone feller that I'm top dog now Marvin's gone, and I'll be comin' back for Tess. She ain't goin' to be his whore."

"Boone cares for her. He'll marry her and take good care of her."

"Shit! He ain't going to marry a woman like her. She been ruint."

"Why do you say that? She's as nice a woman as I've ever met," Annabel said firmly.

"She ain't either nice. Ya don't know what yo're talkin' about. She ain't nothin' but a whore, even if she is a Carter." Calvin's voice was a harsh whisper. "She'd honey up to an oak tree if'n it had a branch in the right place. She ain't fit to be no man's wife—"

Annabel felt Corbin's hand on her arm and snapped her mouth shut before she made a caustic reply.

"Here comes the wagon." Calvin pulled the long-barreled gun from his belt. "It'll be just like shootin' fish in a barrel. Sons-a-bitches! I'd like to roast 'em over a slow fire for gunnin' Marvin down." A minute later he said sharply, "Go!"

Corbin hurried Annabel to the hole in the floor. He went down first and guided her feet to the rungs on the ladder. Each holding tightly to the other's hand, they scrambled out the back of the barn and ran across the cow pasture toward the woods.

Safely amid the dense growth of bushes, Corbin turned

back toward the homestead to see four men with guns at the ready coming up out of the hay in the back of the wagon. There was a blast of gunfire from the wagon and from Calvin, who was shooting from the door of the hayloft. Benny and Lester never got off a shot. The Carters continued to shoot into the bodies as they lay on the ground.

Corbin put his arm around Annabel. She turned and clung to him.

"Is it over?"

"Part of it is. We'll wait and see what the Carters are going to do now."

As they watched, Calvin came out of the barn with the man from the stall.

"Looky what I found," he shouted. "Ain't he pretty?"

Chapter 24

Hᴏᴡ ʏᴀ ꜰᴇᴇʟɪɴ'?" Boone had come to stand beside the bunk where Spinner lay. His face was cut and bruised. He took shallow breaths through his open mouth.

"Like . . . I been run over by a freight train," he gasped.

"Ya look like it too."

"Where's the boy?"

"I sent him out to look around. When he gets back, I should get on down to the house and see about Annabel."

"Murphy ought to be back by now."

"He'll have a run-in with Appleby when he learns that she's been with him all night and that there's somethin' goin' on between him and Annabel." Boone chuckled. "I'd like to see it. Appleby can hold his own. He's 'bout as bullheaded as Murphy."

Spinner grunted and spoke with difficulty. "Ain't no man goin' to be good enough for that girl to Murphy's way a thinkin'."

"Annabel's stuck on him. Murphy might just have to back off."

Tess came to stand beside Boone. "Can ya eat somethin', Mr. Spinner?"

"Lass, ya been pokin' that stuff down me since I woke up. I'm so damn full of broth my eyes is crossed."

Tess bent down and looked into his eyes. "They're no such thing," she exclaimed. "You need to eat and get your strength back."

"Why? I'm doin' just fine a-laying here lappin' up all this waitin' on . . . by a pretty woman."

"This pretty woman belongs to me," Boone said gruffly and put his arm around Tess. His black eyes shone with pride. "Let the old goat lay there and starve," he murmured in her ear but loud enough for Spinner to hear.

"He don't mean it, Mr. Spinner."

"Hell, I don't. Ya been fussin' over him like he was somethin' special."

"Pay him no mind," Tess said and dug her elbow in Boone's ribs. "If you want something, call out. Hear?"

Boone moved Tess toward the door. They stepped out into the bright sunlight. Tess's face wore a worried look.

"What are ya frettin' about?" Boone asked with concern.

"I keep wondering how Leroy is doing. Marvin might of got him away from the doctor."

"I doubt that. Doc Perkin's got sand. He'll not give him up till he's able to go."

"This is a pretty place," said Tess. "I wish Leroy could see it. He would be good at fixing up a place like this."

"Is this the kind of place you'd like to have?"

"Who wouldn't?"

"It'd be lonesome up here."

"Not for me. I love the woods. Course, I like to go to town once in a while," she said, her amber eyes twinkling with mischief.

"Are you wantin' to go to town now?"

Tess bit her lip and thought about it. "Are you?"

"I don't want to, but I ought to go back to the house. Marvin may have sobered up enough to try something. Appleby won't stand for crowdin' Annabel."

"Let me go with you."

"Are ya 'fraid yore brothers will find ya here?"

"When the Carters spread out, they can find a safety pin in these hills. They're going to be awfully mad, but I'm not afraid if I'm with you."

"I'd only be gone a few hours . . . unless there's trouble of some kind."

"Don't you trust Mr. Appleby to take care of her?"

"Yes, but her papa left her in my care. If he's there, I'll be glad to turn the chore back to him and come right back."

"Let me go with you." She had that fear in her voice again. Her arms went around his waist and she hugged him tightly to her.

Boone buried his face in Tess's hair, as if to close out the world and enjoy the pleasure of her soft body against his. His hand came up to rest at her waist, then moved in a slow glide over her back and down to her hips, stroking with loving possession.

"Sweet girl, I can see the writin' on the wall. You're goin' to twist me 'round yore little finger." His voice was a breathless whisper before he bent his head to find her lips with his. His kiss was long and sweet.

"Do you mind me . . . doing that?"

"Twistin' me 'round yore finger? It means I got to watch my step, or I'll be doin' handsprings ever' time ya blink them pretty eyes."

She laughed. It made her look like a young girl. Then the smile left her face and she sobered.

"I just love you so much, Mr. Boone. When you're out of

my sight, I get to worrying that you won't come back and I'll never see you again."

"How can you love me?" he asked, feeling as if he were holding the treasure of the world in his arms. "I'm just a big old ugly bugger that knows nothin' but riverboats and boot-leggin'."

"You're not ugly! Not old! And . . . you're smart. We can get us a chicken farm or . . . something." She framed his face with the palms of her hands. "You're the prettiest and the sweetest man in the whole world."

"Well . . . what do you know about that?" Boone could hardly talk for the pounding of his heart and the warm tide of tingling happiness that washed over him.

"How can you love me . . . knowing . . . what you know?" she asked hesitantly.

"Knowin' what I know makes me love ya all the more. Yo're a woman who come through a troubled time with her head held high." He lifted her off the ground and swung her around. She squealed and clung to him. "I'm not wantin' ya to worry, darlin'. I'll send Jack to see about Annabel."

"If you think you should go, I could go with you."

"We'll stay here and look after Spinner. Appleby could have taken Annabel to town by now. It's what he wanted to do. After you poke some more broth down Spinner, we'll walk Jack down to where we left the truck. I'm not sure he could find it."

Not wanting Annabel to see what the Carters might do to the man he had left tied up in the stall, Corbin quickly turned her away from the homestead.

Minutes later, as they were going through the woods toward the road, a hoarse scream came from the direction of the house.

Annabel stopped. "What was that?"

"I'm not sure," he lied. "Let's get on down to the road. Boone or Jack may come along and we want to stop them before they go up the lane to the house."

When a volley of gunfire sounded, Annabel stopped again and grabbed Corbin's arm.

"They . . . killed him!"

"We don't know that. They could be shooting the chickens. Come on, honey."

"I'm not so dumb that I believe that! The Carters are killers, just like the men with Mr. Potter. They'll kill Papa or Boone. They're not even civilized!"

"They live by their own code of right and wrong. We might not have made it out of there without them."

"But . . . did you hear what Calvin said about Tess, his own sister?" Shock and anger had made Annabel forget how tired she was. She walked so fast, Corbin had to tug on her hand to slow her down before she exhausted herself.

"Like I said, they live by their own code. Boone will take care of Tess. He fell for her like a rock, just as I fell for you, my sweet and pretty girl."

She was so worked up that a spate of angry, loud words spewed out of her mouth. The Carters were the focus of her agitation.

"I still say they are savage, uncivilized, ignorant hillbillies who lie and steal and make corn liquor. I'm sorry that Marvin is dead, but he didn't have two ideas above a goat if he thought I'd even consider going out with him. He had the manners of a lout, a guttersnipe, a yokel. I doubt that he ever brushed his teeth or said thank you in his entire life." Words rushed out of her mouth like water from a dam.

"And that's not all! He didn't even want to take Leroy, his own brother, to the doctor when he was hurt—and it was his fault the kid was hurt. Tess said Leroy could have died if she and Boone hadn't taken him to the doctor." Annabel took a deep breath and continued. "Tess is the only decent one of the bunch. And Calvin, the 'top dog' now, as he put it, said that Tess was unfit to be a man's wife. I suppose he thinks he's fit to be a husband and beget babies on that poor woman who married him. They say he's got six and he's younger than Marvin. The Carters are a clannish, mean bunch of . . . of vulgar, rough, ignorant people!"

Corbin, realizing that Annabel was on the verge of hysteria, didn't interrupt her litany of accusations against the Carters. She had endured more yesterday and today than most women had to endure in a lifetime. This could help ease her frustration.

"They'd better not hurt Papa or Boone or Jack," Annabel continued, walking faster, her voice rising, her anger still focused on the Carters. "If they as much as harm a hair on their heads, I'll get a gun and shoot every damn one of them. I'll—" She stopped suddenly and clapped her hand to her mouth.

She looked up at Corbin, her eyes bright and as green as shamrocks. Suddenly her face crumpled, she gasped and burst into tears. Without hesitation, she threw herself into his arms. He held her close to him while racking sobs shook her slender body. She wrapped her arms around him and hid her face against the curve of his neck. He let her cry until her sobs turned into pitiful whimpers.

"Ah, sweet girl," he crooned to her, holding her tenderly and whispering endearments. "Shhh, darlin', sweetheart, don't cry, love. We're going to be all right now." He kissed her wet cheeks, her forehead, her eyes.

"Corbin . . . I love you—" she gasped between sobs.

"And I love you, honey. Don't carry on so, sweetheart. You've been a brave girl. The bravest I've ever known."

"I don't know what to do . . . about Papa."

"There isn't anything we can do right now, sweetheart. We'll wait down by the road. If he comes, we'll stop him before he goes to the house."

"I've got this feeling that he's not going to come back. He always sends word if he's delayed so I won't worry."

"He's not that late. A lot of things could happen to cause a delay. Car trouble, for instance." He pulled his handkerchief from his pocket and wiped her eyes. "Let's get on down the road and find a place to sit down in the shade."

The place they found was the spot where Jack had spent the night he was sick. They had a view of the house on the hill and of the road in each direction. Beneath the shade of a tree well back from the road, Corbin sank down on the grass and pulled Annabel into his lap. She curled up in his arms like a little lost puppy. He cuddled her to him, smoothing her hair back from her face. She fit so perfectly in the nest made by this arms and his thighs.

She looked up into his eyes. "You've lost so much and been through so much because of me."

"I wouldn't change a minute of it."

"I must look a sight."

"Not to me. Never to me."

Corbin gazed at her upturned face. Her eyes were teary bright and full of love . . . for him. His arms tightened and he slowly lowered his head to hers and kissed her puffed eyes and wet cheeks. The yielding sweetness of her mouth, the softness of her body made him tighten with desire. This woman was his life. It was as simple as that. He loved her with every breath and, if it came to that, would give his life to keep her safe and happy.

They sat quietly for a long while. Corbin, deep in thought, recalled the words he had overheard. Neither Potter nor the other two men mentioned looking for Murphy Donovan, only Boone and Annabel. It was as if they knew that Murphy was no longer a problem for them. If they had already killed him, it would be a crushing blow to Annabel.

They had been sitting there for a couple of hours when Corbin was jarred from his thoughts and shook Annabel.

"Get up, honey. The black car is coming down the lane."

They scrambled back behind the bushes and peered out. The big car moved slowly as if the driver were not sure how to drive it. At the road he stopped it with a jerk by slamming his foot down too hard on the brake pedal. Calvin Carter, at the wheel, looked neither left nor right as he concentrated on driving the powerful car. It turned down the road, leaving a trail of dust in its wake.

"They're stealing it," Annabel exclaimed.

"I don't know who has a better right to it, honey."

They went back to sit beneath the tree. As the hours passed, they moved with the shade. Several cars passed, but not one they recognized, and Corbin was afraid to flag them down. It was suppertime when Annabel admitted her thirst.

"I wish we'd brought the jar of water."

"Sweetheart." Corbin put his hands on her neck, his thumbs gently caressing the line of her jaw. "I know you're thirsty. It's going to be a while."

"I know. I can wait. Maybe when it's dark—" She suddenly broke off her words to listen. "Do I hear a car?"

Corbin stood and shielded his eyes with his hand. The truck coming down the road looked like the one Boone drove, but he waited to be sure before he stepped out into the road.

"It looks like Boone's truck. Stay here, honey, until I

make sure." As the truck approached, Corbin stepped out and waved his arms. "Are we glad to see you!" he exclaimed when Jack stopped.

Annabel came out of the bushes and hurried to the truck.

"Is Boone all right, and Tess and . . . Spinner?"

"They're fine. Spinner is banged up, but he'll be all right. Boone sent me to see if Mr. Donovan was back. What're you doing down here by the road? Where's your car?"

"It's a long story. Do you have any water? Annabel is awfully thirsty."

"It just so happens that I do. Boone keeps a keg in the truck just in case the engine gets hot."

Jack pulled the truck off the road. After they drank the water dipped from an oak keg with a fruit jar, they stood in the shade of the truck while Corbin told him what had happened to them last night and today.

Jack shared the information he had about the men coming to the cave and beating Spinner, trying to get him to tell where Boone was. He described how Spinner had crawled to the plunger to blow up the cave, then dragged himself back to the cabin where they found him.

"Boone went up and looked around. He said the whole side of that rock cliff caved in on them. Spinner had done a good job setting the charge."

"They were hired killers. So were the ones who came to the house with Potter," Corbin said.

"Why did they shoot Marvin?"

"Just because Potter told one of them to kill him. He was going to help me get Annabel out."

"You never told me that," Annabel said. "I thought he was going to help both of us get out."

"He was . . . both of us," Corbin corrected the statement, then changed the subject. "There's been no movement up there at the house since Calvin drove the car out. If you'll stay here with Annabel, Jack, I'll go take a look around."

Annabel got into the truck. "You're not leaving me here."

Corbin followed her. "It'll be an ugly sight up there, and I don't want you to see it."

"I won't look."

"Be reasonable—"

"No. Get in, Corbin. I've been with you every minute and I'm not going to leave you now just because of an ugly sight."

"There could be . . . more. Now the Carters have the tommy gun."

"I'll take my chances along with you and Jack."

Corbin looked at her dear, stubbornly set features for a long while, then ducked his head into the cab and kissed her mouth.

"I can see that I'm going to have my hands full with you. Jack, do you have the rifle?"

"I've got it and it's loaded."

"Give it to me. I'll get in the back and stand behind the cab. I can see better back there. Drive slowly and keep your eyes open. If I want you to stop, I'll pound on the top of the cab. Annabel, if that happens, you get down on the floor. Is that understood?" he said sternly. Then, without waiting for a reply, Corbin grabbed the rifle and climbed up into the truck bed.

The sun was behind them as they went up the lane to the house on the hill. The only movement they observed was the swaying of the tall grass alongside the lane. The front door of the house was closed. Jack drove the truck alongside the house and stopped beside the back porch.

Corbin searched the area and saw absolutely nothing one wouldn't normally see in a house yard. There were no bodies, no wheel tracks. The chickens were gone, the barn door was closed, as was the door leading into the back of the house. The yard had been swept clean. It was as if what had happened here a few short hours ago had never taken place.

Corbin jumped out the back of the truck and stood beside the window of the cab.

"I figured they'd take . . . Marvin. But what did they do with . . . the others?" Annabel asked.

"Stay in the truck while I look in the barn."

Corbin cautiously opened the barn door and darted inside. When he came out, he closed the door and went to the shed. He looked inside, then circled the barn before he came back to the truck.

"Nothing in there but the cow."

"She wasn't milked this morning."

"She's been milked," Corbin said. "She was in a stall eating hay."

"Forevermore! The Carters are the darnedest people I ever did see. I'll never understand them. Kind one minute, mean as sin the next."

"I'm still going to beat the hell out of that kid who was wearing my shirt," Jack said. "He knows what happened to my ball glove."

"This kid's got a one-track mind," Corbin said to Annabel and winked. "I'll take a look in the house."

When he came out, he was carrying the water bucket and went to the pump.

"It's just as you left it. Come get a drink of water."

Annabel made a trip through the house and declared that as far as she could tell, nothing was missing. In the kitchen, she took out bread, butter and cheese. They ate quickly while planning what to do.

"I don't think we should stay here," Corbin said. "Potter

may come back with his partner and his own bunch of thugs. He'll want to know what went on out here. Annabel, pack the things you'll need for a while. We'll go to town and find a preacher to marry us so I can keep you with me in my hotel room. I'm not letting you out of my sight."

"Why don't we go up to Spinner's place," Jack suggested. "It's well hid."

"We can't hide out indefinitely. I'll send a wire to Marshal Sanford as soon as we get to town."

"But what if Papa comes?"

"Leave a note here on the table. Just tell him that he knows where he can find Boone and Spinner and that you're all right and that you'll get in touch with him later."

"What about Mildred?"

"How about giving her to the Carters? They've already taken the chickens. We'll stop by and tell them to come get her."

"They might shoot you on sight," Jack said.

"I don't think so. Maybe next week, but not today. When is Boone expecting you back?"

"He said if I couldn't get back before dark to wait until morning—that is, if things were all right here. I don't know if I could find my way back through the woods to the cabin after dark."

"When we get to town, you can go to the telegraph office and send a message to Marshal Sanford. It'll be a coded message. Annabel and I will stay out of sight as much as possible."

Annabel looked at him strangely. "Boone was right: You *are* a lawman!" she said quietly.

"No, I'm not." He took hold of her shoulders and looked her in the face. "I've not lied to you."

"Then why would you be sending a coded message to the marshal?"

"I know Marshal Sanford. When I first came to town, I met him at the hotel. He asked me to take notice of some of the merchants in town while I was here. He suspected that one or two of them had ties with mobs back East. As we discovered this morning, he was right."

"I know the marshal too," Jack said. "He was all the law we had in Fertile until Corbin came."

Annabel wrapped her arms around Corbin's middle and hugged him.

"I'll never lie to you and I'll always tell you everything, no matter how bad it is." He kissed her forehead.

"I believe you."

"I'll get your violin out of the woodpile while you pack. I know you'll want to take it with you."

"So much has happened, I almost forgot about it. I do want to keep it with me."

"You'll be my wife before this day is over and I'll have every right to keep *you* with me."

Chapter 25

When they came to the lane leading to the Carters', Jack slowed the truck.

"Are you sure you want to go up there? They're well armed now that they've got the tommy gun."

"I'm sure," Corbin said confidently. "I want to thank them." He looked down and spoke to Annabel sitting between him and Jack. "Folks like the Carters make bitter enemies; but if you can get them on your side, they are loyal friends."

The truck rounded the corner of the house. A heavyset man in overalls stepped off the porch. He carried a bucket. Ignoring them, he waddled out into the yard and threw a handful of grain to a flock of white hens picking out undigested tidbits from animal manure and scratching in the grass for insects.

"Those are my chickens!" Annabel whispered angrily.

"Sshh—the chickens aren't important." Corbin got out of the truck and approached the man.

"Are you Bud Carter?"

"Yup."

"I'm Corbin Appleby." Corbin held out his hand. "I want

to thank you for what you did today." Bud, hesitantly, shook Corbin's hand.

" 'Twas for Marvin."

"I know that. But for you, however, they would have killed us. It was a brave thing you did, coming in with that hay wagon."

"We . . . couldn't let it go by."

"Of course not. You did what you had to do."

" 'Twas for Marvin," he said again.

"Miss Donovan is leaving and is unable to take her cow. It would be a favor to her if you would go get her. She's become fond of her and wants her to be where she'll get good care."

"Tess did the milkin', but I know how."

"Can I tell Miss Donovan that you'll get the cow?"

"I guess so."

"Thank you. It will take a worry from her mind. And again, let me say that we're sorry about Marvin."

Corbin came back and got in the truck. As they drove past Bud, Annabel waved. He stood as if frozen to the ground, the bucket in his hand and the hens clucking around his feet, a blank expression on his face.

"You're a good and smart man, Corbin Appleby," Annabel said when they were on the road again. "You're wiser than I am. I wouldn't have thought to go there and thank them and let them think it was a favor to me for them to take my cow."

Corbin grinned at her. "Good and smart? In the years ahead, I'm going to remind you of those words."

"Have you decided where we're going when we get to town?" Jack asked.

"Stop here for just a minute and let's talk about it. I don't know of anyone in town whom I can trust. Potter has a partner. It could be any one of a number of people. I'm only half sure I can trust the butcher. He was in my army unit in France . . . he says. I'm afraid to take a chance on him."

"The preachers wouldn't be connected with Potter," Annabel said.

"We've got to trust one of them to marry us, but I don't want to involve them in something that could be dangerous to them or their families."

"Boone liked the doctor. He said he was a man to ride the river with, whatever that means."

"I thought of him, sweetheart. He may be our best bet. But first I want to find a preacher to marry us. There's a Baptist church on the west edge of town. Is that all right with you?"

"It's all right with me, but are you sure you want to do this?"

Corbin's arm pulled her tightly against him. "Are *you* sure? It's a lifetime commitment. I don't want to rush you into anything because we've found ourselves in this fix."

"I wanted to marry you before we got into this fix." Her hand went to his cheek.

"It isn't the kind of wedding a girl dreams about," he said quietly. "The groom needs a bath and a shave. His clothes are dirty. But he has a heart full of love for his bride."

"That's what matters."

"I don't have a ring."

"You can tie a string around my finger until we can get one."

As the worry left his face, he laughed and kissed her. "I'm going to have you with me every night for the rest of our lives, so we'd better get married."

"Mush!" Jack snorted. "Kissy, kissy. You're just like Julie and Evan before they got married."

"When you fall in love, Jack, my boy, I'll give you some lessons in kissing."

"Better yet, why don't you donate your grandpa's book on courting to him?" Annabel smiled impishly.

"Good idea. It worked for me, didn't it?"

Jack turned down a side road before they reached town and paused in front of a small frame church. He motioned to the two boys playing catch in the middle of the road.

"Where does the preacher live?"

"Right there." The boy pointed to the house nearest to the church. "He's my pa."

"Much obliged." Jack moved the truck to the side of the road and turned off the motor.

"I'll go talk to him." Corbin got out, went to the house and knocked on the door. When it opened, he stepped inside. It seemed hours to Annabel but could only have been minutes before he came back out to the truck. "Come on, sweetheart. You too, Jack. You and the preacher's wife will be our witnesses."

Annabel got out and smoothed her skirt down with her hands and looped her dark hair behind her ears.

This is my wedding day, this is my wedding day . . .

"I told him that we were eloping," Corbin's voice penetrated into her mind. "I said that your father wanted you to marry a Catholic, but we were in love and wanted to be married before we yielded to temptation and did what would possibly result in a child being born out of wedlock."

"You didn't say that!" She could feel the heat that came up her neck to flood her face.

"I did. He was very understanding."

"I'll not be able to face him."

Corbin laughed. "Sure you will. Honey, you're adorable when you blush."

"How did you know Papa was Catholic?"

"He's Irish, isn't he? All you have to do is say the word *Catholic* to a Baptist to get him going. I was lucky to think of it."

The preacher, a serious-faced man with sparse light hair, met them at the door and led them to a table behind the piano, where he asked Corbin to fill out some papers. Annabel was surprised that he remembered her telling him that she was born on Christmas day. He completed the paper and handed it to the preacher.

"Annabel Lee Donovan and Corbin Joseph Appleby, both legal age." He nodded, went to stand in front of the podium and motioned for them to stand before him. His wife had quietly come in the back door of the church.

"We are gathered together here to unite Annabel Lee Donovan and Corbin Joseph Appleby in holy matrimony."

With her hand clasped tightly in Corbin's, her eyes on the preacher's face, Annabel listened, as if it were happening to someone else, to the ceremony that would make her Corbin's wife.

"Do you, Corbin Joseph Appleby, take this woman to be your lawful wedded wife? Do you promise, before God, to love and cherish her in sickness and in health until death do you part?"

Corbin heard the words, his eyes on the face of the woman who had become dearer to him than life.

"I do promise."

"Do you, Annabel Lee Donovan, take this man to be your lawful wedded husband? Do you promise, before God, to love and cherish him, to honor and obey him, in sickness and in health, for better or for worse, until death you do part?"

With her eyes locked with Corbin's, she whispered, "I do."

"The ring, please."

"We haven't had time to buy a ring. This will have to do."

Corbin reached into his shirt pocket and pulled out a short piece of twine. His eyes smiled into hers as he wrapped the string twice around her finger and tied it. He then lifted her hand to his lips and kissed the symbol of their union.

"By the right invested in me by the church and by the law of Missouri in this year of our Lord, nineteen hundred and twenty-five, I declare you man and wife. You may kiss the bride."

The ceremony that changed their lives forever was over in a matter of minutes. Corbin looked into Annabel's face, then slowly pulled her into his arms.

"Hello, sweet wife." His lips whispered against the far corner of hers.

Hers parted warmly. "Hello, husband."

He kissed her then, gently and reverently.

A smile stripped the tiredness from his face. Unmindful of the preacher, his wife and Jack, Corbin held her against him, looking at her. In her eyes was a look of adoration. Her love was so great a miracle that all he could do was wonder how he had lived until now without this special girl who had come so suddenly into his life.

Jack's voice finally broke into the silence. "Don't I get to kiss the bride?"

Corbin released her reluctantly, watched Jack kiss his wife, then pulled her close to him again. The preacher went back to the table and put his finger on a document.

"If you will both sign, the witnesses will affix their signatures." He dipped the pen in the inkwell and handed it to Annabel. She set her name to the paper and passed the pen to Corbin. After the preacher's wife and Jack signed, the preacher waved the paper to dry the ink, then handed it to Annabel. "The marriage will be recorded at the courthouse the first thing in the morning."

"Thank you, sir." She folded the paper carefully and said, "Thank you too, ma'am."

"I wish you a long and happy life together."

"Thank you. And . . . good-bye."

After Corbin pressed some bills in the preacher's hand, he and Annabel walked back down the aisle as man and wife. Jack trailed along behind them. Out in the golden afternoon, she smiled up at her husband.

"Thank you for my beautiful ring." Mischief lit her eyes.

"You're welcome. I asked the preacher's wife if she had a short length of twine. I wish it were a diamond as big as a hen's egg."

"I don't. It's perfect. I may never take it off."

She hugged his arm and matched her steps with his. She hadn't known that there was this much happiness in the world. She loved this man and he loved her in return. She could tell by the look in his eyes when he gazed at her as he was doing now. Even the expectation of her father's anger, when he learned that she had married without his permission, failed to dim her happiness.

"What now?" Jack asked after he had started the truck moving.

"The depot. This is suppertime. Not many people will be out on the street. I'll write out a wire and you can take it in."

"You don't have any paper," Annabel said.

"You do." He reached for the wedding paper the preacher had given her.

"Oh, no! You're not using that."

Corbin laughed, pulled a tablet and pencil out from

under the seat and began to write. When he finished, he tore the page from the tablet and handed it to Annabel. She read it aloud: "'Mrs. Ned Wicker, Jefferson City, Missouri. Aunt Maude is sick. Dying. Medicine from drugstore didn't help. Urgent you see her. J. Jones.'"

"Who is Mrs. Wicker?" Jack asked.

"Marshal Sanford. Hang around until you see the operator sending it. Here's some money." Corbin held out a bill.

"Will the marshal know what you mean about the medicine at the drugstore?" Jack stuffed the bill in his pocket.

"He'll know."

There were no cars or wagons at the depot. Jack parked the truck, got out and walked along the plank walk to the door with the sign TELEGRAPH above it and went inside.

Corbin's arm arched over Annabel's head and pulled her closer to him. His lips caressed her cheek before moving to her mouth. His lips fell hungrily on hers. They were demanding yet tender.

"Someone will see."

"I don't care. Do you?"

"Not a bit."

"Kiss me, wife."

She did, her lips clinging moistly to his. After a minute or two, she leaned away. Her eyes danced lovingly over his face and she laughed.

"What are you laughing at?"

"You. How are you going to teach Jack to kiss?" She cocked her head to one side and wrinkled her nose at him. "Are you going to let him practice on me?"

"Hell, no! If I find any man kissing you, I'll twist his tail off. Even Jack."

He cut her laughter off with a kiss, which she took thirstily. His fingers moved up into her hair, their touch strong and possessive. His lips pulled away, but he kept her close.

"You're sweet and brave and sensible. I love everything about you, Mrs. Appleby," he said quietly.

"I love everything about you."

"You're truly mine now."

"And you're mine. I'm so glad."

"The telegram is on its way," Jack said, pulling open the door. "It cost twenty-two cents. They charge by the word. Here's your change." He got in and started the truck. "Where to? The doctor's?"

"I've been thinking about that. I'd rather not involve him if I don't have to. If Annabel and I can hole up in the hotel until Marshal Sanford gets here, we'll be all right. It occurred to me that Potter knows this truck and so does his partner, whoever he is. The sooner we get it out of town, the better."

"You're probably right. Not many trucks in town can carry as heavy a load as this one."

"I don't want you to go back to the house, Jack. When Potter fails to hear from the men he met out there, he's going to go looking for them."

"But Mr. Potter doesn't know that we know he was out there when Marvin was killed."

"That's right, honey. It's one advantage we have."

"What do you think the Carters did with the men they killed?" she asked.

"I'm thinking that they'll never be found. The car will disappear too."

"Are you going to tell Marshal Sanford?"

"He's the law. He has the right to know."

"Will he arrest the Carters?"

"After I explain the situation, I think he'll let sleeping dogs lie. The Carters did him a favor in a roundabout way."

"I'll go back to where Boone leaves the truck and wait in it until morning. He'll be fit to be tied when he learns all that's happened." Jack's eyes were full of merriment. "I can hardly wait to tell him you're married."

Corbin grinned. "I'd like to tell the big, mule-headed bozo myself."

"He won't be as surprised as you think," Annabel said with a sly smile.

"Tell him to stay put, Jack. When this is over, we'll come up. If I can't find the cabin, I'll fire three rapid shots and he can find us."

"Papa will be here by then. He'll know how to find it."

"What will you do for a car?" Jack asked.

"The marshal will help me get one."

"Jack, I'm worried about you going off by yourself. Will you be all right?" Annabel asked.

"Sure, once I'm out of town."

"Turn in here, Jack, and let us out in the alley behind the hotel. We'll go up the back stairs."

Corbin's eyes swept the area before he stepped out of the truck and held out his hand for his new wife. For a long minute he allowed his eyes to feast on the woman standing beside him. His intense blue gaze clung to her thick, tousled hair, her passionate mouth and tight, slim body. The fact that she loved him was a joy of ever-expanding proportions.

"They'll think I'm sneaking a fallen woman into my room," he teased while they were getting her bag and violin case out of the truck.

"I'll wave this wedding paper in front of their noses if they do." She spoke to Jack. "Tell Boone not to worry and that I left a note for Papa."

"Have you got enough gas to get back?" Corbin asked.

"I'm sure I have. There's an extra large tank on this truck."

Annabel and Corbin moved close to the iron stairway attached to the back of the hotel and waited until the truck was out of sight.

"Do you think he'll be all right?"

"He's a bright boy with a level head on his shoulders," Corbin said by way of an answer.

Carrying her bag in one hand, his other hand cupping her elbow, Corbin ushered her up the stairs and into the upper hall. It was deserted. A dim bulb burning at the end of the hall was the only light as he took out his key and unlocked the door to his room.

"Stay here, honey," he whispered and lifted the violin case from her hand. He set it and the bag inside the room, then scooped her up in his arms and carried her inside. He backed against the door to close it.

"This is our first home together, sweetheart. I wish I could have taken you on a honeymoon to Niagara Falls. We would have spent our first night together in a fancy compartment on the train. Instead we're here in this small-town hotel room. It's not exactly what I wanted for my bride."

Her fingers went up to his lips. She giggled happily.

"You lucked out, Mr. Appleby. The swaying of a train makes me sick. I would have spent the night throwing up."

"What do you know about that?" With his eyes on her smiling face, he let her slide down his body until her feet reached the floor. His arms tightened around her and the words he muttered were scattered from her ear along her jaw to her mouth. "I wanted you to spend your wedding night in a pretty place with a soft, sweet-smelling bed and banks of flowers beside it."

"The bed is soft and clean and I can do without the banks of flowers if you can."

"Annabel Lee, my Annabel Lee, you're wonderful."

"I'm no such thing. I'm hungry."

He was delighted with her.

"*She* was a child and *I* was a child,/ In this kingdom by the sea,/ But we loved with a love that was more than love—/ I and my Annabel Lee."

"You really like that poem, don't you?"

"It has played over and over in my head since the first time I met you. It's as if it was written for us."

Her lips parted with a soft sigh. As if it were the signal he'd awaited, Corbin captured her lips in a kiss that was rich and deep; a kiss she desperately welcomed. His mouth moved over hers in a loving way, tasting and caressing, responding to her response with an ever-tightening embrace. His hand moved from her back to her hips, molding her to his silently clamoring body.

It was all he could do to make himself draw away from her.

"Do I frighten you?" he whispered.

"No. I frighten myself. So many . . . new feelings."

"We'll take it slow, sweetheart." He let his arms fall from around her so that he could think clearly. "There's a water closet at the end of the hall. If you want to use it, I'll take you there. You can take a bath, or if you'd rather, you can wash here in the room. After we've had a chance to clean up a bit, I'll go down to the dining room and bring up something to eat. You haven't eaten much today."

While Annabel was using the water closet down the hall, Corbin washed, shaved and changed his clothes. He gave her the key to the room and cautioned her not to open the door for anyone but him. Reluctant to leave her even for a short time, he hurried down to the hotel lobby. The young desk clerk called out to him.

"Mr. Appleby. Several people have been in today looking for you."

"Really? Who?"

"Mr. Travis was here early this morning."

"Craig Travis, the butcher? Did he say what he wanted?"

"He said he hadn't seen you for a while. Said to tell you to stop by. Mr. Potter came by with a prescription he'd filled for you, and Mr. Brighton, the postmaster, brought you a letter." The clerk placed a letter on the counter. "You must have pull with that postmaster to have him walk all the way over here with a letter."

Corbin fingered the envelope. "What did Mr. Potter have to say about the prescription?"

"He said he would leave it in your room and then changed his mind when I offered to take it up. He said he'd better give it to you himself and to tell you to come to the drugstore no matter what time you got back. He's very accommodating."

"Yeah, he is. Can you keep a secret?" He winked at the clerk.

"Of course, Mr. Appleby."

"I was married today. My bride is in my room. We've got to keep it a secret from her father for a few days. He wanted her to marry a Catholic." The lie that had worked with the minister came easily to Corbin's lips.

"Congratulations."

"Thank you. Can I trust you not to give away our secret until her father comes to accept it?"

"Absolutely, Mr. Appleby. I'll not tell a soul. My sister almost married a Baptist. I tell you, our Catholic parents were not pleased."

"If Mr. Potter comes back, tell him . . ." Corbin tapped the letter he was holding on the counter while he was thinking of an excuse. "Oh, just tell him that I'm not back yet."

"He asked if I knew where you'd gone, as if I'd ask a guest where he was going when he went out." The clerk made a helpless gesture with his hands.

"I'd like to get a couple plates of food to take up to the room. We've been driving all day and my bride is worn out."

"Of course, Mr. Appleby. I'll take care of it myself."

While the food was being prepared, Corbin opened the letter. It was from Julie Jones Johnson back in Fertile. The family had been relieved to learn that Jack was all right and would be coming home soon. Her letter was newsy. Her brother Joe and Thad Taylor were still in Oklahoma. Jill was looking for a teaching job. The town of Fertile had not hired a police chief, she wrote. They were holding out the hope that he would come back.

Corbin put the letter back in the envelope. It was good to know that he had a job if he wanted it. He had a wife to support now.

Chapter 26

THE WORRY ABOUT HER FATHER'S FAILURE TO RETURN on time was pushed to the back of Annabel's mind by the wonder that she was married and that she would spend this night and every other night with her husband.

Although she had known him for a relatively short time, she felt that after all they had been through together, she knew everything about him. He was not only handsome, he was open and honest and capable and brave.

He was wonderful!

Just thinking about him made her feel vibrant and alive, more attuned to life than she had ever been before. From the first, she had felt comfortable with him, so right in his arms, so very right that she had known in only a short time that they were indeed meant for each other.

She wanted to look her best for him. After brushing her hair until it shone, she dabbed a bit of Evening in Paris perfume behind her ears and added a tiny bit of Tangee lipstick to her lips. Satisfied it was the best she could do, she put on her nightgown. Although sleeveless, it was modest, with a tie at the high neck. She looked down at herself and noticed that the outline of her nipples and the dark brush of her pubic hair showed through the thin material and hurriedly pulled from her bag the gingham wrapper she wore sometimes when her father, Boone or Spinner were in the house.

While she waited for Corbin to return, she repacked her valise, putting away all of her intimate garments, then spread her wet towel and washcloth on the towel bar to dry. She busied herself tidying the room. She moved a pair of Corbin's boots over beneath his clothes, which hung on a rod in the corner of the room. While there, she buried her face in his shirt. The scent of him was new, raw and shockingly heady.

At the sound of a bump on the door she went quickly to press her ear against it.

"It's me, honey. Open the door."

Corbin came in carrying a heavy tray, which he set on the bed. It was the only flat place in the room other than the floor. Annabel closed and locked the door, leaving the key in the keyhole. Corbin had told her that if someone tried to unlock the door, the key would fall to the floor and alert them.

"Something smells good," she said.

He turned to her. "Oh, honey. You're so pretty. I'm not sure that I can eat a bite. You are something."

"So are you, Mr. Appleby. And do you mean that looking at me takes away your appetite? That's not very flattering," she chided.

"You know what I mean!" He gave her a leering look and twisted an imaginary mustache. "My dear lady, do not forget that you are at my mercy."

She laughed. "Sir, if you have plans to ravish me, at least let me eat first." She whipped the cloth off the tray of food and sat down beside it. "Chicken pie. My, it looks good. Oh, and bread pudding and cream. A feast before ravishment. A girl couldn't ask for more than that."

While they ate, Corbin told her about what he had learned from the desk clerk.

"Potter came here on the pretext of delivering a prescription I had ordered."

"What would he have done if you'd been here?"

"I don't know. I doubt he would shoot me down in the lobby in front of everyone."

"Do you think he'll try to do that? Shoot you? He doesn't know that we saw him at the farm."

"Face it, honey. About now, he's desperate. He's got to answer to the big guys in Chicago. The men they sent here didn't do the job. They let your father's men outwit them, and they lost thousands of dollars' worth of bootleg whiskey. One of the two who came looking for me, either the postmaster or Craig Travis, could be his sidekick. I hate to think of it being Travis. He has a nice wife and a small boy."

"How will you find out which one it is?"

"I'll lay it all out to the marshal when he comes and let him figure it out."

"When do you think he'll be here?"

"Noon tomorrow, unless he leaves Jefferson City tonight. He'll come here to the hotel."

After they finished eating, Corbin carried the tray down to the dining room, then hurried back to their room. Annabel let him in, then rushed to the bed, scooted to the far side and got under the sheet. Corbin got only a glimpse of an outline of her breasts beneath her nightdress before he turned to lock the door and to wedge a straight-backed chair beneath the knob.

He tried not to look at her, knowing that she must be nervous and feeling shy. He kept his back to her while he removed his shirt for another reason too. His arousal was embarrassing to him, and he feared it would be frightening to her. He removed his shoes and socks, then switched off the light before he removed his trousers.

Standing beside the bed in the pitch-dark room, Corbin felt not only a strong sexual desire for his bride, but a strange fear that she might reject him and despise a physical relationship with him. He was awed by the responsibility he had to introduce her to the ways in which a man loved a woman with his body. He wished they'd had more time to build up to this.

God, help me to do this right.

"Corbin?" her voice came out of the darkness.

"I'm here, sweetheart."

He lifted the sheet and got into the bed. The bedsprings were not strong and he rolled toward her, his arms reaching to surround her. He held her to him, flattening her breasts against his chest. Hungry mouths searched, found each other, and held with fierce joy. Her skin was smooth and soft. His hands couldn't stop sliding up and down her back.

"What do I do?" she whispered when her lips were free.

"Don't worry about it, sweetheart," he crooned in a voice deep and soothing. "When the time comes, you'll know what to do. I'm going to enjoy holding you for a while."

"The feelings inside are all so new. I love you," she murmured between kisses.

"It's the love that we share that makes this so special." Corbin held his dire need in check, carefully keeping his lower body away from her so as not to frighten her with his rock-hard erection while his hands and mouth made her ready for him.

When he kissed her, his tongue entered her mouth, preparing her for the other entry that was to come. She responded with rising desire, and with a feeling of great joy, he knew that she'd given herself into his care.

Her arms encircled him and her hands caressed the smooth skin of his back. He felt so good. His scent was all male, fresh and clean. His chest was warm and she could feel the heavy beat of his heart beneath her cheek. His arms holding her tightly—this was just the way she craved to be held.

"I've wanted to hold you like this, kiss you and feel your breasts against my chest."

"Do . . . we leave our clothes on?" she whispered.

"We can . . . if it's what you want."

"What do you want?"

"I want you naked in my arms. Is it too soon?"

For an answer, she pulled away from him, lifted the gown up over her head and lay back down. A deep longing compelled her to meet his passion equally. The driving force of her feeling took her beyond herself into a mindless void where there were only lips, hands and Corbin's hard demanding body.

When his beloved weight pressed her gently but securely to the bed, she could feel the pounding of his heart against her breast. Without hesitation their bodies joined in mutual, frantic need. She welcomed the hard insistent pressure when he entered her body, and an almost unbelievable pleasure swept through her.

She was aware of nothing but the broad shoulders she clung to, heard nothing but the low murmur of love words that poured from his mouth before it covered hers. Then she was beyond seeing or hearing as she slipped into uncharted but beautiful oblivion.

Minutes passed before Corbin, still deep inside her, raised himself on his elbows and gazed into her face. He brushed back her hair with gentle fingers.

"Well, what do you think, Mrs. Appleby?"

"I think I made the perfect choice when I chose you to be

my husband." She giggled happily. Her tongue darted out to taunt a tiny spot at the corner of his mouth before retreating.

"I wanted it to last longer."

"If it had, I might have died of pleasure."

"I was afraid that I'd hurt you so badly, you'd never want me again."

"Fat chance of that. It did hurt, but only for a minute. It doesn't hurt now. It feels wonderful. Do you suppose we made a baby?"

"We could have. Would you mind?"

"I want lots of babies. Your babies. I wished for brothers and sisters when I was growing up."

Corbin moved to her side and gathered her to him, cradling her head on his chest. His hands stroked her body gently, his breathing slower, his heart quieter beneath her palm. They fell into a warm, languid silence, both of them awed by the glorious thing that had happened between them.

More content, happier than he could remember ever being, Corbin molded Annabel to his side and pulled her arm across his hard, flat stomach. His hand caressed her breast. She captured it and held it there.

"Corbin." Her voice came drowsily from beneath his chin. "I'm so happy."

"So am I, love." He moved his other hand down her side and patted her bare bottom affectionately.

Feeling wonderfully loved and happily relaxed, Annabel closed her eyes on the most wonderful night of her life and drifted into a dreamlike state halfway between sleep and awareness, her mouth uplifted in a tired but happy smile.

Annabel was awakened by a tickling on the end of her nose. Drowsily, she realized she was lying on her back and

Corbin, propped on an elbow, was looking at her and teasing the end of her nose with the tip of his finger.

"You're mean."

His laugh was low, tender and happy. She felt his breath on her face, then his lips. They moved over her chin to her mouth. The tip of his tongue traced her lips before he kissed her.

"Mornin'. Did you have a good sleep?"

"I hardly slept at all. A man kept waking me up."

"What was he doing?"

"He kept kissing me and biting me on the neck."

"Did you like it?"

"Ah . . . it was all right, I guess."

"Only all right?" Corbin's fingers skimmed over her ribs. She squirmed and giggled.

Suddenly aware the sheet had slipped down to her waist, she reached for it to cover her breasts. His hand stilled hers.

"Don't be shy with me, sweet wife. Let me look at them. They're so pretty. You're so pretty." His voice was low and tender. "Open your eyes, love."

She watched as he ran his fingertips over her breasts, then bent his head to kiss them. A strange and exciting feeling unfolded in the center of her being, and she let out a little gasp of pleasure.

His eyes held hers as he pulled her over until her soft stomach was pressed to his hard one, and suddenly he was inside her again.

"How did that happen so fast?" she murmured, her lips seeking his and opening over his mouth with drugged sweetness.

"Did you want it to happen?"

"Uh-huh." The pressure inside thrilled her. She whispered incoherent words of love and tightened her arms about him. "Does it feel as good to you as it does to me?" She arched against him.

"It's pure . . . heaven. You're so incredibly sweet. Sweetheart, I want never, never to make this trip to heaven alone. I want you to always be with me, feeling this with me."

Her body felt boneless. He fit every inch of it against his. This was her husband, her lover, her mate for life. She felt herself being swept away on a cloud, climbing, climbing into the sky until they reached that sunlit moment of glorious shared completion.

Chapter 27

AFTER DECIDING THAT THEY COULDN'T KEEP their presence in town a secret for much longer because the hotel staff would spread the news about their marriage, Annabel and Corbin ate breakfast in the hotel dining room. They decided the best protection they had until the marshal arrived would be to make sure they were among other people.

There was little comfort in knowing that Arnold Potter was unaware that they knew of his connection with the mobsters or that he had a sidekick in town. He had seen Corbin's burned-out car, and Marvin had said that he was there to see Annabel. To make sure that he had a means of defense, Corbin carried his gun in a shoulder holster and wore a light coat to cover it.

After receiving the congratulations of the hotel staff, Corbin and Annabel wandered out onto the hotel veranda and watched the activity on the street. People were coming into town. Saturday was a busy day in Henderson.

"Shall we walk, honey, or would you rather stay here?"

"I'd rather be moving. It'll make the time go faster."

With her hand tucked firmly in the crook of his arm, they walked toward the center of town. Corbin's heart swelled with pride. This was the first day of their married life. They would live out the rest of their days together, grow old together. Never again would he awaken to a day of loneliness stretching out before him. He wanted to shout to everyone they passed that this wonderful, vibrant girl was his wife.

They passed the barbershop. The two chairs were occupied. Stoney Baker, the sheriff, sat with his back to the window reading the paper. The shoeshine boy lounged in his chair, waiting for a customer.

"Shine, mistah?"

"Not today." Corbin flipped him a penny and received a broad smile in return.

A lady stepped out from the millinery shop and eyed them curiously. Corbin tipped his hat and they walked on. When they reached the picture show, they stopped to read the poster advertising the film: RUDOLPH VALENTINO IN "MONSIEUR BEAUCAIRE" WITH BEBE DANIELS.

"He's handsome, but not as handsome as you." Annabel tilted her head and smiled up at him.

"Are you flirting with me?" Corbin asked with a serious frown.

"Whatever gave you that idea?"

"Honey, Mr. Potter is headed this way," he whispered quickly.

"Oh, no! What'll we do?"

"Nothing. He'll not do anything here."

"Hello, Mr. and Mrs. Appleby. Let me offer my congratulations." Potter approached them with his hand extended.

Corbin shook his hand. "Thank you. Word gets around fast."

"Good news travels fast in a friendly town. I hope you plan to make your home here." His eyes focused on Annabel.

"I warn you, my dear, I'm determined that you play in my band. A violin would be a wonderful addition."

"I don't think so. I . . . couldn't." Annabel shook her head and shrank against Corbin.

"My wife is bashful," Corbin said with a laugh. "I'll see what I can do about persuading her. She plays beautifully."

"I'd love to hear her play sometime."

"We must be getting on. We have errands. Good day."

"Same to you folks. Will you be leaving soon?"

"We haven't decided."

"I hope you stay. Good day to you." Mr. Potter tipped his hat and walked on.

Corbin turned back to look at the theater poster so that he could watch Potter out of the corner of his eye. When the chubby little man turned into the barbershop, Corbin urged Annabel on down the walk. She was shivering.

"How can that evil, nasty man be so . . . so friendly to us? Yesterday he told that man to kill Marvin with no more concern than if he told him to step on an ant. He would've had him kill us if he'd known we were there."

"Don't fret, sweetheart. Marshal Sanford will know how to handle him."

At the end of the block they crossed the street and looked in the window of the photo studio. Displayed in the window were family pictures, wedding and baby pictures.

"Let's go in and get our picture taken. We'll have one to remember the day after our wedding."

"Oh, no. Corbin, I look a sight. My hair—"

"You look just right. I want to remember you as you look today . . . all flushed from our loving."

"Corbin!"

"Come on, honey. We'll have a formal picture taken later on."

Before Annabel could protest further, Corbin's hand was on her elbow and he was ushering her through the door. The walls of the studio were covered with pictures in large square or oval ornate frames. Camera equipment, background screens, chairs, stools and other props were at the back of the room. A small table, cluttered with albums and a variety of small tools, stood beside one wall.

Alex Lemon, whom Corbin had seen at the barbershop, came to the door from a room at the back.

"Hello, folks. Look around. I'll be with you in just a minute."

"We're in no hurry. Take your time."

Annabel looked at herself critically in the mirror that hung over the table. She removed the barrette from her hair and placed it on the table while she combed her short hair back with her fingers. Pulling it aside and holding it with one hand, she fumbled with the other to find the barrette on the table. Failing to find it, she looked down when her fingers moved over a heavy object on a pile of papers. Forgetting about the hair fastener, she picked up the object and froze.

She had seen and held a heavy brass object such as this many, many times since her childhood. Her father had carried one with him. She turned to look at the end. Then she dropped it onto the stack of papers and grabbed Corbin's arm.

"Come on! Please—" She tugged him toward the door.

"What is it? Honey?"

"Let's go!"

"I'm sorry to have kept you waiting." The voice came from the end of the studio.

"My wife . . . has decided to wait. She's not happy with how she looks. We'll come back another time." Corbin tossed the words over his shoulder as he hurried out the door to catch up with Annabel. "Honey, wait." After several quick steps, he was at her side and peering into her face.

Tears streamed from her eyes.

"What is it? What has upset you?" He turned her so that her back was to the street.

"Papa's . . . brass knuckles are in there."

"Are you sure?" He took her arm and they moved around the corner.

"I'm sure! I'm sure! He always carries the knuckles with him. He had them with him when he left for St. Louis. I saw him put them in his pocket."

"How do you know they are his?"

"There was a knife blade on one end at one time. Papa had it taken off and . . . complained it was not a very good job. One end was rough. I know they are Papa's. How did that photographer get them?"

Corbin pulled his handkerchief from his pocket. "We'll go back to the hotel, but first wipe your eyes, honey. We don't want folks to see you cry. They may start wondering about us, and we don't want to attract undue attention."

"What'll we do?" Her eyes pleaded with him.

"We'll wait for the marshal, then he and I will talk to Lemon." He hurried her past the barbershop and on toward the hotel.

"Papa has been gone a week," she said as they went up the steps to the veranda. "I'm afraid something has happened."

"Has he been gone this long before?"

"A few times."

A touring car had stopped in front of the hotel. Corbin edged Annabel toward the small cluster of people on the porch. He watched as four men got out of the car. One untied the canvas tarp that covered the rack on top of the car. He handed down a couple of suitcases and cases that obviously held musical instruments. Corbin took them to be a traveling dance band; but after a closer look, when he recognized the big man who wore a battered big-brimmed hat, he moved Annabel toward the door.

As the group approached to go into the hotel lobby, Marshal Sanford looked directly at Corbin.

In their room, Corbin locked the door before he turned to Annabel, who had sunk down on the side of the bed.

"Marshal Sanford is here. He was one of the four men in the touring car—the one with gray hair."

"He didn't look like a marshal."

"No, he didn't. I think he has federal marshals with him. They are traveling as a dance band."

"You've got to tell him about that man who has Papa's brass knuckles."

"I will. Don't worry so, sweetheart."

"I can't help it. Papa wouldn't have given away those brass knuckles willingly."

"We'll lay it all out to the marshal. He'll know what to do."

The words had no more than left Corbin's mouth when a knock sounded on the door. He unlocked and opened it, expecting to see the marshal. Jack stood there with a silly grin on his face.

"Jack. Come in."

"Sorry to bust in on the honeymoon."

"What's happened?"

"Spinner took a turn for the worse last night. This morning Boone and I carried him down to the truck and brought him in to the doctor. He and Tess are over there now."

Annabel got to her feet. "Is he that bad off?"

"Boone thought so."

"Maybe I should go over there."

"Let's talk to the marshal first. That's probably him," Corbin said as another knock sounded on the door. He opened it. Marshal Sanford and another man came into the room.

Corbin introduced Annabel as his wife and received the marshal's congratulations. Marshal Sanford remembered Jack from Fertile. They shook hands. The stranger was Bill McGiboney, a federal marshal out of the St. Louis office. Annabel, Corbin and the marshal sat down on the edge of the bed. The other marshal took the chair; Jack squatted on his heels.

It took Corbin a half hour to tell everything he could remember about what had happened the past several days. He called on Annabel to help fill in details. Jack told what he knew about Spinner being almost beaten to death, about his blowing up the cave and then making it to the cabin.

Corbin expressed his feelings about the Carters. "Marshal, the Carters saved our lives. They acted in self-defense against a couple of guys with a tommy gun. They had seen their brother shot down like a mad dog. It was a brave thing they did, coming in there in a hay wagon. I doubt that even a trace of those men will ever be found. I'll testify in court for the Carters if they're brought to trial."

"I'm marshal for the state of Missouri. I don't see any need for a trial. Do you, McGiboney?"

"You said it. You're the marshal for the state. I've got bigger fish to fry."

"We have one more piece of information. I told you that my wife's father has been in the bootlegging business and was trying to get out. He was rather small-time compared to

George Remus and some of the others. He left for St. Louis to complete the deal. He was due back a couple of days ago.

"This morning my wife and I were in the photographer's studio, and she spotted her father's brass knuckles. She says that he has always carried them with him. He doesn't carry a gun and uses the knuckles if he finds himself in a tight spot. We need you to ask Alex Lemon, the photographer, how they came to be in his possession."

"Boone will tell you that they are Papa's," Annabel added.

"How can you be sure they are your father's?"

Corbin answered for Annabel. "They were a special pair to start with. At one time a knife blade was on one end. It was removed, leaving that end rough."

"We'll see what we can find out, ma'am."

McGiboney spoke. "We need to confront Potter with the fact that you were in the hayloft at Donovan's and saw what went on while he was with the hit men. We need to get him to lead us to the other contact here."

"Before we do anything, I want to make sure my wife is in a safe place."

Jack spoke up. "I didn't get a chance to tell you. Boone said to bring Annabel to the doctor's office. She can stay there with Tess. I told Boone what happened. He has things he wants to say to you about marrying Annabel." Jack grinned.

"I bet he does." Corbin snorted.

McGiboney got to his feet. "No point in waiting around. This is going to be easier than I thought. Seems that Donovan's men and the Carter clan did most of the work for us."

Corbin pulled the thin leather belt from under his shirt. He took out the papers and gave them to the marshal.

"These are the notes I took on each of the men you wanted me to observe."

"Thanks. After what you've done, I think the state should reimburse you for the car you lost. I'll see what I can do. If you want to walk your wife and Jack to the doctor's office, we'll mosey along behind and keep an eye open."

Annabel was quiet as they left the hotel. She walked along beside Corbin and Jack and didn't speak until just before they reached the doctor's house.

"Jack, did you tell Tess about Marvin?"

"I told her everything."

"How did she take it?"

"She just kind of closed up and didn't say much. She just fretted about Leroy."

The marshals remained on the street corner when Jack went into the house. A minute later he returned with Boone and Tess.

"Ya sneakin' polecat." These were the first words out of Boone's mouth. "I ort to strip off yore hide and hang it to dry."

"Go ahead and give it a try, you mud-ugly sidewinder," Corbin answered belligerently.

"I knew the minute I turned my back ya'd do somethin' underhanded."

"Underhanded?" Corbin sputtered. "I'd put my fist in your big mouth if I—"

"Hush up! Both of you," Annabel snapped. "Aren't you happy for me, Boone?"

"Of course I am, sugar. I just have to let this brayin' jack-ass know that I knew what he was up to."

Annabel spoke to Tess. "What'll we do with these two?"

Tess smiled her quiet smile and snuggled her hand into Boone's.

"I'm afraid something has happened to Papa, Boone."

Boone patted her shoulder. "You and Tess stay here with

Jack. Doc says Spinner should make it all right. And Leroy is better. I'll go along with the stinkin' pole—"

"Say it and I'll flatten you out right here."

"Take him to see the brass knuckles." Annabel looked pleadingly at Corbin. "He'll know that they're Papa's."

"I will. Stay here with Jack and Tess. As soon as we know anything, we'll be back." Corbin looked beyond Annabel to Jack. "Jack, take care of the women."

"Be careful," Annabel pleaded.

"We're not alone now, sweetheart. We've got the marshals and the ugly sidewinder now." He bent his head and kissed her.

Boone snorted.

Jack snorted for a different reason. "I guess we'll have to put up with a lot of that kissy stuff now."

"Just wait, young scutter. I hope I'm around when you fall in love. I'm going to make your life miserable."

Annabel stood on the steps holding Tess's hand and watched her tall husband and the shorter, huskier Boone walking down the street. They joined the marshals and introductions were made. The marshals shook hands with Boone; then, after a few minutes of conversation, the four men headed for Main Street.

Corbin peered into the photographer's studio to make sure there were no customers before he opened the door and the four men entered. Alex Lemon came out of the back room.

"You're back. Did your wife change her mind?"

Corbin took the brass knuckles from the table and handed them to Boone. As soon as he heard the oath that came from Boone's mouth, he made a grab for Lemon's shirt and hauled the startled man up close to him.

"You son-of-a-bitch! Tell me where you got those knuckles or I'll bust up every piece of equipment you have in this studio after I work your pretty face over with them."

"What? Who— Stop that!"

"Stop what? I haven't even started. Tell me where you got the knuckles, or your sweety, Mrs. Zeadow, won't recognize you the next time you go crawling, like a slimy little worm, to her bed while her husband is away." Corbin tightened his hold on the neck of Lemon's shirt and shook him.

"What do you . . . want to know? Stop. You're choking me."

"I told you, dumb-head! Are you deaf as well as stupid? My wife saw those knuckles this morning. They belonged to her father."

"I got them . . . got them . . ." He pulled on Corbin's wrist to loosen his hold so that he could breathe. Then he took a deep, gulping breath. "I bought them at the mercantile."

"From whom?"

"Whom do you think? Luther Hogg." Lemon was breathing hard. "I told him that I'd always wanted a pair. He said that the man that had them wouldn't need them . . . that he'd gone downriver. I paid two dollars."

"What did he mean by 'gone downriver'?" Boone asked.

"How do I know?"

"What else did he say?"

"I asked if the man would be back for them. Luther laughed and said not unless he came back on Halloween as a ghost. I took it that the man had died."

"You're out two dollars. Sit down." Corbin pushed him toward a chair and went to speak quietly to the marshals.

"What do you think?"

"Godamighty, Appleby. You 'bout scared the shit out of

him. A few more minutes and he'd have confessed to killing his own mother with her standing in front of him."

"Surprise. It's a technique I learned while dealing with misfits in the army."

"I think he's telling the truth. Hogg may be our man, but all we've got is his connection to brass knuckles. We'll have to get Potter to turn on him."

"I'm keepin' these." Boone held up the knuckles, then slipped them into his pocket. "What ya goin' to do 'bout him?"

"We'll have to keep an eye on Lemon to stop him from getting to Hogg." McGiboney went to the door and beckoned. "I'm glad I brought two extra men. One of them will stay here and keep an eye on our Romeo friend. Does he really bed the married ladies in town?"

"I've been told that he does. Frequently."

"The lucky little shit." McGiboney stepped out the door and spoke to one of his men. While the marshals were conferring, Corbin and Boone left the studio and waited on the sidewalk.

"The sons-a-bitches killed Murphy. It'll be a blow to Annabel. He's all she's got," Boone said with a sad shake of his head.

"You're wrong. She's got me now. If it's true he's been killed, we'll have to help her get through it."

Chapter 28

MARLYS PERKINS, the doctor's wife, took Annabel in to see Spinner. Had she not been told who he was, she would have been hard-pressed to recognize him.

"Spinner?" she said softly. "Oh, Spinner, I'm so sorry this happened to you."

"Howdy, youngun." His cut and puffed lips barely moved when he spoke. His bony nose was swollen to twice its normal size.

"The doctor thinks you'll be all right."

"They was dead set on bringin' me here. Ya know how Boone is when he gets his neck bowed."

"I know. He was right this time."

"I'da been all right. That ride pert-near killed me."

"Did Jack tell you that Corbin and I are married?"

"He told me. Ya needed a steady man, youngun. I ain't seen him but a time or two. But he seemed like he could stand up to Murphy."

"He is steady, Spinner. I hope Papa will like him."

Mrs. Perkins came into the room with a small glass of water and held a straw to Spinner's mouth.

"This will let you sleep for a while. When you wake up, I'll bring you something to eat."

"If it's beefsteak, you'll have to get the dog to chew it for me."

"It won't be beefsteak. It may be beef broth."

He made a derisive sound. "Tess is been jammin' me full of that stuff."

"Good for her. It may have saved your life."

"Tess and I will be close by." Annabel leaned down and placed a kiss on Spinner's forehead.

"Thanky for that, youngun. Hit's been a spell since I been kissed by a pretty girl."

"Then we'll have to do it more often."

Annabel went back into the room where Tess waited. "How is Leroy?"

"He's better. Much better. But I didn't tell him about Marvin. I told him that I wasn't going back home, that I was staying with Boone."

"What did he say?"

"He said he didn't want to go back there either."

"Where is Jack?"

"Sitting out on the steps."

Annabel leaned back in the chair. The thought came to her that all down through history it had been the woman's fate to wait for her man to come back from the wars. What Corbin and Boone were involved in was a war . . . of sorts. And she could only pray that her papa was not already a casualty.

They waited until the only clerk Potter employed left the store to go home for dinner. Then Marshal McGiboney sent his deputy into the drugstore to signal to them when Potter was alone.

When the two marshals, Boone and Corbin entered the store, Corbin closed the door, shot the steel bolt and turned the "Closed" sign facing the street.

"Mr. Appleby, good to see you again. What can I do for you gentlemen?" With a friendly smile on his face, the dapper little gray-haired man came from behind the prescription counter.

"There's a good deal you can do, Mr. Potter."

"I'll help you in any way I can. How is your charming wife?" Potter glanced nervously at the strangers who had moved to surround him.

"Alive and well."

Led by Bill McGiboney, the four men began to crowd Potter into the back room.

"What's going on here? Gentlemen, my clerk has gone to dinner. I must watch the store."

"You won't have any customers," Corbin said. "I locked the door."

"I . . . I don't understand."

"You will shortly."

"Is this a . . . holdup? There's the safe. It's open." Sweat had popped out on Potter's face. His rosy cheeks became rosier.

"We're not after your money. I'm Federal Marshal Bill McGiboney." The marshal produced his badge. "This is Missouri State Marshal Sanford. You know who the other two gentlemen are. My deputy is at your front door."

"How do I know that you're a marshal? You don't look like one. Explain yourself, please." Mr. Potter tried to draw a cloak of dignity about him.

"Be glad to. We understand that you have connections with the George Remus operation in Chicago."

"Remus? Who is that?"

"You've never heard of him? That's strange."

"Why . . . would I? Where did you get the idea . . . that . . . I know him?" Potter stammered.

"From a couple of fellows out of Chicago who say that Remus pays you a pretty penny to keep this area clear for him. You inform him of the competition, and he blows them away."

"That's the . . . silliest thing I ever heard of. Who . . . said that?"

"Lester and Benny. You know who I'm talking about."

"I never heard of anybody named Lester and Benny."

"Your memory is short, Potter." Corbin could hardly keep his hands off the man. "Yesterday you told Lester to kill Marvin Carter. When he did, you told him it was good shooting. Then you said for him not to get a big head because anyone could hit the side of a barn."

Potter's face went white and still after his jaw dropped. The expression of utter surprise on hearing his own words repeated back to him would have been funny if it were not such a serious matter.

"Why . . . that's . . . that's a lie!" Potter looked pleadingly at the marshal.

McGiboney shrugged and looked at Corbin. "The man says you're a liar."

"Are you calling me a liar?" Corbin moved forward and towered over the shorter man.

"No, no. You're mistaken, is all. I don't know how those men could say . . . such things. I don't even know them."

"You lying little shit-head. Isn't that what Marvin Carter called Lester just before you told Lester to kill him?" Corbin's hand leaped out and fastened on Potter's shirt so fast it threw the shorter man off balance. Only Corbin's hold kept him on his feet.

"My wife, the former Miss Donovan, and I were in the hayloft out at the Donovans'. We could see and hear everything that happened in the yard below. We saw you drive in, saw you go through the house, saw you waiting for Benny and Lester. We heard you say that you were in charge, that they had botched the job they had been sent to do and it had cost the boss fifty thousand dollars' worth of whiskey."

"I . . . never—"

"Goddammit, you did! Stop your damn lying or I'll mop the floor with you even if you are old . . . and fat! I was there. I heard you tell Lester to kill Marvin Carter and so did my wife."

"You . . . misunderstood—"

"Bullshit! You were out there looking for Boone. You'd had orders to kill him for fear he'd start up and be competition to Remus. You'd decided to kill my wife and get her out of the way. You asked Benny if he was too chicken to kill the girl."

Potter began to shake. The skin on his face was deathly white beneath the red blotches. Corbin continued to hold him up with his hand fastened to his shirt.

"They . . . would have killed me. I didn't want to hurt anybody."

"You are the lowest piece of humanity I've ever come across, and I've seen plenty of the sorry side of life." Corbin stiffened his arm and threw him. Potter landed sprawled in a chair. "I could kill you for the hell you've put my wife through, for what you forced her to witness."

"Don't kill him . . . yet." Boone stepped in front of Corbin. "I want to work him over with these for what his friends did to Spinner." With his hand covered with the brass knuckles, he nudged Potter's chin.

Potter cringed. "Where did you . . . get—"

"The knuckles?" McGiboney asked. "He got them from your friend Hogg, who else?"

"That stupid bastard! I told him to get rid of . . ."

"Of what, Potter? We know he had Donovan killed. Did you have a hand in that too?"

"No! It was his job."

"Did he do it himself?"

"He hired some fellows down south of here. When they came to collect, they brought the knuckles. I've never hurt anyone." Potter now only seemed interested in saving his own hide and continued to babble. "I never wanted to get mixed up with that kind of lowlife. Hogg told me I didn't have to do anything, just keep my eyes open and report to him."

Marshals McGiboney and Sanford exchanged glances. McGiboney gestured and Sanford followed him to the front of the store.

"Have we heard all we need to know?" Sanford asked.

"More than enough. With Appleby testifying, he'll be sent up for a good long while. Appleby's a damn good man. I'd like to have him working with me."

"Do you want me to go along with you to get Hogg?"

"I'll take my two deputies. Tell that wild man Boone to be careful with those brass knuckles. We don't want any broken noses."

"We don't?" Marshal Sanford took his hat off and scratched his head. "Hell, McGiboney, you take the fun out of everything."

Fifteen minutes later, Sanford unlocked the door of the drugstore. McGiboney and his deputies came in with a hand-cuffed Luther Hogg.

"I demand to know what's going on. What will folks

think seeing me like this? I have a position to uphold in this town." He held up his cuffed hands.

"You should have thought of that before you got mixed up with Remus."

"Dammit, I told you that I didn't know anyone by that name. I have a store to run, and this is a busy day."

"Ease up," McGiboney said calmly. "Your wife is there. She can handle it. Come on back. We have a friend of yours here who wants to see you."

Luther Hogg stopped as soon as he entered the back room and saw Potter huddled in a chair. The man who stood over him wearing the brass knuckles was systematically pounding them into the palm of his other hand.

"You smart-mouth know-it-all! I told you to get rid of those knuckles," Potter shouted angrily. "This is your fault . . . all of it."

"You weak little worm! You've spilled your guts!"

Hogg made a dive for Potter and came up against Boone. With one hand Boone pushed him back, with the other he swung. He struck Hogg square in the mouth with the brass knuckles. The force of the blow would have felled a horse. Hogg flew back and crashed into the wall. Blood spurting from his mouth and nose shot out over his face and shirt. Uprooted teeth hung from his broken, bloody mouth. He slowly sank to the floor.

"That was for a damn good man who never did anything more than sell a little bootleg whiskey." Boone walked over and spit on the man on the floor. He looked up at the federal man. "Hell. I wanted more than one shot at him."

"The one you got in was a good one." McGiboney shook his head and squatted down to look at the unconscious man. "He'll never again be eatin' corn on the cob or beefsteak. Not that he'd be getting that where he's going."

"Guess this winds it up," Sanford said. "What are you going to do with these two?"

"Take them to St. Louis in the morning. They can spend the night in jail here. My deputies will take turns watching them. I've heard that the sheriff here is none too reliable."

"That's an understatement," Corbin muttered. "I'd like to get back to my wife if we're no longer needed here."

"We'll be getting in touch." McGiboney stuck out his hand. "If you want a job, look me up."

"Thanks, but I'm thinking of getting into the newspaper business and using my training as a journalist. It's not quite so hard on the nerves."

"Good luck." McGiboney turned to Boone. "Do I have to put your name on the Feds' wanted list?"

"Not unless ya want ta give me a job. I'm handy with brass knuckles."

"I can see that." McGiboney shook Boone's hand.

Luther Hogg was moaning on the floor and Potter was crying when Corbin left the room. The sight of the two of them sickened him. Now he had the chore of telling his sweet wife that her father was dead. He wasn't looking forward to it.

It was late afternoon.

"I want to go home, Corbin."

"All right, honey. We'll have to wait for Jack to come back with the truck. He took Boone and Tess to the same preacher who married us."

"They were getting married today?"

"They would rather have been married on a happier day, but it was necessary. Boone wanted the right to keep her with him in case the Carters decided to come and take her."

Corbin hadn't told Annabel about her father until they

were alone in the hotel room. After seeing the brass knuckles, she had been halfway prepared for the news. Yet she had cried until she was exhausted. Afterward she had lain on the bed with Corbin holding her for a long while.

"What are we going to do, Corbin?" She sat up and pushed her hair back from her tear-wet face.

"Honey, there isn't any rush for us to do anything right away. We can go out to the farm if that's what you want. I need to get a car. It's unhandy not having one. I've had one for several years and I'm spoiled."

Annabel got up from the bed, opened her violin case and took out the violin. She pulled the felt lining loose to reveal a layer of hundred-dollar bills—at least ten of them.

"Papa put the money in here in case I'd need it. Take what you need for a car."

"No, honey." Corbin carefully replaced the lining and then the instrument. "Marshal Sanford said he'd see if the state would replace my car. Meanwhile, I have money to buy one. In a few days I'll look around and see what I can find."

Knowing that she grieved for her father and that there was not much he could do but wrap his arms around her and kiss her, he did that now. He sat down on the bed and pulled her down on his lap.

"I'm glad you're here with me," she whispered.

"Where else would I be, sweetheart? I'm your husband."

He took her hand to his mouth and kissed the string he had so proudly tied on her finger.

"I love you."

Her arms looped around his neck, her eyes level with his. She touched his jaw and the scar that notched his eyebrow. Her lips were soft and sweet when they caressed his.

"I love you too."

Chapter 29

THE TOWN OF HENDERSON WAS ROCKED by the news that two of their leading citizens were crooks and had been taken to the federal prison to await trial. It had come out that Annabel's father had been bootlegging, but that was petty compared to murder: his and that of Marvin Carter.

After it became known that Spinner had been beaten badly by the hit men from Chicago, a collection was taken up to help with his medical expenses.

Annabel and Corbin returned to the Donovan farm. Jack took Boone and Tess to the hills, where they would spend the first few days of their married life in Spinner's cabin. When he returned, for the lack of something to do, he worked in the garden he had planted earlier.

Grieving for her father, Annabel moved about the house, quietly showing little emotion except at night when she was in her husband's arms. Basking in his love, she nestled close to his chest as he found her deepest warmth and crooned soft words of love and reassurance to her. Then, arching helplessly against his hardness, she would strain toward that something new and wild and wonderful.

They made several trips to town to see Spinner; and on

the first one, Corbin made arrangements for an Oldsmobile to be sent up from St. Louis. He explained to Annabel that the Olds was a good, heavy car, one that would last them for a long time, and he wanted her to learn to drive it.

Another time they met Calvin Carter, who had come to take Leroy home. The only words that were exchanged were when Calvin slapped money in Corbin's hand.

"That feller that married Tessie paid for Leroy. Tell him we Carters ain't takin' no charity from the likes a him."

"Are you sure you don't want to tell him yourself? He's your brother-in-law now."

"Sh-it! What kind a man'd marry a whore?"

On the way back to the farm, Annabel showed more life than she had for days.

"The Carters are so ignorant they wouldn't know a bee from a bull's foot. Wouldn't you think they'd believe their own sister over that awful man who raped her? If Boone catches up with him, he'll not leave him with the equipment to rape another girl."

"Ouch!" Corbin exclaimed, then grinned at her. "Calvin has his own code of what's right and wrong. It would be better if Boone and Tess moved away from here. Tess's relatives are never going to accept her."

"I want to leave here, Corbin."

"Where do you want to go, honey?"

"Not to a city."

"What do you think about moving to Fertile? It's a nice town and needs a newspaper. I know a man in Springfield who has worked for years at the *Gazette*. He knows the business in and out and would like to go out on his own. He was a good friend of my father. When I was there we talked about starting a small semiweekly paper somewhere. He'll go partners with us if we say the word."

"Do we have the money?"

"I have money left to me by my father. If it isn't enough, I can get a loan at the bank in Fertile."

"Would the money from the farm be enough?"

"I want you to save that, honey. We'll use it only if we should get down and destitute."

Over the course of the next few weeks, preparations were made to move. The bank had been put in charge of selling the farm when Boone and Tess declared that they did not want to live near the Carters. They decided that when Spinner was up and around and able to take care of himself, they would take one of the trucks, go to Minnesota and visit Boone's sister.

Later, Boone said, they'd decide where they wanted to settle down, and it might very well be near their friends in Fertile. Annabel whooped with delight and threw her arms first around Tess, then around Boone.

Jack and Corbin loaded the truck and the car with everything Annabel wanted to take to their new home. The rest was left for Boone and Tess if they wanted it.

Jack was reluctant to leave Henderson without his baseball glove, but he was eager to get home. He would drive the truck, following Corbin and Annabel in the car. Somewhere between Henderson and Fertile they would spend the night.

At dawn, three weeks from the day Annabel and Corbin were married, they left the house on the hill to begin their new life in Fertile. At the end of the lane Annabel looked back.

" 'Bye, house. 'Bye, Papa. I'll never forget you." Tears filled her eyes and she held tightly to Corbin's hand.

It was hard for her to let go of her father. She didn't have a grave to put flowers on. Corbin had taken her down to the river. She had stood on its bank and said her good-bye. Her memory of her papa would be his smile and his kiss on that bright sunny day when he had driven down the lane to the road and had not come back.

Jack's eyes drank in all the familiar sights as they neared his hometown of Fertile. Corbin had sent a wire to Jethro Jones, Jack's father, giving an approximate time of their arrival. Jack's excitement built as they passed through town, then passed the ball diamond where he'd had the lucky hit against the traveling league who had come to play the hometown team. When they crossed the railroad tracks and started up the rocky hill to the farm, Jack couldn't keep the smile off his face.

It was so damned good to be home.

Even Corbin had the feeling of coming home when he saw the Jones family gathered on the porch and in the yard awaiting the return of one of their own. He stopped the car behind the truck and he and Annabel watched the family rush out to meet Jack.

Amid tears and hugs and slaps on the back, he was welcomed home. Watching from the car, Corbin tried to identify the family members for Annabel.

"The pregnant girl is his sister Julie. She was the hub of the family while the kids were growing up. She's married to Evan Johnson, the big blond fellow carrying the boy. They live on an adjoining farm.

"Jack's father is the one wiping his eyes with his handkerchief and the lady beside him is his wife, Eudora. Julie took over the house after their mother died. Jethro didn't remarry until a few years ago. The kids all welcomed Eudora into the family.

"That little tyke with her arms wrapped around Jack's

legs is Joy, the youngest Jones. Julie is the only mother she has ever known, and she lives with Julie and Evan. And there's Jill. She's the pretty girl in the blue dress. She's about seventeen now, I think. She graduated from high school this year. She's a little younger than Jack but I don't know how much.

"I don't see Joe. He's a couple years younger than Julie. He might still be in Oklahoma. And there's Jason. He's the tall kid in the white shirt. Lordy, he's growing like a weed. He's darn near as tall as Jill. He has a misshapen foot that gave him some problems when he was younger. Evan, Julie's husband, found a place in Kansas City that makes special shoes. He wears them, and that has helped him a lot. He hardly limps now.

"Did you notice that all the Joneses have names starting with a *J*? Jethro, Julie, Joe, Jack, Jill, Jason and Joy."

"I think that's nice." Annabel reached for her husband and kissed his cheek. "Our kids could have names starting with a *C*. Catherine, Connie, Carl, Claude . . ."

"Only four?" He hugged her. "I think they should start with an *A*. Alice, Ann, Albert, Arnold . . ."

"Only four?" she teased. Then, looking wistfully at the family in the yard, "It must be wonderful to be part of such a family."

Corbin hugged her to him. "We'll have one like that some day. The next best thing, sweetheart, is being a friend of such a family. Come and meet them, honey. They are special, like you."